# Jason h...
# to the co...

❖❖❖❖❖❖❖❖❖❖❖❖❖❖❖❖❖❖❖❖❖❖❖❖❖❖❖❖❖❖

The night sounds were drowned out by the sound of his ragged breathing and the furious pounding of blood in her ears. Autumnfire could feel his hungry eyes take in every inch of her bared body, tracing a warm path from her knees to her face. Why didn't he get it over with? She shut her eyes tighter still and cringed as she felt the weight of his leg come off her.

"Damn you, Meghan O'Brian!" The hoarse words ripped unwillingly from his throat. "Damn you to hell for doing this to me. What is there about you...?"

She opened her eyes. Jason was still crouched above her, but the fury in his eyes had been supplanted by pure and driving hunger. He reached out a hand and gently cupped a cold bare breast, and Autumnfire surprised herself by not flinching away. His warm calloused hand felt good, felt right as it moved over her sensitive flesh. The slow burn that had ignited earlier flared up suddenly into an aching need. A whimper escaped her throat. Jason stood and with hasty movements shed shirt and trousers...

❖ ❖

*Autumnfire*

*Also by Emily Carmichael*

◆

*The Devil's Darling*

**Published by**
**WARNER BOOKS**

# Emily Carmichael
# Autumnfire

**WARNER BOOKS**

A Warner Communications Company

WARNER BOOKS EDITION

Cover illustration by Tom Galasinski

Warner Books, Inc.
666 Fifth Avenue
New York, N.Y. 10103

**W** A Warner Communications Company

Printed in the United States of America

First Printing: December, 1987

10 9 8 7 6 5 4 3 2 1

# Chapter One

A coyote howled at the moonless sky, his eerie song reverberating through the black prairie night. Before the echoes of his howl faded, his fellows joined in, sending a chorus of high-pitched howls and yaps bouncing over the gently rolling grasslands.

Meghan O'Brian hugged her knees more tightly to her chest and stared with wide green eyes into the darkness that pressed against the edges of the campfire's comforting glow. In all her nine years of life she'd never heard anything so haunting. The coyotes had serenaded them most nights since the wagon train rolled onto the endless, empty prairie, but she still wasn't used to the sound. And tonight, the wild song floating through the dark stretches of the night seemed more lonely than ever.

Sitting beside Meghan, her mother Mary Catherine stirred restlessly and pulled her shawl more tightly around her thin shoulders. "Lord above! I don't think I'll ever get used to that unholy sound! Sounds like the very dead awailing from their graves. That it does!"

The ruddy glow of the big campfire softened the fine lines that etched her face and made her appear once more the young girl who'd been the most sought-after beauty in County Cork, Ireland.

"No need to worry, missus." A dry chuckle floated across the fire from old Joseph's throat. "There's no harm in the little critters. Not if those sounds is really comin' from coyote throats, that is." He chuckled again to see the look of alarm come into the faces of the several women who sat in the circle around the fire. The grizzled old scout enjoyed giving these greenhorns a jolt now and again.

Wagon master Dick Simmons threw another log on the faltering fire and sighed in exasperation. "Joseph's just joking, Mrs. O'Brian. There hasn't been any fresh Indian sign in days. Isn't that right, Jason?" Simmons looked for confirmation toward Joseph's young partner.

"Been no Indians through here in a while," Jason agreed. That didn't mean, he thought silently, that there wouldn't be a whole pack of them through here tomorrow or the next day, but unlike his older counterpart, he didn't like to worry innocent folk who had enough on their minds dealing with the hardships of the long trail from Missouri to California.

Meghan tried to let the sound of adult conversation shut out the howls and yaps that echoed over the prairie. The night beyond the circle of wagons was both awesome and frightening to a girl whose only concept of wide-open spaces was the dirty street in front of her old home, a rundown clapboard house in St. Louis, Missouri. She rested her little pointed chin on her knees and took comfort in the quiet conversation that passed around the men squatting by the fire, letting their voices keep the darkness and emptiness of the prairie at bay. The warmth of the campfire lulled her bone-weary little body into a state of dreamy peace.

It had been a long journey, and Meghan's mind was numbed by the thought of the long stretches of prairie and mountain still ahead of them. At first it had been high adventure, and the sense of adventure had overshadowed the wrench at leaving the little house in St. Louis, where she had lived ever since she could remember. The steamboat ride up the great Mississippi and Missouri rivers to Independence had been exciting, but their arrival at Independence the first of April had been a disappointment. Instead of immediately setting out for California, they had to wait until the wagon master of their party judged the prairie grass to be well enough grown and greened to support the animals and livestock on the crossing. For more than two full weeks Meghan had waited, bored and impatient, until finally, April nineteenth, her family had rolled out of Independence in their newly purchased "prairie schooner," bumping over the ruts behind their team of fat oxen, their goat tied to the back bleating in protest.

Meghan had been thrilled. But the thrill had rapidly worn off on the long and monotonous trail to Fort Kearney, and the even more monotonous trek along the Platte. For Meghan the trip had turned from adventure to a grinding chore, moving slowly westward, eating the dust of the wagons ahead, wearing blisters on her sore feet from walking beside the no longer new wagon and no longer fat oxen, or enduring the bruises on her backside from riding the hard and jouncing seat beside her father and mother. Now, two weeks from Fort Laramie, she felt worn to the bone.

"Meghan." Mary Catherine's gentle voice roused her from her reverie. "I think there's still dishes to do at our own fire. And the water should be hot by now." Mary Catherine got to her feet and looked at Meghan expectantly.

Meghan grimaced, screwing up her elfin face into an expression of distaste. This whole trip was nothing but chores—chores and endless walking and endless dust and endless bouncing on the wagon! But she unfolded her arms and legs and stood up, a gawky collection of knees and elbows, all angles, no curves. Brushing the dirt from the back of her skirt, she started to follow her mother out of the circle of firelight.

"Hey, squirt!" Jim Petrie called laughingly as she passed him. "You still got your dinner on your chin."

Meghan scrubbed at the dried beans on her chin as the others around the fire chuckled good-naturedly. She wrinkled up her pert nose at Jim, whom she liked. He sometimes let her help care for the fine string of horses he was taking to Wyoming Territory.

"Can't eat beans and bacon without getting some on you somewhere. And that's all we have to eat around here," she commented saucily, checking first to make sure her mother was well out of hearing.

Tod Cameron, whom Meghan liked less than Jim, added bitterly, "If these two gents"—he nodded at Old Joseph and Jason—"would find us some fresh meat . . ." Meghan knew Todd had been a gentleman down South before the war had wiped out his family and his landholdings. She figured he was more used to good food and luxury than the rest of them. That didn't make her like him or his complaining any better though.

Old Joseph grunted. "Goin' out tomorrow, ain't we Jase." He grinned at Meghan. "Maybe you'll have something other than beans to put on your chin tomorrow night, baby girl."

"Meghan!" Mary Catherine's impatient voice calling from beyond the circle of firelight reminded her that the chores were waiting. She flashed an elfin grin at the group around the fire as she trotted off to do her mother's bidding.

Mary Catherine was pouring hot water over a pail full of dirty tin plates and cups when Meghan reached their wagon. She greeted her daughter with a frown of irritation.

"I heard that sassiness back there, young miss! Indeed I did! You shouldn't be bothering the menfolk with your prattle, Meghan O'Brian. You'll do well to keep your saucy comments to yourself."

"They started it." Meghan wrinkled her nose, unconcerned by her mother's censure. "Besides, they like me. I didn't say anything so bad. Everybody's tired of eating just beans, bacon, and hardtack."

"You should be grateful you have that to eat," Mary

Catherine admonished as she stirred the dirty dishes in the hot water with a long-handled ladle. "Here"—she handed the ladle to Meghan—"you do this. I have a whole pile of clothes to wash out." She added a few more buffalo chips to the small but aromatic fire that burned under the iron kettle. "If your da and I had eaten so regular and good in Ireland, we'd not have left."

"Aren't you glad you did?" Meghan stirred the dishes with a marked lack of interest.

Mary Catherine strained to wrestle the heavy kettle of hot water to where the pail and washboard sat a few feet away.

"I don't know, Meghan," she sighed when she'd managed to pour the water into the pail and set the kettle back over the fire. "I miss all the green. . . . Well, I suppose you wouldn't know, since you've not seen it. Every step we take toward the west I feel I'm farther away from the old country, from home. Even after ten years away, I still miss it.'

There was a catch in her mother's voice that made Meghan look up from where she was dawdling with the dishes. She was suddenly struck by how tired her mother looked. Her hair, a faded version of Meghan's own fiery red mane, was pinned back severely in a bun at her nape. The fine, classic features of her face were almost hidden by the worn mask of worry and weariness. Meghan couldn't remember a time when her mother hadn't looked old and tired. Even though to Meghan thirty years seemed a ripe old age, other women who were just as old didn't look so ancient.

Mary Catherine pushed the last of the soiled laundry into the hot, sudsy water in her pail and dried her chapped, red hands on her apron. She turned to her daughter and affectionately tugged a rusty-colored braid, noting how many strands had managed to escape confinement and curl wispily around the small face. She could remember a time when her hair had been as bright, her skin had been as fresh and flawless, her eyes as clear. So long ago.

"Maybe you'll get to go to Ireland someday," she said softly. "I'd like to think you would love it as much as I do."

"Sure Ma," Meghan answered, not quite understanding why her mother looked so sad and so far away.

"Well." Mary Catherine shook herself free of her mood. "No more of this woolgathering. You get to the dishes. I've got the mending to do while those clothes soak. You get those dishes clean, you hear. Not like last time, when I had to wash half of them over myself before I could serve your father his dinner."

Meghan screwed up her pert face as her mother disappeared into the wagon, then hastily wiped off the frown as her mother's head poked out from the canvas flap.

"If Mrs. Petrie comes by, you tell her the goat's milk is hanging on the side of the wagon in the milk can. Her new babe's been doing poorly since her milk dried up, and she wants to see if goat's milk will go down easier than cow's milk. And don't you forget to milk old Heather in the morning. We'll need more milk for Mrs. Petrie, and you waited so long this morning that Heather's bleating woke your father."

"Yes, ma'am." Meghan wrinkled her upturned, freckled nose as her mother disappeared once again. Milking Heather was not her favorite chore. The goat would try to kick the stuffings out of anyone who got near her precious teats, but if she wasn't milked on time she set up a fuss to wake the whole wagon train.

Meghan gave the dishes another stir, then cautiously tested the hot dishwater with one finger. Finding the water cool enough for bare skin, she immersed her hands and humming a little tune to herself, pulled them out and watched with childish interest the patterns made in the dust by the droplets falling from her fingers. Then, hearing a rustle in the wagon and fearing a sudden reappearance of her mother, who for some reason had little patience with her dillydallying, she plunged her hands back into the warm water and started scrubbing in earnest.

The tin cups and plates were dented and scratched, not much different from the dishes used by most of the wagon train. Meghan knew some of the ladies on the train had brought along fine china though, because Mrs. Nelson had once showed her some, reverently unpacking one cup and saucer so she could see the delicate decorations and colors. Meghan had never seen such beauty before. The dishes the O'Brians had used in St. Louis had been no better than these she was now banging around in the washpan.

From some of the fine clothing, furniture, and dishes the other members of the wagon train had packed away in wooden boxes that lined the floors of their wagons, Meghan realized that the meager belongings packed in the O'Brian wagon were shabby indeed. Perhaps that was what it meant to be poor. Her mother was always telling her father that they were poor. Yelling at him about it, in fact. Of course he yelled back, and sometimes, when he was good and drunk, he did more than yell. More than once Meghan had gone to sleep at night to the sound of her parents' fighting, and when she woke up in the morning her mother would have a swollen and discolored eye or lip or fresh bruises on her thin arms. Meghan herself had quite often felt the weight of her father's hand, or the dreadful sting of his belt as it whipped across her shoulders and back. For all her tender years, the bruises and welts had simply made her more defiant. But her poor mother seemed somehow diminished by every mark her husband put on her fragile body.

There would be no more fighting, though, Meghan figured, when they got to California. They would be rich. And people who were rich had no reason to fight or to be mean to each other. Her father had promised her mother that they'd be rich, and though her mother didn't believe him, Meghan did. Before they had started on this journey, there had been a fight to end all fights, Meghan thought as she distractedly swished the dishrag over a greasy plate. She could still remember the frantic words that had wakened her from a sound sleep on her screened-off cot by the wood stove.

"We're what?" Mary Catherine demanded of her husband, who at one in the morning had just stumbled through the door and made his grand announcement. Meghan had peered around the corner of the screen and seen her mother in her flannel nightdress, faded hair flying loose around her thin face, hands on hips, facing her father with the light of despair in her eyes.

"I tell you, Mary Catherine, it's the chance we been waiting for. Sent from heaven above, it is!"

"Lord have mercy!" Mary Catherine had wailed. "First it's moving from Ireland to New York when you lost the farm. Then it's from New York to St. Louis when your gaming debts got too high. And now to California? You win a piece of paper in a poker game, probably a crooked game at that, and you want us to risk our lives and go to some unknown, untamed land across the continent? We're living on the edge of the world as it is. And now you want us to jump off!"

"But Mary Catherine!" Meghan still remembered the crestfallen look on her father's face. "It's a deed to a gold mine. A working gold mine, and two other claims besides. We're rich!" His voice pleaded for her approval. "All we've got to do is get there!"

"All we've got to do is get there," Mary Catherine repeated sarcastically. "We're running away again, Daniel. We came to this land for its opportunities, not to fall victim to its vices."

"But Mary Catherine! It's a gold mine!"

Meghan had felt like shrinking back behind her curtain at the bitter look on her mother's face.

"And what if it is a gold mine? How would you work it? You who only know drinking and gambling and, yes, whoring, while I try to provide us with a roof over our heads and something to eat by scrubbing other people's dirty clothes!"

Daniel's face was still bright with elation and with

liquor in spite of his wife's bitter words. He didn't bother to deny her accusations.

"I told you I'd win some day!" he crowed. "And now I have!"

"You've won nothing but a worthless piece of paper. You're too drunk to know when you've been cheated."

"You'll see," he insisted. "You'll see when we get there. No more laundry for you. And maybe we can put Meghan in a school—turn her into a proper little lady. You'd like that, wouldn't you, love?"

"We're not going anywhere!" Mary Catherine was adamant.

"We'll use the rent money to get us to Independence and buy us an outfit. Damned moneygrubber charges us too much anyway. Lousy house isn't worth half what we pay!"

"Get your hands off that money!" Mary Catherine shrieked as Daniel lifted her money jar off the shelf to examine its contents.

"You got more than this hidden away somewhere. You go get it so we can count it."

"You have no right!" Mary Catherine's face had already taken on the sad look of defeat though.

"Go get it."

The tone of her father's voice told Meghan the liquor was wearing off and her father was getting mad. She prayed that her mother would do as her father said. She didn't want to think about what would happen otherwise.

"Go get the money." Daniel's face had taken on the stony look Meghan knew so well. Mary Catherine knew it too. She still bore bruises from their last argument. She sighed in sad resignation as she went to get the money she'd put away for the next month's rent.

The sound of raised voices coming from the wagon interrupted Meghan's reverie. Her always active curiosity piqued, she strained to hear what her parents were saying. Silently she moved closer to the wagon, figuring if she was discovered eavesdropping, she could claim she was on her way to the fire to fetch more hot water.

"You're too soft on the girl!" her father was saying. "Always running about, never seeing to her chores. Needs a switch taken to her, that one does. Not that it's ever done any good before."

Mary Catherine's voice was tight with strain. "Aye, and you've taken the switch to her often enough, Daniel O'Brian. You'll not lift a hand to that child again, you hear. You snatch her from the only home she's known, make her follow us on this godforsaken trail, and expect her to be an angel."

Daniel made a rude sound. "An angel she'll never be. She's a little hellion, thanks to your sparing the whip."

"The child inherited your temper," Mary Catherine commented bitterly. "No amount of whipping is going to drive that out of her."

"Aye, my temper she's got. And your wild looks!" Daniel spat. "Three years from now she'll have every boy-stud in California sniffing after her. She'll be nothing but trouble unless we do something about it now."

Mary Catherine hissed. "Lower your voice! Do you want the whole train to hear our family business? And Meghan is right outside, washing the dishes."

Daniel mumbled a terse reply, but lowered his voice to the point that Meghan could no longer hear. Curses! she thought to herself. A body shouldn't have to endure knowing such a conversation was going on without being able to hear. It wasn't fair! And what right did her father have in calling her a hellion! Just because he couldn't get her to give in when he whipped her.

She crowded close to the wagon, placing one ear up against the canvas. But the only thing she heard were unintelligible murmurs. She screwed up her face in frustration and climbed up on one wheel, pressing her ear to a more likely spot. It was in this improbable posture that her father found her as he stepped down from the wagon bed.

A cuff on the side of her face was the first hint Meghan had of his presence.

"Ow!" she wailed, lurching back from her perch and clapping a hand to her stinging face.

"That'll teach you to mind your own business, missy!"

A defiant gleam sparked in Meghan's eyes. "You were talking about me! That is my business!"

"Damned cheeky twit! I'll wipe that look off your face!" Daniel raised his hand for another blow, but he was interrupted by a feminine voice coming out of the darkness, followed by the plump presence of Caroline Petrie.

"Oh!" she exclaimed uncertainly. "Did I come at an awkward time?"

Meghan shot her father a look of childish triumph as her mother, alerted by the sound of Caroline's voice, emerged from the wagon.

"I came to see if you have any goat's milk you could spare," Caroline said hastily, trying to ignore the fireworks shooting between the eyes of father and daughter.

Mary Catherine looked at her husband and daughter and her mouth tightened to a grim line.

"Meghan," she instructed, "get Mrs. Petrie the milk can that's hanging on the side of the wagon."

"Yes'm." Meghan grinned at her father and made her escape. Mary Catherine gave her husband a grim look of reproach. Caroline cleared her throat awkwardly. "Lovely night, isn't it. Other than those coyotes yammering. They woke me up at some unholy hour last night. Did you hear them?"

"Yes, indeed," Mary Catherine replied politely. Meghan ran around the corner of the wagon, milk can swinging from one hand.

"Here's the goat's milk, Caroline. You're welcome to the whole thing, and we'll have plenty tomorrow too, if your little one takes to it." She handed her the pail. Caroline smiled her thanks and with a slightly embarrassed nod to Daniel, turned and disappeared into the darkness. Meghan moved into the shelter of her mother's skirts.

"Well, now," Daniel hesitated, seeing both females ranged against him, stuck together solider than rock, he figured. To hell with it, he thought. He'd go down to John O'Donnell's wagon and have a swig or two. More pleasant than staying here. Old John always had a bottle handy and was always willing to share with a fellow Irishman. "To hell with you both!" he mumbled, jamming his hat on his head and turning to leave.

"Daniel!" Mary Catherine called after him. "When will you be back? We have . . ."

"When I damn well please!" he rasped. "That's when!"

Mary Catherine sighed and squeezed Meghan's shoulder. "Do you want to tell me what happened?"

"Nothing," Meghan lied. She had no desire to add to her mother's burdens, or to her own by admitting she was eavesdropping. Even at her tender and inexperienced age she could tell her mother was near the breaking point.

Mary Catherine stuck a finger experimentally in the dish pail. "Meghan!" she scolded gently. "You've not even finished the dishes. And here the water's all cold."

"I'll get another kettle," Meghan sighed.

Her mother looked at her sadly as she hauled the kettle from the fire to the pail. "Can't you try to get along with your father, Meghan?"

"I don't like him," Meghan admitted without hesitation as she poured the steaming water over the still-dirty dishes. "He's always mad, and he hits me."

"That's nonsense. Of course you like him. He's your father. And he only hits you because he loves you."

Meghan remembered that it was her beloved mother she was talking to and choked back the rude noise that leapt into her throat. "Does he hit you because he loves you too?"

Mary Catherine refused to meet her daughter's eyes. "Some men just can't help themselves, Meghan," she tried to explain. "Your father's got a temper. Much like yours." She smiled and reached out a hand to brush the curly wisps of russet hair from her daughter's freckle-splashed face. "And he can't always help what he does."

Meghan made an unpleasant face. "Maybe he could help it better if he wasn't always drunk."

Mary Catherine's sigh came straight from her heart. "How wise you think you are, and all of nine years old." She looked at her daughter sadly. "Maybe when you grow up you'll realize things are not always as simple as they seem. Finish the dishes now, then go to bed. We've another long day tomorrow." She turned before disappearing into the wagon, adding an afterthought. "And do try, at least, not to make your father mad. At least for a few days."

Meghan scrubbed the plates with a vengeance, taking out her temper on the helpless tin. Life would be so pleasant, she thought, with just her sweet mother and herself. If her father would just disappear from the face of the earth life would be so simple. Her mother and she could go to California and be rich and happy. They'd never have to worry about her father and his temper and his drinking and hitting.

She put the clean dishes in their box on the side of the wagon, then used the leftover hot water to scrub her face and arms. She collected her tarp and blankets and rolled herself up snugly under the wagon. Tired as she was, the hard ground felt like a feather bed. She wondered, as she drifted off to sleep, if what her mother said was true. Would she see things differently when she grew up? If so, she wasn't sure she wanted to grow up. She was certain the way she saw things now was right.

In the darkness of the night, not very far away from where Meghan lay rolled in her blanket, savage men were making savage plans—bloody plans that made it very unlikely that Meghan O'Brian would ever grow up to find out if her mother's words were true.

# Chapter Two

"Goddamn horse! Move!"

Jason Sinclair shoved against the broad red-brown rump that threatened to pin him against the wagon. The big bay stud jerked against the halter rope in irritation and sidestepped deftly as Jason gave him a hearty swat on the flank.

"Wouldn't have that trouble if'n you'd teach that damn stud to behave like a civilized horse 'stead of some crazy wild stallion," Old Joseph observed from a safe distance, saddling his own dun gelding.

"More use to me this way." Jason grunted as he hefted the heavy saddle in one hand and quickly maneuvered it onto the back of the bay stud before he could think up any more tricks. He tightened the cinch, giving the big bay a final pat on finishing. The horse blew loudly in disgust, his warm breath steaming in the cold predawn air.

From under bushy gray brows Old Joseph observed Jason and the stud as he finished tightening the girth on his own mount. He figured the boy was right about the horse. Those two seemed to belong together somehow, the stud being no more untamed and unruly than the boy who rode him.

Joseph had never met an older eighteen-year-old. In spite of his few years, there was very little of the boy about Jason Sinclair, a fact Old Joseph had noted in his favor when he agreed to take the kid on as an assistant of sorts in scouting for the Simmons train. He was glad he had, because with every passing year the ground seemed to get harder, the nights colder, and the food worse on these emigrant trains. This one was his last, Old Joseph figured, and the boy had taken a load of work off his shoulders. Still, there was something odd about Jason that set Old Joseph to wondering. His shoulders were broad, and his hard-muscled torso evidenced a physical strength greater than most grown men's. That in itself wasn't so strange, Joseph acknowledged. Some boys hardened up faster than others. But there were other things. The kid had come along with him to learn, but it turned out there was little the experienced old scout could teach him. The boy had skills that rivaled those of the best frontiersman Old Joseph had ever met. He was a dead shot with a rifle and carried a long-bladed knife in his belt with a confidence that made chills run down Joseph's spine. But the eyes were what completed the impression—deep-set, light whiskey brown bordering on amber—eyes that no eighteen-year-old kid should have. Combined with his bronze hair streaked blond by the sun, they gave him the look of a yellow puma tom stalking his prey, just as cold and just as hard. Old Joseph wondered what had happened in the boy's short life to give him the look of a hardened savage. But he wasn't about to ask. The kid didn't take kindly to personal questions, and his right hand hopped in a nasty reflex toward his pistol on the slightest provocation. Old Joseph figured it was a mite healthier to keep his curiosity to himself.

"Think I need another cup before we set out," the old scout grumbled. "My old bones are still creaking from the cold." He walked stiffly over to their little fire and poured a cup of strong black coffee. Jason joined him, bending over to pour himself a cup of the steaming brew. Joseph noted with envy the fluid grace of Jason's movements and the supple play of muscles against his snug buckskin shirt. Youth! he thought. We never appreciate it until we lose it. He rubbed his stiff neck and grimaced.

The rosy glow in the eastern sky was brightening as a molten sliver of sun made its appearance above the gently undulating horizon. The wagon train was beginning to stir. The clang of pots and pans heralded the start of breakfast, and an occasional whine or shout from a child's throat shattered the peace of the prairie dawn.

"We better get a move on." Old Joseph tossed the remainder of his coffee into the dust. "We get any of these greenhorns fussin' around us we'll never get off."

"Too late." One of Jason's tawny brows quirked slightly as he observed the approach of a little calico-clad redhead who trotted toward them with barely contained eagerness. "Here comes trouble."

Meghan woke early to the sound of birdsong from a nearby thicket, the cheerful carols heralding the imminent arrival of dawn. From her hard bed beneath the wagon she could hardly make out the shapes of other wagons in the circle. Dew had condensed on her blanket, and she was cold and stiff from sleeping on the ground. Her first inclination was to huddle under the blanket and go back to sleep, but then she remembered that Old Joseph and Jason were going hunting this morning. Maybe if she caught them before they left, she could persuade them to take her with them.

Screwing up her face against the first shock of the cold morning air, Meghan threw off the blanket and pulled on her stockings and boots. She crawled out from under the wagon to the outside of the circle and squinted through the uncertain gray light, trying to locate the scout's fire. Nothing was to be seen, but she did catch a hint of conversation carrying through the crisp morning silence. Without bothering to rebraid her unruly red hair or smooth the wrinkles from her faded cotton dress, she trotted toward the sound of the voices.

Jason was less than glad to see little Meghan O'Brian bouncing up to their campfire, the sun rising behind her and transforming her into a fiery-haloed pixie. Having never experienced a real childhood himself, he had little time or patience for children. This kid in particular could be a total nuisance, though he couldn't help but feel a little sorry for her. He didn't like her overbearing, drunken father, and he had to pity her mother, a woman used up before her time and totally ineffectual, it seemed, in protecting the child from the father's vagaries of mood and temper.

The ungainly little pixie lurched to an awkward halt beside their fire and smiled up at Jason with all the charm, he thought, of a mosquito preparing its tiny but irritating attack.

"Going hunting?" she asked needlessly.

"Yeah," Jason mumbled, downing the last of his now cold coffee and setting the coffeepot off the fire. He picked up his rifle and shoved it into the scabbard on his saddle, trying to ignore Meghan's persistent presence. The big stud laid back his ears in irritation at this evidence they were about to be on their way. Jason turned and found Meghan on his heels.

"Don't get close to that horse," he cautioned. "He doesn't like people much."

Meghan's eyes grew wide as the stallion regarded her with malevolent eyes. Obedient for once, she backed off.

"Why do you ride him if he's mean?"

"I didn't say he was mean," Jason said shortly. "I just said he doesn't like people much. We get along okay." He didn't bother to explain that they probably got along because Jason didn't like people much, either.

Meghan watched him as he tightened the cinch for mounting. "Can I go with you?"

Old Joseph chuckled, sitting astride the placid dun and watching the two of them with eyes twinkling under his gray brows.

"No," Jason said, swinging easily up to his saddle. The stud snorted in irritation and sidestepped.

"Why not?" Meghan's lower lip crept out in a pout. "You took Jimmy Nelson with you two weeks ago."

Jason cursed the female memory. "Jimmy Nelson is thirteen. Besides, he's a boy. He can ride and shoot like a man."

"I can ride," Meghan fibbed.

''You can't go,'' Jason declared with finality.

Meghan squared her chin and lifted her freckle-dusted nose higher into the air. ''It's not fair! Jimmy Nelson's no better than me! You just like him 'cause he's a boy. That's not fair.'' A small tear spilled out of one eye and trickled down her cheek.

Jason cursed inwardly and looked to Old Joseph for help. The old scout immediately found something interesting to gaze at somewhere out on the prairie.

''You can't go, Meghan,'' he repeated with a sigh. ''But I'll give you a ride back to your wagon.''

Her complaints forgotten, Meghan was immediately all smiles. ''Really?''

''Come on. Climb up.''

Meghan approached the big bay horse cautiously, remembering Jason's warning of moments before. When she placed one foot in the stirrup and grasped Jason's hand, the stud flicked his ears in annoyance but stood still for her scrambling climb into the saddle. Jason lifted her onto the pommel in front of him, her skirt pushed up around her knees and her thin bare legs flapping on either side.

When the stud responded to the pressure from Jason's legs and moved out in a gentle trot, Meghan grasped the saddle horn for dear life, immediately giving the lie to her claim that she could ride. Jason steadied her with an arm wrapped around her narrow waist, sending a strange thrill of excitement through her. She leaned back against his chest experimentally, and when he didn't object, she snuggled even closer, deciding that Jason Sinclair was the nicest, handsomest, bravest man in the world, even if he wouldn't take her hunting. He'd make a good brother, she decided as they trotted slowly around the circle of wagons. A big brother like Jason would never let her father beat her mother, or her either. Or better still, maybe when she grew up in a few years she'd marry him. Yes, she decided, that would be a lot better. A brother would be nice, but a husband was forever. In a few years maybe she'd be beautiful, as her mother was when she was young. Jason would see how beautiful she was and marry her. And he would never let anyone yell at her or hit her again.

Meghan's fantasies had hardly begun when they arrived at the O'Brian wagon. Mary Catherine looked up in surprise when the big bay stud came to a halt beside her cooking fire.

"Meghan?"

"Hi, Ma!" Meghan grinned, her green eyes sparkling with excitement.

"Morning, Mrs. O'Brian." Jason touched the brim of his hat in greeting. "Hope you don't mind my giving Meghan a little ride. She was keeping us two bachelors company this morning."

Mary Catherine smiled uneasily as Meghan slid down the side of the horse, assisted by Jason's strong grip, and lit ungracefully on the ground, tousled but in one piece. "I hope she wasn't bothering you, Mr. Sinclair, Joseph." She greeted the two men politely, then looked disapprovingly at Meghan's unwashed face, uncombed hair, and wrinkled dress.

"Not at all, ma'am," Joseph assured her. "She's always welcome at our fire." He turned to Jason. "We better be going, boy. Sun's well up. Shoulda been gone an hour ago."

Jason touched the brim of his hat again. "So long, Meghan. Have a good day, Mrs. O'Brian."

Jason was silent as the stud's long strides brought him even with Joseph's dun. But Old Joseph wasn't about to let the boy off that easy.

"Seems you got all the women on this train swoonin', boy," he chuckled dryly. "Shoulda seen that little gal's face when you lifted her up in front of you. And the mother wasn't much different when you rode up to that fire." He went on, ignoring the irritated gleam in the boy's eye. "Course, one's too young, and the other's a bit old." He grinned knowingly. "Then there's that Nelson girl— Jimmy's sister, isn't she? She's about the right age. Good tits on that girl, too. 'Spect you know that, though.

Somethin' about those redheads though . . . Never did care much for freckle-faced redheads myself. But that Mary Catherine O'Brian ain't a bad-lookin' woman, and that little girl's goin' to grow up a real beauty.''

Jason merely grunted and regarded the older man malevolently. "Kid's a pest."

"All kids are pests," Old Joseph agreed. "Females never grow out of it. A female's a pest from the day she's born till the day she dies, mostly. They got some uses, though. Figure you've found out about that."

Jason was silent.

"Course, that little Meghan's a particular kind of pest. That little gal's goin' to be a wildcat one day. Glad I'm not goin' to be the man to have to handle that."

Jason allowed himself a tight smile. "That one will be lucky to find herself a man. There's getting to be enough women out here that a man doesn't have to pick the roses with all the thorns."

Joseph grinned at him. "You're gettin' downright poetic, boy."

The two men drew rein on a low, grassy bluff and looked back at the wagon train. From this distance the train took on the aspect of a long, white, segmented snake as the wagons pulled out of the night circle and started to move out along the well-worn wagon trail. A hundred or so yards beyond the train, the North Platte gleamed like a silver ribbon in the morning sun, guiding the emigrants ever westward to Fort Laramie and beyond, well into the heart of Wyoming Territory.

Jason pulled his hat down to shade his face. The sun, now a blazing ball a good three fingers above the horizon, was quickly dispelling the morning cool and promised a hot June day to come.

"Don't feel real easy about riding away from the train today," Jason commented. "My gut tells me something isn't quite right."

Old Joseph grunted. Any other eighteen-year-old kid he'd have totally ignored. Jason Sinclair—well, Jason was different. So Old Joseph thought a moment before he answered. He, too, felt a mite jumpy this morning. But he attributed his uneasiness to old age and shot nerves.

"Your gut's tellin' you those cold beans you ate for breakfast ain't settin' right. That's your problem."

"Could be," Jason admitted.

"Ain't seen no fresh Injun sign for days. No redskins for miles around, seems. Don't know why. You'd think that horse herd of Jim Petrie's would be pullin' 'em in like shit draws flies."

"Seems like it's almost too quiet," Jason added. "The Cheyenne and Sioux have been working bloody hell ever since that fool Chivington's attack at Sand Creek last November."

"Well, wherever they're at, they ain't around here. I been either fightin' 'em or living with 'em for twenty-five years. I can smell an Injun ten miles away."

Jason grunted acknowledgment, but he was still uneasy.

"We need to pull down some game today. Buffalo would be nice, if'n we're lucky. Antelope would be nicer."

"Well"—Jason turned the bay stud and set his heels to its sides—"let's go, then."

It was the last time Jason Sinclair would trust another man's judgment above his own.

Meghan figured the morning had started out about even. She hadn't convinced the men to take her hunting, but then she'd gotten to ride with Jason Sinclair halfway around the circle of wagons. The thrill of sitting astride that big horse with her hero's arm around her had made up for the disappointment of having to stay with the train while the scouts were out having fun. And all the other kids had been wide-eyed to see her perched upon that big bay stud in front of the handsome young scout. Her status would certainly go up a couple of notches after that! Things had gone downhill rapidly after she had returned to her wagon, though. As usual, she had neglected to milk Heather when she'd gotten up this morning, having more important things on her mind. She'd just plain forgotten about that nasty old goat. It hadn't been on purpose. But her mother had scolded her soundly as soon as the two scouts were out of hearing, not only for forgetting to milk Heather and letting the goat wake the whole train with her bleating, but for bothering the scouts as well. And of course when she finally did milk the goat, the old nanny fidgeted and fumed and tried to kick her—revenge, no doubt, for being forgotten.

As if all that wasn't bad enough, just before the wagons were ready to roll her father had returned from who knows where, bleary-eyed and rumpled and smelling of smoke, sweat, and whiskey. Meghan wrinkled her nose when he first came near and received a sharp cuff for her sassiness. The hurt look on her mother's face when he appeared was worse than any blow from her father, though.

The strained silence that stretched between her parents for the rest of the morning made Meghan's mood even worse. Since her father had not gotten up enough nerve to square himself with her mother, he took out his temper on her. Everything she did seemed to be wrong, drawing his sharp criticism and sometimes a blow for good measure. Mary Catherine, sunk in the gloom of her own thoughts, spared little attention for her daughter's plight.

By the time the train was stretched out once again along the trail, the sun was a blazing furnace in the eastern sky. Meghan wished that just once there might be some middle zone between the cold of night and the heat of day. Her fate on this trip seemed to be either to shiver or to sweat. She'd rather be shivering than sweating, she decided as she trudged along just behind their wagon, Heather trotting placidly beside her. This morning she preferred the goat's company to that of her parents, who sat together, silently and stiffly, on the seat of the wagon.

The morning grew hotter, and Meghan could feel trickles of sweat running down her back and sides under her cotton bodice. Dust churned up by a thousand hooves hovered in the still air and made breathing a chore. Meghan's head ached from the heat and the remnants of Daniel's most recent parental blow. The blankets hadn't been shaken out to his satisfaction, and the milk can not tied securely enough to the wagon. Finally, she risked drawing her parents' notice by clambering into the back of the moving wagon. Mary Catherine turned a cautious look on her as she scrambled to find a seat among the wooden packing boxes, but said nothing, her very silence warning Meghan not to disturb her father.

The shade of the canvas-covered wagon was welcome after the heat of the sun, though in the dim light Meghan could still see that even here the air was thick with dust. When she wiped the droplets of sweat from her face, her hand came away smeared with dirt. For the hundredth time that morning she thought with envy of the two scouts, riding in the fresh air away from the dust and away from the stink of the livestock. She hoped they brought down something good to eat. That, at least, would be something to look forward to tonight—something other than beans, bacon, and hardtack for dinner.

Meghan had drifted into a torpor induced by the heat and the sway of the wagon when she was jerked to alertness by a sharp, grinding jolt, followed by a string of curses coming from her father. The wagon shuddered mightily, then abruptly tilted, coming to rest with a crash, listing to one side like a grounded ship. Meghan screeched as packing boxes came flying at her from across the wagon bed, threatening to crush her legs before she could lift them out of the way of danger.

Mary Catherine's pale, dusty face appeared at the back wagon flap. "Meghan, are you all right?" She reached up and helped Meghan from her perch.

"Sure, Ma," Meghan assured her as she awkwardly slipped to the ground through her mother's arms. "What happened?"

Her question was echoed by Dick Simmons, whose

horse slid to a dust-roiling halt beside their wagon. Daniel, being busy filling the air with curses, didn't answer, but the question was rhetorical anyway. A broken wagon wheel was all too familiar to the travelers who journeyed along this road.

Simmons pushed his hat back on his head and sighed, wiping the dust and sweat from his forehead with the back of his arm. "Shit!" he spat, then looked apologetically at Mary Catherine. " 'Scuse me, ma'am.''

Daniel looked ready to take the wagon and wheel apart with his bare hands when he noticed Simmons's presence. "Broken wheel!" he explained unnecessarily.

"So I see. Bad luck."

The wagons behind them were pulling around, shouting at their oxen to catch up to those ahead. Soon the O'Brian wagon would be the last in line, having to eat the dust of all the others.

"Guess we'll call an early nooning," Dick decided. "I'll get a few men back here to help you. Maybe we can be back on the road in time to make some miles today."

"Thank you, Mr. Simmons." Mary Catherine smiled at the wagon master, seeing that her husband was still too sunk in bad temper to be decently courteous.

An early nooning was a welcome break on such a hot morning. The meal was no treat. Though some families, most families in fact, were better provisioned than the O'Brians, many were making do with beans and bacon for most meals. A few families still had strips of dried beef or buffalo meat hanging from their wagons like odd tassels, but the O'Brians had none. Game was scarce along the well-traveled emigrant trail; and with the Indian threat, men were reluctant to stray far from the protection of the train to search out fresh meat. So Meghan had grown accustomed to very plain and meager fare, which in truth was not so much different from what she'd eaten in St. Louis. For a poor family, fresh meat and vegetables were luxuries.

The noon meal was at least filling if not tasty, and after

eating, Meghan felt revived enough to wander curiously over to where her father and two other men were working to put the repaired wheel back on their wagon. She was forestalled by her mother, however, who shoved a water bucket in her hand and pointed meaningfully toward the river.

"Awww!" she whined.

"Meghan!"

Mary Catherine's tone warned Meghan that trying to weasel out of hauling water would be a losing battle, so she settled for assuming her best abused-child look and set out for the river, the bucket swinging from her hand. She wrinkled her nose in distaste as she scrambled down the muddy banks to get near the water, if water it could be called. The North Platte looked more like a river of mud than a stream of water. The smell of the sluggish waterway was noxious, and Meghan felt like holding her nose as she dipped her bucket to be filled. It would be a little better, she knew, after some of the mud and silt had settled out, but she could almost understand her da's preference for whiskey to what passed as fresh water on the wagon train. Almost every man, woman, and child on the train had been plagued with the trots ever since they had left Fort Kearney.

Meghan's arms ached by the time she hauled the bucket back up the slight slope to the wagon trail. Now, she hoped, she'd be allowed to watch the men at their work. It wasn't much for entertainment, but it was better than doing chores. Her hopes were for naught, however, for Mary Catherine was determined to keep her out of her father's way.

Water was steaming over the fire for washing dishes, and when she was done with that, her mother told her in no uncertain terms if there was still time, she could take the sack and collect buffalo chips for the supper fire. There looked to be enough around here to occupy her with that chore until the train was moving once again. Meghan pushed her lower lip out in her best pout, but her mother was adamant.

Collecting buffalo chips was Meghan's least favorite chore. Trailing a burlap sack behind her, she wrapped an old apron around her hand in order to pick up the dried but still malodorous dung piles. Her mother had been right. There were enough piles in this area to keep her well occupied until the train rolled. There would be no shortage of fuel for the fire tonight.

For fifteen minutes Meghan diligently combed the area near the train where the grass had been grazed off by the livestock of numerous passing wagons. Her sack was almost full when she drifted farther afield to where the grass still stood chest high to one of her short stature. She spent several minutes searching through the high grass, then with a sigh of boredom and disgust with her task straightened to stretch, her back aching from the continued bending.

The air was hot and still. For a change, no birds were singing in the thickets. Meghan wiped the beads of sweat from her brow with the back of her arm and looked back at the train, wagon after wagon stretched out in a line along the well-worn trail, people still bustling around the cookfires, trying to get organized to hit the road for another long afternoon. She could see Jim Petrie in one of the wagons closest to where she stood. His herd of fine horses was clustered by his wagon, kept from straying into the higher, more succulent grasses by his little sheepdog turned horse-herder.

A slight movement brought Meghan's attention back to the prairie where she stood. She frowned. She could've sworn the grass about a hundred feet from where she stood had rippled slightly, yet there was no breeze at all. There it was again! Just the slightest shiver of the coarse blades.

A chill ran down Meghan's spine as she stood frozen. Wild animals very seldom came close to a train, especially with all the activity that was going on now. But what else could be causing that movement? Her imagination? She moved in what she hoped was a casual manner to a better vantage point. A tiny break in the vegetation gave her a better view in the direction of the movement. Out of the corner of her eye she spied a splotch of color. Her breathing quickened into short gasps of fear as she realized the color was the gaudy war paint on a Sioux warrior.

Meghan's heart pounded so that for a moment she was dizzy. Studiously she avoided looking at the spot where the Indian crouched, hoping against all reason that the warrior didn't realize she had seen him. Every fiber of her nine-year-old body screamed for her to run, but she knew that would mean certain death. Casually she wandered away from the Indian's hiding place, making her way slowly toward the wagons, dragging her gunnysack behind her and occasionally forcing herself to bend and pick up another buffalo pile. When she reached the grazed-off apron of ground adjacent the train, she could no longer contain her terror. She broke into a desperate run for the nearest wagon.

"Indians!" she screamed at the top of her voice.

People looked up from their work, smiling and shaking their heads at the child's imagination. The smiles were wiped from their faces when a line of warriors materialized as if by magic out of the tall grasses two hundred feet from the train. A moment followed in which the earth itself seemed to hold its breath, the emigrants regarding the Indians in stunned silence and the warriors standing as if menacing statues, only their fierce grins showing that they thought their surprise a hugely successful joke. Then all hell descended.

Women screamed and children cried, not understanding what was happening but reacting to the fear in the air. Shouts and curses competed with the war cries of the Sioux and Cheyenne as men urged the oxen and horses to pull the wagons into a closed defensive circle. Meghan was still screaming her warning as she leapt between two wagons of the half-formed circle. An arrow thudded into a wagon bed close to her head as she made a desperate lunge for the relative safety of the closing circle.

The circle was only half closed when the leading warriors reached it. Fortunately the open portion faced away from the attack and toward the river, but still some Indians were able to leap through the narrow openings between the closed-up wagons before the defenders could take their places. One brave, intent on taking a bright red scalp from the girl who had screamed warning, leapt between the wagons close on Meghan's heels. He was quickly dispatched by a shotgun blast to the head at short range.

Meghan screamed and covered her ears as the sound of the shotgun deafened her. She turned to see Jim Petrie, shotgun in hand, standing over the mangled body of a young Indian. "Cheyenne," he said in a tight voice, "but there's Sioux out there too."

Meghan just whimpered.

"Meghan!" Mary Catherine's desperate voice was edged with tears. "Oh, thank God!" She grabbed Meghan, who stood stunned and staring at the bloody piece of meat that used to be a man, and hugged her to her spare bosom.

The Indians who had gotten through the circle were quickly dispatched, and the circle was closed with wagon tongues overlapping to form a defendable barrier. None of the emigrants had been hurt, though Jim Petrie had lost two horses that he hadn't managed to drive into the protective circle in time. The defenders began to take heart, thinking the small band that attacked them could never break through the organized front the wagons now presented. Then the main body of Indians appeared. A line of mounted warriors rose over the ground swell that hid the horizon from view. They were painted and stripped for battle, each brave having a bow slung over his bare shoulder and a rifle in his hand.

Tod Cameron groaned as he took in the scene. Beside him, Dick Simmons looked grim. "That first party must've been the advance scouts or some young braves who wanted some extra glory. They were forced to attack prematurely when Meghan gave warning. Otherwise, we'd have been caught by this bunch with our wagons all strung out.''

"Might as well have been," Tod commented bitterly. "What chance do we stand against a force like that?"

"Not much," Simmons acknowledged calmly. "Not if they really mean business. And they look like they do."

Mary Catherine urged her trembling daughter back to their wagon, where Daniel, sober now but with a face gone pasty white with fear, crouched with a rifle. Mary Catherine climbed in the wagon and pulled Meghan after her. Frantically she pulled at the heavy wooden packing boxes that held all their worldly possessions, making an empty space just large enough for a small girl.

"Get in here." Mary Catherine pulled Meghan toward the space.

Heart pounding frantically, Meghan obeyed, crouching down until she was all but hidden by the surrounding boxes.

"Don't you come out until I come for you, or one of the other people on the train does. You understand?"

Meghan nodded mutely, for once in her life at a loss for words.

"Don't you make a sound, no matter what happens." Mary Catherine's voice faltered as her green eyes, so like her daughter's, filled with tears. "You do just as I say, or I swear by all the saints I'll whale the living tar out of you myself, then give you to your father to finish the job."

Meghan stared at her mother wordlessly as Mary Catherine looked down at her, tears streaming freely now down her windburned cheeks. Her face showed that she longed to say something else, but she didn't. She threw a blanket over Meghan's hiding place, arranging it so that it looked as if it covered a solid pile of boxes. Meghan felt the wagon sway slightly as her mother swung herself down to the ground, leaving her in her stifling cubbyhole, afraid to move an inch.

Her hot, dark hiding place was her own private splinter of hell, Meghan decided as her cramped muscles screamed for relief. The smell of her own sweat became unbearable. An eternity passed, which was in reality no more than an hour. For that long Meghan held to her mother's command. She crouched with silent tears of terror coursing down her cheeks, listening to chaos erupting around her. The sharp reports of rifles, both the Indians' and the emigrants', tore through her aching head while the screams of terrorized women and children tore through her heart. She shut her eyes tightly and brought up her hands to cover her ears in an attempt to shut out the sounds crashing in upon her, but to no avail. Then, after an eternity had passed, she could stand it no longer.

She turned in her cubbyhole, forcing her stiff and burning muscles to move until she was facing the side of the wagon instead of the packing boxes. Slowly and carefully she lifted the canvas that was lashed to the wagon bed, fastening her eye to the tiny slit she'd produced. The scene that met her eye set terror to grip her anew.

The emigrants were in panic. Sioux and Cheyenne warriors had broken the barrier of wagons and now wreaked havoc inside the circle. The emigrants, inexperienced and ill-prepared for this kind of savage fighting, were easy prey for the braves who ran or rode unhindered where they wished. The fierce grins on their faces evidenced the great good time they were having with their cat-and-mouse games as they played with the terrified white people. Several wagons were afire, sending columns of smoke toward the pale blue sky.

Meghan longed to burst out of her hiding place, jump down from the wagon, and run away from the sight of her friends fighting for their lives, and losing, but her mother's stern command echoed in her mind. Don't move, no matter what happens. Don't move. Don't move. Don't move.

The wagon lurched as someone jumped on board. Meghan crouched down into a trembling ball as booted footsteps pounded on the wagon bed beside her little den, then stopped as the wagon swayed under a second man's weight. Her father's voice cursed, then grunted something as a meaty thunk was accompanied by a savage victory scream. The fall of Daniel's body shook the wagon; Meghan tasted her own salty blood in her mouth as she bit her lip in an attempt to keep silent. Then the frantic beating of her heart was accompanied by wet ripping sounds as the Indian stripped her father's head of its hair. Another short eternity passed before she felt the brave swing down.

Terror was giving way to numbness in Meghan's mind. She wished she could die right now rather than have to listen and see any more of the bloody massacre. But still she crouched in her hole, crying openly now as she watched her friends murdered. When fear turned to anger she never knew, but when she saw Mary Catherine being dragged kicking and screaming by the hair across the bloodied ground by a grinning brave, something snapped inside her. A great stillness settled upon her soul as she felt the anger swell inside her, expanding into something white-hot and explosive, something that demanded release. Then she let go.

Angry Bull grinned widely as the red-haired white woman he held screamed and kicked like a mad banshee. This was the best time he'd had in a long while. If his wife, Red Buffalo Woman, weren't so jealous, he might take the red-hair with him as a captive. As it was, he'd have to have his fun here then throw the woman away. He had no trouble subduing the woman with one hand while unfastening his breechclout with the other. All hindrance aside, he threw Mary Catherine to the ground and landed on top of her. Hastily and brutally he pushed her skirts up around her waist, ripped off what flimsy cloth remained, prized apart her thighs, and thrust himself into her. But just as he started his furious pumping into the moaning woman, a demon landed on his back, screeching like an evil spirit. With a cry he was up off the red-hair in an instant, casually splitting open her head on a nearby rock so he was free to turn on his tormentor. His quick

movements flung the demon from his back, and it was
revealed to his amazed eyes to be nothing but a half-grown
girl-child, a girl-child with red hair and green eyes like
those of the one he'd just pleasured himself on. He
laughed.

Angry Bull's laugh was premature though, for he'd
never met Irish fury head-on. Meghan saw her mother
lying still as death where the brave had thrown her, but she
felt no grief, not now. Now she only felt rage, a rage that
ate at her insides and made her hurt and want to hurt in
turn. The brave was grinning, laughing, stalking her as if
they were playing a game where only he could be the
winner. She backed away cautiously, knowing she was
going to die and not caring—knowing she was going to
die and caring only about taking this Indian with her. Her
foot struck the knife Angry Bull had discarded with his
breechclout.

Meghan grinned a wholly unchildlike grin and stooped
to pick up the knife. The smile of triumph didn't leave the
Indian's face, not until she lunged at him and, due partly
to luck and partly to Angry Bull's confident carelessness,
scored a bloody gash over his ribs. The Indian lurched
back in surprise, then lunged forward in an angry rush. No
longer enjoying the game he'd started, he determined to
bring it to a quick end with his bare hands. But a guttural
order brought him up short.

Standing Antelope repeated his order and gestured with
his war spear for Angry Bull to back off, leaving Meghan
watching them both warily, holding her knife poised in
front of her. For a long moment the warbonnet-clad newcomer sat like a statue on his pony, regarding her with
impassive eyes. Then he turned to Angry Bull.

"You will not kill this little one."

Angry Bull shouted his objection.

"No!" Standing Antelope faced him down. "She is a
warrior in a girl-child's body. Look at the hate in her eyes.
Look at her courage—facing death with the ferocity of a
she-cat. She is worthy to be *Tsistsistas*, one of the People."

Angry Bull sneered, but turned sulkily away. Standing Antelope dismounted and walked quickly up to Meghan, deftly avoiding the ineffectual thrust of her knife. Closing his long brown fingers around her wrist, he ignored her kicking and twisting and squeezed until the weapon dropped from her nerveless hand. Meghan still fought as he lifted her onto his pony and mounted behind her.

Jason kicked in disgust at the burned-out shell of the Cameron wagon. The string of oaths he rattled off didn't come close to expressing his feelings at seeing the pathetic remains of the Simmons train left behind by the Cheyenne and Sioux—the smoking ruins of wagons and the bloody ruins that had once been people who, while not exactly his friends, had at least for the past two months been his comrades.

"Well"—Old Joseph rubbed his bristly jaw in thought—"I figured when we saw that column of smoke that there was big trouble. I didn't exactly figure it was this big, though. Didn't leave much, did they?"

Jason didn't reply, just tilted his head back and looked into the hot, blue sky, as if seeking an answer there.

"Don't take it so personal, boy. If we'd have been here things wouldn't have been no different. We'd just be lying here with the rest of 'em."

"Maybe." Jason conceded.

"No maybe about it."

Jason looked down at Mary Catherine O'Brian's still form sprawled beside her wagon, her face drooping sadly without the support of a scalp. His gut clenched and threatened to rebel.

"You found anything that looks like it could be the O'Brian kid?" he asked.

"The O'Brian girl?" Joseph repeated. "Naw, can't say as I have."

"Neither have I. I don't think she's here."

"Could be they took her. Wouldn't be unusual."

Jason felt a wave of guilt and nausea as he thought of Meghan, with hair uncombed and dress wrinkled and unbrushed but with eyes full of mischief and life. She'd begged to go with them this morning. If he had said yes . . .

Old Joseph saw the look in Jason's eyes. "Don't get any fancy ideas about going after her, son. We wouldn't stand a ghost of a chance against a band of riled-up braves big enough to take on a train this size. Besides, she's probably dead already. If she's not, she might get lucky and get adopted. But for sure if those braves sight us followin' 'em, she'll be dead before you can shake a stick at a snake."

"Yeah," Jason acknowledged reluctantly. "I guess so." It was difficult to curb his first impulse for immediate action, preferably violent action to dull the sharp edge of frustration biting into his soul at the sight before him.

"We'd better get goin'." Old Joseph swung up onto the dun. "Sooner we let the army know about this, the sooner they'll do something about it, and Fort Cottonwood is a far piece down the road." He thought privately that the army wouldn't do very damn much, but they would do more than two men alone could.

Jason took one last look at the scattered bloody remains of the people who'd depended on him, in part, to guide them safely to California. He turned and mounted the bay stud, who for once didn't object, sensing the mood of his rider. Wordlessly he pulled abreast of the dun. The two men pointed their horses' noses toward the open prairie, neither looking back at the sight they'd never forget. As their hoofbeats faded, the only sound breaking the peace of the prairie was the relentless buzzing of feasting flies.

# Chapter Three

"Old Bedlam" it was affectionately, or at times not so affectionately, called by the men who lived there. Of the buildings that bordered the Fort Laramie parade ground, it was easily the grandest, being a two-story, whitewashed frame house that could have easily passed as a modest mansion in the more civilized parts of the country. The social life of Fort Laramie revolved around the gracious building, which was the only building on the military post that had room for a full-fledged ball, or at least what passed for a ball west of the Mississippi. More important, it housed the post headquarters and the unmarried officers assigned to the post. For a short time it also housed, courtesy of the post commandant, one Jonathan O'Brian, who now sat behind the desk of his modest room, puffing on an expensive cigar and regarding Jason Sinclair with speculative eyes. His face showed only a hint of uneasiness when his gaze dropped to the animal lying calmly at Jason's feet, a silver-gray wolf with eyes much the same color as Jason's own.

"Can't tell you how glad I am to find you here, Mr. Sinclair. Most fortunate coincidence for me that you were passing through. The army's been no help. No help whatsoever."

Jason regarded the man opposite him with mild interest. He bore little resemblance to his late brother, the drunken, violent Irishman who'd perished ten years ago with seventy-odd other souls on the Simmons train. Still, Jason decided,

35

in spite of the lack of physical resemblance, the hint of Irish blarney was there, same as it had been in Daniel O'Brian. The man was hiding something behind his facade of bluff earnestness.

"Unbelievable!" John continued. "Here it is 1876, and those wild savages are still roaming around causing trouble up north. And what's the army doing? Not much of anything that I can see. Oh, they're very polite. Yes, sir! Very polite! But that damn commandant won't raise a finger to get my niece back from those red hooligans."

Jason lifted one tawny brow a fraction of an inch and interrupted the tirade. "You don't know for sure that the woman sighted with the Northern Cheyenne is your niece, Mr. O'Brian."

"Who else would it be?" O'Brian snorted. "Red hair, and the age is about right. That girl is Meghan O'Brian, my niece. And I want her back, dammit!"

Jason sighed, tilting back in his chair until only two legs were on the floor. He was uncomfortable in this building, with all the trappings of civilization around him. He felt hemmed in by the walls, stifled by the pungent smoke issuing from O'Brian's cigar, and suffocated by the still, too warm air of the room.

"All right," he admitted cautiously. "Suppose that woman is your niece. You think you're doing the right thing by trying to get her back? After ten years' living with the Cheyenne, she's probably forgotten she's a white woman. Probably very happy."

He smiled to himself. If the woman really was the little girl who was carried off years ago from the ill-fated Simmons train, she was probably happy as a duck in water. At nine years old, he remembered, that kid had more wild Indian in her than old Crazy Horse himself. Whether the Cheyenne were happy with her was another question. Those braves may have bitten off more than they could chew when they carried off that little wildcat.

"I realize what you're saying," O'Brian acknowledged. "I'm not as ignorant of Indians as you may think, Sinclair."

"I'm not meaning to say you're ignorant." Jason leaned forward abruptly, slamming the front two legs of his chair onto the floor with a loud crack. "I'm just saying that it may be difficult, maybe impossible, for a woman in these circumstances to come back and live with white people like nothing had happened."

O'Brian regarded Jason more closely. He hadn't anticipated this hesitancy. The man was uncivilized, as uncivilized as the beast that kept him company. He was a notorious hell-raiser who skimmed along just on the inside of the law. His deadliness was almost legendary, and he was feared from Wyoming to the Pacific Coast. A man like Jason Sinclair generally didn't quibble about niceties when a chance for a profitable venture arose. He'd expected the man to jump at the sum being offered him to bring Meghan back from the Cheyenne, and here he was sitting there arguing why the project should be dropped.

"Meghan belongs with her own people," O'Brian said stubbornly. "I'm a rich man. I can give her all the advantages—everything she needs. In the long run, she'll thank me, and you, for bringing her back."

Jason had private doubts about that. But no matter. It wasn't his business. He had no intention of dancing to the tune of Jonathan O'Brian's whim and chasing all over the Powder River country for his red-haired niece.

"Well"—Jason picked up his hat off his lap. The silver gray wolf beside him stirred. "I figure you're doing what you think is best, O'Brian. But I'm not the man to do the job for you. I'm tied up."

"Untie yourself then," O'Brian said in the voice of a man accustomed to being obeyed. "I'm offering you a thousand dollars, Sinclair. That's more than the job is worth. And for a man like you, who knows Indians, who's lived with them even—the risk isn't that great."

Jason looked at the older man with cold amber eyes. "I

lived with the Pawnee, not the Cheyenne. The two are deadly enemies. Have been for generations.''

"No matter. An Indian's an Indian. You're the man for the job.''

"Sorry, O'Brian. Get yourself another errand boy.'' Jason unfolded his tall body from the chair and stood up. Standing, he seemed to make the room smaller, not only because of his size, which was considerable, but because of the wild-beast restlessness that radiated from him. He reminded O'Brian of a captive panther stalking the boundaries of his cage. But there were ways, O'Brian thought, for a smart man to tame even the wildest of beasts.

"Sit down, Sinclair.''

Jason regarded O'Brian impatiently. As far as he was concerned, their talk was finished.

O'Brian disregarded Jason's glare. "I think you've a responsibility to that unfortunate girl.''

Jason put one booted foot on the chair and leaned his arm on his thigh, shaking his head in half frustration, half amusement. "As far as your niece Meghan is concerned, O'Brian, I'd more likely call the poor brave who kidnapped her unfortunate. Ever try to tie down a tornado?''

O'Brian drew himself up indignantly to his full height, which was just a sliver below Jason's. He was a man of considerable bulk, mostly muscle, but beside Jason he looked only of average size. "I have no wish to discuss my niece's temperament. I've never met the girl. And I don't believe you've seen her since she was nine years old, when the wagon train for which *you* were responsible was attacked and slaughtered. I hardly think that after ten years you would know what her circumstances or feelings are.''

Jason sighed and looked down at his hat. "All right, O'Brian, I get your point.''

"Good.''

"I guess in a way I am partly responsible for what happened to her.'' Jason thought again of the red-haired pixie who'd wanted to go hunting with him and hadn't been allowed.

"Then you'll go after her?"

"Well," Jason hedged, "I'll tell you what I'll do. I'm headed up to see General Crook at Fort Fetterman. He's going to take some troops up the Powder River country to try to teach the Sioux and Cheyenne a lesson about bothering all those innocent"—a sarcastic smile pulled at his mouth—"innocent white miners who're after all that gold on Indian land. Expect we'll be seeing a lot of Cheyenne. If I see Meghan I'll make sure she gets back to you. That's about all I can promise."

"That's good enough," O'Brian conceded, his hearty manner back in force. He would've liked to have won a more definite commitment, but hesitated to press his luck. He needed Meghan back, if she were indeed still alive. And there were more ways than one to ensure her return.

The "hog ranches" that attached themselves like leeches to the boundaries of frontier military posts were named for the dubious charms of the soiled doves who plied their trade there. The establishment of Adolph Curry and Jules Escoffey, three miles upriver from Fort Laramie, Wyoming Territory, was no better and no worse than the majority of such places. It was certainly one of the busiest, however.

Though in 1876 the stream of emigrant trains rolling westward along the California-Oregon trail had long since stopped, Fort Laramie was still the primary military post in the frontier west. And the men of Fort Laramie, hard playing as they were hard fighting, eagerly took advantage of the various vices that Curry and Escoffey had to offer. And now that the Black Hills had been opened at long last to gold seekers, the rough tavern found that business had at least doubled. Happy coincidence had run the stage route from Cheyenne into the Black Hills right past the tavern door.

So on this night the place was jumping. Booze flowed like water, and the girls, seasoned campaigners tough as the soldiers they serviced, found their wares in great demand, sometimes even fought over. Only one man in the tavern seemed oblivious to their appeal—the broad-shouldered fellow in buckskin who sat alone at a corner table, back to the wall, nursing a half-empty bottle of what passed for whiskey in Curry's place. Beside his chair a silver-gray wolf reclined, seeming oblivious to the surrounding confusion and crush of bodies.

Even the most cynical of the tavern's girls could not still a slight flutter of the heart at the sight of that hard-muscled torso revealed by the form-fitting buckskin shirt. The bronzed face with its tawny cap of unruly sunstreaked hair was enough to melt even those female hearts hardened by too much booze and too much time spent servicing a crowd of uncaring men. The firm jaw, straight nose, and broad, high brow above deep-set eyes could have been cast in bronze for a statue of masculine perfection. Only the eyes ruined the picture. Cold they were. Cold and hard. Devoid, it seemed, of the capacity to mirror human emotion, as if the man had none. Deep amber, like the eyes of a hunting cougar. A hard-edged look from those eyes could cut like a knife, send fear quivering through a strong man's gut, and desire through to a woman's very core.

Jason Sinclair had no interest in his effect on the whores of Curry's place tonight. He'd had his fill of their services since he came to Fort Laramie two days ago, and his appetite for their dubious charms had burned itself to ashes, leaving only a bitter taste in his mouth. He shouldn't have stopped at Fort Laramie on his way to Fort Fetterman, he thought. Should have kept straight on. Then he wouldn't have been spied by John O'Brian, wouldn't have been reminded of things he'd rather forget.

After ten years, the Simmons train was still a bitter memory in his mind. He hadn't been close to anyone in the train. But he'd approached comradeship more closely with those people than he ever had before or since. He'd been responsible for them, in part, and he should have been there when their need of him had been the greatest, even if that help would've been to no avail. Now Jonathan O'Brian had come along to remind him of his responsibility to the only surviving member of that train, that little Irish hellcat Meghan O'Brian, if it was indeed she who had been spotted with a band of Northern Cheyenne in Montana. He'd be goddamned if he was going to chase all over Montana because some railroad surveyor had seen a flash of red hair among the black.

"Well, I'll be a poleaxed prairie chicken! I cain't believe my tired old eyes! If'n it ain't ol' Jason Sinclair!"

A gravelly voice brought Jason up from the well of his thoughts. There, pulling a chair to his table, not bothering to wait for an invitation, was a face out of the past he'd just been recalling, a weather-beaten face framed with wisps of dirty gray hair and decorated with wildly sprouting tufts of bristly brows. He'd have thought Old Joseph would be long in his grave by now.

"Hullo, Joseph."

"Hullo, yourself, boy." Only a man of Joseph's advanced age could have gotten away with calling Jason a boy. If there had been little about the boy in the Jason Sinclair of ten years ago, there was absolutely nothing now. The man sitting across the table from Old Joseph was even broader, stronger, and if possible harder-eyed than the prematurely hardened boy Joseph had known before.

"Funny thing meetin' you here." Joseph echoed Jason's own thoughts. "I was jest thinkin' about old times when we was scoutin' together for the Simmons train."

"That so?"

"Yeah. Got myself an offer from an uncle of that brat who got carried off by the redskins. Remember her?"

"I remember. Think I got the same offer myself."

"Yup. That's what I figured when I saw you in here. Figured the guy took hisself out some insurance. If'n one of us don't bring the girl back, maybe the other one will. He sure does figure to get that girl back, one way or t'other."

"Looks like," Jason agreed.

"Cain't figure it, myself." Joseph poured himself a glass from Jason's bottle of whiskey and seemed to settle in for a long chat, with or without an invitation. "Kid was peskier than most females even. Probably didn't grow up any better."

"If she grew up at all," Jason added doubtfully.

"From what that survey party said, I figure she did. No Cheyenne brave bred that red hair from no Injun squaw. Figure it's the girl, all right."

"Didn't much sound like her, the way that guy described her. I read the letter this fellow sent the commandant. Only thing that woman had in common with that kid was the color of her hair."

Old Joseph chuckled. "Well, sharp-edged, skinny little girls do tend to soften up and fill out a bit with the years, you know. I suppose that little Meghan could've grown up to something that could get a man that enthusiastic."

"I doubt it." Jason's memories of Meghan O'Brian, all planes and angles, knees and elbows, didn't leave room for the possibility that the awkward little brat could have blossomed into a wildflower under the less than gentle nurturing of the Cheyenne. "You goin' after her?"

Joseph laughed. "Not me! All the money in the world wouldn't make me take up that kind of chase, though I was hard put to convince that fellow of that. He seemed to think I owe it to him, just because I was unlucky enough to be scout on that train. I don't owe him or that girl nothing. And I'm too old to go chasin' after Injuns like I did when I was a sprout. I'm here on business with the sutler, that's all. Soon's I'm done I'm headed back to St. Louis. Got me a nice little business goin' back there, doin' supply work for the army."

Joseph gave the younger man a canny look. "I imagine you're headed up there, though."

"Maybe. Might do some scouting for Crook. Haven't made up my mind."

"Man's offerin' a decent reward for that girl. If'n I was younger, I wouldn't pass up a pile like that."

"Don't exactly need the money, but if I run into a red-haired Cheyenne, I'll probably bring her back just to get that fellow off my back. He's an insistent cuss."

Old Joseph poured himself another glass and settled back in his chair, giving Jason an assessing look. "Don't exactly need the money, huh? You got yourself quite a reputation since we last met, but I ain't heard anything about you being rich."

Old Joseph had followed with interest the notorious career of the man who'd been for a short time his protégé. He knew the boy had drifted awhile after the emigrant train massacre, getting into gunfights now and again, winning himself a reputation as a mean son of a bitch that a man didn't want to rile, a dead shot with pistol and rifle and just as deadly with the long-bladed knife he carried at his belt. Less than a year after the Simmons train incident, he'd taken up with the Pawnee. Must have lived with them for nigh on five years, and the story was he'd taken a Pawnee wife, leaving the tribe only when his wife died giving birth to a stillborn son. The stories about him since then—a deadly bronze-haired man who was accompanied everywhere by a wild silver-gray wolf—had almost reached the point of legend.

"I wouldn't say rich," Jason answered, giving the older man a knife-edged look that let him know that personal questions weren't exactly welcome. "Got lucky with a gold claim on Clear Creek, down in Colorado. Have an honest partner who runs it right. It's doing okay, but money isn't much use to a man unless he wants to settle in one place."

"Heard something about a horse ranch down on the South Platte," Joseph continued.

"Nosy son of a bitch, aren't you."

Old Joseph chuckled dryly. "Us old farts, you know. We ain't got any business of our own left, so we got to get into everybody else's."

"Bullshit. You've always been too nosy for your own good." Jason cracked a smile, remembering his avoidance of the old man's garrulousness when they were scouting together. "Bought a horse ranch with some of the money from the mine. Thought I could settle down. Big mistake though. Got a manager to run it for me before I'd been there a year."

Joseph felt a stab of pity for the young man across from him, though it was strange that he should feel sorry for a man with all the advantages—youth, strength, money. But he'd met men like Jason Sinclair before, throwbacks to the day of the wild mountain man. The boy showed all the symptoms—restless, watchful, mistrustful of everything and everyone around him, obviously uncomfortable even in such a scantily civilized place as this. Such men had no roots, distrusted civilization, and despised its ways. And civilization was advancing rapidly across the frontier, even faster now that the railroad had come. Men like Jason Sinclair were becoming extinct; they were looking for a way of life that no longer existed. Joseph, old as he was, had adjusted. Young Jason would have to do the same, or wander the rest of his life in search of something that was gone.

"Got to settle down sometime, boy."

Jason only grunted, not really interested in the old man's opinion, even though it echoed his own. He'd made his attempts to settle down, realizing that his violent and restless way of living was leading him nowhere he wanted to go. But he didn't know where he wanted to go. He had no anchor—nothing and no one to hold on to.

He'd been wandering literally all his life. His parents had dragged him to California during the Rush of '49, when he was two. They'd wandered from one supposed strike to another for several years, his father always optimistic that a fortune was to be made just around the next bend. After a few years his mother, tired of being married to a loser, tossed her husband out on his ear and took up a profession she had a true talent for—whoring—and made a great deal of money touring the mining camps and burgeoning towns of California. When Jason was ten he took out on his own. Tired of the succession of perfumed, opulent rooms above noisy casinos and gambling houses, tired of the not-so-sweetly-perfumed succession of men in and out of his mother's lodgings, he figured he'd be better off on his own. So he packed his bundle one afternoon and set out with childish faith to make his own fortune. His mother, as far as he knew, had never bothered to look for him. His childish optimism had soon been beaten out of him by the harshness of reality. It was replaced by an animal cunning that was the only thing that allowed him to survive those young years. As he grew to manhood and his way grew easier, the optimism never returned, and the cunning never left.

Old Joseph had lapsed into a rambling account of his own early days trapping for the American Fur Company, his tongue loosened by the downed half of a second whiskey bottle that had somehow appeared on the table. His voice scarcely penetrated Jason's thoughts, but the loud voices of a couple of soldiers sitting at a table across the smoky room did cut through his musings. He had an animal instinct for danger. A seasoned troublemaker himself, he recognized trouble at the first hint, especially when it was pointing his way.

"Seems as though a few of the boys have had a bit too much to drink," Jason commented through Joseph's narrative, casually taking a last swallow of the watered-down whiskey and tilting his chair back so he could stretch his long legs out in front of him. "Though how anyone could get drunk on this horse piss I don't know."

Old Joseph abruptly cut his chatter. He was no amateur himself when it came to trouble, and the three boys in army blue sauntering in their direction spelled trouble if he'd ever seen it. The crowd parted for them, sensing their intentions and hoping for a good show, the more violent the better.

The leader, a big unshaven man whose bulk was as much muscle as it was fat, leaned a hamlike fist on the table and favored Jason with a slightly woozy grin. "Evenin'," he slurred.

Without moving his chair from its precarious tilt, Jason looked the big man over with seeming carelessness. "Evenin'."

"My friends and me"—he waved vaguely toward his two grinning comrades—"we saw you sittin' over here. We said to ourselves"—his bulk jerked with a hiccup— "we said to ourselves—that's Jason Sinclair sitting over there, bold as brass. Couldn't be no one else. Big, yellow-haired son of a bitch with a dirty dog wolf follerin' like some sort of pup." He swayed slightly, waiting for Jason's answer.

"So?" Jason answered calmly, though he longed to spring up and get this over with. He knew what was coming, and he was tired of this repeated scene. How many times in the past years had this happened?—the frequency increasing as his reputation grew. Some lout, or in this case louts, recognized him and figured to prove what a tough guy he was by beating him up or gunning him down. Only it never quite worked out the way they had planned. He was getting tired of leaving a trail of dead or beaten fools behind him.

The lout smirked, as did his companions backing him. "So are ya?"

"Might be," Jason admitted. "Who wants to know?"

The lout was too drunk to read the warning in the cold amber eyes that had suddenly hardened to knife-edged sharpness.

"A better man than you," one of the secondary louts tossed in.

"Yeah," the third companion added. "We don't like your dirty wolf. Figure it don't belong in with people who're eatin' and drinkin'. Maybe you don't either, from what I've heard."

The crowd, avidly listening, collectively held their breath.

Jason was as relaxed as ever. He always was most relaxed before a fight. He motioned Joseph to move away, and the old man hastily obeyed, realizing sadly that he'd come to the point in his life where he was more hindrance than help in a fight.

Jason seemed to ponder a moment, then regarded the chief lout with a smile. Any man who'd dealt with him before would've backed down right then, for Jason Sinclair was at his deadliest with that friendly-looking smile spread across his face.

"Well, now," Jason began. "Wolf here doesn't seem to take offense at your rudeness, mister, him being pretty good-natured as wolves go. Me now...I'm one of the touchiest sons of bitches you'll ever meet. I think you better take your dirty carcasses, you and your little friends here, and hightail it back to your barracks before you find yourselves in deep trouble."

The lout's grin widened, and his friends fairly chortled.

"You got any balls to back up your words, Sinclair?"

The tavern crowd held its breath in gleeful anticipation.

Jason signaled a command to his furry companion to stay out of the coming ruckus, then he turned his attention back to the three who were so generously offering themselves as outlets for the day's maddening frustrations.

Jason's smile was pure happiness as he placed one booted foot on the edge of the table in front of him and rammed it into the offending body on the table's opposite side, catching the big man in the general vicinity of his groin, and causing a purpling grimace to replace the challenging grin of moments before.

"Still have *your* balls, friend?" Jason asked with a friendly grin as the man stumbled backward, toppling the two who'd sheltered behind his bulk and drawing an approving "Aaaaaaah!" from the crowd.

Jason sat relaxed and seemingly amused as the three men desperately tried to untangle themselves from each other and the various pieces of furniture that had followed them to the floor. When they finally succeeded, they shook themselves free of confusion and charged him en masse.

Onlookers in the crowd said later they'd never seen a

man move so fast, like quicksilver. One moment Jason was sitting, still casually tilted back in his chair as the three louts charged like maddened bulls, heads down and arms outstretched to grab and crush. The next moment the three were plowing into the wall behind where Jason had been sitting, and Jason was regarding them with ill-concealed contempt from five feet away, leaning on a pillar as though he were an onlooker and not one of the combatants.

"Fun's over, boys," he told them. "Let's get down to business and forget this fooling around."

Without further preamble he charged, driving his knee into the chief lout's stomach and catching the chin of one of the others with a rock-hard fist. While he was thus employed, the third lout, smarter than the others, circled around behind him, grabbing a chair as the first weapon that came to hand.

Jason turned and ducked just in time as the heavy chair barely missed his head, ruffling his tawny hair with the wind of its passing. He grunted with effort as he drove his fist into the man's hard belly, putting all the considerable power of his arm behind the blow. He followed with a fist to the jaw. The man dropped as if he'd been poleaxed.

The two secondary louts were out of action for a good long while, but the chief lout showed his mettle by picking himself up off the floor and regarding Jason with an ugly grin as he bent and pulled a wicked-looking knife from his boot.

"Want to get nasty, do you?" Jason answered the challenge by pulling his own long-bladed knife from its sheath. His opponent's confident smile faded a bit when he saw the ease with which the weapon slipped into Jason's hand, as if it were a familiar and well-loved extension of his arm.

The knife duel was a short one. The avid crowd of onlookers could barely follow the action as the two men feinted and dodged, the flashing silver blades weaving a pattern of death between them. But even from what little they could see, it was clear the lout was outclassed. He ended up pushed against the wall, gasping for breath and afraid that his next movement would be his very last. The razor tip of Jason's knife pressed against his throat, drawing a thin line of red wherever it touched.

Two years ago, the lout's blood would have been spurting onto the floor by now. But tonight there was a weariness in Jason's eyes that had nothing to do with physical exertion. He was tired of killing men. He was tired of being forced to kill men to defend his own life, just because some yahoo thought he'd be a bigger and better man for outgunning or outfighting Jason Sinclair. This man, smelling of booze and fear, made his stomach turn. He didn't want his blood on his hands. He had too many men's blood on his hands already. He looked steadily into the terrified lout's eyes, letting him stew in his own fear. Then he twisted his hold on the man's shirt collar until his eyes bugged out.

"Be grateful I'm in a generous mood tonight, friend. But don't try me again. Understand?"

The lout gaped at him wide-eyed, giving the barest hint of a nod as the knife point pressed more tightly against his jugular.

"Good!"

Jason pulled him forward abruptly, then slammed him back into the wall with a force that would knock a bear senseless. The lout slithered down the wall to the floor to join his friends. The few catcalls that erupted in the crowd to protest this show of mercy were quickly silenced by a glance from the cold yellow eyes.

The silver-gray wolf regarded the three felled men with deadly interest, but made no move from his spot until Jason signaled him to his side. As they exited the room together, the onlookers, in recounting the tale later, said they couldn't pick which was the more deadly, the man or the wolf.

The cool evening air of spring felt good on Jason's face as he mounted the fiery black that had replaced the aging bay stud two years ago. But it would take more than the cool kiss of night air to make Jason feel clean after the past hours spent in Curry and Escoffey's tavern. The night had been a mistake. The stop at Fort Laramie had been a mistake. He felt more disgusted with civilization and its hangers-on than ever before. Tomorrow at first light, he vowed, he'd be on his way to Fort Fetterman to join General Crook in his expedition to lands not yet completely under the sway of the white man. He smiled. The irony of his fighting to wrest this last wild frontier from the Indians to put it in the hands of the invading horde of civilization did not escape him.

# Chapter Four

Autumnfire Woman floated motionlessly in the little pool of Reno Creek, a dappling of shade from the overhead canopy of leaves playing over her sun-browned body and the still green surface of the water. A short walk upstream, the bustling activity of a Cheyenne camp shattered the midday stillness, but here at the shaded pool the occasional call of a bird or the buzzing of an insect only emphasized the silence. Autumnfire closed her eyes against the cloud-less sky burning blue above her, enjoying the cool wash of the slow-moving creek water against her hot skin. Hair the color of fiery autumn leaves fanned out behind her, tugged gently by the sluggish current.

The day was unusually hot for June, but the sun that burned down so intensely from the pale blue sky held no sway in the cool glade where Autumnfire took respite from her chores. All morning she'd labored over the hides that her mother had set her at in the early hours of dawn. She deserved this break, she thought. The sun had beaten down mercilessly all morning, making even her sun-browned skin feel as if it were burning, and giving birth to a light sprinkling of tan freckles across her nose and cheeks. This afternoon she would go with the other women to gather wood for the night fires. But just now she didn't want to do anything but savor the coolness of the water against her naked body.

Her pleasant reverie abruptly ended as a small tidal wave of creek water lifted her from her motionless state then inundated her, pouring down her nose and mouth and bringing her choking and sputtering to her feet. She opened her eyes in time to see Magpie, her eight-year-old sister, climbing from the pool and preparing another cannonball jump to whip the formerly peaceful pool into churning chaos.

"Magpie!" Autumnfire waded toward the bank and caught the little girl's ankle. Magpie giggled and twisted free, knocking Autumnfire on her rear in the shallow water and scurrying toward the high bank that overhung the deeper pool.

"Here I go!" her high-pitched voice declared.

The pool erupted into foam and waves as her tightly curled little body splashed through the surface.

Autumnfire picked herself up off the sandy creek bottom and dived into the deep pool, her slim sun-browned body slicing cleanly through the still-tossing water. She broke surface next to where Magpie was happily churning the water around her, bobbing and diving like a small brown otter in the green water.

"Brat!" the older sister scolded. "How did you slip away from Mother?"

Magpie looked into her sister's clear green eyes and laughed at the irritation she saw there. "Mother was busy." She giggled and slanted her sister a sly look out of dark brown eyes. "I knew you'd be down here. Red Shield was looking for you, but I didn't tell him where you were."

She smirked as the delicate line of Autumnfire's eyebrows drew into an irritated pucker. Then, for safety's sake, for she knew her sister's fiery temper, she dived beneath the surface, stroking out to a safe distance before surfacing. Autumnfire was still treading water where she had left her.

"Did he say what he wanted?" Autumnfire smoothed the irritation out of her voice, hoping to coax some useful information out of her mischievous little sister. Red Shield was a subject that interested her very much.

Magpie fairly twinkled with joy at being able to be the teaser for once instead of the teased. "He didn't say. But I'll bet I can guess." She grinned at Autumnfire's impatient glare. "He had that moony look. You know." She rearranged her little brown face into a fair imitation of the love-struck expression that the noted warrior Red Shield had worn lately whenever he'd been around Autumnfire Woman. "I bet he wanted to corner you for the young people's dance tonight."

"Pooh!" The older sister's blush was visible even under her tan.

"Pooh yourself!" The fountain of water set up by Magpie's hand spurted full into Autumnfire's face, followed by tinkling cascades of little girl giggles.

Autumnfire sputtered. "Wait until I get my hands on you, you hopeless ninny. You'll be sorry you ever left the camp. Your little rear's going to be so sore . . ."

Magpie bounced out of the creek well ahead of her sister. She disappeared into the bushes before Autumnfire could finish her sentence, leaving only the echo of mischievous laughter behind her.

Autumnfire frowned into the foliage for a moment, making sure her little tormentor was gone. Then she stretched out once again on the pool's calm surface, grateful to have her privacy back. The luxurious sense of relaxation had fled, though, and eluded her attempts to call it back. Her body was on edge, waiting for another surprise cannonball from Magpie. With a sigh of regret she turned over and stroked for the bank, pulling herself up on a sandstone ledge that overhung the water. The sandstone, worn smooth by the scouring of countless spring floods, felt good against her bare skin as the hot sun dried the droplets of water that beaded her body. She stretched in sensual ecstasy, reveling in the feel of the warm sun and the cooling touch of a playful breeze that riffled the smooth water of the pool and danced through the green leaves roofing the glade. She felt as free and uninhibited as the sleek brown female river otter she'd seen playing in the creek just the day before.

Few would have recognized a vestige of Meghan O'Brian in the young woman sunning herself on the ledge. The angles and planes of the child's body were gone along with the gawky awkwardness. Autumnfire Woman was tall and slender, but her slenderness, with ripe and perfectly formed breasts, tiny waist, gently flaring hips, and long graceful legs, enhanced her femininity rather than detracted from it. Bright red hair burnished with gold framed a fine-boned face with high forehead, small straight nose, and delicately molded mouth. The sun-browned skin was smooth and clear and boasted a hint of freckles across her nose and cheeks. Clear green eyes looked out from behind dark lashes.

The red hair and green eyes belonged to the little girl whom Standing Antelope had carried off from the ruins of a wagon train ten years ago, but in spite of looking like an Irish wood sprite, the woman sunning herself beside Reno Creek was totally Cheyenne. Her past was all but forgotten; and when her memory occasionally dredged up some scene from her life with Daniel and Mary Catherine O'Brian, she viewed it as one might remember a fleeting glimpse from a half-forgotten dream. Her life, her family, and her happiness lay with the Cheyenne.

Dark lashes fluttered downward to rest against fine high cheekbones as the warm sun coaxed Autumnfire toward sleep. But only a few seconds passed before they flew upward again and delicately winged brows drew together in a frown. She pushed herself up to a sitting position and looked suspiciously around her. No sound disturbed the peace of the glade other than the soft ripple of the creek. No movement caught her eye other than the innocent flutter of leaves in the breeze. Still, she knew herself watched.

"Who's there!" she demanded, unafraid but vexed.

Red Shield didn't bother to conceal himself any longer. Smiling, he stepped out of the thick foliage.

With a squeak of dismay, Autumnfire jumped to her feet and grabbed her buckskin tunic, hastily pulling it over her head. When she was halfway decently dressed, she turned around to face the grinning warrior with emerald fire in her eyes.

"How dare you sneak around while I'm taking a bath! Of all the low, dishonorable . . . !"

Red Shield's grin grew wider as he watched her struggle to put her leggings on. White teeth flashed against his brown face and his dark brown eyes sparkled with unabashed appreciation of the scene before him. His breechclout, the only garment he wore on such a hot day, couldn't begin to hide his masculine reaction to the wealth of feminine charms that had just been on display.

"I came only to make sure you were well protected," he protested halfheartedly. "You take too many chances, walking alone so far from camp. There are some who might take advantage."

"Hmph!" Autumnfire lofted her small nose into the air. "And who's going to protect me from you, Red Shield?" She pointedly turned her back on him to fasten the protective rope under her tunic, wrapping it around her waist, bringing it back between her thighs and winding the extra length halfway down to her knees. The crude chastity belt was worn by all young maidens at night and during the day whenever they were abroad. No right-minded Cheyenne warrior would violate the sanctity of the protective rope for fear of severe retribution from the tribe. The rope in place, she turned and faced Red Shield with more confidence. It was with some satisfaction that she noted the hint of desire in his eyes and the air of possessiveness with which he regarded her.

"You don't need protection from me, my little dove." He smiled confidently. "Someday we will marry. There is nothing wrong with my admiring the charms of my wife-to-be."

Autumnfire felt a delicious tingle between her legs as she ran her eyes appreciatively over his broad brown shoulders, narrow waist and hips, and long, well-muscled legs. Red Shield was the handsomest man she knew, and a warrior of great skill and renown. Already, stories of his cunning and courage circulated around the fires and within the lodges. She was proud that he'd been her suitor for over a year. Enough time had passed now that it would be proper for him to make a formal offer for her. She would be proud to be the wife of such a great man and had a most unmaidenly eagerness to be initiated into the mysteries of womanhood. Still, she shouldn't let him become too confident. The light of mischief ignited a green sparkle in her eyes as she moved closer to where he was standing, letting him appreciate the sway of her hips.

"You presume too much. We are not yet man and wife." She allowed a gentle smile to soften her words. She certainly didn't want to discourage him unduly.

"Soon," he replied simply. This was an old game between them. He took her arm and guided her onto the trail leading upstream to the village.

She turned and looked back at him, one impish brow raised. "I have other suitors, you know."

Red Shield refused to be nettled. He sent her an indulgent smile. "So you have. And most of them you've turned down. You've broken the hearts of more warriors than any other maiden in our village."

She sniffed indignantly at the hint of disapproval in Red Shield's voice. "I'm particular." Her eyes told this warrior, however, that should he send someone with an offer he would not suffer the same fate.

"So am I."

He put a strong brown hand on her arm to stop her. She read his intentions in his eyes as he pulled her against him, but she made no move to stop him. His mouth tasted good on hers, though he was rough. His arms tightened around her until she feared her ribs would crack. His kiss grew deeper as his tongue thrust into her mouth, making her want to choke. Autumnfire began to struggle against the unwelcome invasion. The still swollen evidence of his desire pressed against her stomach, frightening her with the sudden intensity of his arousal. No decent Cheyenne maiden allowed liberties beyond a simple kiss, and Red Shield was slipping past her ability to control as he snaked one hand inside the wide-cut armhole of her tunic and roughly began to fondle her breast. Summoning all her strength of will, she pushed him away. Her eyes flared to anger as she straightened her garment, but she said nothing, knowing that she was as much at fault at he. Slowly they resumed their walk up the trail, an awkward silence stretching between them.

After a few moments of letting her suitor regret his misbehavior, Autumnfire deigned to break the strained silence. "How many horses will you offer for me when you go to my father?" Her voice bantered, trying to lighten the mood between them and at the same time let him know that no more such incidents would happen between them until they were safely bound.

He visibly relaxed. "Unless you behave," he chuckled, "I might only offer two. Your friends will all laugh. It will be said in all the lodges that Autumnfire Woman is not worth much as a bride, even though she is the daughter of one of the highest lodges in the camp."

Autumnfire cocked one brow and laughed. "And unless you behave I will send those horses galloping back to your lodge, and the whole village will pity Red Shield, who cannot find a wife who will have him."

They laughed together, the awkward mood dispelled. Red Shield took her hand in his as they walked together up the trail.

"I will do you great honor," he told her in a more serious voice. "I will send my father's brother to offer your father many horses for you to come to my lodge. The whole village will know how I honor you. In my eyes your white blood does not make you less worthy. I will have no other besides you for a wife."

Autumnfire's face immediately darkened. She pulled her hand out of his. "I am not white. I am as much Cheyenne as you are," she insisted haughtily. "More perhaps. I am better with a bow than you. And I ride as well as any warrior in the village."

Red Shield drew back from her anger, but was not about to stand there and allow himself to be chastised by a mere woman. "You work too hard at a man's skills." He remembered his embarrassment at the several raiding parties that Autumnfire Woman had insisted on participating in. It was not unheard of for a Cheyenne woman to ride to war with the men, but he didn't want his wife to be such a one. "You would do well to concentrate on being a woman, so you can please a man." He looked at her sternly down his hawklike nose, hoping to see her show proper meekness in the face of his disapproval. He was doomed to disappointment.

Autumnfire's Irish temper flared to life. How dare he expect her to play the meek and mild mate to his domineering maleness. "If I'm not woman enough for you, you can just keep your flea-bitten horses. There are other braves who would be more than happy to receive my favors and are more appreciative of my worth!"

Satisfied with having put Red Shield in his place, she turned and flounced down the trail. She was not above cocking an ear for the sound of his following, though. This was a common argument between them, and she knew he would always back down in the face of her anger and rejection.

She was right—almost. Red Shield hastened to catch up with the lilting hips and fiery red mane that fascinated him so. He fell into step with her, noting the angry set of her jaw, and wondered what it would take this time to placate her. He tried the ploy that had worked last month.

"I'm only trying to protect you. It is the man's place to ride into danger and the woman's to welcome him home and give him children."

It didn't work this time. She froze him with a glare of green ice.

"I don't need protection," she declared hotly. "I, Autumnfire Woman, ride as well as any warrior in camp. And I shoot as well with a rifle or bow."

"That's true. You have the skills, as you say." Red Shield tried to be conciliatory. They were nearing the village, and he didn't want the camp to see them arguing. He'd lost this argument so often, though, that he couldn't resist just one more try. "You should think on this though. Tagging along on raiding parties is all very well when you're an unattached maiden. But a wife should guard herself, tend to her home and children. A wife can't be as free as an unmarried girl-child."

She pushed her nose higher into the air as they entered the great circle of lodges. "Maybe *your* wife can't."

He frowned, his dark expression warning her that this time she was approaching the limit of his patience.

She ignored him. Caution was not part of her nature. "You're not my husband yet, Red Shield, and you may never be if you don't change some of your silly ideas."

He opened his mouth for an angry retort, but she continued before the words left his throat.

"So just you don't go telling me what to do!" She arched a triumphant brow, showing her disdain for his displeasure. "I just may go with Little Hawk on his next raiding party to get horses from the white ranchers. My father won't deny me. He knows how much help I am on those raiding parties."

Red Shield's thin lips tightened in anger. "Then Stone Eagle is a fool!" he said hotly. "He allows you to wander where you will and fly wild and free like a bird with no cares and no duties. Someday he will regret not keeping you closer to home!" Before she could get in the last word he walked away, stiff-backed and angry. She tossed her fiery mane and smiled knowingly at his back. He would come around to her way of thinking, she thought. And if not, they would find a compromise. In spite of her heated words, she knew she would not send back the horses he would offer.

Red Shield's stiff-backed, prideful stalking relaxed when he was out of Autumnfire's sight, but his features were still stiff with disapproval. He was less confident than Autumnfire that the two of them could work out this basic difference. Their arguments on the subject had been growing more and more heated over the last few months. He wanted Autumnfire as his wife. Her beauty and spirit held him fast in a fascination that amounted almost to obsession. He wanted to possess her more than he'd wanted to possess any woman in his entire life. He was willing even to brave the stern disapproval of his parents to make her his.

Ten years ago, Standing Antelope had brought back his captive girl-child and given her to his brother, Stone Eagle, to replace the daughter he'd recently lost to the coughing sickness. Stone Eagle and his wife, Long Stepping Woman, had immediately welcomed the girl into their family, not as a white slave, but as a beloved daughter. As she grew up in Cheyenne ways, the village accepted her as part of their band in spite of the red hair and green eyes that declared her white heritage—most of the village, that is. Red Shield's father was one who didn't. The girl's presence was a constant reminder to him of the loss of his eldest son in the raid on the Simmons train. Whenever she passed by him he turned his face away, refusing to acknowledge her existence. That his son Red Shield, a worthy warrior who could have any maiden of his choosing, paid court to this spawn of the white menace that poured over their country was a continuing source of grief for the old warrior, and a frequent cause of heated arguments with his son.

Red Shield was prepared to bear his father's anger for his attentions to Autumnfire, but somehow he had to convince her to become more conservative in her thoughts and actions. Her flamboyant ways were really no worse than the antics of some of the other young unmarried maidens, but with her unusual hair and eyes, and her eye-catching beauty, she was more noticeable than the others. He was weighing the merits of offering for her immediately, making his life easier by taking her in hand as husband instead of trying to mend her ways as a mere suitor, when a stir of excitement in the village caught his attention.

Little Hawk galloped his pony triumphantly through the village, howling like a wolf and holding his war spear high over his head. The three other young braves who rode with him did the same, riding and whooping through the camp until the entire village was astir to hear their news.

"What is it? What is it?" Excited children crowded at the warriors' horses, agilely avoiding the prancing hooves as they jumped for glee and begged to be told the news. But Little Hawk, leader of the party, waited until the war chiefs and most of the camp had gathered around before he told of what they'd seen on their raiding party to steal horses.

"White soldiers!" he declared with a fierce grin. "So many they darken the plain. The light from their cooking fires turns the night into day."

A graying war chief didn't look happy, in spite of the exultation of the younger man. "Where, Little Hawk?"

"Where Rosebud Creek makes its great bend. They make their fires where Muddy Creek joins Rosebud Creek."

The old war chief sighed. "They have come for trouble. Always it is the same. The white man will not stop until our hunting grounds are all trampled beneath the hooves of his cattle and our mother earth is everywhere violated by their shovels that seek the yellow metal."

Little Hawk took his cue from the old man's indignation. He raised his war spear above his head and shook it fiercely. "We must fight! We must kill them now, before they come to our camp, destroy our lodges, and kill the women, children, and old men!"

His battle cry was taken up by the eager crowd, the young warriors giving voice to gleeful howls and yips and the women shouting encouragement.

Another chief raised his arms for silence, and the tumult slowly died. "We must fight. Yes. We must fight, and our young men will gain much honor. But we must win! We must show these invaders that the Cheyenne and their friends the Sioux cannot be defeated. We must show them that they must go forever from our land. They must take their railroads and shovels and cattle and leave us in peace. We are not reservation Indians, to be starved and bullied into submission, to be pushed here and prodded there like dogs. We are Cheyenne! We are Sioux! We are invincible!"

One by one the chiefs and noted warriors of the camp had their say, decrying the evils the invaders were bringing to their land and extolling the honor to be gained in the coming fight. The crowd cheered for each speaker. Autumnfire Woman, standing with her best friend, Buffalo Calf Road Woman, cheered as loudly as the rest. Her face was flushed with excitement as the crowd finally broke up, the warriors going to prepare their mounts and weapons for the coming expedition and the women to ready packs of dried food to sustain the warriors on their journey.

"Come with me!" Buffalo Calf Road Woman grabbed Autumnfire's arm and urged her to follow. Her dark eyes snapped with excitement.

"Where?"

"To my brother's lodge. We'll see whose band he's going with. If he's in a good mood, he'll let us come with him. He has extra war ponies. Enough for both of us."

"You're going with the war party?" Autumnfire's voice was incredulous and excited. Small raiding parties were one thing, but even she was shocked by her friend's intention to join a major war expedition.

Buffalo Calf Road Woman turned with challenge in her

eyes, the same that had burned there when the two of them were small girls each daring the other to top her feats of foolishness. "Are you afraid?"

"Of course not!" Autumnfire lied. "But Stone Eagle will never let me go. He complains even when I go with the horse-stealing parties."

Buffalo Calf Road Woman sighed in exasperation. "Don't tell him! By the time we return, we will have gained so much glory that he will say nothing. He will be proud you are his daughter. He has no son to send to war. So you go. Bring honor to your family!"

It didn't take much to persuade Autumnfire Woman. The deciding factor was Red Shield, who interrupted his own battle preparations to find her and absolutely forbid her going. After a heated discussion with him, the gods themselves couldn't have kept her from joining Buffalo Calf Road Woman and her brother Chief Comes in Sight as they gathered with the other warriors to receive the words of blessing and encouragement. The Medicine Arrows, the most sacred of the Cheyenne holy objects, were with their brothers in the south. It was unfortunate that the keeper of the Medicine Arrows could not be consulted on this most important occasion, but the medicine men and older chiefs had performed the necessary ceremonies to bring victory in battle. The signs were all good. They would win a great victory. The braves were silent and solemn as they heard the words. The time for cheering, for celebrating, would be when the victory was won, when the white men were dead or had flown from this land. Now they husbanded their energy and spirit for the task before them.

Chief Comes in Sight and the two girls fell in with Two Moon's party of two hundred warriors. They were but a small part of the total war party, which boasted over a thousand Cheyenne, Ogalala, Miniconjou, Sans Arcs, Brulé, and Hunkpapa Sioux. The night was well gone when they finally moved out of the camp, and Autumnfire was already tired and wondering how she would last the night on the back of the fractious war pony Chief Comes in Sight had assigned to her. She bolstered herself with visions of the excitement to come once they reached their destination. She and Buffalo Calf Road Woman would be honored by warriors and women alike when they returned. And Red Shield would be proud of her and finally see that he couldn't force her into the mold of meekness and subservience that he thought was required in a proper Cheyenne wife.

She never paused to consider that she might be riding toward trouble, not honor. The medicine men had seen victory for the Cheyenne, but the fate of a fire-haired, green-eyed Irishwoman from St. Louis had never entered their visions. She rode on, knee to knee with her black-haired, brown-eyed comrades, blissfully ignorant of the future that awaited her.

# Chapter Five

The Cheyenne war party rode the entire night, using the dim moonlight to pick their way first up the south fork of Reno Creek and then down Corral Creek to where it joined Rosebud Creek. The canyons were rocky, steep, and cut frequently by side ravines. The sturdy, surefooted Indian ponies were accustomed to such travel, however, and moved steadily and swiftly over the treacherous terrain. Autumnfire Woman, riding in the rear of Two Moon's party with Buffalo Calf Road Woman, allowed herself to doze off and on while her pony followed docilely in line with the pony ahead.

The stars in the eastern sky had begun to fade before the

false dawn when Little Hawk called a halt. Autumnfire wearily slid from her pony's back, surprised that her rubbery legs and stiffened muscles consented to support her. She unfastened the small pouch of jerked beef and hard bread from the saddle pad and found a place by the stream to sit and breakfast. She was joined shortly by Buffalo Calf Road Woman.

"Aren't you glad you came?" The Cheyenne girl's face was an indistinct blur in the predawn darkness, but the twinkle in her eyes seemed to spark in the night.

"Yes," Autumnfire agreed with somewhat less enthusiasm, shifting to try to find a more comfortable spot for her abused posterior.

Buffalo Calf Road Woman laughed. "You've let yourself get out of shape. Last summer with Crooked Toe we rode all night and into the day, and I was the one who was sore, not you."

Autumnfire smiled ruefully. "You're right. I've stayed home too much this summer."

"You let that overbearing lout Red Shield tell you what to do. If you marry him, you'll never have fun anymore, you know."

The two girls were silent for a moment while both concentrated on chewing the tough jerky that might be their only nourishment for the day. When the last morsel of bread and meat had been washed down with cool, clear creek water, Autumnfire stretched out on the creek bank on her back, folded her arms beneath her head for a pillow, and watched the paling sky through the pine branches. Her friend stretched out beside her.

"One must marry sometime." Autumnfire resumed their conversation as though there had been no break. "Red Shield is handsome, and a fierce warrior. He'd make a good husband. He'll give me many strong children." She thought of the evidence of his urgent desire pressed against her when he'd kissed her so fiercely. The thought set off a mild tingling between her legs and made her heart pound with feelings she didn't quite understand. Was it worth giving up so much of her freedom to become fully a woman in Red Shield's arms?

"Bah!" Buffalo Calf Road Woman had no such romantic notions. "You could find a man who wouldn't coop you up in camp all day. I've seen other braves looking at you. In fact . . ." She trailed off significantly as her brother approached their resting spot with silent footsteps.

Autumnfire Woman pushed herself into a sitting position and hastily brushed the twigs and leaves from her hair when Chief Comes in Sight squatted down beside them on the stream bank. He smiled, white teeth flashing in the darkness.

"You're supposed to be resting, you pair of jabber mouths, not gossiping like a pair of silly maidens."

Buffalo Calf Road Woman flashed a teasing smile at her brother. "Don't worry, my brother. We'll be ready when the time for battle comes."

"See that you are." His voice lost its banter. "I will have no time to watch over you once the battle begins. You must watch over yourselves and stay out of trouble." He addressed them both, but his eyes were for Autumnfire only. "You, Autumnfire Woman, must take special care. I answer to myself for my sister. But if you should take hurt in this adventure, then I must answer to Stone Eagle, your father. He values you greatly and wouldn't go easy on the man who allowed hurt to come to you." His eyes told her that Chief Comes in Sight would not himself take it lightly should she sustain injury in the coming fight. Her heart flip-flopped at the warmth in his eyes, and it didn't stop its tumbling until his tall form had disappeared into the brush.

Buffalo Calf Road Woman cocked a knowing black brow. "As I was saying, there are other warriors . . ."

Autumnfire felt her face grow hot, knowing her friend had no doubt observed the silent byplay with her brother. Comes in Sight was a fine-looking man, a brave warrior well respected throughout the entire tribe. He was almost as handsome as Red Shield and had a higher status as well. But she loved Red Shield, she thought. How could she love Red Shield and react so quickly to a single heated glance from another man? She sighed and settled herself once again onto the soft creek bank vegetation.

"Maybe I just shouldn't marry!" she complained. "I can't seem to settle my mind on any single one I want, and every man who's offered for me seems to have a different idea of what I should do and what I should be. Sometimes I think men are impossible." Her face fell as she regarded the slim Cheyenne girl lying beside her, so resembling her brother that Autumnfire's heart fluttered recalling that other one's face. "But I don't want to remain a maiden forever!"

Buffalo Calf Road Woman laughed. "Men are not so impossible when you learn how to handle them." The Cheyenne girl spoke from considerably more experience than her fire-haired friend, for she was several years older. "We'll have a talk when we return from the village," she promised the younger girl. Her eyes danced with delighted mischief as she settled more comfortably into the soft grasses. "Perhaps we will become sisters in truth, as well as spirit." The blush that suffused Autumnfire's face at her remark was most satisfactory, Buffalo Calf Road Woman thought.

When the red glowing orb of the sun crested the hills to the east, the band was on its way once again. Now that day had come, there was no talking and joking between braves as there had been the night before. Even the ponies' footfalls were quiet as the wary Cheyenne and Sioux carefully guided their mounts where their unshod hooves would fall only on soft vegetation, avoiding stone and twigs that might make noise and give the as yet unseen enemy warning of their coming.

The sun was still low on the horizon when the band reached the clearing on Rosebud Creek where Little Hawk had spotted the soldiers two days ago. Two Moon raised his arm, signaling his band to stop, then rode back along the line, pulling out four men, two Cheyenne and two Sioux. After a brief conference with Two Moon, the four set out at a swift gallop down the trail ahead.

Autumnfire Woman, intent on watching the four disappear, was surprised to find that Chief Comes in Sight had reined in beside her. He flashed his sister a grin, but his eyes were only for Autumnfire. She saw in his eyes the hint of fire that had warmed her a few hours before.

"Two Moon has sent his scouts to locate the white soldiers," he explained. "Soon we will be in battle."

Autumnfire was silent.

On Two Moon's signal, the line began to move forward again, this time at a slower pace. Comes in Sight stayed beside her, riding knee to knee with her as Buffalo Calf Road Woman discreetly dropped back behind them.

"Pay heed to what I have said," the young chief said quietly, careful that his voice shouldn't carry to the others around them. "Guard yourself in the coming fight."

Autumnfire looked at him boldly, fighting the urge to avoid his gaze like a bashful child. "I will heed your words. But my father, Stone Eagle, will not lay the burden at your door should I be hurt." Her eyes twinkled momentarily. "He knows my stubbornness well."

Comes in Sight grinned. "You are much like my sister. We will talk, you and I, when this battle is won and we return to our village."

Any answer Autumnfire might have given was forestalled by the crack of shots being fired up ahead. The scouts had found the white soldiers. It sounded as though the soldiers had also found the scouts. A ripple of excitement coursed through the party of Indians. Comes in Sight gave Autumnfire a last eloquent look and then he was gone, urging his pony through the crowd ahead.

Autumnfire had no time to ponder the significance to that last look or worry over the romantic dilemma that seemed to loom in her future. Buffalo Calf Road Woman was beside her the moment her brother left.

"Hurry! Do you want to get left behind?" The Cheyenne girl's voice fairly crackled with excitement as she urged her mount forward and prodded her friend to do the same.

The band of warriors was surging around them now, all

pushing to get to the front, anxious to cover themselves with glory by being one of the first to count coup on the enemy. The need for silence was over, and the dull thud of ponies' hooves mingled with the warbling war cries of braves eager to leap into the fray. As the sporadic gunshots up ahead became a steady fusillade, the excitement increased to a desperate tempo. Little Hawk's band, in the van of the Indian party, had engaged the enemy. The battle had begun in earnest.

Autumnfire's pony caught the fever of excitement that flashed through Two Moon's band. Trained for war by Comes in Sight himself, he needed no urging from his rider to push his way through the press of ponies around him, scrambling off the beaten path over rocks and logs and twisting through the trees to stay abreast of the main body of the band. Autumnfire let him go. The battle fever was beginning to beat in her blood also. She ignored scrapes and scratches as they pushed through bushes and around trees, anxious as any warrior to plunge into the fighting up ahead.

She was in the middle of Two Moon's band when their group of two hundred warriors broke out into the open. Before them stretched a wide, gentle valley bordered on either side with steep bluffs. Gunfire echoed off the surrounding hills, and through the dust churned up by the ponies' flying hooves, Autumnfire could see a line of blue standing fast against the Indian attack. A yell and signal from Two Moon veered the band of two hundred from their course and sent them toward the bordering bluffs.

Autumnfire urged her pony to greater speed as they veered off toward the hills. Fear and fatigue fled before the excitement that heated her blood. The rhythmic pounding of her pony's hooves, the smooth surge of his muscles beneath her strongly gripping legs, all seemed to synchronize with the beating of her heart and the pounding of blood through her brain. She could see Buffalo Calf Road Woman stretched low over her pony's neck not far ahead of her.

The level grassy floor of the valley gave way to the rocky slopes of the bordering bluffs, and they were forced to slow their pace to scramble up to the heights where Two Moon awaited them. Autumnfire reined to a halt beside Buffalo Calf Road Woman and looked over the edge of the bluff to the fighting below. The white soldiers were still in a disciplined line, firing steadily and advancing across the valley floor. Little Hawk's band feinted and rushed, using bow and rifle to good advantage, but still they were being slowly pushed back against the bluff by the soldiers' relentless advance. Soon they would be pinned against the rocks with no room to maneuver.

Two Moon grinned fiercely and raised his rifle above his head, shaking it and loosing a great war cry. On his command, the entire band set heels to their ponies and charged down the bluff in a rush of flying hooves and dust. The two women didn't hesitate. Reins in one hand and rifle in the other, Autumnfire loosed an exhilarated cry of her own and plunged down the slope in the midst of the warriors. She'd forgotten she was a woman. For the moment her fierceness equaled that of any other brave in the band. She was a warrior, her blood hot to fight, to avenge the relentless invasion of the whites into her territory, her home, and her way of life.

A brave beside her screamed as a bullet tore through his throat, but his dying scream blended into the war cries of his fellows, and Autumnfire didn't turn her head to watch him tumble from his horse. Little Hawk's band, revitalized by Two Moon's reinforcements, turned from their retreat and charged with the newcomers. The line of soldiers broke. Some of the whites ran to take cover in the rocks, picking off any warrior they could get within their rifle sights. Others stayed to fight the oncoming Indians hand to hand.

As their furious charge ended in a confused melee of whites and Indians, the first flush of excitement passed, leaving Autumnfire breathless and weary. The moment of choice had passed though, and now it was either fight or die. In the heat of battle the fragile barrier of her sex was no protection, and her inexperience in the arts of war was serving her ill. This was nothing like the raiding parties she'd gone on. This was war—ugly, brutal, merciless. Her lungs were choked with dust and the smell of warm blood. Her ears were pounded by the screams of dying men and horses, the deafening explosion of firearms all around her.

A soldier loomed up out of the dust. He grabbed at her pony's bridle as the horse reared and plunged. She fought to bring her rifle to bear, but too late. The man was already dead, struck by her faithful mount's deadly hooves. A bullet whizzed past her ear like an angry hornet, then another. An Indian beside her fell, his head shattered by the explosion of lead in his brain. Another bluecoat tried to pull her from her horse. This time she was ready. She fired her carbine full in his face. The results made her stomach heave up into her throat.

A brief respite followed as the warriors pulled back to regroup. Dead bodies littered the battleground, both red and white, but the warrior's battle fever was still at high pitch. The Indians were winning. The tide had turned.

Autumnfire sagged over her pony's neck. Sweat ran down her brow and into her eyes. Her tunic was spattered with dead men's blood. Her mind was fast becoming numb from the sights and sounds and smells around her. She heard Little Hawk's war cry and automatically turned her pony for the second charge, but a hand jerked the reins from her fingers.

"Go back to the rocks." Comes in Sight's tone brooked no refusal. "You should have stayed there. There is no place for you in this."

Autumnfire's pride pushed its way through her sick numbness. "I didn't come to hide in the rocks." She fixed him with a level gaze, hoping he couldn't see in her eyes the sick horror inspired by her first real experience of war. A Cheyenne woman didn't shrink from such things. War and fighting were a way of life.

"You will be more use to us in the rocks with a rifle in

your hands. You're one of the best shots we have." His face softened for a moment, regarding her blood-spattered tunic and her sweat- and tear-stained face. "I don't question your courage, Autumnfire Woman. But you must learn how to take orders. Don't disobey me."

He dropped her pony's reins and set his heels to his horse, disappearing in the dust of the charge as he caught up to the rest of the band.

For what seemed hours, Autumnfire crouched in a rocky perch above the level of the valley, watching the progress of the battle and firing into the melee whenever she could pick out a target. She found that watching men fall from her fire at long range was almost as stomach-wrenching as at short range. Where did this weakness come from? she wondered. Buffalo Calf Road Woman attended to the same task from behind a nearby rock and chortled with glee every time her bullet found its mark.

The battle raged both below them in the valley and above them in the hills, but only twice in the hours they'd been here had the enemy approached close enough to see them in their rocky nooks. One had paid with his life, a bullet from Buffalo Calf Road Woman's rifle ripping off the top of his head. The other had escaped, but if he had told of their whereabouts, no one deemed them important enough to pursue. The soldiers had their hands full enough with the warriors in the valley and on the bluffs to worry about two women taking potshots from the protection of the rocks.

Time became a blur as Autumnfire watched charge after charge of warriors cut the soldiers' lines time and time again. The white men were sustaining many more casualties than the Indians, it seemed to her. Surely the whites would soon admit defeat and run to lick their wounds. Whites were supposed to be cowards, after all, not fit to be called true warriors. Perhaps her white blood was the source of her unwarriorlike squeamishness. She had a sudden urge to hide the golden red of her hair and smear dirt over her lightly freckled face to hide its lighter than

Cheyenne hue. The women in the village would laugh at her, and Stone Eagle, her beloved father, would be ashamed, if they knew of her faintheartedness at the sight of blood and death. And Red Shield would wear a smug I-told-you-so look on his handsome face. Chief Comes in Sight had seen it in her eyes, she knew, though he'd not chided her for it. She could only hope he never told anyone that she'd been sick and numb after only one charge at the white soldiers' line.

Autumnfire leveled her rifle with determination as the Indian charge began once again. The white soldiers were close to finished now, she guessed, for a great number of them turned to run at the renewed Indian attack. Some rallied though, holding their places and firing at the on-coming braves. She saw Crooked Toe go down, his horse falling on top of him. When the pony heaved to its feet and galloped away, Crooked Toe didn't move. Autumnfire choked back a sob as she took aim at the bluecoat who'd shot him. She squeezed the trigger, and missed. Cursing, she reloaded.

A scream from the nearby rocks brought her attention sharply around to Buffalo Calf Road Woman. Her friend's eyes were wide and wild as she pointed to the fray. Autumnfire squinted into the sun to see where she was pointing. Chief Comes in Sight was down, trapped beneath his horse, who flailed in bloody death throes from the bullet lodged in his chest. Comes in Sight fought to free himself as a bluecoat gleefully advanced toward him to personally attend to the kill.

Autumnfire crouched behind her rock and steadied her rifle. This time she couldn't miss. She slowed her breath-ing and willed her heart to quit its pounding, then squeezed the trigger. The soldier dropped his rifle and clutched at his chest, falling facedown in the dust not ten feet from the trapped Indian. She saw Comes in Sight glance in her direction, though he couldn't see her, and grin. Finally he succeeded in pulling his leg from beneath his dead pony's body.

Autumnfire stopped thinking and starting reacting. There would be other soldiers anxious to count coup on a downed warrior of such renown. She ran toward the horses and got there barely ahead of Buffalo Calf Road Woman, who had the same idea. They raced toward the battlefield, Autumnfire Woman in the lead. She fastened her gaze on Comes in Sight, who stood with legs spread, ready to leap up behind her when she reached him. So intent was she on her purpose that she hardly felt the jolt of a bullet plowing into her pony's chest and ripping through his heart. The valiant horse faltered, momentarily recovered, then plowed his nose into the dirt, launching Autumnfire from his back and sending her flying to an ungraceful landing ten feet from where he slid to final stop.

Autumnfire picked herself up slowly and dizzily, shaking her head to clear it from the ringing that swelled above the cacophony of battle. Her vision cleared in time to see Buffalo Calf Road Woman wheel her horse around her brother, who grabbed her arm and swung gracefully to the pony's back behind her. Comes in Sight screamed at a warrior who galloped toward him with the same intention as the women's, and the brave diverted toward Autumnfire. Only when she saw him racing toward her did she notice she was closer to the whites than the Indians, and that several bluecoats were taking aim with her heart as their target. She dove for the dead heap that had been her horse and took shelter behind his bulk, picking up her rifle from where she'd dropped it in the fall. The soldiers were discouraged by several accurate shots from her rifle before she rose abruptly to meet the brave who was rushing toward her, heavily muscled brown arm extended for her to grab. Rifle bullets tore past them as she swung up behind him, then held on for dear life on the wild gallop toward the bluffs. He dropped her beside Comes in Sight where he stood beside his sister in the shelter of the rocks.

Comes in Sight grinned warmly as he thanked Autumnfire's rescuer, a middle-aged Sioux warrior she didn't recognize. "Thank you for bringing this one back to me, my friend."

The Sioux grunted and regarded Autumnfire suspiciously, noting the red hair and green eyes. Her face burned under his scrutiny, and suddenly she wanted to hide the evidence of her white blood. But the Sioux warrior's eyes lit with a different light as he continued to boldly rake her with his eyes.

"Your women have courage," he addressed Comes in Sight with approval. "The one with green eyes—she is your woman?"

Comes in Sight warmed to the challenge. "Not yet."

The Sioux's harsh face softened to an almost boyish grin. "It is good, my brother." He raised his arm in salute and farewell. "After the battle is won."

The battle was almost won. Comes in Sight rode out briefly and came back with two riderless Indian ponies and gave them to the girls. Then he left to participate in the final cleaning up. The white soldiers were retreating to their camp downstream. The day had been a glorious victory for the Cheyenne and Sioux.

Buffalo Calf Road Woman was ecstatic, flushed with her own private victory over the white soldiers and the glory she knew would surround her for saving her brother's life. She couldn't hold still as she watched the final skirmishes of the day, excitedly pointing out one brave's coup, and then another's courageous rush. Finally she left to climb to the top of the rocky bluff for a better view. Autumnfire Woman declined her urgings to go along. Her head still rang from her tumble off the horse, and every muscle in her body felt as if it had been pounded to a bloody pulp. She was very content to sit in the shade of a lone pine and let her friend scramble up the hill to watch the rest of the day's glory.

The sounds of Buffalo Calf Road Woman's footsteps had barely disappeared up the hill when the sound of drumming hooves brought Autumnfire from her near doze. The hoofbeats had the sound of a steel-shod horse, not a barefooted Indian pony. She jumped to her feet in alarm when the rider came in sight over the rise—not a soldier, but a man clad in buckskin riding a big black stud. He hesitated at the sight of her, then urged the big black forward straight for where she was standing.

Autumnfire was too tired to be much afraid. Her first thought was amazement at the stupidity of the white man, coming toward an armed Indian without a hint of cover to protect him from her marksmanship. Did he think because she was a woman she couldn't shoot? She raised her rifle and confidently took aim at the moving figure. Suddenly the man crouched low over the horse's neck, and she could no longer distinguish man from animal. She hated to risk hitting such a magnificent horse. She frowned and aimed again. No time for mistakes.

A miss! The rider seemed to read her mind, knowing exactly when she would fire. He started to weave in and out just in time to avoid her bullet. She fired again, this time wildly. Her heart was beginning to pound with fear. The rider was much too close. No time to reload for another shot.

Autumnfire dropped the rifle and ran toward the horses, half expecting a bullet to tear through her back as she ran. Her exhaustion made her easy prey to panic, and her heart was racing so swiftly that the pounding in her ears all but drowned out the drum of hoofbeats behind her. With a quick over-the-shoulder glance to check her enemy's distance, she swung onto the nearest horse and whipped it into a frenzied gallop. She let the pony run blindly, fear having blocked out all common sense. She couldn't think. Her mind was spinning in circles. Where could she go for help? Her comrades were out of reach, her nemesis close behind. When the pony veered into a steep-sided ravine, she let him. In only seconds she realized her mistake.

There was nowhere to go. The ravine ended a hundred yards farther on in an unclimbable wall. The steep sides offered no avenue of escape. She yanked her pony around, only to face oncoming death. The big black stallion was on her almost the moment she turned. Her horse gave way and was forced against the rocks at the edge of the ravine.

He stumbled, knees buckling under the weight of the larger horse, and slowly went down. Autumnfire was trapped. She looked up to see the glistening black chest and foam-streaked neck heaving above her and braved herself to feel the weight of the huge beast settle down on her, crushing the life from her suddenly fragile-seeming body. But before that could happen, she was lifted from the saddle pad by an iron-thewed arm and brought up hard against a broad, firmly muscled chest. She screeched her anger, twisting and turning violently as she tried to reach the knife sheathed against her leggings. The long arms that imprisoned her were like steel, and she heard her captor actually laugh at her struggles. Enraged, she sank strong white teeth into one of the arms that immobilized her, eliciting a satisfying yelp from her tormentor. Momentarily free, she slid the knife from its sheath and pushed herself back from the man who held her, ready to thrust the knife deep into the broad chest in front of her. As she wrenched free, her head came up and she looked at her enemy for the first time, his face now exposed to the full light of day since his hat had flown from his head during their struggle. Poised to drive her knife home, she looked him full in the face. There she froze. Tawny, sun-streaked hair. Amber eyes set off by bronzed, hard-planed features. A face from the dim past, a past so dim she barely remembered. But the face she remembered, like a specter from a recurring dream suddenly and unexpectedly brought to life.

She hesitated only an instant, but that frozen instant was fatal. His arm lashed out like lightning and struck her wrist a numbing blow. The knife clattered uselessly to the ground. In the next moment she found herself draped belly down across the saddle in front of her captor, watching the ground fly past her face as the big black pounded away from the battle, carrying her far from any hope of rescue. Most infuriating of all, Autumnfire heard a distinct chuckle from the man who held her as his hand swung sharply against her vulnerable rump in an ungentle swat.

# Chapter Six

"Well, if it isn't little Meghan O'Brian in the flesh!" Jason Sinclair grinned. To Autumnfire's eyes the expression looked more feral than friendly. "You've grown some."

She stood on the sand of a dry creek bottom where Jason had finally allowed her to slide down from his horse. The sound of the battle had long since faded in the distance. Here there were only the two of them. She regarded him with clear green eyes, no longer quite as frightened as she had been.

He'd grown some himself, she noticed. He was bigger than she remembered, with a broadness well-proportioned to his considerable height. His buckskins didn't hide the heavy muscles in his chest, arms, and legs, but every part of him flowed so well together that he didn't give the impression of great bulk, though his height was well over six feet and his weight over two hundred pounds.

It was his eyes that caught and held her attention—those deep-set amber eyes that reminded her of a hunting cat. Had they always been so cold? His face—bronzed and chiseled to near masculine perfection—had it always been so hard? Her nine-year-old's memory had left out those details when, in her first few weeks of captivity, she had dreamed of Jason Sinclair's coming to her rescue, carrying her off from the frightening savages who surrounded her and bringing her to a place of warmth and security where they would dwell together happily evermore. She dreamed of him until she no longer wanted to be rescued, until she discovered the joys of being the beloved daughter of a respected Cheyenne chief, of being a happy-go-lucky child among the warm-hearted and fun-loving Cheyenne. As months passed, then years, she forgot Jason Sinclair, forgot Daniel and Mary Catherine O'Brian, forgot Meghan O'Brian, forgot everything about herself that labeled her as foreign to the way of life and the people she'd come to love.

Autumnfire stood silently and impassively, refusing to acknowledge Jason's words. She tried to push the name he called her out of her mind, along with the memories that name conjured up from her past.

"Don't play games with me, you little Irish hellcat!" Jason demanded, his frown making him look even more fearsome. "You speak English as well as I do."

Had she actually heard this man laugh as he'd carried her off? There was no humor in that hard, bronzed face as he regarded her now. She tilted her chin at a stubborn angle and flashed him a haughty ice-green look that belied her growing fear. Suddenly he seemed very large, towering head and shoulders above her, his broad chest blocking out the afternoon sun. She felt very small, very vulnerable. This wasn't the Jason Sinclair of her dim childhood memories. This was some stranger, a white man, the enemy, and she was weaponless and helpless before him. She saw the spark of anger in his eyes at her defiance and guessed that she was looking into the face of death. She vowed to meet it as a daughter of Stone Eagle should, without a flinch or tremor. Jason moved a step toward her and she backed up warily until she felt the hard rock lip of the ravine cut into her back.

"Stop looking like a damned martyr!" he said gruffly. "I'm not going to hurt you." He came closer and took her by the shoulders, looking thoughtfully into her face. "You're Meghan O'Brian right enough." He fingered one of the heavy russet braids that hung down almost to her waist. "Who would've thought that gawky little pest could grow up to look like this."

Angrily she twisted out of his grasp, disturbed more by the jolt his touch sent through her body than his words.

She tossed her russet braids defiantly and fixed him with what she hoped was a regal stare. "I am not the one you speak of. I am Autumnfire Woman, daughter of Chief Stone Eagle and Long Stepping Woman. I am Cheyenne!"

A smile quirked the corner of his mouth, softening the harsh features of his face for a brief moment. "No doubt you are all of that. But you're also Meghan O'Brian, daughter of Daniel and Mary Catherine O'Brian, carried off in a raid on a wagon train ten years ago."

"No." Ice frosted her voice. "I am . . ."

"All right, all right! Don't press your luck. I'm in no mood to split hairs with a stubborn Irish hellcat who thinks she's an Indian."

"I am not a . . . a hellcat." She stumbled over the unfamiliar word. She'd spoken English often with the white captive wife of Gray Wolf. Hellcat hadn't been in their vocabulary. "I am . . ."

"Yeah, I know." A gleam of sympathy flashed in his eyes and then was gone. "I'm glad your uncle gets the joy of taming you and not me."

He took her arm and led her back toward the black, who snorted impatiently at their approach. "Are you going to be a good girl, or am I going to have to tie you to the saddle?"

She dug her feet into the sand and refused to budge. "Where are you taking me?"

His tawny brows drew together in an impatient frown, but his voice was still calm. "We're going back to General Crook's camp. Then I guess I take you to Fort Laramie."

"You'll have to kill me first." She drew herself up proudly. "I will be no white man's prisoner."

He sighed. Why hadn't he just ignored Private Bailey's report of a red-haired woman sniping from the rocks? "I'm taking you to your uncle—your father's brother. He's gone to a lot of trouble to find you."

"My father's brother is Standing Antelope. He is right now killing your soldiers in the valley below."

"Your real uncle, dammit!" Jason's patience was beginning to fray. "You have an uncle, an aunt, and a whole host of cousins waiting for you in California. You have a nice home and a good deal of wealth just waiting for your return."

"You lie!" She watched her captor's lips tighten into a grim line as she stubbornly persisted. "My home is with Stone Eagle and Long Stepping Woman. If you wish to return me to my family, take me back to the valley where you found me." She waited for him to hit her. She could see it in those cold amber eyes and the clenching of his big hands. But he only grabbed her by the arm and pulled her toward the horse.

"Damn stubborn Irishwoman! I'm not going to argue with you. Come on!"

"No!" She panicked when she felt those steel fingers close around her arm. A wild swing of her small fist caught him full in the face, and out of surprise more than pain he released her. She took her chance, knowing somehow it would be the only one she'd get, and sprinted down the sand wash along the path her fleeing pony had followed a few moments earlier. Gouts of sand spurted from beneath her flying feet as she raced for the mouth of the wash. Already her lungs burned with the effort, and she heard heavier footsteps pounding close behind her.

Jason downed his little captive in a flying tackle that sent them both sliding along the gravelly creek bottom. When they slid to a halt, Autumnfire found herself pinned securely to the ground with her captor's long hard body stretched out on top of her. He showed no desire to move as she heaved up under him, trying futilely to throw him off.

"I wouldn't do that if I were you." His voice had a strange huskiness that hadn't been there before. She continued her struggle until his hands found her wrists and pinned them to the ground, and his weight bore down on her and held her immobile. She looked up into amber eyes that burned down into her own, and she recognized the animal heat that fired their depths. He smiled a not very pleasant smile of warning. "I'm not a saint, little Meghan. And you have grown some."

In the space of a heartbeat a new fear grew, a woman-fear of the man who held her down. She was suddenly and acutely aware of the power in the muscle-taut body that stretched over hers, of the helplessness of her own spread-eagled position, and most of all, of the hard rod of desire that pressed against her inner thigh. She froze, afraid to move, afraid to look into his eyes again and see the panting beast that stared at her out of those burning amber orbs.

"That's better." He eased himself off her, careful to never completely release his grip and give her a chance to run away again.

She rose from the ground warily, eying him with a new knowledge of her vulnerability. There were things less pleasant, less honorable than death.

General Crook's camp looked like a charnel house when Jason and his prisoner arrived an hour later. The tents were still orderly, strung out in neat rows where Muddy Creek flowed into the larger Rosebud Creek. Soldiers still moved here and there about their business, but a pall hung over the camp. Everywhere there were bodies, dragged back from the battlefield upstream to be given a military burial. Where the ground wasn't littered with bodies, the wounded lay in rows to be tended by the overworked camp surgeon and their fellow soldiers. A chorus of groans and an occasional scream rent the otherwise peaceful evening air as Jason guided his horse between men and tents and halted in front of a complex of larger tents that Autumnfire assumed was the lodge of the war chief.

Jason swung to the ground and reached up to pull his prisoner down with him as an orderly hastened to take the reins and lead the big black away.

"Careful with that horse," Jason warned. "He's got a mean streak with strangers."

"Yessir," the orderly acknowledged, giving hooves and

teeth a wide berth as he led the black toward the picket line.

Jason's fingers closed around Autumnfire's arm in a viselike grip as they paused before the entrance to the largest of the tents. "Behave yourself, little Meghan," he warned in a low voice, squeezing her arm in gentle but unmistakable pressure. "This is a man who isn't too fond of the Cheyenne right now. He lost a lot of good men today."

She refused to acknowledge his warning with either word or look and only stiffened her back and tilted her head higher. Jason sighed and shook his head, then pushed aside the tent flap for her to enter.

General George Crook was not quite the monster Autumnfire had expected. He was a middle-aged man sporting an impressive black crinkly beard that parted in the middle and swept out from either side of his cheeks. Dark hair was trimmed very close to his head, so close that it stood up like a black bristly brush. It emphasized the squareness of his face, which right now sagged with exhaustion under a layer of streaked dirt and dried sweat. He sat behind a plank that served as a desk, squinting through the dimness inside the tent as he scratched his quill along the paper in front of him. He didn't look up as Jason and Autumnfire entered.

Jason cleared his throat. The general jerked as if he'd been startled out of sleep.

"Oh, Sinclair. Glad to see you're back. Thought maybe we'd lost you in the scuffle."

"No, sir. I got diverted is all."

"Goddamned horrible day it's been." Crook massaged his forehead with a grimy hand, then rose wearily from his seat and took a half full bottle of bourbon from its place on the cot and poured himself a glass. "Have some?"

Jason declined, but waited patiently while the general finished his.

"Lost fifty-seven men today out there," he finally rasped. "Dead and wounded. Fifty-seven damn good men.

And I'd wager the savages didn't lose half that number. I've never seen the devils fight with such tenacity, damn 'em!'' He slammed his glass down on the makeshift desk. "Fifty-seven fine men!"

His eyes swung up abruptly and fastened on Autumnfire's face. "What's this?"

Autumnfire choked back angry words as Jason's fingers tightened around her arm in warning. His grip was gentle, but spoke of strength not yet exerted. She didn't like being referred to as a "what," and she was tired of hearing her people called savages and devils.

"This is the girl I mentioned to you a couple of weeks back," Jason explained. "Her uncle was at Fort Laramie a couple of months ago. He'd heard a white woman was sighted in Montana with a band of Northern Cheyenne. Private Bailey spotted her a ways from the battlefield and I rode over to pick her up."

Crook picked up one bright red braid that rested on her breast, and Autumnfire's eyes ignited with fury. She jerked back, raking him with a hot gaze full of contempt. He merely chuckled.

"Guess she's white all right. You sure this is the right one? Seems you said that gal was taken a long time back."

Jason nodded. "She's Meghan O'Brian right enough. I was scouting for the train she got taken from eleven years back. She may be older"—he grinned—"but she's got the same temper. I promised to see she got to her family if I found her, so if you don't mind, I'll be starting for Fort Laramie in the morning. With any luck her uncle will still be there. I can dump her and come right back."

Crook looked thoughtful. "Is that who you are, girl? Meghan O'Brian?"

Autumnfire fixed the burly, dark-bearded man with a haughty stare. She couldn't decide whether to ignore his question out of disdain, or to demand that he set her free. The alternative of pleading with the man for her freedom never entered her mind.

"I am Autumnfire Woman, daughter of Chief Stone

Eagle, daughter of Long Stepping Woman, friend of Little Hawk and Two Moon.'' She thought she'd throw in the two well-known chiefs for effect. If the white war chief thought she was under the protection of the men who'd just defeated him, maybe he'd be more likely to grant her freedom.

''Is that so?'' General Crook didn't seem impressed. ''Could it be that you were one of the women sharpshooting at our men from the rocks today?''

She didn't flinch from his accusing gaze. ''That was I. I and one other.'' She admitted her part in the battle with pride, forgetting the sick disgust she'd felt earlier in the day when she'd watched the bluecoats fall under her fire.

The look of black anger that came to the general's face only made her tilt her chin more defiantly.

''Do you think it was without honor to shoot at your soldiers while hiding in the rocks?'' she asked with a sneer. ''Where was your soldiers' honor when three moons ago they rode through Two Moon and Old Bear's peaceful camp. They burned the lodges and robes, took the food, and stole the horses from men, women, and children who wanted nothing but to live in peace, even though the night was very cold and the children and babies had nowhere to find shelter. Where was your honor then?''

Crook's eyes fell briefly. He was all too familiar with the incident, even though he himself had not been present at the one-sided fight.

Autumnfire pulled against the restraining hand of her captor, feeling as though she would like to spring at this white man who was harassing her people so mercilessly. ''I tell you, white war chief, we will fight you however we can. You will learn that the Cheyenne and Sioux are not dogs to be kicked or old women to run in fright at your coming!''

The anger faded slowly from Crook's eyes. He chuckled. ''She's a little firebrand, isn't she? A regular little Cheyenne hellion.''

'' 'Fraid so. Guess she fit right in with the Cheyenne.''

A mocking smile twisted Jason's chiseled mouth as she stiffened in tight-lipped hauteur. "Figured she might, way back when they first took her."

"Well"—Crook grimaced, massaging his brows again as he dropped into the seat behind his desk—"take her to Fort Laramie if you want. You're a civilian. I can't hold you. But get back here as soon as you can. I've got plenty of scouts, but I don't have many like you."

The tent that was commandeered for Autumnfire's use that night was hot and stuffy. Several dirty but serviceable blankets lay scattered on the floor, and a lantern glowed dimly from a peg on the tent pole. Though she couldn't see him, she knew a guard sat directly outside the tent flap. Occasionally an unmelodic whistling from in front of the tent reconfirmed her jailer's presence.

When food was brought into her she refused to eat, refused even to answer the friendly greeting of the young soldier who brought the meal. Miffed by her stony silence, the boy set the tin plate of stew and biscuits on the ground and left her in peace.

Jason, however, wasn't so easy to discourage. When he entered the tent an hour later and discovered her dinner untouched, he regarded her with an impatient glare.

"Eat!" he ordered.

She stared at him in hostile silence.

"We have a long trip ahead of us. You're going to do your share of the work, so you'd better eat."

One of her softly molded lips twitched in a sneer.

Jason's bronzed face relaxed into a dangerous smile. If she'd known him better, Autumnfire might have relented, seeing that easy-looking smile that didn't reach the cold amber eyes. He picked up the plate and held it in front of her. "Do you want this stuffed down your throat, little Meghan?"

Her eyes gleamed emerald with challenge. "Try it," she invited.

"You'd tempt a saint to murder. Do you know that, girl?"

"You're certainly no saint," she sneered.

His eyes snapped dangerously. "All the more reason for caution on your part, little Irish Indian."

He set the plate beside her and picked up an unsavory-looking piece of meat. She could see in his eyes the full intention of carrying out his threat to stuff the stew down her throat. No doubt it would be a messy fight. Worth it if she could win. Humiliating if he managed to overpower her, which she admitted was the most likely outcome.

She forestalled him with a hand on his chest. "I'll eat." She cast her eyes down in what she hoped was an expression of humble defeat. She wasn't sure. She hadn't had much practice in humility.

"About time." Jason set the plate beside her and started for the tent flap. "Tell the guard when you're done and he'll take the plate." With much difficulty she continued to look humble. "And don't get any funny ideas. There'll be someone outside this tent. . . ."

The plate of stew landed in his face in the middle of his sentence, leaving him with meat, potatoes, grease, and broth coating his face and dripping down onto his neck and chest. Autumnfire no longer looked humble. She openly smirked, green eyes alive with the joy of this small revenge.

The string of epithets hurled her way had no effect. She didn't know what most of them meant anyway. But when Jason wiped the grease from his face and she saw the expression there, her heart jumped in alarm.

In two long strides he was beside her and had her in his hands. Ignoring her screech of outrage, he pulled her up and threw her backside up over his lap.

"Someone should have attended to this a long time ago!"

His big hard hand landed with a painful smack on her

shapely little rear. Her screams of pain and anger didn't deter him. His hand rose and fell again and again until she sobbed with hurt and humiliation. Then he turned her until she faced him, pinned down on his lap and held firmly by his iron grip. His lips drew into a tight line as he looked down into her tear-stained face. Autumnfire's breath caught in her throat as his eyes caught hers and she saw the fire that burned there.

Anger, fear, and reluctant desire warred for ascendancy in Autumnfire's breast as Jason lowered his mouth to hers. His lips were hard and unyielding, hurting her as they forced her mouth to open and accept the caress of his tongue as it thrust inside. She froze, unable somehow to fight, ashamed at her body's rampant demand to yield. His kiss grew gentler, no longer bruising her tender lips as his tongue explored the sweet inner recesses of her mouth. It ended finally with a gentle brush of his lips against hers as he lifted his face from hers. In contrast to his caress, his eyes were hard, hiding all the emotion he was feeling behind opaque amber. Without a word he set her aside and stalked out, leaving her to fume, wipe the grease from her face, and muse on the impossibility of understanding a white man.

No man among the Cheyenne would have dared raise a hand to her, knowing he had Stone Eagle to deal with for her hurt. Autumnfire was beginning to realize that this man who had her in his power was not one to be dealt with lightly. He had strength and cunning enough to make a formidable enemy, and dark passions hidden beneath that cold and impassive facade that she didn't care to face. She had to break his hold on her, to get away before returning to her family and her people became an impossibility. She had to escape tonight. She would escape tonight, she vowed.

With stoic patience she waited for the night to grow old. She sat motionless and relaxed on the pad of blankets that was the only covering on the dirt floor. Dire speculations flitted worrisomely on the edges of her mind, but Indian-like she gathered the self-discipline to push the anxieties from her consciousness, concentrating on the problem at hand. As she sensed the camp growing quiet, she rose and doused the single lantern that hung from a peg in the tent pole, then returned to her quiet repose, garnering her strength until the time should come to implement her plan.

The camp was quiet except for the occasional moan from the surgeon's tent or the rustle of her guard shifting to a more comfortable position. Autumnfire searched inside herself for a sense of the amount of time that had passed since she'd first been escorted to her canvas jail. She decided it was well past the time for the moon to be down. The night should be velvet dark, and if she was lucky, she thought, the clouds that had been building on the horizon when she'd come out of the war chief's tent would have spread their robes across the night sky, and even the stars would be hidden from view. The night would be dark and thick. Now was the time to act.

She rose from her seat, sternly trying to quell the rapid pounding of her heart. She loosed her hair from its braids, mussing it as though she'd been sleeping, then calmly opened the tent flap and gestured to the guard. This man was not the one who'd been sitting here earlier, she noted. This was barely a man, more of a boy. His cheeks were more downy than bearded. His hair fell in light brown curls over his forehead. Autumnfire couldn't picture him as the enemy. But he was.

She gave him a tremulous smile, the one that had worked so well on occasion with Red Shield. With a maidenly show of fright and a practiced quiver in her voice, she told him a small snake had slid under the tent wall and into the pile of blankets on which she was sleeping. She was too frightened to look, and certainly she couldn't sleep knowing there was something slithering around the tent. Would he please come see?

The boy's face turned red as he gulped down his embarrassment at being so close to a female in such unconventional attire. And a right good-looking female at that, the boy noticed. He didn't care much for freckle-faced redheads, but this one was different. Her hair was soft and full, haloed by the light of his lantern. It fell down to her waist in bright red waves shot through with molten gold, still crimped in places from the braids she'd shook out earlier. Her skin was a soft golden brown, smooth and without blemish. The light dusting of freckles across her nose gave her a girlish look. She looked young and helpless, innocent and frightened. The emerald green eyes were wide with worry, clear of deception. He swallowed the bait without even feeling the hook as he ducked through the tent entrance to help this fair lady in distress.

The unfortunate soldier had hardly set his lantern down when Autumnfire deftly relieved him of the army-issue knife at his belt. His gun went skittering across the floor as she knocked it from his hand. Before the befuddled young soldier knew what was happening, the winsome redhead was at his back with her slim brown arm locked against his throat. He could have easily broken her grip except for the knife blade resting with threatening firmness against the column of his throat.

"Make a single noise and I cut your throat!" Her voice was barely a whisper in his ear, but the meaning carried well enough.

She maneuvered him awkwardly against the tent pole, keeping the knife pressed against his windpipe. "Sit!" she commanded with quiet intensity.

Reaching behind her, she grabbed the strips of blankets she'd torn earlier. Once the boy was securely tied to the pole, she used the last of the strips to stuff his mouth and gag him. Then she doused the lantern.

Armed with her guard's pistol and blade, she slipped out of the tent into the dark velvet night. The moon was down and not a star relieved the blackness of the sky. The neighboring tents had finally doused their lanterns. The dark was like a palpable blanket blotting out the camp, just as she had hoped it would be. Unerringly she crept in the direction of the picket lines, having memorized the layout of the camp as she'd ridden in with Jason. No alarm, no disturbance indicated that her struggle with the guard had been heard or that the boy's absence had been discovered, but still her heart pounded in a loud drumbeat of fear. Her moccasined footsteps were muffled by the dust. The only sound she heard in the silent blackness was the strained sound of her own breathing.

As her eyes adjusted to the dark, she could just make out the dim shapes of tents around her. She counted her steps. The picket lines should be just to her right, she decided. Just a short way to go. Freedom was just a few minutes away, just over the hill. Let her get that far with a good horse under her, and Jason Sinclair would never catch her, even if he tried. She heard the soft whicker of a horse. She stopped, letting the animals get used to her presence. A step closer and she started ever so softly to croon the tuneless sound that had always brought horses to her command. One horse stamped uneasily in the darkness. Another huffed an indignant breath through distended nostrils. Other than that, they were quiet. She picked out a long-legged dappled gray who looked as if he could run and stepped silently toward him.

As she stepped closer, the horse nearest her rolled his eyes and jerked back on his tether. Instantly he was joined by his fellows. She tried quickly to calm them as a frightened whinny broke the night silence and threatened to wake the camp. Then she noticed it wasn't her presence they were objecting to. The rolling, white-rimmed eyes were all focused on the thick blackness just beyond the picket line.

Autumnfire turned and stared hard in the same direction. Her heart stopped for an instant as the huge shape of a silver-gray wolf glided out of the dark, a nightmare in the flesh. She froze as the big wolf halted not ten feet from where she stood. Behind her, the horses had surprisingly grown quiet, as if now that the wolf was in the open, they thought he was no danger—almost as if they recognized him. The beast stared at her, yellow eyes seeming to glow in the night. He seemed more watchful than hostile. All the same, Autumnfire felt like a tasty morsel about to be snapped up by his powerful jaws.

An eternity of several seconds passed as neither she nor the wolf moved. Autumnfire could hardly believe the evidence of her eyes. No wolf walked boldly into a camp of men, no matter how hungry. And this beast didn't have the look of hunger about him. Even in darkness she could sense the thick lustrous fur and the muscles rippling in shoulder and haunch. The beast couldn't be real. He was a nightmare with no place in reality.

Autumnfire gathered her courage. If this was a phantom from her imagination, it could be banished. Emboldened by the quiescence of the horses, who were behaving as if they didn't see the specter, she stepped forward. A single step and the wolf's lips rippled in a snarl, revealing most unphantomlike fangs. A low growl of warning rumbled like deep thunder in his chest. Autumnfire halted, her heart in her throat.

"Have a problem?" Jason seemed to materialize out of the night beside the wolf, who visibly relaxed, licking his chops and greeting the man calmly.

Autumnfire opened her mouth, but nothing came out. She pointed mutely to the huge beast who now lounged at Jason's side, scratching casually at an itch under his formidable jaw like a tame hound.

Jason's mouth twitched in a grim smile. His face was as dark as the night around him. "This is a friend of mine. Wolf, meet Meghan O'Brian. She'll be traveling with us to Fort Laramie." His frown deepened and his mouth settled into a hard line. "That is, if she's still in one piece when I discover what she's done with her guard."

He stepped toward her and grabbed her arm in a painful grip, turning her roughly and pushing her in the direction from which she'd come. The wolf trotted calmly after them.

"Let me—"

"Save it!" he snapped, dragging her with him when she

couldn't match his long-legged strides. "We'll just see what bloodthirsty Cheyenne tricks you played on your guard, since I'm pretty sure he didn't agree to your little nighttime stroll."

The guard, still securely trussed and gagged when Jason stormed into the tent, greeted them with a look of acute red-faced embarrassment. His eyes shot daggers at the one responsible for his humiliation, and she returned his look eye to eye, refusing to flinch from his youthful anger. Releasing the boy, Jason tried hard to suppress the laughter that threatened to burst to the surface at the sight of them battling each other with their eyes.

"Git!" he ordered the embarrassed youth. "I'll guard her from here on out."

The boy ducked out of the tent with one last malevolent glare.

"I can see you're not the Cheyenne you thought you were," Jason chuckled.

Autumnfire whirled on him in a fury. "I am—"

"If you were," he interrupted calmly, "that boy would be lying here with his throat cut instead of stomping through the camp cursing green-eyed redheads. Guess that's what I thought I'd find when I saw you'd gotten free. Glad I didn't."

"You—"

"Lie down," he ordered, his voice edged once more with steel.

"What?"

"Lie down. I intend to see you stay here the rest of the night."

"What are you going to do?" She eyed him suspiciously as he went to extinguish the lamp.

"Nothing. If you behave yourself."

He lay down beside her and Wolf curled up comfortably by their feet. His arm circled her waist like a steel band and drew her snugly into the curve of his long, hard body. She stiffened, every muscle tautly objecting to this intimacy.

"Relax." His breath was warm on her hair. "Go to sleep."

"Let me go."

"No."

She sighed in frustration and strained against the encircling arm that held her prisoner firmly against him. "What do you think you're doing?"

He chuckled unpleasantly. "You can't move without waking me up. And if you try to escape again, I'm going to tie you to the tent post in the most uncomfortable position I can think of. Do you understand, Meghan O'Brian?"

Stubborn silence.

"Meghan?"

"My name," she answered between clenched teeth, "is not Meghan. I am Autumnfire Woman, daughter of—"

"Bullshit!" He shifted abruptly, dumping her on her back. His bulk loomed threateningly above her. "There is no Autumnfire! She's gone. She's dead, a thing of the past. From now on you're Meghan O'Brian, the name you were born with, the name you'll wear for the rest of your life. You may as well get used to it right now!"

She returned his glare with one of her own. The stubborn set of her jaw did not lessen.

"What is your name?" he asked in a tense, low voice.

She glared.

"Say it!" He shook her, not hard, but hard enough to remind her of the contained power of the arms that pinioned her.

"Say it!" he demanded again.

"Meghan," she gritted out reluctantly.

"Again."

Her eyes sparked with jade-green fury. "Meghan," she spat.

"What is your name?"

"Meghan!" She took a great sobbing breath and fixed him with a look that would have shriveled green grass. "May the gods above and below curse you. May the four spirits of the earth make your life a living hell. May you dry up and grow old and feeble before your time!''

He released her and sighed in frustration. ''If I have to spend much time with you I certainly will!''

He pulled her back into the curve of his body. ''By the way,'' he breathed against her ear, grinning as she tried unsuccessfully to turn her head away, ''you won't be needing all those spirits anymore. You're not Cheyenne, remember, Meghan. And I doubt the spirits that guard the Cheyenne have time to listen to a mere Irishwoman.''

He laughed as she tried to dig her sharp elbow into his ribs, pulling her more tightly against him. ''Give up, little Meghan,'' he advised with a chuckle. ''You've met your match.''

Autumnfire suffered his intimate nearness in stiff and angry silence. She fought an insidious languor as the warmth of Jason's flesh seeped into hers. She didn't want to relax or sleep. She wanted to mourn. Her past was gone, her future uncertain. Autumnfire was dead, a creature of the past, all because of the big tawny-haired man whose body curved so closely against hers. Because of him Autumnfire had perished, and a stranger named Meghan O'Brian lay in her place. Meghan stared into the dark and wondered who was the greater beast, the wolf curled sleeping at her feet or the man beside her on the blankets.

# Chapter Seven

The rolling Montana grasslands were still green from the spring rains. Later in the summer when the dry heat of July and August came searing down from the sky, the rolling expanse would be yellow-brown and parched. But now the grasses were still soft and verdant. The trees bordering the streams that splashed their way north to the Yellowstone were still lush with the vigor of new foliage. The world seemed fresh, young, and fertile as Jason and Meghan rode south.

Meghan began the trip in frozen hostility. Underneath a facade of proud disdain, she was confused and terrified. She felt helpless and terribly vulnerable in the grip of events that were changing her life. She hated the white soldiers who had looked at her with mixed curiosity and hostility the morning she and Jason had ridden out of camp. She hated her faraway white uncle, and aunt, and cousins. She hated herself for getting into this mess. But most of all, she hated Jason Sinclair, who seemed impervious to her curses, her glares, and her sullenness. He rode beside her with calm self-possession, seldom speaking, seemingly hardly aware of her presence. On their first day's ride, his casual lack of concern tempted her to contemplate escape once again, but before she could yield to temptation she felt his eyes on her. A mocking smile twisted his mouth.

"I wouldn't, if I were you," he said without anger. "I promise you wouldn't like the consequences."

She bit back an angry reply, knowing he'd read her with infuriating ease.

Jason Sinclair also was not entirely happy with the turn of events. He was beginning to regret bitterly his halfhearted promise to Jonathan O'Brian. What had been the chances he'd run across the little twit while scouting for Crook? One in a thousand? One in a million? And why had he persisted in thinking of her still as a gawky nine-year-old with a dirty face and uncombed hair? What a difference ten years could make! Little redheaded, freckle-faced girls were merely pests. Fire-haired, green-eyed temptresses were a real danger! One he would just as soon avoid.

Jason had never lacked for attention from the fairer sex.

The cold, opaque eyes that gave a sensible man pause gave most women a yen to get 'closer. His dangerous reputation and the ruthless reality of his presence drew females like moths flirting with the danger of a hot flame. He took what they offered and gave nothing of himself in return. He used them without regard to class, connections, age, or at times even attractiveness. A woman was a woman. One was much the same as another. They served their purpose and assuaged his physical appetites. In all other things he had little use for them. He regarded with ill-concealed contempt their flirting and posturing, so reminiscent of his mother as she plied her age-old trade. Not that he despised the memory of his mother. Whores at least were honest in their demand for gold in payment for their services. Most "good women," he'd found through experience, were just as anxious as any whore to open their legs for his pleasure, but they were less honest about their demands. After the deed was done, they placed a high price on what they'd offered for free. His soul and his heart were what they demanded, much more precious commodities than gold, and a price that he was willing to pay to no one.

But now there was this fire-haired Meghan O'Brian riding by his side. She didn't fit into any category. Therefore she was dangerous. More dangerous still because she was no ordinary female. Her beauty was wild and untamed, flamboyant and at the same time completely natural. Every move she made was filled with unconscious sensuality. Her air of innocence was unstudied and completely genuine. She was at the same time earthy and ethereal, a true daughter of the wild plains and mountains of Montana.

He respected her hatred. It was something he could understand, something he figured he deserved in a way. What he couldn't understand was the effect she had on his senses. The first time he'd touched her a shock of desire had run rampant through his senses. Not ten minutes later, when he'd tackled her in the sand of the dry wash, his body had been ready to take her right then and there. When he found her at the picket line trying to escape, he'd been ready to strangle her. He'd also been ready to throw her to the ground and avail himself of the tender flesh he knew he'd find under that tunic. The rest of the night, her firm little rear tucked up against his hips, was exquisite torture. He felt like a hot-blooded stud led to a mare in heat, then tethered just out of reach.

He'd been without a woman for two months, ever since he'd left Fort Laramie. That could explain part of it. But there was something more disturbing than the lust that heated his blood at her proximity. There was something more than lust, something he didn't care to examine too closely. It might be sympathy for her plight—a confused and lonely child-woman dragged from family, friends, and familiar surroundings and being delivered up to an alien and hostile society. It might be admiration for her courage, or compassion for one who was more of an outsider even than he was. It might be any of those things, or all. But he didn't like the emotions that lurked beneath the more easily understood, more easily dealt with, animal lust. He wouldn't let himself fall prey to this little wildcat. He was the predator, and he liked it that way. He would deliver her to Jonathan O'Brian at Fort Laramie, then be on his way back to General Crook. Meghan O'Brian would be gone and forgotten, disrupting her uncle's life, not his.

As the two of them rode south, one day followed on the heels of the day before with pleasant monotony. The sky was cloudless blue and the burning midday sun was always allayed by cool breezes that riffled through the grasses and set the prairie in undulating motion. At night a sea of stars swept from horizon to horizon, and Meghan night after night stretched out on her blanket and followed with sad eyes the shining span of brighter stars that belted the sky, the Hanging Road that led to Seyan, the land of the dead. Sometimes she wished she could follow that road with her soul as well as her eyes. Better to cross over to that land of eternity than face a future apart from the people, the life, and the land she loved. Better to dwell in the land of the dead than with the enemy who was claiming her as one of them.

Day after day they traveled through a land that seemed as virgin as the day the earth was born. The birds serenaded them by day and the coyotes by night. Life abounded, but of man there was no evidence. Jason deliberately avoided the few spots that sprouted human habitation. The gold rush and the great Sioux reservation was to the east of them, and settlers and ranchers in this last stronghold of the Indians were few and far between. The farther south they traveled, however, the more frequent were the signs of the white man's incursion.

Two days out of Fort Laramie Jason drew rein on a low bluff overlooking a small sheltered valley. A creek ran along the opposite bluff. Trees grew thick along the banks, and the water that chuckled merrily over the rocks was all but hidden by a tangled overgrowth of gooseberry bushes. At the head of the valley, resting in the shade of three enormous birch trees, stood a house—the first real house Meghan had seen in ten years.

Jason jerked his flat-brimmed hat down to shade his eyes from the glaring noonday sun and squinted at the house for a long moment. Then he turned to Meghan with an air of resignation.

"Guess it's time to try out your city manners." His smile was half mocking, half sympathetic. He noted the panic that flooded her eyes.

"We're stopping? Here?" Her voice was colored with alarm.

"That's right."

"Why?"

"That latigo of yours is about worn through. You're going to land on your butt any day now. And the horses could use a little rest. We've been pushing 'em pretty hard." Lame excuses, Jason admitted to himself.

"Bullshit!"

Jason sighed and regarded her ruefully. "I can see I'm

going to have to give you a lesson in proper English for females.''

''I'm just following your example!'' she shot back in a tart voice.

''Yeah,'' he sighed. ''I can see that.''

''Why are we stopping?'' she demanded, stubbornly steering him back to the question at hand.

'' 'Cause I'm the boss and I say so.''

''Bull—''

''Would you quit cussin', goddammit!''

She burned him with an emerald glare.

''We're a couple days out of Fort Laramie,'' he finally relented. ''Figure it's time for you to try out some of your white manners. It'll be easier here with just a few folks than at Fort Laramie with all sorts of curious people floating around.''

''I don't have any white manners,'' she insisted.

He lifted one thick tawny brow. ''That's what I'm afraid of.''

He ignored the rebellious set of her face and turned his back. ''Wolf, you're on your own for a while. And don't you go near those chickens, understand?''

The big silver-gray wolf looked at the man intently, as though he really did understand.

''Now git! And stay out of trouble.''

As they trotted slowly down the little valley toward the little house, Meghan had time to examine the structure. It didn't look nearly as inviting as the cozy buffalo hide lodges where she had spent the last ten years of her life. The walls were of stone, the roof of timber and sod. A small neat vegetable plot flanked it on one side, and several rickety henhouses of scrap timber crowded up to the other side. Set off from the house and pushed up against the steep sheltering bluff, a corral held two horses who looked as if they'd seen better days, many better days. A barn badly in need of repair ran along the side of the corral.

Their approach didn't go unnoticed. A small woman in

a faded print dress rose stiffly from where she'd been working in the garden and regarded them curiously, and a bit cautiously, as they drew rein at the front of the house.

Jason casually touched the brim of his hat as she approached. "Howdy," he said briefly.

"Howdy, yourself." The woman's eyes took in the well-worn buckskins, the long-barreled pistols resting on his thighs, and the knife at his belt. Then they came to rest on his face and softened somewhat. Meghan recalled some soldiers joking about Jason's way with women. Was this what they meant?

"We were passing this way, heading toward Fort Laramie, and hoped you might see your way clear to letting us use your barn for a few hours. Got a repair job to do on the lady's saddle."

The woman's gaze shifted to Meghan. Her eyes narrowed as she noted the buckskin tunic and leggings, the tight, Indian-style braids that confined the fiery hair.

"That's the strangest getup for a 'lady' that I ever did see." She eyed them both suspiciously. "What's all this? Where you folks from?"

Jason swung lightly down from his saddle and respectfully removed his hat. Tawny waves sprung free to frame his sun-browned face. The dark amber eyes were as innocent as a preacher's in Sunday school. He could radiate charm when he wanted to, Meghan noted. And even this worn-out middle-aged husk of a woman fell prey to his good looks, broad shoulders, and the ready smile that curved his lips but never reached his eyes.

"Just come from General Crook's army up in the Powder River country, ma'am. This lady here's had a hard time of it. Got carried off by a band of Cheyenne some time ago. We got her loose from those savages and I'm takin' her back to her family. Didn't have time to get her looking like a decent white woman again."

Meghan bristled at his words, but the woman was instantly all sympathy. "You poor dear!" In her rush of emotion she failed to note the look of contempt in Meghan's green eyes as she looked at her "rescuer." "What did you say your name was?"

Jason cleared his throat and thought fast. "Uh . . . I'm John Sawyer, ma'am. The lady's Meghan O'Brian."

"Well, Meghan O'Brian," the woman clucked, "you get off your horse right now. You're welcome to use the barn or anything else you need. And why don't you step in the house while I heat up a pot of tea."

As Meghan stepped down, the woman waved a hand toward the house. "Junior! You can come out now. Everything's fine."

A boy holding a shotgun appeared from around the corner of the house. "My boy, Carl Jr. Can't be too careful, you know. Never know who's going to come riding up with all the riffraff pouring into the country these days."

The boy ambling toward them wore a grin that seemed to split his face in two. He was awkwardly adolescent, and his frame had obviously outpaced his coordination. Raggedly trimmed light yellow hair stuck out of his head at awkward angles. Long arms flapped as he walked, and large feet landed in a dangerously haphazard manner with every step. Meghan suspected the boy would trip over a dust mote if given half a chance.

"My two girls are in the house," the woman told them as Junior lurched to a halt beside them. "They'll be right glad to have a couple of new faces to jabber to. Honey, why don't you come in and freshen up while Mr. Sawyer here takes your animals to the barn and does whatever it is he thinks needs doin'?" She placed a chapped and leathery hand on Meghan's arm, a maternal gleam lighting her eyes.

Meghan's head swam with the possibilities the woman's suggestion offered—Jason in the barn and her in the house. The horses in the corral looked as if an amble was their top speed, but that might be good enough if she could get enough of a head start. The prairie was a big place.

Finding her would be difficult if she didn't want to be found.

Jason saw the wheels turning in her head though, and his chiseled features softened in amusement as he crushed her newborn hopes.

"Mrs. . . . uh . . ."

"Mrs. Karr. But my friends call me Grace."

"Well, Mrs. . . . uh . . . Grace. Meghan, here, she's not quite right in the head right now. You know—she's been through a lot with those devil Cheyenne." He tried to conceal a smile as Meghan's eyes shot jade fire. "She'll be fine," he hastened to add at the look of horror on Grace's lined face. "Soon as she gets back to the loving arms of her family. But right now she sometimes goes off her head and thinks she's one of those savages. So I'd just as soon keep her within arm's reach. Just in case."

As Jason towed her and the weary horses toward the dilapidated barn, Meghan furiously searched her mind for a torture appropriate to the man's insults. She failed to find one gruesome enough.

"How dare—"

"Tch, tch!" He didn't let her finish. "Mind your manners. You're among civilized people now." The laughter in his voice was unmistakable.

"You're a toad! A worm! Why did you tell them such a lie?"

"Not so much a lie, was it?"

"I'm perfectly all right in the head! If you ask me, it's your mind that needs mending! And why did you lie about your name?"

He pulled her into the cool dimness of the barn and tied the horses to a rusted iron horseshoe that had been set in one beam as a hitching ring.

"My name gets around. Never can tell when the name Jason Sinclair's going to make otherwise sensible people do crazy things."

"What do you mean?" she asked warily.

"Just what I say. Why don't you sit down over there and

be quiet while I take care of this latigo strap. When I'm finished we'll go in the house, wash up, and maybe we can weasel our way into getting some of that stew I smell cooking."

"What do you mean your name gets around and makes people do crazy things?"

Jason sighed and pulled the saddle off her bay mare. "Persistent cuss, aren't you. Seems to me I remember your being that way when you were a kid, too. Pest."

"Are you some kind of an outlaw?" she demanded with a frown.

"No," he answered truthfully. "Outlaws don't get jobs scouting for the army."

"What, then?"

His mouth tightened into a grim line. "I'm fast with a gun. Killed a few men in gunfights in my younger days. Now they seem to hunt me out. Word gets around. Some places I'm about as welcome as a wolf in a henhouse. Lots of folks seem to think I'm about as deadly, too. Guess I can't really say they're wrong."

Her eyes flickered, and for a moment Jason thought he saw a trace of alarm. But they steadied in a level gaze that carried a hint of contempt.

"Should I be frightened?" she sneered.

His amber eyes caught her green ones and held them captive. For a change there was no shade of mockery there. "Maybe you should," he said quietly, "if you had an ounce of sense in your head."

She couldn't think of a rejoinder. The gravity in those strange but compelling amber eyes frightened her more than his earlier confession. Her heart thumped unreasonably as she tore her eyes away from his face.

The delicious stew Grace Karr put before them once they had finished washing up was almost enough to make Meghan glad they'd stopped. She even felt a twinge of relief when Jason accepted the woman's invitation to stay a few days.

"Place is mighty run-down," Grace explained. "Haven't

had a man around for near six years now, ever since my Carl Sr. took his death of pneumonia. Junior could sure use a hand at some of the chores, and I know the girls and I would take good care of little Meghan here.'' She flashed Jason a significant look while Meghan's face tightened in resentment.

''We could use a break.'' Jason's smile sent Grace's two girls, Amy and Christine, into spasms of giggles that were instantly quashed by a threatening glance from their mother. Junior smiled happily. The rest of the meal he sat seemingly dumbstruck at his place and stared furtively at Meghan, his eyes full of puppyish worship. Meghan's face relaxed into a reluctant smile. She admitted she'd rather deal with these few people here for a while than face what was waiting for her at Fort Laramie.

The next three days were a wonder of revelation for Meghan. Grace and her two giggly daughters treated her with kid glove caution, as though expecting her to explode into a wild war dance at any moment. But just the same, the warmth, laughter, and affection they shared among them was infectious. It made Meghan think sadly of her Cheyenne family—Stone Eagle, Long Stepping Woman, and Magpie. That a family of the dreaded whites could show much of the same joy, laughter, and affection was an unexpected thought.

Grace Karr was a woman of unusual strength of both spirit and body, in spite of her diminutive size and worn appearance. She made it immediately clear to her buckskin-clad guest that no funny business of any kind would be tolerated, then proceeded to treat her like a much-loved daughter. Meghan recognized her match when she met it and reluctantly gave up her budding plans for escape, for the time being at least.

Meghan must have a decent dress, Grace insisted. It wouldn't do at all for her to ride into Fort Laramie and let her uncle see her got up like a savage. Meghan resisted mightily. The buckskin tunic and leggings were the last vestiges of her former life. She resisted, but she lost.

Grace and her daughters all fussed about Meghan as if she were a doll to be dressed. Christine donated a length of cotton print she'd been saving, and Amy contributed several yards of lace ripped off an old dress she claimed was ready for the dustbin. They bustled about taking measurements and discussing patterns until Meghan thought she would scream. She decided with little doubt that white women had it all over their men when it came to torture.

Between fittings and discussions of suitable styles, Grace took it upon herself to give Meghan a crash course in the basics every white woman should know. Her skill at sewing hides for lodges and clothing was no help in producing the delicate stitchery Grace thought necessary to construct a white woman's garment. Her fingers grew sore from innumerable pricks of the needle, but the giggles of Amy and Christine, both considerably younger than she, prodded her to greater effort to prove she could top any skill they could master. She learned about the baking of bread with a queer substance that made it airy and light instead of dense like the breadcakes she was used to baking on a stone heated in the cook fire. Her ignorance of reading and writing went unnoticed, for none of the three women could boast of those skills either, but her free use of the English language as spoken by Jason Sinclair brought an unaccustomed sternness to Grace's usually mild features.

"A decent woman doesn't use such words, Meghan O'Brian!"

"Why not?" Meghan asked in all innocence. "I just say what I feel."

"Just the same, you'll not be using them in this house, or I'll be taking a switch to you, guest or not. And if your uncle's a right-minded man, he'll do the same."

Meghan shrugged, not willing to argue over such a minor point. She liked Grace Karr, and she liked her two silly daughters with whom she shared a bed in the little loft upstairs. If it upset Grace that she spoke as she did, she'd do her best to mend her language. The trouble was, she wasn't at all sure which words Grace didn't like. She'd have to severely limit her vocabulary in the future.

Their stay lengthened to a week as Jason worked diligently with Junior. Twice Jason and the boy rode out to count and examine the few scrawny head of cattle that the Karrs ran on the grasslands surrounding their little valley. At all other times, sometimes even late into the night, the valley rang with the sound of their hammering and sawing. The house, barn, corral, and henhouses began to take on a new look as the week drew to a close.

Seldom was Meghan able to escape from the house and her forced domesticity to watch Jason at his labor. She didn't miss his company, she told herself, in the long days she spent with the females of the house. She got occasional glimpses of him working with Junior or alone, bare-chested and sweating in the sun. There was nothing wrong with admiring the sheer masculinity of his form, she told herself. It was only natural to notice the hard muscles rolling in his back as he sawed a plank to fit a gap in the barn wall, or the flexing of his heavily muscled arm as he hammered the plank home. It didn't mean she despised him any less because she recognized a certain bold appeal, a certain animal attractiveness about him. She could still loathe the man and admit he was a magnificent creature, a virile male beast who could set the blood of any healthy female to racing. Meghan O'Brian, whoever she was, whoever she would discover herself to be, was not going to be a woman controlled by her animal urges. Especially when her animal urges had her fantasizing about a man who represented everything she hated, a man who had ruined her life and her happiness and gloated constantly, reminding her of her predicament.

She couldn't understand why it irritated her so much when Amy and Christine fluttered around Jason like giggling butterflies. Meghan liked the two younger girls, but a hard core of resentment grew within her at their silly antics to gain his attention. Their mother wasn't that much better herself. Not only did she not put a stop to her daughters' foolishness, she herself wasn't above looking at the big tawny-haired man with a softness to her otherwise sharp eyes. Meghan told herself she didn't like to see the girls' making fools of themselves. She found Jason's attitude of tolerant amusement especially annoying, as though he was accustomed to this sort of treatment from females and accepted it as his due.

The fourth day of their stay, Meghan's dress was finished, complete with chemise and petticoats. Amy and Christine, exceedingly proud of their handiwork, insisted on preparing Meghan as a surprise for Jason when he returned in the evening. He and Junior had ridden out to look at some of the cattle, so he was safely away from the vicinity of the house. The girls could do their worst.

Meghan was grateful for all the girls' work and genuinely touched by their kindness, but she balked at letting them get her "gussied up," as they put it. Jason didn't care what she looked like. All he wanted was to get to Fort Laramie and dump her so he could get back to killing Indians. She promised to wear the dress when she got to Fort Laramie. Yes, it was a lovely garment, and she liked it very much, but no, she didn't want her hair and face messed with. She preferred to stay just the way she was. Grace and her daughters, however, were not to be discouraged.

Hot water was poured into a wooden tub in Grace's bedroom, the only room in the house that afforded any privacy. Meghan found herself soaking in sudsy water up to her neck with two giggling handmaidens attending to her every need and guarding against any attempt to escape their ministrations. It felt good to be clean all over, to feel the warm water sift through her hair and carry away all the accumulated dust and grime of the past days. But she had serious doubts about the flowery-smelling oil the girls dribbled into the tub, a forbidden purchase, Christine confided, from their last trip to Cheyenne a year past.

Bath complete, Amy sat her reluctant victim down on a stool in front of a cracked mirror and brushed the fiery strands of her hair until they were dry. Then, to Meghan's horror, she took a pair of shears and shortened the thick mass by several inches, evening and trimming until her hair fell in an even line just below the middle of her back.

"God, I wish I had hair like that!" Plump, mousy-haired Christine sat on Grace's bed and watched the transformation with envy. "And skin! If I looked like you, know what I'd do? I'd go into Cheyenne or Denver and find me a rich man! That's what I'd do. I'd never have to weed the garden or slop the pigs or scrub the floor again!"

Amy snorted. "You're too young to have a man." From her vantage point of being two years older she felt wonderfully superior to her younger sister. "You don't even know what you're talking about." She parted Meghan's hair and carefully began to plait it into several tightly woven braids.

"I do so!" Christine insisted. She sighed theatrically. "At least I know enough to know I'd sure like to ride off with that Mr. Sawyer. Now there's a man who's a man!"

Amy glared at her, but Christine was unmoved by her sister's silent plea for discretion.

"Are you and Mr. Sawyer going to get married, Meghan?"

Meghan's head snapped toward Christine in surprise, pulling a braid out of Amy's fingers. "No! Of course not!" Amy turned her victim's head impatiently back toward the mirror. "What makes you ask that?"

"Women don't generally go around alone with men unless they're married or going to get married."

Amy's mouth pursed in exasperation at her sister's thoughtlessness. "Meghan's different."

"Why?" Christine persisted obtusely.

"Because!" Amy paused in her braiding and turned a contemptuous look on her sister. "She's been living with the Indians." She didn't bother to elaborate that any woman having lived with those savages was assumed to be irredeemably soiled. Meghan had no reputation to worry about protecting.

Meghan didn't understand half of the conversation going on around her. She fidgeted impatiently while Amy took her carefully braided strands and wove them into a shining coronet on top of her head.

"There!" she said with satisfaction, patting the last wisp into place. "Now for the dress!"

The chemise, petticoats, and bright cotton print dress with its snug waistline, prim neckline, and narrow sleeves trimmed with lace felt strange and uncomfortable, though the fit was perfect, the girls declared. Uncomfortable also was Meghan's first sight of herself in the mirror. There was no trace of Autumnfire in the woman she saw reflected. In her place stood a prim and proper white woman, smelling faintly of lilac, covered in flower-sprigged cotton from neck to toes, hair neatly braided and pinned on top of her head. It was a woman whom Meghan didn't know.

"You're gorgeous," Christine sighed.

"Beautiful!" Amy agreed. "You'd knock any man's eyes out."

Meghan examined the reflection in the mirror. They said she was beautiful, but she couldn't tell. Her hair and skin, so envied by Christine, had always been her bane. Her skin, paler than that of her Cheyenne sisters, had that loathsome sprinkling of freckles that always appeared when she was too long in the sun. Her hair was a flaming banner that proclaimed her alien to the people she most loved. Her eyes, the green of a deep, cool pond, were so unlike the soft brown of Stone Eagle and Long Stepping Woman and Magpie. The men had pursued her in spite of all this, but she'd thought it was because she was different, not because she was especially attractive. Yet these girls called her beautiful. Perhaps among the white men she would be considered so. For herself, she could see no special beauty in the woman who gazed at her out of the cracked mirror; she saw only foreignness.

Jason, though, apparently saw something to his liking when he came back to the house that evening. He and Junior had just washed up at the pump behind the house and were sitting down to a meal of fried chicken when Amy and Christine pushed a reluctant Meghan into the room. He glanced at her, then stared. Color rose to Meghan's cheeks as he continued to stare.

"Well?" Christine demanded. "Isn't she beautiful?"

Jason choked on the food that had gone unheeded in his mouth. He took a moment to recover, all the while taking in the miracle before him. The dirty Indian ragamuffin he'd dragged with him from Montana had been transformed into a primly garbed, neatly coiffed, sweet-smelling, ravishingly beautiful young white woman. He'd had trouble enough guarding against the charms of the ragamuffin. How would he cool his hot blood alone in the night with this utterly beautiful, painfully innocent, achingly female creature standing before him?

"Very nice," he growled. With determination born of despair he wrenched his eyes from Meghan and turned back to the plate full of food.

"Is that all?" Amy demanded.

Junior stared at the transformation with wonder in his eyes. "Yer gorgeous. Lord, Meghan, yer the best-looking girl I've ever seen!"

"Sit down, girls," Grace instructed, giving Jason a knowing look. "You look wonderful, Meghan." She squelched another slobbering approbation from Junior with a threatening glare. "Do you like it?"

Meghan studied her dinner plate with unwarranted interest. Her cheeks were still warm with color. "I don't know. . . . I mean, yes." She didn't really expect Jason to fall all over her with praise, but something more dramatic than 'very nice' would have been encouraging. Still, what did she care what he thought? "Amy and Christine were very nice to go to all this trouble for me." For the world she wouldn't let these people know she felt as uncomfortable as a trussed-up cow in this getup.

Grace looked at her, a sympathetic smile softening her careworn face. "You'll get used to it, dear. Never fear."

By the time they were ready to leave for Fort Laramie, Meghan had gotten used to the different mode of dress, though she still had trouble keeping the long skirts out of her way. Amy and Christine had labored over another dress and finished it the night before they were to leave, in spite of her protests. She needed an extra, they insisted. Lord only knew when she would be able to make or purchase the clothes she would need.

The Karrs' generosity and warmth touched Meghan with emotions she wanted to avoid. She had tried to remain aloof and hostile with these people, her enemies, the dreaded whites. But they had welcomed her with a kindness that was impossible to resist. As they embraced in farewell, Christine's and Amy's tears wet the shoulder of her new dress. Meghan herself came embarrassingly close to a very un-Cheyenne-like display of emotion. She was still stiff-faced and clench-jawed from holding back disgraceful tears when the house and the little valley disappeared from sight behind them.

# Chapter Eight

The day was blisteringly hot. Meghan felt wilted and confined in her unfamiliar white woman's garments. The tight sleeves and snug bodice were not nearly so cool as her loose tunic, and the skirts were not nearly so practical in the saddle as her sturdy buckskin leggings. They twisted and pulled and bunched up most awkwardly as she sat astride her saddle. The most practical, and comfortable, part of her clothing was the last-minute gift from Grace Karr, a too-large pair of trousers worn under her skirts and held up at her waist by a length of rope. To preserve her modesty when she had to ride astride, Grace had told Meghan as she'd handed her the pair of Junior's outgrown pants. She didn't care much right now about preserving her modesty, but the trousers were the only part of this white woman's fashion that she approved of. If she was forced to remain among the whites, she vowed she'd wear only trousers and dispense with the frilly dresses.

At the start of the morning Jason had been relaxed and in a light mood. He'd played boisterously with Wolf when the big silver-gray animal had joined them in the early morning. He'd teased Meghan unmercifully about the dress, and then about the trousers, and then about her stubborn insistence on returning to her Indian-style braids, despite Amy's best efforts to persuade her otherwise. Mid-morning his mood darkened. The amber eyes grew watchful. The chiseled planes of his face settled into a mask of wariness. Conversation ended, and he constantly scanned the surrounding landscape for some sign that all was not as it should be. Wolf also seemed edgy, frequently twisting his head to look over his shoulder and staying much closer to them than was his wont.

"Is something wrong?" Meghan finally asked, puzzled by his behavior.

"Nothing's wrong yet," he told her with a hint of worry in his voice. "But it might soon be. We're being followed."

A brief flicker of joy lit up her face before she could hide it.

He lifted a brow at her reaction. "Friends of yours maybe?"

She flashed him a look of irritation. "How would I know?"

"You wouldn't, I guess. Figure we'll find out soon enough."

"Couldn't it just be someone traveling the same direction we are?" she asked, though she sincerely hoped not.

"Unlikely. They're going to a lot of trouble to hide themselves."

They rode on in silence, Meghan as watchful now as Jason. Her heart leapt with the hope that Stone Eagle had sent someone after her, or perhaps even come himself. Or maybe Red Shield had come to rescue her from the white men, or even Comes in Sight. How could she have thought her people would forget her, would let the white man take her from them with no effort to bring her back? She couldn't help wondering what had taken them so long, but that didn't matter as long as they were here.

Meghan's respect for Jason's acute senses increased tenfold in the next hour. She could detect no sign they were being followed, but he grew more and more certain. Meghan was about convinced that Jason's imagination was playing tricks on him when she heard a distinctive five-note bird trill repeated twice. Her heart caught in her throat. She knew that call. No bird caroling over the rise sent that whistle lilting through the air. Someone from Two Moon's band was signaling her their presence. She stole a furtive glance at the big man riding beside her. He showed no sign of having noticed the bird call, and in truth, unless one knew the call was the identification signal used between warriors in Two Moon's camp, there was no reason to suspect it had not come straight from the throat of a bird.

"Are we still being followed?" she asked innocently.

"Haven't seen 'em in a while. But I figure they're still out there, whoever they are."

"I think you're imagining things," she said loftily and turned away with apparent lack of interest.

Jason scanned the horizon with wary eyes. "Think what you want. But if those are your friends out there and you don't want them to get hurt, you better hope they hotfoot it back where they came from."

Meghan faced him with wide-eyed innocence, wondering if he knew more than he was letting on. "I don't know who's out there," she lied. "Or if anyone's out there. I think you've been in the sun too long without a hat."

A grunt was her only answer.

"And what makes you think you could take on several Indians and win, anyway? If those were Cheyenne out there, you'd be lucky to escape with your scalp, white man!''

A wolfish grin curved his lips. ''Do you think so?''

''I know so!'' She was irritated by his calm assurance. ''You may think you're a tough guy among the white man, but if there were really Cheyenne out there, you'd be dead meat!''

He lifted one brow at her agitation, but the unpleasant smile on his face didn't fade.

The setting sun brought a rumble of hunger to Meghan's stomach, and she was grateful when Jason trotted into a tree-lined wash and dismounted.

''Guess this is as good a place as any to camp,'' he said.

Meghan dismounted, stiff from the long day's ride and weary from the tension that had hung between them all afternoon.

''I'll go hunt us up a rabbit or two.'' Jason grabbed his rifle and checked the loading. ''Wouldn't go anywhere, if I were you.'' He said it casually, but his meaning was clear.

''I've nowhere to go,'' she said truthfully. The temptation was great, with help so close by. But to run while it was still light, when he would follow her tracks with no effort at all, was foolish. She had no desire to see Jason's blood stain the ground, and she knew that would happen should it come to a fight.

So she was still there when he came back carrying two rabbits. Meghan suspected there'd been more, for Wolf was licking his chops with a very satisfied look in his eye. Without a word she took the rabbits, skinned them, cleaned them, and spitted them over the fire she'd started. Soon the juices were spattering on the coals and the aroma was making both their stomachs growl with impatience. In the meantime she took some of the flour that Grace had given them and started a batch of biscuits.

''You're very efficient tonight,'' Jason commented.

''This is our last night out, isn't it?''

"Maybe. If we put in a real long day tomorrow, we might get to Fort Laramie by sundown."

Meghan stole a glance at her big tawny-haired captor as she checked the sizzling rabbits. If she succeeded in stealing back to her rescuers tonight, she'd never see Jason again. If she failed and they arrived at Fort Laramie tomorrow, then she would never see him again either. Strange the tug that gave her heart. He was the enemy. He'd stolen her from her people, humiliated her, threatened her, made fun of her, and still she found a tender place in her heart that leapt whenever he looked at her the way he was doing now.

"Rabbit's ready." She avoided his eyes, hiding her regret behind thick, dark lashes. Pride demanded that she never let him suspect that she cared one tiny bit about being parted from him.

The night was peaceful. They sat in silence eating their rabbit and biscuits, watching the stars pop out one by one in the darkening sky. There was no sign that there was any other human being for miles around. A coyote howled. His lonely song rose against the clear and moonless sky. Wolf looked up, his eyes alert, then rested his head once again on his forepaws.

Meghan was aware of Jason's eyes on her, regarding her with an enigmatic look she couldn't fathom. A frown creased his forehead and drew a deep line between his brows. Did he suspect there might be help waiting for her out there in the brush? Meghan hoped not. He would only come to harm if he pushed her rescuers into taking her by force. Finally he spread out his blankets and yawned, seeming to have come to a decision.

"Going to be a long day tomorrow," he said, stretching. She couldn't help but admire the play of muscles in his back as the thin cotton shirt stretched across his broad shoulders. His buckskins had been packed away and replaced by cooler clothing. The expanse of chest and arms bared by the light cotton shirt Grace had given him had tempted Meghan's eyes all day.

She rolled out her blankets a decent distance from his. He eyed her with amusement, but didn't object. Before reaching the Karr ranch, they'd slept in the same intimate arrangement he'd insisted upon at Crook's camp.

"There's nowhere for me to go," she snapped, seeing his look.

"True enough." His answer seemed unusually mild, and she frowned in suspicion as he moved to his pack and rummaged through the contents.

"Thought I remembered putting this in here." He smiled, pulling out a length of lightweight rope. "Just in case," he explained as he moved toward her. "Wouldn't want to lose you on our last night out."

She looked at the rope in his hands and the mocking look in his eyes, and her face flushed with anger. "You scum-blooded toad! That's . . . you wouldn't!" Her eyes shot green sparks at him. "How can I sleep trussed up like a cow!"

"Don't know about you." A hint of amusement flickered in his eyes. "But I'll sleep a hell of a lot better." His smile was infuriating.

Meghan knew better than to resist as he tied her hands in loose but inescapable bonds. Fighting would only make him tie her tighter, she knew, and all was not yet lost. Let him think he'd won, for the moment. Just the same, she was infuriated that he would do this to her, and after all the charitable thoughts she had had about him this day!

"That ought to do it," he said with a satisfied smile, giving the knots a last tug. "That shouldn't be too uncomfortable."

"Pig!" she spat.

"Sweet little Meghan." His head cocked as he looked at her, an almost affectionate warmth in his regard. Then, unexpectedly, his mouth came down softly on hers. His big hand at the back of her neck held her gently but firmly as his lips moved over hers in a tender, almost chaste caress. He released her after what seemed a confused, heart-pounding eternity to Meghan. His eyes were opaque again, his mouth set and hard, unlike the soft caress it had just rendered.

"You'll have your uncle eating out of your hands in no time," he told her in a flat voice. "You'd be quite a woman if you only learned to control that temper of yours." He stood up and eyed her with what struck Meghan as unbearable superiority.

"Black-hearted dog!"

A smile twitched at his mouth and relaxed the hard-planed set of his face. "Pig, dog, scum-blooded toad. Any more animals come to mind that I remind you of?"

She shriveled him with a haughty look, difficult to do tied hand and foot, lying at the feet of her tormentor. "If any do, I'll let you know!"

"I'm sure you will." He laughed good-naturedly. "Go to sleep, little Meghan. Tomorrow's going to be a long day."

Meghan didn't go to sleep, though she closed her eyes and gave every appearance of doing so. She listened to Jason's even breathing coming from across the campfire. She listened to the splash of the streamlet that ran down their little ravine. She listened to the occasional movements of the hobbled horses as they nibbled on the lush grass beside the stream. The sound she most longed to hear didn't come.

An hour passed, then two. The regular rhythm of Jason's breathing didn't falter. Wolf had gone off about his own business, no doubt indulging himself in a late-night hunt. No untoward sound broke the nocturnal stillness.

Meghan opened her eyes. Stealthily, willing herself to make no noise, she groped in the folds of her blanket where she'd hidden one of Grace's kitchen knives the morning before they'd left. After what seemed an eternity, her searching fingers closed around the wooden hilt. It took only a few minutes to saw through the rope that bound her hands, and once her hands were free the strands around her ankles were cut through in a few seconds. Nevertheless, perspiration beaded her brow and upper lip from the strain. Rising to her feet, the knife clattered from her lap to the ground. She held her breath, heart pounding so loud she was sure that in itself would wake her captor. But Jason remained quiet, his broad chest rising and falling in the easy rhythm of slumber. Meghan allowed herself to breathe once again.

She resisted the temptation to linger for a last look at Jason's face. She was a fool, she told herself harshly. He was the enemy. There were men just as attractive, just as capable, just as masculine, among the Cheyenne. Of course they didn't have those amber eyes that could hint of warmth, humor, and passion hidden behind an opaque wall of coldness. They didn't have the tawny hair that fell over his forehead in a confused profusion of waves. How often had she longed to reach out a hand and brush back those unruly golden strands from his brow?

She shook herself mentally and forced herself to think of her family—Stone Eagle, Long Stepping Woman, and Magpie—who would welcome her so warmly back to her home. She thought of her friend Buffalo Calf Road Woman and Red Shield and Chief Comes in Sight. Both of those handsome warriors would make her forget any attraction she'd felt for the treacherous tawny-haired white man.

Her resolve more firm with every step, she stalked silently out of camp, pausing every couple of steps to listen for signs that Jason might have heard her. She was momentarily tempted to take the horses, but the risk of waking Jason wasn't worth it. But it seemed forever until the camp was out of sight, even longer until it was out of hearing. Finally she stopped. Stepping swiftly out of the cotton dress and petticoats that Amy and Christine had labored over, she pulled her buckskin tunic over her head and yanked on her leggings. Good thing she'd remembered to pull these out of her pack at the last moment. It wouldn't do to appear before her Cheyenne rescuers garbed as a white woman. As she hid the dress and petticoats beneath a bush, her heart gave an unexpected tug. The dress had become a symbol of the warm friendship Grace,

Amy, and Christine Karr had showered her with. She almost hated to leave it, but she had no choice. And she certainly didn't have any use for it where she was going.

Meghan felt considerably more Cheyenne when she resumed her flight, now suitably dressed in Indian attire. The moon was down, but the stars gave plenty of light to find her way up the narrowing ravine. She felt free again, and reveled in the feeling. Once more she felt close to the earth, close to the night animals that skittered through the brush away from her path, close to the owl she could see circling above, a blacker shadow against the black velvet sky.

For a quarter hour she walked, her delight in her escape making her all but forget the man she'd left behind her. Finally she stopped. No indication of human presence intruded on the night, but somehow she sensed a change. She pursed her lips and whistled the five-note bird call, copying exactly the one she'd heard earlier. She followed it immediately with another.

The answer came almost immediately. Meghan could barely contain her excitement. After all these miserable days, rescue was finally here.

Her joy diminished somewhat when she saw who walked out of the thick brush clogging the ravine in front of her. Mad Buffalo, son of Standing Antelope. In the Cheyenne way of reckoning kinship, this son of her father's brother was her brother. She'd never been able to find any sisterly affection in her heart for this young warrior though, even though he was well regarded among the men of the tribe as an upcoming war leader. The women of the tribe had little liking for him, thinking him a swaggerer and boaster. They warned their daughters away from him, saying his haughty, hawklike features hid a mean and petty heart. Even some of the old men of the tribe thought him a foolish hothead, without the wisdom to listen to the advice of men with more years and experience.

"Little sister," he greeted her.

"My brother," she acknowledged. How good it felt to

once again speak Cheyenne, as if she were already home. "You've come for me."

"We've come." He smiled. "And since you are here, it is good that we can bring you back to your father."

She was confused by his answer. "You didn't come for me?"

Mad Buffalo shrugged. "We are here. Myself and three others. We come to hunt."

"This far south?"

"We come to hunt the white man. The Sioux and Cheyenne have won a glorious victory. The white men attacked the camp of Crazy Horse on the Little Bighorn. We fought with glory. Our medicine gave each man the strength and cunning of ten. None of the white men were left alive."

Meghan was stunned. Knowing Mad Buffalo's boastful nature, she didn't believe the battle could've been that one-sided. But still, so much bloodshed. She found that after visiting with the Karrs she couldn't hate the white man with the intensity she'd known before.

Mad Buffalo mistook her silence for awe.

"Now we separate for the summer hunt," he continued. "The others hunt the buffalo, the antelope, the elk, and the moose. We, myself and Spotted Robe, Horse Walking, and Running Elk, we hunt the white man. There are more white men south than north, so we come south."

Meghan bit back the comment that they were fools. She recognized the names of the three hotheads who accompanied her "brother," and they weren't company she'd choose to be in, given a choice. She didn't have any choice though.

"You will take me back to Stone Eagle?"

Mad Buffalo readily assented. So far, the hunt for white men in this area had proved futile, and returning Autumnfire to her family would bring much honor. "First we will go cut the throat of the one who took you away. We will avenge you, my little sister."

"No!" Meghan said hastily. Too hastily from the look

of suspicion on Mad Buffalo's face. "There's no need. He's not worth staining your knife with his blood. Let him ride into the fort of the white men without his prey. His humiliation will be more revenge than giving him the honorable death of a warrior."

Mad Buffalo frowned. "He will follow."

"Perhaps," she agreed casually. "But what can one white man do against five Cheyenne?" She slanted him a crafty look. "Are you afraid?"

He grunted his contempt. "Let us go, then."

The eastern horizon was barely stained with pink when Meghan started north again with her escort of four Cheyenne braves. She rode behind Mad Buffalo on his pony, having none of her own—a humiliating position for one who had ridden to war with Two Moon himself. But all that was important, she kept telling herself, was that she was riding toward home and leaving that big, troublesome, lion-eyed white man and his stupid wolf far behind.

They rode swiftly, not sparing the horses. Toward midday Horse Walking, who rode in the lead, reined in on a bluff. Meghan's heart sank as Mad Buffalo's pony pulled abreast of the others and she found herself looking out over the peaceful valley that housed the Karr ranch.

As one, the Indians wheeled their ponies and sought cover in a tree-shrouded draw that led into the main valley.

Spotted Robe grinned maliciously. "A fat side of beef would taste good tonight. And there are two horses down there. Autumnfire can have her own mount, and there will be one extra besides. We will make much better time back to our people."

"It's about time we found some fun," Horse Walking commented.

"No!" Meghan was desperate. She could think of nothing that could keep these hotheads from attacking the home of her friends. "We do not need this delay!"

Mad Buffalo laughed. "It won't take long, little sister. You could join in, but I have no horse to give you. Soon we will give you one of the horses of the white man."

She decided to appeal to reason. "My brother, I know these people. I lived with them for a week, ate their food, slept in their bed. They were kind to me. Leave them alone."

He looked at her sternly. "No whites are friend to the Cheyenne. All will be driven from this land or killed."

She felt like hitting him in frustration. He wasn't on a mission to regain the land for his people, he simply wanted to raise a little hell and shed some blood. "There's no honor in this," she persisted. "No glory. There are only women down there! Women and a boy who is not yet nearly a man. Leave them alone! Let us go back to our people!"

Mad Buffalo sneered, his brown, hawklike features twisting into a mask of contempt. "White women breed more white men. Enough of this! I never listened to the father of Red Shield when he said Autumnfire was more white than Cheyenne, but now I think perhaps it is true. I think perhaps those are your people down there."

"No!"

"Then cease!"

"This is a coward's deed!" She grabbed his arm as he walked toward his horse. "There will be only shame for what you do!"

His face livid with fury, Mad Buffalo caught her by the open neck of her tunic. The back of his big fist landed with a solid thunk on the side of her head. She dropped without sound.

The three other braves looked on the scene with expressions ranging from surprise to horror. True, Autumnfire was behaving foolishly, but a Cheyenne brave didn't treat women in such a way, especially a sister. Mad Buffalo eyed them belligerently, his face turning darker as his friends' eyes filled with contempt. Meghan lay unmoving on the grass and leaves that carpeted the bottom of the ravine.

"My sister has been with the white man too long," he grunted. "Such foolishness must be beaten out of her."

Horse Walking lifted his lip in a sneer of disbelief.

"Get on your horses!" Mad Buffalo snapped. "Have you forgotten the fat cows and fine horses waiting in the valley?"

"If they befriended your sister . . ." Running Elk started.

"They are whites!" Mad Buffalo almost screamed. "Death to the whites who have invaded our hunting grounds, laid rails of steel across our land, killed our women and children, sent their soldiers to burn our homes, steal our horses, destroy our food! Death!"

The others sprang to their horses and raised their rifles above their heads, shaking them in fury. The drumbeats of their ponies' hooves faded down the ravine, and only the sound of Meghan's shallow breathing marked the time that passed as the sun inched slowly across the sky.

The first sliver of the morning sun crested the horizon and burned into Jason's closed eyes. He squinted and turned on his side, but it was too late. He was irrevocably awake. The dream had faded into the unreachable recesses of his mind. Only the image of Meghan remained.

He opened his eyes and groaned. What was he doing dreaming about that little hellcat? No wonder he was so tired. At the thought of Meghan he grimaced sourly. She was going to be in an unpleasant mood today after spending the night tied up like a hog ready to be spitted. He rubbed the sleep from his eyes and got to his feet. Finally, his gaze came to rest on the empty blankets where Meghan had made her bed. The cut lengths of the rope he'd used to tie her lay scattered on the blanket.

"What the . . . !" He turned quickly to where the hobbled horses were peacefully grazing on the stream bank. Both were there.

"Meghan!"

No answer.

Damn little idiot! She couldn't be meaning to run off

without a horse! Probably just wanted to scare him. Probably out in the brush that closed over the streamlet up the gulch, laughing her fool fire-colored head off, getting revenge for his tying her up last night.

"Meghan! You come out this instant or I'll turn you over my knee and swat you so hard . . . !"

No answer. Birds in the brush twittered to greet the rising sun. The stream gurgled peaceably through the rocks. A breeze whispered through the birch leaves and stirred Jason's hair. No sound but the quiet sounds of nature awakening to a new day.

"Goddamn, muddleheaded, stubborn, freckle-faced squaw! What does she think she's going to do without a horse? Where does she think she's going to go?"

The answer hit him like a bolt of lightning. They'd been followed yesterday for a short time. At least Jason had only detected them for a few hours during the morning. In the late afternoon he'd seen and heard no more sign. Had they really left, as he'd finally assumed, or just gotten more careful? It looked as if Meghan had known all along they were there. And she knew who they were, somehow— or hoped she knew.

At that moment, that painful moment of enlightenment, if it had been physically possible to kick his own tail around the campsite Jason would have. As it was, his choice of words to release the frustration swelling in his head even made the horses look up from their grazing. How could he have been such a stupid greenhorn! Outfoxed by a slip of a girl! He'd never live this one down! When he caught up to that redhead and her Indian friends, he was going to kick ass so hard those Cheyenne weren't going to stop running until they got back to the Powder River!

He kicked dirt over the coals that still glowed from the evening's banked fire. Without pausing to eat, he broke camp, packed, and was riding out before the sun had risen another finger's width in the sky. It was easy to find Meghan's trail. The overconfident little twit hadn't bothered to conceal it. It took only five minutes to find the dress stuffed under a bush, ten to find the spot where she'd met

Mad Buffalo. He found the Indian campsite within another five minutes. The prints of four horses, one carrying a double load, led away from the camp like a well-marked road. No one was bothering to hide anything. Four Cheyenne and one stubborn Irishwoman figured they didn't have anything to fear from a solitary white man. A grim smile touched Jason's face, thinking how wrong they were.

For three hours Jason followed their trail. With each passing hour he felt more uneasy. He didn't like the direction the trail was taking. He didn't like it one bit. A little past midday he saw the column of smoke rising lazily to the northwest. He knew with gut-wrenching certainty what it was. Cursing out loud, he kicked the black stallion into a gallop, leaving Meghan's mare with the packs to follow at her own pace.

It was much too late when he got there. With a feeling of sick helplessness and black rage he looked down from the bluff. The charred remains of the Karr ranch smoldered like a ghastly black wound on the green valley floor. Reluctantly he rode down the bluff toward the scene that only two days ago had been so peaceful.

The bodies of the women, Grace, Amy, and Christine, were easy to find. They lay sprawled in indecent heaps, their faces still twisted in the grimaces of the agony that had marked their last moments. Each buck had taken his turn upon them, from the looks of the bodies maybe several times. Flies buzzed around the slaughtered live-stock. The milk cow and one pig was butchered. The other carcasses had been left to rot. Both horses were gone.

With face turned to granite and amber eyes turned to hard resin, Jason buried the dead. For once in his life he wished he'd studied harder that winter when he was twelve and had lived with a preacher man and his wife. It would be nice to know what to say over the graves of these gentle and God-fearing women. Nothing came to mind but curses for the savages who'd done this deed.

Junior was nowhere to be found. Jason searched the charred remains of the house and the barn. He called until he was hoarse, hoping the boy had somehow managed to run off. No answer. No trace. Nothing.

Only when the work was completed did Jason allow his iron control to crack. He leaned against a birch trunk and heaved until he felt turned inside out. Sweat dampened the sun-streaked hair that fell over his brow. The amber eyes were no longer opaque, but hot with misery.

Jason Sinclair had witnessed much worse than the burning of an insignificant ranch and the rape and slaughter of three woman. He'd lived with violence all his life, generating much of it. These women had been friends of a sort. That made it bad. What made it worse was the thought of Meghan's participating in this orgy of blood, as she'd participated in the battle on Rosebud Creek. Could she have watched calmly while these women who'd befriended her had met such fearful deaths? Could she have helped her warrior friends burn the house where she'd been offered friendship and hospitality? His gorge rose again, and he leaned weakly against the smooth white bark of the tree.

"Goddamn it to hell!" he finally rasped. "Goddamn it all to hell!"

He'd catch up to those savages if he had to search the whole Cheyenne tribe, Jason vowed, and Meghan too. If she wanted to live like a redskinned savage, she could damn well be treated like one!

# Chapter Nine

The afternoon wore on endlessly for Meghan. Her head ached abominably, and her face where Mad Buffalo's fist had landed had started to swell.

She'd been furious when the four braves returned to the dry wash towing the two Karr horses behind them, one laden with freshly butchered beef and pork. Their whooping and howling filled the ravine, and a full five minutes passed before the noisy confusion died down enough for her to be heard.

"Fools!" she screamed above the racket. "What have you done?"

Running Elk, the youngest of the band, postured himself before her in a manner he thought befitted a warrior freshly returned from victory. His elation subsided at the look of contempt on her face.

"What is all this?" she demanded with narrowed eyes.

The look in her angry green eyes convinced him the whole truth was not necessary at this very moment. "As you see, Autumnfire," Running Elk answered, much of the bravado gone from his voice, "we butchered a cow and a pig."

"Is that all you butchered?"

"Quiet!" Mad Buffalo rode to where they were standing and regarded her haughtily down his hawklike nose. "A warrior does not have to answer to a woman!"

She whirled on him in fury. "You braying jackass! You go beyond yourself, Mad Buffalo! Stone Eagle will hear of this, as will Comes in Sight, and even Two Moon. See how cocky you feel then!"

Mad Buffalo's haughty demeanor slowly melted to a tolerant smile. As the battle fever subsided, his confidence was cracking. "Hear about what? We stole a cow, a pig, and two horses. We need food for the coming journey. Would you deny us that?"

"Is that all you did?" Her voice rang with disbelief.

"That is all, my sister."

Second thoughts were beginning to niggle at Mad Buffalo's mind. He knew Two Moon would disapprove of his attacking a helpless homestead, especially when Autumnfire had claimed the people as her friends. But his lust for blood and battle, brought to a higher pitch by the recent battles in the north and the frustration at his fruitless hunt for blood in the south, had overcome his sense of caution. The story of the slaughter of the white women must never reach Two Moon.

"I'm sorry I lost my temper with you, Autumnfire." He gestured toward her discolored face. "But you have strange ideas since your journey with the white man."

She ignored his apology and regarded her rescuers with an angry sweep of her eyes. Mad Buffalo still looked somewhat tight-lipped and stern, in spite of his apology. The other three were silent, somewhat shamefaced now that the excitement of the kill had worn off. Meghan desperately wanted to believe what Mad Buffalo told her about the raid on the ranch. She prayed Grace, Amy, Junior, and Christine would not be thrown into hardship because of this loss of livestock, but there was no way she could undo what had been done. She supposed she should be grateful that her white friends were left with anything at all—including their lives—considering the temperaments of her four "rescuers." Why couldn't she have been rescued by Red Shield or Comes in Sight or even Stone Eagle himself instead of this band of miscreants? At best they were the worst troublemakers in the village. At worst they were vicious animals.

The rest of the afternoon was spent in constrained silence. Meghan and Mad Buffalo ignored one another. Running Elk tried in vain to flirt but was promptly discouraged by her ill-tempered rebuff and didn't try again. Spotted Robe and Horse Walking, being older than Running Elk and more experienced in the moods of women, kept a safe distance. They would all be glad when the camp of Two Moon was within sight and they could give Stone Eagle back his fractious daughter.

They made camp with the setting of the sun. In the custom of the Cheyenne, it fell to Meghan to set up camp, unload the meat, tether the horses, make a fire, and fix the evening meal. In this one thing, she grumbled to herself, she found the white man's ideas superior to the Cheyenne. At least Jason had not balked at doing his share of the camp housekeeping.

The thought of Jason brought an expected twinge to her heart. She missed him. She'd grown accustomed to the feel of his eyes following her every move. She'd grown to value the rare smile that softened his face. She'd come to almost like the rush of warmth that flooded her body at his rare touch and the tingle that set her blood afire when she sensed the aroused beast that sometimes stirred behind those cold eyes. Damn! She even missed Wolf, who had occasionally condescended to accept from her the scratches and thumps that he thought of as friendly.

By the time the evening meal was finished, the last hint of light had disappeared from the sky. The stars were obscured by a heavy blanket of clouds, and the air was sticky with the threat of rain. The four men sat by the fire and lit their pipes, while Meghan cleaned up the last of the dinner mess. Finally through with the chores, she came to warm herself by the fire. A cool breeze from the north carried the smell of rain. She was glad the wood she'd gathered was piled under a tree where it would be safe from the weather.

"Tomorrow we will ride hard," Mad Buffalo announced after many minutes of silent puffing on his pipe. "We will break camp before the sun shows itself in the east. There will be no lagging or complaining. I am leader here, and my word will be obeyed."

He scowled pointedly at Meghan as he got up, wrapped a blanket around his broad shoulders, and retreated toward a soft spot under a tree. She snorted her scorn as he settled comfortably in a bed of pine needles, and the others got up to find similar resting places. Horse Walking made a noticeable detour around her as he ambled over to his sentry post.

Meghan carefully banked the dying fire, then wrapped a blanket around herself and settled beneath a tree to go to sleep. She stared into the quiet night, wondering about the capricious jokes of fate. She'd wanted nothing more than she had wanted to go home. And here she was on her way back home and all she could do was lie here and miss the devil white man who'd taken her away.

Jason, Wolf crouched quietly at his side, watched from his hiding place in a gooseberry thicket as Meghan rolled herself in her blanket beneath a tree and gradually became still. Whatever she and that Cheyenne butcher had between them, it looked like the hot-tempered redhead was giving him as much trouble as she'd given Jason. If the scowl the Indian had given her had been any indication, little Meghan had better watch her back from here on out. Of course, Jason figured, these braves weren't going to be around long enough to cause her any trouble. But he certainly was.

Tracking the little band as they'd made their way north had been child's play. The fools were so confident of their safety they hadn't even attempted to conceal their trail. They probably figured Jason wouldn't dare pursue, or even if he did, what could one man do against four braves in the prime of their strength? But Jason had no intentions of letting these hooligans leave a trail of murder and havoc all the way back to Montana. These blood-happy miscreants needed killing, and Jason was the only one around to do it.

Several hours passed as Jason maintained complete stillness in his thicket. His muscles cramped, and worst of all, his nose itched, but he gave no thought to the discomfort. Many times in his life stealth, patience, and quiet endurance had saved his neck and made it possible for him to accomplish feats that other men would never try. Self-discipline was second nature and had saved his life as many times as his fast gun and skill with a knife.

The little band slept soundly, confident of their safety. The fire died down until it was a mere glow, but Jason's sharp eyes could still plainly see the sentry across the campsite, who'd sat in one place for the several hours he'd been on duty. He wasn't taking his task very seriously, and no doubt uppermost on his mind was impatience for his shift to be over. Occasionally his head nodded for a moment until a snore jerked him back to bleary consciousness.

There would be no better time than right now, Jason figured. The sentry was off guard. A light rain had started to fall, pattering softly against the leaves and the ground and sputtering in the dying coals of the fire. It would muffle any noise he made in moving around to the sentry's position.

He gave Wolf a signal to stay, then silent as a ghost he slipped from the thicket. Carefully he stalked around the perimeter of the camp, fading from tree to bush, every movement planned, every sense alert. Finally only ten feet of open ground separated him from the bored sentry. He crouched, knife in hand, lithe and dangerous as a stalking panther. Horse Walking never saw the white man behind him. He made no sound as the keen blade of the knife opened his throat, spilling his blood on the ground in a crimson flood.

Jason lowered the sentry quietly to the ground. No one stirred. Three against one now—three and a half if he counted Meghan. He figured the odds were fairly even. He was feeling reckless. This silent killing in the night was against his nature. To hell with stealth.

"You want to fight, you bloody bastards?" he challenged, his voice ringing through the quiet night. "Let's see how you like fighting a man instead of helpless women."

The four on the ground jerked from sleep instantly. All reached instinctively for their weapons. Mad Buffalo was the first on his feet but maintained that position for only seconds before a flying kick from Jason sent him sliding on his back along the ground. His head came to rest against a tree trunk with a sickening thunk. Running Elk closed in on Jason with a yell and met hard steel slicing into his heart. Spotted Robe, a more experienced fighter, circled warily, his knife weaving a lethal pattern for his opponent's eyes to follow.

Meghan backed up against a tree, confused by this sudden explosion from sleep to battle. This wasn't a violent dream. This was really happening. Jason had burst into camp bold as life. Two of their band were already dead, maybe three, from the looks of Mad Buffalo. Spotted Robe would soon join them, if Jason had his way. And then her?

The two men circled watchfully, each sizing up his opponent. Jason recognized a deadly fighter when he saw one. The man facing him showed no hint of fear or panic, in spite of three companions already downed. A savage grin bared crooked and stained teeth, and the gleam in his eyes showed him anxious for the kill. Jason watched his eyes, not the knife that was weaving a hypnotic pattern in front of his face. He watched the eyes fill with hate and bloodlust and contempt.

The eyes signaled before the Indian leapt, and Jason was ready. He dodged out of the knife's way—not quite fast enough. He felt the burning trail of the blade slice along his ribs, then ignored it. Spotted Robe's momentum carried him past his opponent and left him off balance for a short time—time enough for Jason's knee to connect with his backside and send him stumbling to the ground. Jason was on him then, his knife at his throat, his cold amber eyes hard and merciless.

"How do you like this taste of your own medicine?" he snarled, remembering the gaping throats of the three Karr women. He momentarily ignored his own rules disdaining vengeance as he drew his blade swiftly across the Indian's throat.

Meghan felt helpless as she watched the two struggling men go down. In her hand now was a keen-bladed knife, but the nearest pistol was fifteen feet away in the hand of the unfortunate Horse Walking. She started toward it when something materialized out of the dark to block her way.

Wolf took up a position in front of her and regarded her matter-of-factly. When she took another step toward the pistol, a low growl rumbled in his chest. The black lips rippled back to reveal awesome fangs. It was hard to believe this fearsome creature had cozied up to her, begging a piece of her lunch just one short day past. Now he looked prepared to tear her apart if she moved from the spot. She gave up the idea of retrieving the pistol.

In truth, she didn't know how she would use it, or against whom. Her emotions were swinging wildly. Spotted Robe was a vicious bully who she'd avoided since childhood. But he was Cheyenne. Jason was the enemy, but she didn't think she could bring herself to send a bullet plunging into his body. Her mind and heart warred painfully as her eyes strained through the darkness to follow the struggle.

Two figures had dropped to the ground, one on top of the other. Only one rose. By the breadth of his shoulders and his height, she could tell it was Jason. Slowly he turned toward her, a feral gleam in his eyes. Her heart seemed to hang suspended between beats.

"White man!" The voice growled from across the dead fire. Mad Buffalo crouched, knife in hand. "I am not dead, white man. Come try to kill me, if you can!"

Jason's lips drew back into a grin that was as savage as Wolf's snarl. He still stood tall as he turned to meet this new challenge. But even in the shrouding dark, Meghan could tell he was tired. Blood from his side was soaking through his shirt, and his movements lacked their usual coiled-spring litheness. Mad Buffalo wasn't in his best form, either. His jaw was swollen where Jason had kicked him earlier. His tunic was shredded and bloody where he'd slid across the ground. Meghan's hands tightened around the hilt of her knife until her knuckles were white. If only there were some way she could end this madness! If only she could reach the pistol! But the sleek silver-gray wolf showed no signs of relenting.

Jason and Mad Buffalo circled each other warily. The

Indian was a few inches shorter, but had more bulk to his frame than the taller, leaner white man. Jason made up in length of reach what he lacked in bulk. Both men were determined to make an end to his opponent, no matter how he had to do it.

"You'd better start singing your death song, Cheyenne," Jason taunted. "This is your day to die."

Mad Buffalo grinned evilly. "I will sing a song of death, but it will be yours!" The words were not out of his mouth before he lunged. His knife came within an inch of slicing through Jason's gut, but the white man saw what was coming and nimbly stepped back just the right distance, at the same time bringing his own knife down in an arc that left a red trail diagonally across Mad Buffalo's chest. The Indian didn't seem to notice as blood oozed from the shallow wound.

"Were those your women back at that little ranch, white man?" Mad Buffalo leered. "You fight no better than they did." He feinted again with his knife, but his wrist was caught in a grip of steel. He reached out with his left hand to grab at Jason's arm, immobilizing the white man's weapon before it could be brought into play.

"Will you scream for mercy when you are about to die, like they did?" he taunted through tightly clenched teeth as they both strained to break the other's grip. Jason's eyes flamed with anger at the Cheyenne's words, but his concentration, and his grip, didn't falter.

Both men were panting, both exerting all their strength to halt the descent of the other's knife. The muscles in Jason's back and arms bulged and sinewy cords stood out in the strong column of his neck as he matched brute strength with the heftier man. Finally, in a herculean effort, he shoved the Indian back, throwing him off balance so that he landed butt first in the dead fire. Jason threw himself on his opponent before he could gain his feet.

A few live coals still glowed underneath the pile of damp ashes. Mad Buffalo yelped and bucked as one came in contact with his bare skin. The two men rolled, struggling for ascendancy. They stopped with Jason on the bottom, looking up at a wicked length of steel that was aimed for his throat. The muscles in his arm and shoulder burned as he strained to hold the blade off, but he was tiring fast. The loss of blood from his side was beginning to tell.

Mad Buffalo's grinning face leered down at him. "You will die easier than your women, white man. They died with my manroot between their legs, like a knife, tearing them apart inside. It was a long time before I put an end to their screaming."

Jason answered from between clenched teeth, feeling strength return in the heat of anger. "You will find me not so easy to kill!"

With superhuman effort he reared up and threw off the heavier man, coming down on top of him with his own knife clenched in his hand. His weapon descended with terrible inevitability. His free hand pressed against the Indian's throat in a stranglehold.

"I should let you live, you bloody butcher," Jason rasped. "I should cut off that useless flesh that hangs between your legs and send you back to your tribe like a squaw, bleeding like a virgin. We'd see how many innocent women you rape then."

Mad Buffalo turned white under the swarthiness of his skin. He read grim intent in the white man's lion-colored eyes. He gasped for breath as the hand against his throat tightened. The knife disappeared from his view, and seconds later he felt the cold kiss of its razor edge pressed up against his genitals. Words came into his throat of their own accord. Whether words cursing the white man or pleading for his mercy Mad Buffalo never knew, for he hadn't enough breath to speak them out.

Jason could smell the other man's fear. A hoarse croak issued from his abused throat, and his eyes, just minutes ago glittering with viciousness and victory, were now wide with supplication.

"Shit!" He lifted the knife from its terrible resting place

and drew it quickly across his opponent's throat, but not quickly enough to miss the look of relief that flooded the Cheyenne's eyes. Now at least he would go as a whole man to meet his ancestors.

Meghan stood in confusion and horror. She'd overheard the grunted conversation between the combatants with horrified disbelief. The women Mad Buffalo was taunting Jason about—the women he'd cruelly raped and killed— they had to be the Karrs, her friends. The realization hit her like a physical blow, and her stomach threatened to heave into her throat. Then suddenly the battle was over. Mad Buffalo was in a heap on the ground and Jason was walking toward her, a darker shadow in the dark night. As he approached, Wolf slunk into the bushes as if wanting no part of his human friend's temper this night. She couldn't make out his features or the look in his eyes, but something about his bearing frightened her terribly. He slowly came toward her, like a shadowy being from a nightmare. And just as in a nightmare, she stood frozen to the spot, unable to move for the fear paralyzing her limbs. Then he was in front of her, not a foot away. The stony hardness of his face made her last hope fade. His amber eyes that looked at her with no feeling at all belonged not on a flesh and blood man, but on some creature of the night bent on hunting and death.

"Now you," he whispered as if to himself. "Did you think you could run with a pack of curs and escape their dirt?"

Like lightning his hand flew out and grabbed her tunic by the neck. She gasped as the material tightened about her throat.

"Did you sit by and laugh as the people who'd befriended you were tortured and killed?" His voice was cold, devoid of emotion. It was as though he were asking her the time of day. That very lack of feeling frightened her more than anything else. "Did you enjoy yourself? Were you entertained?"

"I didn't . . ."

He pushed her back viciously so that she almost landed on the ground. The paralysis of fear left her as she regained her balance. If he wanted to believe she'd done this thing, then so be it. He was the enemy. He always had been. He'd killed four men tonight, and he was going to kill her unless she did something very soon. She tightened her grip on the knife she held, then without giving fear a chance to close in on her again, she lunged, feinting with the knife while attempting to bolt past him.

He deflected her blow with ease, sending her knife clattering to the ground and roughly pushing her back. Cradling the wrist he had cruelly twisted, she backed off, trying not to whimper as she read her fate in his eyes. She would not die like a mewling coward. She would give as good as she got!

"What to do with you?" he wondered aloud in a quiet voice. "What to do with such a vicious little bitch?"

She dodged away from him as he grabbed her again, but it was useless. His hands closed around her upper arms like steel clamps.

"Do you know how it feels, what they went through?" His voice was relentless, shredding her nerves to raw fragments. "Brutally raped until they were torn and raw and bleeding. Can you guess how they felt? Having their throats slit might have been a relief, except your friends' fancy knife work didn't let them die quick." His face grew even harder at the memory of those pathetic bodies.

"No, no!" She shook her head back and forth, trying to keep the images of the Karrs' horror from claiming her mind.

He smiled, a feral smile reflected in the savage glitter of his eyes. "Maybe you should learn what they felt like."

She looked at him in disbelief, her eyes wide with horror.

"Only I'll give you a fighting chance, unlike Grace and Christine and Amy. I'm a nice guy. I'll let you run for it. Maybe you can manage to escape."

At that moment she couldn't move, much less run.

"You heard me, you little savage! Run!" He gave her a hearty push in the direction of the bushes. "Run, goddamn you!"

She turned with a cry and ran, her heart beating a desperate tattoo that had nothing to do with exertion. She, who had once recklessly boasted to Buffalo Calf Road Woman that she was afraid of nothing, would cower before no man, ran with the hounds of terror nipping at her heels. The night became a nightmare and closed in around her, choking her with darkness. Rocks sprang up to trip her feet, branches reached out to grab and hold her. She could feel the hot breath of death panting on her neck.

For ten minutes she plowed her way through the jungle of thickets that lined the dry wash where they'd been camped. The gentle drizzle still falling from the sky made the rocky ground slick. Her knees bled from several falls. Her face stung where branches had whipped viciously across her forehead and cheeks. Gasping for breath to fill her burning lungs, she leaned against the gnarled trunk of a tree. No more than a few seconds passed before she heard the sound of her pursuer closing in. She pushed herself away from the tree and stumbled forward once again.

So it went for what seemed like hours. She ran until she dropped, then was forced to run again by the sound of approaching fate—her own personal nightmare. Every time she stopped to draw breath, she heard Jason pounding behind her. He never really drew any closer, but was always close enough to make sure she couldn't get relief for her burning legs and lungs. He was playing with her, she knew. But sooner or later she would drop and not get up, and then he could do what he would to her without even having to fight her in the process. She wouldn't let that happen, she vowed.

She ran on, knowing finally that this would be her last run. Her legs were screaming, threatening to cramp every step she took. Her head swam dizzily from lack of breath. Still she was certain Jason was behind her.

The mouth of the little wash, where it joined a much larger river valley, was just ahead. The rain had stopped, and the sky was beginning to show a sprinkling of stars. She could just barely make out the terrain around her. Suddenly she realized where she was. They had passed this very spot not long before stopping to camp. On shaky legs she climbed up the gentle slope of the wash and headed cross-country for the spot where she knew the land would drop abruptly down into the larger valley below. She would cheat Jason of his victory yet! If he could track her across this stony ground, then as a last resort there was always the steep bluff. But she didn't have to think of that yet.

She was barely out of the wash and onto the hard stony slope before she heard Jason's footsteps dogging her. She climbed on, but her legs gave out before she reached her goal. Twenty feet from the edge of the high bluff her legs cramped and froze. She stumbled onto her face, but kept crawling forward. One thing dominated her desperate mind. It was better to die cleanly, by her own hand, than suffer the revenge Jason would mete out. She no longer thought of the Karrs. She thought only of the man behind her and the high bluff in front of her. Her fingers found the edge of the bluff just as a hand closed around her ankle.

"Taking the coward's way out?"

She turned. Jason was a dark shadow looming ominously above her. She twisted desperately in an attempt to escape as he pulled her to her feet. Then, abruptly changing her tactics, she launched herself at him with wildcat ferocity. He dodged the fingers clawing at his face, then watched impassively as she dropped to the ground, her legs cramping and refusing once again to support her.

"Time's run out. You didn't run far enough."

She glared up at him, putting all the hatred she could muster into her gaze. He bent down and roughly threw her over his shoulder as if she were a sack of meal, and she found she had strength left only for a fitful struggle. Her brain told her to give up. She was finished. But her heart told her to fight until life had left her body.

Jason dumped her ungently on her back in the wet sandy bottom of the little wash. Almost casually he unbuckled his belt and pulled his shirt out of his trousers.

"No!" She skittered away, crablike, searching for something she could use as a weapon. Nothing came to hand before he dragged her back.

"Do you know how they died, those innocents you led your band of wolves to?" He pushed her to the wet ground and knelt beside her, pinning her down with the weight of one leg. "Of course you do. You were there, weren't you?"

He jerked up her tunic, easily subduing her frantic twisting and bucking as his eyes drank in the delicate lines and curves of feminine flesh that had always been hidden from his view. Slowly her struggles ceased as she felt the heat of his gaze. Against her will, a slow burn ignited the center of her being and started to pulse outward, combining with her fear to send blood racing through her veins.

"No! Please!" She didn't want to beg, but the words escaped her mouth of their own volition, born of a fear more deeply rooted in a woman's heart than the fear of death—the fear of that unique violence that only a man can perpetrate. She pushed desperately at him, then clawed at his face. He ignored her futile struggles and slapped her hands aside.

Meghan lay back and shut her eyes tight, willing her soul to leave her body before this terrible thing could be done to her. But stubbornly, her soul stayed where it was, trapped in a body that was about to become the victim of this ravening wolf of a man. The night closed in and the world seemed to narrow to just the two of them—her, pinned to the cold ground, him, crouching above. The night sounds were drowned out by the sound of his ragged breathing and the furious pounding of blood in her ears. She could feel his hungry eyes take in every inch of her bared body, tracing a warm path from her knees to her face. Why didn't he get it over with? She shut her eyes tighter still and cringed as she felt the weight of his leg come off her.

"Damn you, Meghan O'Brian!" The hoarse words ripped unwillingly from his throat. "Damn you to hell for doing this to me. What is there about you . . . ?"

She opened her eyes. Jason was still crouched above her, but he was no longer holding her pinned to the ground. His breathing came in ragged gasps, but the fury in his resinous eyes had been supplanted by pure and driving hunger. He reached out a hand and gently cupped a cold bare breast, and Meghan surprised herself by not flinching away. His warm, callused hand felt good, felt right as it moved over her sensitive flesh. The slow burn that had ignited earlier flared up suddenly into an aching need. A whimper escaped her throat, born of fear and confusion and unfamiliar passion.

Jason stood and with hasty movements shed shirt and trousers. As he crouched over her once again, his face was intent, his mouth a tight line of tension and his nostrils flaring with need. The feel of his hard flesh caressing hers was frightening but welcome as he lowered his body onto hers. His mouth covered hers in a bruising kiss, and the last remnants of Meghan's reluctance fled before the wave of passion that washed over her body as his tongue thrust deeply into her mouth. She felt his hips grind against hers as a hand moved to capture a breast, and the other hand slipped insistently between her thighs to find the source of the fire that was consuming her. There was nothing gentle about his passion, and nothing maidenly about her response. The tension that had existed between them from the beginning had reached a crescendo on this dark, wet night. Now it exploded in the form of a blazing desire that held them both in helpless thrall. When finally Jason parted her thighs and thrust the throbbing tool of his passion into her waiting body, Meghan didn't even feel the pain of his brutal entry. She was lost in a world of tormenting, aching need. Wrapping her legs around his narrow hips, she strained to bring him deeper into her body, and his next few pounding thrusts sent her over the edge into the sweet fulfillment she'd reached for. She floated higher and higher in a blissful euphoria, oblivious of the cold, damp night, forgetful of the fear and violence that had marked the last few hours, conscious only of sweet paradise and the man who'd sent her there.

Jason spiraled slowly back to earth, shaking in reaction to the flood tide of fury and passion that had, for once in his life, rendered him out of control. He pressed a soft kiss against the contentedly curved lips of the woman who'd started out as his victim and ended up as . . . what? His lover? No, not a lover. Whatever was between them would never be as gentle as love. He grimaced, remembering the feel of fragile tissue tearing before the onslaught of his manhood, and as he eased himself out of her, his mouth drew into a tight line as he observed the crimson of her virgin blood staining them both.

He'd never dreamed Meghan was a virgin. He knew the Cheyenne women's reputation for chastity, but seeing Meghan running with this wild bunch of misfits—troublemakers and hell-raisers who'd known her well enough to come all this way in search of her—he'd assumed her virtue was long ago sacrificed, that her body was well versed in the ways of men. Now he knew better, and the revelation was enough to douse the warm glow of passion's aftermath and make him bitterly regret the careless and violent lovemaking he'd visited on her vulnerable body. But he couldn't undo what had already been accomplished.

He caught her eyes staring up at him. Mingled in their green depths, visible even in the darkness of the night, were embarrassment and shame. Meghan had fallen back to earth with a painful thud.

"I didn't know you were a virgin," he said lamely.

"There's a lot you don't know, white man."

Now that her passion had faded the anger was flooding in, anger at him and at herself. She felt soiled, degraded, and absolutely shameless. And worse still, she knew if he started again, started doing those horribly wonderful things to her, she would react in exactly the same way. She looked at the long, lean body that had just moments ago brought her to the peak of throbbing pleasure. He looked strangely vulnerable, lying naked and exposed, regarding her with eyes that were hooded and revealed none of his own feelings, if he had feelings. She casually raised herself to one elbow and reached for the long-bladed knife fastened to his discarded belt. She looked at the wicked blade, then looked at him in all his revealed glory.

"I ought to cut it off, you know," she commented dryly. "You deserve it."

His fingers curled around the hand that held the knife. "Don't get personal," he warned with a twisted smile. "Seems a minute ago you were eager enough to make use of it."

Her face tightened in pain at the reminder, and she didn't resist when he pried the knife loose from her fingers.

"I have a better use for this," he said.

She gasped as he placed the sharp tip at her neck, then jumped in surprise as, instead of using it on her tender flesh, he drew the edge down the middle of her tunic, splitting the garment in two.

"You won't be needing this anymore," he told her matter-of-factly, peeling the buckskin off her and throwing it into the bushes. "White women don't dress in buckskin." A fire was lighting once again in his eyes, and to Meghan's distress she felt a now familiar tingling start between her legs.

"You're beautiful, little Meghan." His voice was soft, almost a caress in itself, and held none of the sharp edges that had cut her before. "Who would have thought that skinny little girl would grow up into this."

With one hard-callused finger he leisurely traced the curves of her breasts, leaving a trail of fire in the wake of his touch. When he leaned forward, replacing his finger with his mouth, she gasped. His lips and tongue seared her skin as they blazed a gentle trail over the hills and valleys of her body. When he took a nipple in his mouth and playfully pulled and suckled until it stood rigid in excitement, a flood of warmth rushed through her veins. Her blood pounded in her ears, throbbing out a primitive rhythm of urgent longing that she now understood only too well.

"Noooo!" she wailed, trying to push him off. She could bear his brutality better than this attack on her senses. Her body was aflame with sensations. It was all she could do to keep from pulling him closer instead of pushing him away. "Not again! Leave me alone! Please!"

He chuckled, a deep, throaty sound of male pleasure. "Stop fighting, Meghan. You're going to enjoy this. You know you are, little hellcat."

He was right. She did. She enjoyed every minute of it, even though a voice in the very depths of her mind told her it was wrong, that she was going to be hurt in a way that had nothing to do with his hard body delving so intimately into hers. But the voice finally stilled when he drove her to the pinnacle of need, then beyond, and she joyfully abandoned herself to the ecstasy that surged through her body and pressed him to her even more tightly as with a cry of exultation he pumped his seed within her welcoming flesh.

# Chapter Ten

Meghan woke to a feeling of warm contentedness. Half asleep, she knew something was very right with her world, though she couldn't remember what. She snuggled closer against the warmth that wrapped around her body, burrowed into the hard flesh that formed her pillow.

Wakefulness came slowly. The warmth of her contentment was replaced by the heat of the day. One by one she noticed the discomforts of her hard bed, the pricks of twigs against her flesh, the tickle of a leaf against her bare skin, the moist clamminess of sweat filming her cheek where it lay against warm flesh. Her eyes opened onto a close-up view of the bronzed masculine chest that had been her pillow during the night—sun-browned flesh and sculpted muscles decorated with a sprinkling of golden hair. Memory returned.

With instinctive reaction she jumped away from Jason as though she'd been burned, bringing them both fully awake. Jason pushed himself to a sitting position, searching with wary eyes for what had startled her. Satisfied that everything was peaceful, he frowned at her. Then he smiled, remembering. The smile she saw was the smile of a victor, gloating. She longed to wipe it off his face with a hard slap. At the same time she wanted to reach out, soothe away the tired lines that still etched his face, and bind the wound that bloodied the side of his shirt. In confusion, she voiced a little cry of distress and turned away, huddling into a ball of misery and presenting him with her back.

"Well, good morning to you too," he muttered, taken aback by her actions. Outright hostility he could understand. Hate he could understand. Even passion he could understand. But her actions so far this morning, accompanied by the enigmatic and confused look in her emerald eyes, left him wondering what was going through her mind. Then again, who could understand how females thought?

Meghan listened to Jason clatter around the campsite, building a fire, putting coffee on to boil. A few minutes later part of the side of salt pork Grace Karr had given them two days ago started to sizzle. The sound and smell brought back the memory of the Karr family and the misery of the day before.

A physical pain stabbed through her head at the thought of Grace, Amy, and Christine. And what of Junior, the puppyish boy who'd followed her around with adoration in his eyes? What had happened to him? The horror and senselessness of the Karrs' deaths would haunt her forever, she thought.

She couldn't bring herself to grieve over the deaths of Mad Buffalo and his band. They were Cheyenne, but they were also misfits, troublemakers, and worse. More than once Running Elk and Horse Walking had been reprimanded by the council. Spotted Robe had once been banished, but by the influence of relatives had been reinstated. Mad Buffalo was highly thought of by some and scorned by others. But even for her "brother" she found she couldn't mourn. His words last night, cruel and callous words depicting the fate of her friends, uttered in stark detail to taunt his opponent—those words had sealed her heart against him. She mourned for his father, Standing Antelope, a good man who would feel his son's loss. But for Mad Buffalo she could only feel anger.

For herself also she could only feel anger—anger and contempt. What had happened to her the night before? She'd been a different person, a stranger she didn't know—a stranger subject to feelings and desires and reactions she found horrifying in the light of day. From where came the explosion of sensation when Jason used his body to ignite a flame that had burned mercilessly through her veins, a flame that destroyed all her resistance, all her pride, all her self-possession? Had that truly been herself last night, moaning in his arms, writhing beneath him as he deliberately drove her body to a frenzy of desire? Had it really been her who had wrapped her legs around him, begging him with her body to plunge deeper, yet still deeper, into the core of her? She gave a little moan for the shame of it and wrapped herself into a tighter ball of misery. She had never felt like that when Red Shield had kissed her and pressed against her. Then she had felt only curiosity, and finally something akin to panic. Why was it this man, this harsh, violent, vengeful, cold-eyed killer, whose touch made her lose control? She'd willingly given herself to her enemy, allowed herself to be defeated in the most degrading, humiliating way possible.

For a moment her misery pressed her down further than she'd ever been in her life. She wanted to sink into the ground, be swallowed by the earth, or simply die and never move again, never think again, never feel again. Then, when her spirit hit rock bottom, something inside her sparked. Misery gave way to anger. Anger grew into rage. Nothing she did could wipe out her disgrace. She must learn to live with it, and learn she would. So why was she huddled into a useless ball of self-pity? Was a Cheyenne so easy to defeat? Where was her pride? Where was her strength and resilience? The man who'd done this to her was casually going about the morning camp chores as if he'd not taken the fabric of her being and ripped it into shreds. He must never know how deeply he'd wounded her. He must never see this abject cringing defeat in her eyes.

In one fluid, graceful motion she rose to her feet. Heedless of her nakedness, she walked purposefully over to where Jason's brace of pistols hung over the corner of one pack. Deliberately, her face devoid of emotion, her heart turned to stone, she picked up a pistol, checked the loading, turned, aimed carefully in Jason's direction where he squatted beside the cookfire, and pulled the trigger.

The sound of the shot reverberated through the morning air. Jason jumped, instinctively threw himself to one side, and rolled to the nearest cover. Then, when he discovered the source of the shot, he grated out a string of curses, walked calmly toward the smoking pistol that was still pointing at him, and twisted it out of Meghan's shaking hands.

"You were a better shot than that at the battle on Rosebud Creek."

Meghan looked at him stonily, her heart thudding heavily in her chest. "Next time I'll aim to hit you." She put every remnant of her tattered pride into her voice. "Touch me again, white man, and you'll find my aim good enough to send you to your grave."

His eyes moved from her face and traveled down her slender body. Suddenly she was very aware of her nakedness. She saw his jaw clench, and for a moment those cold amber eyes seemed to burn. But when he met her eyes again his face had turned once more to stone.

"Seems like you enjoyed yourself well enough last night, for all your complaining today." He smiled wickedly and his eyes roved assessingly over her nakedness. "But if you don't want to be touched again, little Meghan, I suggest you get dressed."

She desperately wanted to do something to hide herself from that stony gaze, but she forced herself to stand erect and proud.

"You destroyed my garment—if you remember."

The smile that flicked across his mouth showed he remembered all too well. She was beginning to fear a repeat performance of the night before when he turned and dug into one of the packs. Triumphantly he handed her the cotton dress and petticoats she'd stuffed under a bush during her escape. The dress called up images she didn't want to see—Amy and Christine laboring over the garment, Grace telling her how lovely she looked. She closed her eyes tightly to try to shut out the pain.

"Put it on," Jason growled.

She opened her eyes and shot him a green-eyed glare filled with all the loathing she could muster.

"Put it on!" he demanded again. "Put it on, unless you want to spend the rest of the morning on your back again!"

In silent dignity she turned her back and once more donned the garments of a white woman.

They rode south in cold hostility. The sun had already been high when they had awakened, and it was past noon when they finally got mounted and away. Jason rode hard, forcing Meghan to prod her slower mare continually to keep up with the black stallion. With luck they might reach the vicinity of the Karr ranch again tonight. In two days, if they pushed it, they would get to Fort Laramie. He certainly didn't want to spend any more time than necessary with this wild Irish Indian.

Jason was less than pleased with his actions of the day before. After the first exultation of revenge, something he generally regarded as a fool's errand, there had been no joy in killing those four Indians, vicious brutes though they were. The job had needed doing though, and he'd been the only one around to do it.

But Meghan—that was another story. He'd been enraged at the thought of her taking part in the group's bloody massacre, furious that the girl whose innocence he'd respected, whose essential goodness he'd taken for granted, was running with such vermin and had no doubt run with them in the past. Never before had he been prey to such violent emotions, emotions that pushed him beyond his limits of control. When he'd turned on Meghan the night before, the blood of four men on his hands, the obscene taunts of Mad Buffalo fresh in his brain, he'd been ready to kill her for her part in the vicious events of the day. He believed he would have killed her had a desperate wave of desire not driven all anger from his mind. Death was probably no more than the vicious little bitch deserved. But when he'd seen her delicate, vulnerable body bared and waiting helplessly for his revenge, his burning anger had been replaced with a different kind of burning. The feel of her soft body beneath his drove him to a gentler passion.

That was what bothered him. That was what soured his mood as they rode south. He had forgotten Meghan's crimes as he'd buried himself in the joy of her warm flesh. He'd forgotten his anger in the urgent arousal she fired in his loins. He should have punished her, not wooed her with gentle caresses. He'd seen the terror in her eyes and couldn't help but soothe her fear with the solace of his own body. His anger had evaporated in the wonder of her ardent response, had evaporated and not reappeared until her bullet had ripped past his head this morning. He'd never before lost himself in the loving of a woman, and he was disgusted that he could feel such passion for a woman who'd just helped to massacre three, and possibly four, helpless people—people who'd been her friends. The fact that a bloody-handed little savage had been able to woo him away from justified anger with the charms of her body made him feel a ridiculous fool.

Meghan's anger also fed the icy tension between them as they resumed their journey. She wished the white man had killed her last night. He'd intended to, she was sure. She'd seen her death in his eyes and had been terrified by it. But she was more terrified by the snare he'd caught her in. What had turned his mind from death she didn't know, but the fate he'd visited on her was much worse. He'd shown her how weak she really was, she who'd always prided herself on strength. He'd degraded her and made her enjoy it, humiliated her and made her beg for more. Her body was no longer her own. It had responded of its own will to his intimate touch. She almost wished that instead of sending her bullet to one side of him that morning, she'd sent it tearing through his treacherous masculine heart. Even now, with anger and humiliation burning in her mind, her heart leapt whenever he looked at her, her blood pounded when he spoke, even at the brusque words demanding she keep up. She would never forgive him for what he'd done to her, enslaving her traitorous body to his will while her soul writhed in misery.

The sun rested on the western horizon when they reached the Karr ranch. Clouds were banking in the north, and a cold wind heralded a repeat performance of last night's wet weather. Jason would have liked to avoid the ranch, but the barn, the one building not completely destroyed by fire, offered better protection from the coming rain than the sparse trees of the valley.

Meghan rode into the Karrs' valley with a feeling of dread in her heart. The blackened stone walls of the house where she'd slept, where she'd discovered that whites could be warm and loving, seemed to stare at her in accusation. She felt like crying out her innocence, screaming that she'd had no part in this tragedy. Instead, when she felt Jason's brooding amber eyes on her, she raised her chin and stared straight ahead, hiding her feelings behind an uncaring facade.

While Jason rubbed down the sweaty horses, she automatically went about the motions of making camp for the night. She would rather have spent the night out in the coming rain than have to pass the night with her memories of this place. She was sure this was another punishment her surly captor had planned for her. She would die before letting him see how much the blackened ruins were eating into her heart.

The packs and blankets were all stowed safely in the barn. Jason led the horses to stalls in the back. Almost against her will, Meghan wandered toward the blackened house. Much as a sore tooth will draw the attention of an irritating tongue, the pitiful remnants of what had been home to the only white people she could call friends drew Meghan to wander sadly through the charred ruins. Memories of a conversation here, a scene there, flashed painfully through her mind. It did not seem possible that those happy, loving, laughing people were gone.

As if pulled by some unseen force, her wanderings took her almost directly to the freshly mounded earth of the three graves. There she sat, head bowed, thinking of the three women who rested there. She hoped their deaths had not been as horrible as Mad Buffalo had depicted. He'd been a boastful man prone to gross exaggeration of his own feats. His words had been chosen to inflame Jason to heedless anger and carelessness. Perhaps their deaths had been quick—a moment of fear, of pain, then it was over.

But however they had died, they were at rest now, and she knew in her heart that these good and gentle souls were at peace, wherever they were. She didn't feel they looked down upon her now with anger in their hearts. They would know how sad she was at their fate. In the wisdom granted upon death, they would know she had tried to prevent what had happened.

Jason leaned on a corner of the blackened stone walls of the ranch house. Broodingly he watched Meghan as she sat by the fresh graves. Tears ran unheeded down her cheeks. Her face, no longer frozen into the grim hostility that had served as her mask all day, clearly reflected her grief and turmoil. A growing feeling of uneasiness filtered into Jason's mind as he stood silently watching. Would she sit crying this way if she had participated in the grim attack that had taken place here, as he had imagined? Would her eyes mirror such sadness if she had helped to spill these people's blood just the day before? Remorse mingled with a strange feeling of relief as he realized his terrible error.

He had terrorized then carelessly seduced an innocent woman—innocent not only of sexual knowledge, but innocent of the crimes he'd laid at her feet. Now the truth was obvious. It had, in fact, been obvious all along. Blinded by rage, he hadn't even wanted to see the truth. He'd been too anxious to strike out and hurt someone.

How could he have imagined that Meghan could do this thing? Meghan—who'd spared her guard when she'd tried to run from Crook's camp, who'd taken the time to tie and gag the boy instead of slitting his throat, which would have been far easier and more efficient. Meghan—who, in spite of her wariness, had responded so warmly to the affection the Karrs had offered. How had he fooled himself into believing this essentially gentle-hearted girl could be a cold-blooded killer?

He knew how he'd done it. He'd let lust and anger overwhelm his reason. He'd wanted Meghan from the first moment he saw her, standing so proud and fearless by the valley of the Rosebud. He'd used the first excuse he could to justify taking what she would never give of her own will. And in giving his anger, frustration, and desire free rein, he'd damned the consequences and bent a terrified and inexperienced virgin to his will. Jason felt a sickness twist his guts as he realized just what he'd done, and what the consequences might be for his victim.

"You didn't have anything to do with all of this, did you?"

Startled from her deep absorption, Meghan jerked as if burned by the sound of his quiet voice. He stood not ten feet away, amber eyes fastened on her with a strangely grim expression. How long had he been silently watching? she wondered. And why the questioning sadness in his eyes?

"No," she answered simply, turning her face back to the graves. "I didn't."

"Why didn't you tell me?"

She laughed bitterly and turned to look at him again. "When did you give me a chance to tell you anything?"

He hesitated. She could have sworn he colored a deep shade of red under his normal bronze.

"Afterward?"

"Afterward . . ." She let the word trail off. "What use to tell you afterward? Would you have believed me?"

She turned her face away again, no longer able to face him. The silence was heavy between them.

"I no longer care what you think," she finally said in a quiet voice. "If you think I had part in this"— she gestured to the blackened buildings and fresh graves—"then I don't care. Believe what you want. It makes no difference."

"It makes a big difference."

She didn't answer. The grim planes of Jason's hard face got grimmer. He took off his hat and ran his hand through his tousled, sun-bleached waves, then passed his hand over his eyes, wishing he could wipe out the deeds of the last few days and start over. He looked at the darkening sky as if hoping to find the right words written there. They weren't.

"I've made a big mistake," he finally said.

Meghan could have laughed at his understatement if she had any humor in her soul at that moment.

"I've treated you like no innocent woman ought to be treated. I thought that you . . . well, even if you had . . . that was no excuse. I wanted you. And that's the plain truth."

He was met with silence and the back of her head.

"I don't ask you to forgive, and there's no way I can make it up to you. Just thought I'd let you know I'm sorry."

Finally she turned her face toward him. Jade eyes mirrored emotions that even she couldn't explain or interpret. She only knew that she hurt. That her life, her pride, her very being, was in shambles, and this big tawny-haired man was responsible.

"Touch me again, white man, and I'll kill myself. Better still, I'll kill you."

His eyes lit with the faintest of twinkles. He was a man who could take himself seriously for only so long. "You already tried that, remember?"

"I hit what I aimed at," she assured him grimly. "I mean it. Stay away from me."

He frowned in irritation and stood up. "You can get that martyred look off your face. I have no intention of touching you again," he snapped, irritated more with himself than with her. "There's plenty of women in this world. I don't need to tangle with a wildcat Irish Indian just to get laid!"

"You just remember that, white man!" she said tartly, ignoring his crudity. "Touch me again and one of us is going down. One way or another, you won't be able to deliver me to my uncle and collect your money!"

He glowered, then reached out to take her arm. She drew back with a frown.

"I merely wanted to escort you to our fire," he said caustically. "Or would you rather stay here in the cold?"

With silent disdain she rose, gave the graves of her friends one last look, and walked toward the fire.

Dinner, the remains of the beef butchered by the Indians the day before, was done before any more words passed between them. Jason's irritation, both with himself and with her, had faded. His pragmatic mind refused to dwell unduly on something that was past and could not be undone.

"You should stop calling me white man, you know. You're as white as I am."

She lifted her chin and regarded him coldly. "My heart is Cheyenne."

"Hearts change," he remarked casually.

"Mine never will. I would rather die than forget my people."

He couldn't help but chuckle at the almost ceremonial somberness of her voice. "You won't forget, little Meghan. But you'll change. A year from now . . . maybe two . . . the Cheyenne will seem far away. You'll no longer be a part of them."

"No." Her denial was flat, absolute, certain.

"You'll find out. You were . . . what . . . nine years old when Stone Eagle took you away?"

"Stone Eagle did not take me. Standing Antelope, his brother, took me."

"No matter. You were nine years old. Do you think you were Cheyenne then?"

Cold silence.

"Hell, no! You were a little pesky Irish kid straight from the bad part of St. Louis. You'd never seen a buffalo before your family joined the wagon train. You'd never ridden a horse or shot a rifle or a bow. You'd probably never seen an Indian close up until that war party came and slaughtered everyone on the train."

Her face was stony.

"You changed then," he reminded her. "You learned what you had to learn and got better at being Cheyenne than some of the genuine Indians. You'll change again. You'll learn what you need to learn. Before long you'll be as good at being a white woman as you were at being a Cheyenne.''

Her mouth pulled down into a stubborn pout. "I don't want to be a white woman."

"You don't have much choice, little Meghan. Probably at one time you didn't want to be Cheyenne."

The gathering storm was putting on a fine display of lightning as they prepared to bed down for the night. Yellow-white fire jagged across the night sky, closely followed by the crash and rumble of thunder. The first big drops of rain pelted to the ground and sputtered in the dying fire as they hurried into the barn, swinging the heavy door shut behind them.

Inside the barn the warm animal smell of horse and leather and hay welcomed them. The darkness was complete, and Jason didn't bother to light the oil lamp that hung from one of the rafters. As a result, Meghan plowed into him as he stopped to lay out their blankets.

"Oof!" she grunted as she came up against the hard wall of his chest. "Why don't you light the lamp. I can't see a thing!"

His arms went around her almost automatically as she tried to pull away. "We don't need light. We're just going to bed."

"Let me go."

He hesitated only a moment. She stiffened against him, and he released her from his hold. "The blankets are right in front of you."

"I'm not sleeping beside you."

"Yes, you are," he said calmly. "I'm not going to have you sneaking away in the middle of the night again."

"I've no one to sneak away to, now."

"Somehow I don't think that makes a hell of a lot of difference. You'll sleep next to me, as close as you can get."

She stiffened as he pulled her down beside him, struggling as his strong arms pulled her up against his hard body. Memories of that hard body lying over hers, possessing hers, increased her struggles to near frantic proportions.

"Dammit! Hold still. I'm not going to do anything to you!"

Her squirming didn't stop.

"Not unless you make it impossible for me not to, that is!"

In graphic demonstration of his words, he pulled her back hard against him, letting her feel the swelling of his desire in response to her struggles. Abruptly she stilled. She almost stopped breathing, afraid to move.

"That's better. Now go to sleep. You sure as hell made certain that I won't sleep for a while."

She closed her eyes and tried to still her heart, pounding from fear and something else she didn't want to think about. Her traitorous body still wanted him. Her breasts tingled with longing for the feel of his roving hand, and between her legs an ache throbbed that could be assuaged only by his maleness. She hated her body; she hated herself for feeling this way. She hated him most of all for awakening these unfamiliar, uncontrollable feelings within her.

She wasn't aware of finally falling asleep, but she was awakened by a tightening of Jason's arm about her waist. She squirmed in protest and was about to voice an objection when his warm breath brushed her ear.

"Quiet," he whispered. "We have a visitor outside."

Silently he rose, took the pistol that was always within his reach, even when he was sleeping, slipped the long-bladed knife smoothly into his belt, and walked soundlessly to the door.

"What's—"

He silenced her with a soft hiss. Then he slipped out the door.

Jason glided into the rain-wet night. The darkness was almost absolute. His eyes were useless, so he waited, silent and motionless, for a repeat of the sound that had roused him from sleep. Moments later it came—a quiet rustling, the snap of a breaking twig, the almost indiscernible scuff of a boot on the wet ground. Unerringly Jason moved toward the sound, silent and smooth as a stalking panther, and just as deadly. He approached the brush that bordered the back of the corral between the fence and the bluff. Thumbing back his pistol hammer, he waited once again. A rustle in the foliage revealed how close the intruder was. A form separated itself from the line of brush, a barely visible blacker shadow in the black night. The time for caution was past.

Jason reached out and grabbed the shadow around its neck, pushing the snout of his pistol to the side of the intruder's head.

"Hold real still," he warned calmly, "or this pistol just may go off."

The intruder froze. A whimper escaped his throat. The sound of the whimper was somehow familiar to Jason's ears.

"Junior?"

"Mr. Sawyer?"

Jason released the boy and spun him around. "Goddammit, boy! What're you doing sneaking around the bushes like that?"

Junior slumped. "Thought you was Injuns. Thought I'd sneak up and let ya'll have it." The boy's voice cracked into a sob. "They . . . they . . ."

"I know, boy," Jason said quietly. "Where've you been? I buried your mother and sisters, and I looked for you."

"I hid," he explained in a weak voice. "I was down by the creek. There was all this hollerin', and these four Injuns come ridin' and whoopin'. . . . I lit out. I just lit out. When I came back . . ." The sobs he'd been holding back came pouring out. "I just lit out. I can't believe it. I shoulda stayed. But I just lit out."

Jason sighed. "There's nothing you could've done. I'm sure it made it easier on your mother, knowing you escaped."

The sobs continued.

"Come on in the barn now. Dry off. There's no sense in your sticking around here. You can ride out with us in the morning."

The boy followed him through the darkness toward the looming blackness of the barn.

"Is . . . is Meghan all right?"

"Of course Meghan's all right. Why?"

"I thought . . ." Junior's voice was filled with as much embarrassment as grief now. "I thought maybe you'd run into those Injuns too. I was afraid maybe you and Meghan . . . you and her . . . got . . ." It never occurred to the youngster that the marauders had been Meghan's friends.

"The Indians are dead, Junior."

"How . . . ? All of them?"

"All of them."

"You kill 'em?"

"Yes."

The boy's voice suddenly grew older and bitter. "I hope they hurt. I hope they hurt real bad before they died."

# Chapter Eleven

Jason set his glass down on the bar and motioned to the bartender for a refill. The whiskey didn't wipe the frustration from his mind, but it helped. Of all the rotten luck. Of all the stinking, goddamn, rotten luck! All the trouble he'd gone to, the frustration and irritation he'd had to put up with to bring Meghan O'Brian back to her goddamn uncle, and the uncle wasn't even here!

"Son of a bitch!" Jason mumbled as he sipped on his fourth whiskey.

They'd ridden into Fort Laramie the morning before, he and Meghan and Junior. The post commander had greeted them with some reserve, saying Jonathan O'Brian had left the month before, not saying if he had plans to return. He'd left a forwarding address in Placerville, California, and the commander gladly offered to send a wire informing him of his niece's safe return. But he refused to take responsibility for Meghan until O'Brian could come for her.

The people of Fort Laramie, soldier and civilian alike, were still in an uproar over the recent happenings on the Little Bighorn. Custer's entire command had been wiped out. Crook was busy trying to track down the Indians, who had now broken into smaller bands to spend the summer hunting. Feeling against the Indians was running high. The army had no time to tend to the problems of one young girl "rescued" from the savages and one small boy robbed of his family. So now Jason was stuck with two problems instead of one. And he'd thought Fort Laramie would be the end of this trail!

Jason stared at his whiskey in disgust. What was he going he do? He was a loner, accustomed to the problems of survival in a still-savage frontier. He was not used to the responsibilities of caring for a girl too uncivilized to care for herself in the white man's world, and a child too young to make his own way.

Young Junior was a problem he hadn't counted on, though he couldn't very well have left the boy to fend for himself after his family had been killed. When Junior had learned Jason's real name, he'd been awestruck that he was traveling with an infamous gunman whose name was practically a household word in the West. A severe case of hero worship had set in immediately. One thing the boy for sure didn't need, Jason thought, was to idolize a bloody-handed misfit like himself.

But what was he to do with the boy? The kid said he

had no relatives other than his mother and sisters. Jason couldn't very well just dump him. Though Jason had been on his own for two years when he was Junior's age, he couldn't see the experience had done him much good. Besides, Jason at thirteen was already close to six feet and two hundred pounds. He could shoot a fly off a fence post at thirty paces and stick his knife dead center in any target from the same distance. This coltish runt was lucky to be able to walk straight, much less shoot straight. He needed someone to care for him—some good couple who would bring him up to be a decent, law-abiding man. He didn't need to be following a half-savage outcast who regarded civilization as a curse.

Where Jason could find such a couple was right now beyond his imagination. Fort Laramie was strictly a military post. There were civilians around—the sutler and his wife, the post laundresses, and the folks who ran the establishments around the perimeter of the post that catered to the various vices and appetites of the soldiers. None of these were people who had the interest or the capability to take in a confused, heartsick, painfully adolescent boy. So what on earth was Jason going to do with the kid?

And Meghan—now there was a different problem altogether. At the thought of that emerald-eyed redhead Jason motioned the barkeep for another whiskey. Meghan was a problem indeed. She'd behaved herself well enough so far, much to Jason's surprise. All during the ride from the Karr Ranch to Fort Laramie she'd listened to Junior's spouting his hatred of the Indians. She hadn't said a word, seeming to understand the boy's reasons for hating and his need to air his feelings. The boy appeared to have forgotten altogether that Meghan had spent more than half her life with the Cheyenne and was well acquainted with the savages who'd slaughtered his family. Jason didn't expect continued forbearance on Meghan's part, though. The population of Fort Laramie was incensed over the slaughter of Custer and his men. In addition, they were scared—scared that the Cheyenne and Sioux were a bigger threat than they'd

heretofore believed. All this bred hatred, and hateful
words and pronouncements were plentiful at Fort Laramie
these days. Sooner or later, Jason figured, Meghan was
going to break her uncharacteristic silence and say something exposing her true sympathies. When she was revealed
as a friend rather than a victim of the Indians, all hell was
going to break loose, Jason figured. She'd be lucky to
escape being lynched.

The subject of Jason's worries was at that moment
sitting demurely in the small parlor of the sutler's house.
Bess Carmody, the sutler's wife and a woman with a heart
as big as her ample girth, had insisted Junior and Meghan
stay with her and her husband the minute she heard the
story of their adventures, a story Jason had cleaned up
considerably in the telling. Her home was the only decent
place for the two of them to stay, she insisted, since none
of the officers' wives had come forward to offer their more
spacious and luxurious accommodations.

Two of those same officers' wives sat opposite Meghan
and Bess, drinking tea from the delicate china cups that
were Bess's pride and joy. Bess's face wore a slight frown,
knowing the women's visit was more from curiosity than
courtesy, and knowing that her guest could expect many
more such visits from the ladies of the post. She was at a
loss as to how to defend the poor girl from the cruel barbs
that she knew were bound to come her way.

Cynthia Smythe, the porcelain-delicate wife of Major
James Smythe, smiled at Meghan with a sympathy that
was not quite genuine. "My dear Miss O'Brian," she
started, "I believe you are so brave to have survived
everything you've been through." Her tone implied that a
female of proper sensibilities could never have endured
such an ordeal. "I do believe that I would've perished
living among those savages. I know I would have!"

"Yes, Cynthia dear!" The graying but haughtily dignified woman sitting next to her looked rather bored. "We all know how sensitive you are. Let us just be glad that Miss O'Brian did survive and has returned to civilization safe and sound."

Adele Hutchison, wife of Brigadier General Abraham Hutchison, post commander, was the leader of Fort Laramie society both by virtue of her husband's position and her own formidable personality. She had wasted no time in coming to see for herself the unfortunate creature who'd spent so much time with the savages. It was such a shame, she thought, sitting stiffly erect on Bess Carmody's horsehair-stuffed settee and regarding the girl with slightly narrowed eyes. A shame the girl was such a lovely creature. She was irredeemably soiled, of course. The indignities she must have endured at the hands of the Indians were enough to ruin her forever in the eyes of polite society, no matter how much money her uncle had. And if that weren't bad enough, she'd spent several weeks in the clutches of that awful Jason Sinclair! No telling what that yellow-eyed male animal had done to her. Mrs. Hutchison gave a shudder as much from titillation as from horror, thinking of the delicious possibilities. And there the girl sat in her prim cotton dress like a modest maiden fresh from finishing school. Whom did she think she was fooling?

Bess put out an arm and circled Meghan's shoulders in a motherly fashion. "Of course we're glad she's safe and sound. After all those years of cruel captivity—now she's finally back with her own people, and soon with her own family. No wonder she's overwhelmed." The beginning of a tear collected at the corner of Bess's eye. She did so love a happy ending. There were too few happy endings out in this godforsaken land beyond the Mississippi.

"Yes, of course," Mrs. Hutchison replied with a non-committal smile.

"Bess is right," Cynthia chimed in, wishing they could ask outright what they most longed to hear—an account of all the wretched use the Indian bucks must have made of her during her captivity. "You must be truly overwhelmed,

Miss O'Brian. You must have given up every hope of ever being rescued. How absolutely awful to think yourself condemned to that fate for the rest of your life."

Meghan looked at the two women curiously. She didn't understand these ladies. They were so different from the forthright, outgoing, outspoken Grace Karr. They were different, even, from the kind, stolid, matronly Bess Carmody. That their words didn't say what they themselves meant was obvious in their tone, but why the women would speak those words and mean others was beyond her comprehension. They looked at her with pity and contempt in their eyes, but spoke in terms of sympathy and friendship. They professed horror at her supposed mistreatment, but in their eyes she read avid interest.

She turned to Bess, who at least seemed a decent, honest woman. Bess had been kind to her, in spite of the older woman's confusion at Meghan's recalcitrant attitude toward merging herself back into civilization's ways. Bess smiled in genuine sympathy, concerned with how the women's condescending attitude was affecting her young charge.

"I don't understand, Bess," Meghan said with an irritated little frown. She addressed the sutler's wife as though the other two women in the room were not worth her attention, which she had indeed decided that they weren't. "Why does everyone believe me so fortunate to come here to the white man's fort? I am a captive here and would go back to my people if I only could."

Cynthia gasped and pressed a handkerchief to her lips. The formidable Mrs. Hutchison frowned thunderously.

"You are with your people, child."

Meghan regarded her with calm self-possession. "The Cheyenne are my people."

"Well, I never!"

"You never what?" Meghan didn't like the gray-haired old harridan, and she wasn't shy about showing it.

"I never heard such talk! You wicked creature! You should be grateful that you've been taken away from those savages and that the good and generous people of your own race will accept you back after you've lived with those filthy beasts and been contaminated by their evil and lewd ways.''

"Now Adele!" Bess tried to intercede.

But Meghan didn't flinch from the indignant lady's accusations. Somewhat less shy in sexual matters than a well brought up young white woman, she did not swoon, as Cynthia Smythe looked about to do, at the idea that Mrs. Hutchison considered her soiled goods. Her English was still a bit rusty from lack of use, and she didn't understand all the words Mrs. Hutchison threw at her, but she did understand the gist of the woman's thinking.

"The Cheyenne," she said with a level glare at the incensed woman, "are not evil or filthy. They treat their women with more respect than I have seen from the white man. No Cheyenne warrior would dare to touch me, though several sought me as their wife. Not until I was unlucky enough to fall into the hands of Jason Sinclair was I . . .''

"That's quite all right, dear!" Bess hastened to interrupt. "No one is questioning your virtue, I'm sure." She shot a stern warning look to the two women who sat with shocked expressions on the settee. "You've been through such a bad time, I'm sure everyone understands if your temper is a little frayed."

"But—"

"Of course we understand." Mrs. Hutchison's voice dripped acid. "One cannot expect anyone to have lived so long with the savages and emerge with any notion of proper behavior." She rose to leave, motioning to Cynthia Smythe to do the same.

"Thank you for the tea, Bess." Cynthia smiled hesitantly.

"Yes, thank you. This has been a most enlightening chat." Mrs. Hutchison turned the force of her glare on Meghan, who no longer looked demure, only defiant. "I would urge you, miss, to learn some manners, as well as humility. A woman who has been shamed as you have—

you have no right to hold your head so high in the presence of decent women. I'm afraid you need some lessons in decency before you can fit again into civilized society.''

Meghan's conversations with the other women of Fort Laramie who came to visit went no better. Though she heeded Bess's warning to say no more of Jason Sinclair, in the small closed society of the ''decent women'' of Fort Laramie, Adele Hutchison's verdict on the character of the rescued captive traveled with the speed and force of lightning.

''That old biddy!'' Bess sighed the next day as she shut the door behind three curious ladies who'd sat over tea and biscuits for the last hour. ''She's painted you scarlet. That's for sure! We'll have every officer's and soldier's wife in here gaping at you like a freak in a circus before the week is out.''

''I don't understand.'' Meghan frowned, picking up the china cups and saucers and carrying them to the kitchen. ''Scarlet?''

''Adele Hutchison's a dried-up old prune if I've ever met one,'' Bess complained, following Meghan into the kitchen. ''She's told everyone within hearing range that you're a fallen woman. Course, I 'spect to her any female under the age of forty whose face don't stop a clock is a fallen woman.''

''Fallen woman? You mean . . . ?''

''That's exactly what I mean.'' Bess sighed and gave Meghan's shoulder a motherly pat. ''I guess folks just assume all Indian woman are loose and any white woman who's lived with the Indians has had every buck in the tribe between her legs.'' She caught Meghan's wide-eyed stare of horror and chuckled. ''Don't mind me, dear. My mouth runs away with me at times. I didn't mean to imply that you . . .''

''I'm proud to be Cheyenne,'' Meghan said defiantly. ''The Indians are a much more honest and loving people than the whites I've met.''

Bess dropped her ample frame onto a kitchen chair and regarded Meghan sadly. "You're not Cheyenne, honey. You're white, whether you like it or not. Women like Adele Hutchison are going to make it kinda hard on you, but you're just going to have to face them down. There are a lot of good, kind people who will love you for the sweet girl you are, just like I do. What happened when you were with the Cheyenne don't make any difference to me."

"When I was with the Cheyenne," Meghan explained, taking the chair across the table from the older woman, "I was treated as the honored daughter of a chief. Cheyenne women are expected to guard their virtue, and I did."

"You don't have to—"

"But it's not fair what people think! It was Jason who . . . who . . . dishonored me."

Bess heaved a sigh. "Guess that don't much surprise me. Much as I like that boy, he's not much more civilized than that wolf he hangs out with. But it don't make no difference, girl. You just keep your mouth shut and let people think what they want. You don't go spreadin' the word that Jason done you wrong, 'cause folks will look down on you for it, and Jason sure as hell isn't going to do right by you."

"I wasn't the one who did wrong," Meghan asserted, knowing in her own heart that she wasn't speaking the whole truth.

"Don't matter," Bess told her with pursed lips. "Folks always blame the woman, no matter who lusted after who. It's always the woman who gets the blame." She eyed Meghan knowingly. "You aren't sweet on him are you?"

"What?"

"Sweet on him. You know, in love with him."

Meghan's eyes flickered with what might have been uncertainty, then hardened. "I hate him."

Bess flinched at the vehemence of the simple declaration. "Well, I guess that's for the best, honey. He'd break your heart for sure. That man draws women like honey draws flies. I guess there's something fascinatin' about something as dangerous as he is. But he just uses 'em then sets 'em loose. I think a lot of Jason Sinclair, spite of what folks say. But I sometimes think he doesn't have a heart.''

Just when Meghan believed she was used to the parade of curious women passing through the sutler's house, a more formidable visitor arrived. Commanded by Mrs. Hutchison in a manner more imperious than her husband the Brigadier ever thought of employing, the Fort Laramie chaplain, Joseph I. Greene, paid a call upon the half-savage, shameless hussy, as Adele had termed her. He privately thought the girl deserved a good deal more understanding than the prim and rather narrow-minded "decent" females of Fort Laramie were wont to give. But he dutifully added himself to the parade of visitors before Mrs. Hutchison could complain to her husband about his inattention to his Christian duty. That most Christian lady, he knew, would settle for nothing less than a complete report on his efforts to instill a proper sense of shame into the poor unfortunate girl who had drawn her contempt.

Chaplain Greene was a mild-mannered, somewhat rotund little man who enjoyed the good things in life and whose live-and-let-live attitude put him at odds with many of the hellfire-oriented religious men of his day. He had no desire at all to lecture Meghan O'Brian on the shame and remorse she should feel because of her unfortunate experience with the Indians. He was, however, curious to see this girl who had the ladies of Fort Laramie abuzz with delicious gossip.

The chaplain's first sight of Meghan convinced him that the post ladies' main problem with the girl was that she was simply too pretty. When she walked into the room beside Bess Carmody, the Reverend Mr. Greene was immediately struck by her cool emerald eyes, flawless skin, and the hair that cascaded down her back in waves of gold-streaked fire. The light dusting of freckles across her nose, rather than being a flaw, simply made her human instead of a goddess.

In spite of what wagging female tongues had conveyed,

the girl seemed demure and behaved in a modest manner. He, of course, was careful not to touch on any subject too intimate, because that was not proper between a man and a woman, even a chaplain and a woman whose soul he was supposed to be reforming. She listened attentively to what he had to say, seeming to take in with considerable interest his short verbal essay on the necessity of her forgetting the Cheyenne heathenism.

What surprised him was that, when he had satisfactorily concluded his little private sermon, she expected him to listen to her with the same courtesy she had listened to him. She started a most convincing account of the Cheyenne beliefs about the spirit world, and he found himself caught up in fascination and unable to stop her sinful lecture. Much to his mortification, he discovered he agreed that the Cheyenne concept of Seyan, the great world where after death good and bad alike share in a life that is much like the one on earth, was in many ways more attractive than the Christian concept of the rewards of Heaven and the eternal punishments of Hell. He was about to enter a lively discussion of the merits of the two religions when Adele Hutchison herself sailed through the door and into the parlor.

"Good afternoon, Chaplain Greene." She smiled archly. "It's good to see you here." She spared a glance for Meghan, who had left a sentence trailing in midair on her entrance. "Miss O'Brian," she acknowledged. "I hope you are profiting from the good chaplain's attention."

"Uh . . . uh . . . Miss O'Brian has been most attentive," the chaplain stuttered. He hoped Mrs. Hutchison hadn't grasped the ragged ends of their interrupted discussion. It wouldn't do at all to have the old prune discover him in what she would consider a most unsuitable and unchristian discussion.

"I'm glad to hear it," she said with a queenly nod.

"Chaplain Greene is a most interesting man," Meghan said with a tiny smile. She well understood the gentleman's discomfiture and did her best to look like a properly chastened heathen. She didn't care one whit what The Mrs. General Hutchison thought, but Chaplain Greene was a kind and intelligent man, and if he wanted to look good in the old tyrant's eyes, she wouldn't prevent him.

Much to Meghan's surprise, the commandant's wife had come to deliver a dinner invitation for the following evening. The guests would include Meghan, Jason, the sutler and his wife, the chaplain and his wife, and the assistant post commandant and his daughter. Meghan would have preferred to refuse haughtily, but a warning glance from Bess forestalled her. She had no desire to spend the evening in the company of Mrs. Hutchison and a group of white people who were probably equally unlikable. And she certainly didn't want to see Jason again, though the idea did start a strange quivering in her stomach. She put down the sensation to dislike, though. It certainly couldn't have been anything else.

Dinner at the Hutchisons' house was not a complete success. Bess had conjectured that the general had forced his wife into making the plans, and Meghan had to admit that she was probably correct. The knowledge that Meghan's uncle was rich and influential in California had undoubtedly prompted the general to try to make some gesture of friendship. And if Meghan was included in the company, of course they had to invite her "rescuer" and Meghan's present hosts. Bess had declared tartly that she could see no other reason why she and her husband would have been invited to the post commandant's house.

The gathering was doomed from the beginning for Meghan, who was seated next to Jason at the long dining room table. She suspected that the seating arrangement was a deliberate ploy on the part of her hostess to make her feel uncomfortable. Deliberate or not, it worked. Meghan could feel those opaque eyes assessing her appearance in the frilly dress Bess had brought from her husband's store for her to wear. The feel of his gaze on her was unnerving, even though the dress was prim and modest. Conversation between them was nonexistent. They had nothing to say to each other. But the sensations fired by his proximity made her feel like running from the room. She felt all eyes were on her, witnessing her shameful reaction.

Throughout the first course Meghan managed to keep her outward composure. She had enough on her mind trying to sort out the various eating implements and following Bess's lead in correct table procedures to worry about the man sitting next to her, though worry about him she did. The second course was a cold tomato soup unlike anything Meghan had ever tasted. She wasn't sure she liked its acidity and noticed Jason's bowlful also was barely touched.

Nor was the rest of the dinner much to Meghan's taste. She had appreciated Grace Karr's cooking, as it had seemed not very different from the Cheyenne fare of stews, wild roots, and simple garden vegetables. Bess Carmody's tablefare was similar. Mrs. Hutchison's cook, however, was from New York and aspired to a more sophisticated style of cookery that emulated the European chefs. The dishes were strange to Meghan's taste, and much of her portions went untouched.

The beverages were also strange—a different wine with every course. Meghan had never tasted wine and thought at first it was biting and unpleasant. As she drank more though, she began to understand the allure of this strange liquid. A pleasant warm and woozy feeling had captured her entire body by the time dessert was served. The faces around the table had begun to blur, and the conversation seemed muffled to her ears. Strangest of all, Jason Sinclair's sitting next to her didn't seem nearly as unpleasant as it had at the beginning of the evening. In fact, she couldn't quite fathom why she had ever objected to his nearness. The slight tingle of excitement that buzzed within her at the sight of his tall, strong body and sun-bronzed features was most entertaining.

"Is the dessert not to your taste, Miss O'Brian?" Mrs. Hutchison queried with a raised brow.

Meghan regarded the sweet sugar confection in front of her. "I—" Abruptly, she forgot the question and looked up in confusion. Her head was spinning most alarmingly.

"She's used to simpler fare," Jason interceded, noting with some amusement the slightly unfocused blur of the green eyes that were normally so sharp and clear.

"Yes, of course," Mrs. Hutchison sniffed. "What do those people eat, anyway?"

Meghan looked at Jason rather vaguely as the conversation turned away from her. "I feel . . . so strange." A hiccup jumped out of her throat, and she giggled.

Jason cast his eyes ceilingward as if for divine help, then shook his head helplessly. "I think perhaps Meghan needs some air," he explained to his hostess as he helped the woozy girl out of her chair. He smiled briefly at the others, then guided his charge toward the door. He didn't give a damn what the others thought. He didn't want to be here himself. But he figured he'd made so much trouble for Meghan that he could at least try to get her out of an embarrassing situation before she made a complete fool of herself. It wouldn't do for the niece of the rich and influential Jonathan O'Brian to get roaring drunk at her social debut.

"Where're we going?" Meghan slurred as the cool night air met her face.

"Nowhere. Take some deep breaths."

She followed his instructions, breathing so deeply she almost fell over in the process.

"Better?"

"Yeth . . . yes," she lied.

"Guess you've never had alcohol before."

"Alco . . . huh?"

"Alcohol. That's the stuff in the wine that makes you feel dizzy."

"Who feels dith . . . diz . . . dizzy?"

He chuckled, a rich masculine sound that started a curious tingle in the pit of her stomach. "You feel dizzy, little Meghan."

"Not me," she objected, then put the lie to her own words by grabbing his hard-muscled arm for support as they descended the porch steps.

"No need to be ashamed," he told her with a smile. "Course, you didn't need to drink like a fish out of water, either. Didn't anyone ever tell you Indians can't hold their liquor?" His eyes lit with a faint gleam of humor.

"I didn't . . ." Once again her muddled mind lost the train of her thoughts. They were wandering through the night-black shadows on the spacious lawn by the side of the house. The warmth of his nearness befuddled her, driving all thoughts from her mind but the aching need to bring him nearer. Her earlier inhibitions were forgotten in a haze of alcohol. The barrier that had always been between them seemed to have fallen, and she found herself wanting nothing more than to lay her cheek against the hard muscles of his chest and feel his arms go around her. In her abandoned state she saw no reason why her every wish and yearning should not be gratified.

"Jason . . ." She looked up at him, her feelings warming the green depths of her eyes.

"What—hey!"

She stopped and wound her arms around his neck, then giggled.

"Goddamn, you're drunk! You don't know what you're doing, girl!"

"Oh, Jason." She hiccuped and leaned her body against the hard strength of his.

It was beyond Jason's strength to push her away. Her soft yet firm female body ignited his with yearnings he somehow hadn't been able to assuage at Escoffey's tavern, no matter how many eager women he had taken to his bed. Her lips sought his, and somehow his hand just naturally set itself to hold her head so his mouth could cover hers and still her uncertain swaying.

Their mouths fused with a fury born of desire long denied. Meghan surrendered completely to the giddy longings that his touch inspired. She pressed her body close against his, reveling in the feel of his hard torso, wanting to melt into him completely. His kiss snatched the breath from her. At this moment she was willing to give him her very soul. But even as she felt the hardness of his desire swell against her, he pushed her away.

"Son of a bitch!" he muttered as he looked at her swaying unsteadily in the grip of his hands. His amber eyes glittered with the hard light of desire and a softer gleam of something he wasn't ready to think about. "Thought you never wanted me to touch you again."

She smiled in tipsy abandon and regarded him coyly from under thick lashes. "I shan . . . changed my mind."

His lips drew together in a tight line. "Damn! You don't have a mind right now." He slapped her hand away as her fingers began to trace an exploratory path up the front of his shirt. He didn't know why he didn't push her down into the night shadows and give her what she so obviously desired. Hadn't his body ached for her since that night their mutual explosion of passion had made slaves of them both? She might hate him in the morning, but what did he care? The trouble was, he hated to admit, he did care.

"Jason . . ." Her arms wound around his neck once again, and her body pressed against his in unpracticed but very effective invitation.

"Goddammit!" He ignored the demands of his loins and untangled her body from his. "You'd better never touch another drop while I'm around you, girl. I couldn't do this twice!"

He turned her gently and marched her back toward the door, one arm around her waist to keep her upright. Disappointed but hazily compliant, she allowed him to guide her back into the Hutchison parlor. There, he detailed a servant to summon Bess.

"She's plastered," he announced without preamble as Bess bustled into the room. If that good woman noticed the tense set of his jaw or the heated flush under the bronze of his face, she didn't remark on it. "No amount of air is going to make her fit to join your little party. You'd better get her home. Tell 'em she's sick or something."

Without a word Bess took charge of the now pale and trembling Meghan, who felt with horror that the excuse of her being sick was very soon to become reality.

"Oh, dear!" Bess cried softly as she noted the sheet-pale face and saw the desperation in Meghan's eyes. "Jason!"

Jason took one look at Meghan's ashy color and hurried her out through the door and onto the lawn. Just in time he rushed her to a fairly inconspicuous spot under a spreading pine. The rich food and wine staged their final rebellion, and Meghan bent over and lost every last bit of her dinner onto the pine-needle-carpeted ground.

"Ohhhh!" she groaned and retched again. Jason's hand was firm on her brow, holding her head steady.

"Easy now. Try to relax. That's better," he said as the spasms died. He took out a clean handkerchief and wiped her mouth, then cradled her head against his chest as she groaned again. He'd been sick drunk enough times himself to know exactly how she felt. She burrowed her face into his shirt and began to cry. The delightful giddiness and abandon of a few moments ago had settled into sickness and depression.

"Sweet little Meghan," he crooned with an odd smile flickering over his face. "You're going to hate yourself in the morning. And me, too."

He guided her toward the porch steps where Bess and her equally plump, equally good-natured husband waited.

"You tell me when she can walk straight again," he told Bess as he handed Meghan over into her charge. "It's time we were on our way, her and me and the boy."

"But . . . !" Bess stuttered. The thought that Meghan

would not stay at Fort Laramie until her uncle could pick her up had not occurred to her.

"You tell me!" Jason repeated.

He'd decided what to do, with the boy as well as with Meghan. He sighed as he walked back into the house to say his good-byes. Odd that his mind felt so much lighter now that he'd made his decision. That little Irish Indian was turning out to be more trouble than she was worth, but somehow, he acknowledged, his heart couldn't feel quite as heavy as it should.

# Chapter Twelve

Of the three who rode out the gates of Fort Laramie two days later, only one wore a smile, and that smile rivaled the rising sun in brightness. Junior was delighted when Jason had offered him the chance to ride south with him and make a new home for himself at Jason's ranch on the South Platte River north of Denver. He'd been grinning ever since and talked about nothing else. The sad-eyed youngster who'd ridden into Fort Laramie with his mind on the tragic past was transformed into an ebullient, mischievous lad with eyes fixed firmly on the future. Bess Carmody, who'd tried in vain to comfort the boy when he'd first come to stay at her house, witnessed the transformation with wonder. Jason Sinclair, half-civilized savage that he was, went up several notches in her estimation for being able and willing to perform this small miracle. She'd had some doubts, at first, that a man such as Jason should be allowed the care of a boy not yet out of childhood. But when Jason mentioned to her, with a knowing twinkle in his eye, that Junior would be in the care of the ranch manager and his wife, a steady, reliable couple who had longed for children of their own but had none, her doubts had disappeared. She'd always suspected Jason had more good in him than he cared to have known, and now she was certain of it.

The other two riders in the trio heading south from Fort Laramie wore a quiet glumness that was at odds with the beautiful morning. Jason's face was closed, his eyes hooded and opaque. For the hundredth time since he had made the decision to have Meghan spend the winter at his ranch, then take her to her uncle in the spring, he wondered if he weren't doing something he would greatly regret. Not for the first time he cursed the day he'd met Jonathan O'Brian and had given his halfhearted promise to return his niece. The demons or the gods or the angels or whoever wove the tapestry of men's fates must have had it in for him on that day. Ever since he'd first laid eyes on the fiery-tempered redhead his life had been turned upside down. He couldn't even predict his own behavior when he had to deal with that female imp of the devil.

The morning before the Hutchisons' dinner party a wire had arrived from Sacramento. Jonathan O'Brian had sent his thanks to Jason for snatching his niece safely away from the Cheyenne. Unfortunately, business problems prevented O'Brian from making the journey to Fort Laramie to collect Meghan in the near future. He would see that Jason was well paid to escort the girl to Sacramento, where he would have a trusted employee meet them and take his niece the last short distance to Placerville. Even in the terse, abbreviated wording of the message, it was obvious that O'Brian assumed Jason would carry out his commands without question or hesitation. Jason felt a moment of pity for the girl he was delivering to such a haughty and imperious man. Then he decided it was Jonathan O'Brian he should feel sorry for. He figured that Meghan O'Brian, ex-Cheyenne warrior woman, could hold her own with just about anybody.

After he read the wire, Jason's choices had been limited. He figured it would do no harm to fulfill his promise and see Meghan safely to her relatives in California. He owed her that much. But he couldn't make the trip now. He'd promised General Crook to be back for the fall campaign, and from what he'd heard at the post, that man needed all the help he could get. If Jonathan O'Brian wanted Meghan back, he'd just have to wait until it was convenient for Jason to deliver the goods, which would be next spring, probably. But what to do with the little hellcat in the meantime? He could have left her with the sutler and his wife, but it would've been unfair to Bess Carmody to saddle her with the uncivilized brat. Taking Meghan with him back to Montana was out of the question. The only alternative was to leave her in the reliable hands of Pete and Carrie Wellner, the couple who managed his ranch for him during his almost constant absences. She'd be safe there, and perhaps a winter spent in the company of civilized people would rub off some of the rough edges. Lord knew, if her uncle saw now what he was getting, he'd probably hire Jason to turn around and take her back to the Indians.

Bess Carmody had begged Jason to wait a week or so before taking Meghan from the post. The girl needed time to rest, she argued, and to adjust herself to her new life before having to cope with another new environment. But Jason was adamant. As soon as he could buy provisions and pack they'd be on their way. They'd been here too long already, and the girl was causing nothing but trouble.

The day after the Hutchisons' dinner, while Meghan lay groaning in her bed learning firsthand about the aftereffects of alcohol, Junior returned home from the schoolroom sporting a purple, swollen eye and a cut lip. Questioned by the horrified Bess, he admitted truculently that he'd jumped some fellows who'd been saying bad things about Meghan. One kid had called her a white squaw, he told Bess in tight-lipped anger. Then another boy had chortled that white women who were captured by Indians were always forced to become whores, so Meghan was probably giving it to every soldier on the post. At that point Junior had jumped in to defend his lady's honor with flailing fists. Unfortunately, his fighting skills weren't up to the test, and he'd gotten much the worst of the battle. The schoolmaster had sent him home in disgrace. Even he didn't even have any sympathy for Junior's cause, saying that it was only natural for boys to talk about a woman like Meghan. If the slut liked the Indians so much, she should've stayed with them.

When Bess had related the incident to Jason, she'd been thoroughly ashamed of both the schoolboys and the schoolmaster. But it served to convince Jason that the talk about Meghan was not limited to the chattering matrons of Fort Laramie's polite society. The sooner they left, the better. He didn't say a word of reproach to the defiant Junior for fighting. He couldn't very well chide the boy when he'd been involved in a similar incident himself at Escoffey's tavern. In the middle of eating lunch, at roughly the time Junior was trying to explain himself to Bess, Jason overheard a relief stage driver talking at the next table to one of the tavern hangers-on, one Ben MacCauley by name. Ordinarily he shied away from listening to other people's conversations, believing that sticking your nose where it wasn't wanted only leads to trouble. But Meghan's name on the lips of Big Ben, as he was called, caught his attention, and his ears perked in their direction.

"Right purty little redhead!" Ben was saying. Jason recognized him as a ne'er-do-well who did odd jobs around the tavern and occasionally on the post. He would earn himself enough money to drink himself to oblivion. Then his money would run out and he would have to work again. Right now he was firmly in the grip of the whiskey he'd been consuming for most of the morning.

"Don't care much for redheads." The stage driver sent a stream of tobacco juice spurting to the tavern floor.

"You'd care for this one all right!" the enthusiastic drunkard assured him. "Tall . . ." His hands waved in the air in an approximation of the female shape. "Little light in the tits, maybe, but all that gold-red hair . . . Yessir, I figure that little gal's crotch is just as red as her head. Sure would like to find out for myself."

The stage driver grunted. "Waal, you can be sure every mother's son of a Cheyenne buck has found out."

"That's so. That fella who brought her in is sure one lucky son of a bitch. I bet he got a piece of that tail whenever it struck his fancy. Bet she's taught him all sorts of Cheyenne bitch tricks. Sure like to have a piece of that for myself!"

The two were so engrossed in their imaginations that they didn't notice Jason leave his table and stroll with seeming casualness over to theirs, Wolf padding silently by his side. He woke them rudely from their wishful thinking.

"You boys ought to know better than to dirty a lady's name in a place like this."

"Huh?" Big Ben, entertaining himself with visions of impressing Meghan with his sexual prowess, jerked up in surprise. His gaze was caught and held by the coldest eyes he'd ever seen.

"I said"—a gentle, dangerous smile touched Jason's lips—"that you boys need to learn some manners when it comes to talking about innocent women."

The stage driver squinted at him assessingly, then glanced at the silver-gray beast sitting calmly by his side. "You're . . ."

"That's right," Jason said softly.

"Huh?" the drunkard said, not understanding why his drinking partner had suddenly paled under his tan.

"We didn't mean no harm." The driver pushed back his chair and rose. The rest of Escoffey's customers were following the action by now, hoping for the entertainment of a rousing brawl.

"Who's this?" Ben glowered at Jason and stood up. He was a man of enormous bulk, and he was known for his brute ability to squeeze the life from any man foolish enough to cross him. "Who says we don't have no manners."

"I do." Jason grinned, glad to get his mind off his frustrations and concentrate on bashing in somebody's face. He needed a good fight, he figured. He motioned Wolf back out of the way.

The big man lunged, but his chin connected with Jason's fist. To Jason's amazement, he merely staggered. Any normal man would have gone down from a blow such as the one he'd received. Ben roared and charged again, this time succeeding in wrapping his massive arms around Jason's body. Slowly he began to squeeze.

The other tavern customers were gathering around to watch the fun. At the sight of Jason's face growing red under the relentless pressure of the giant's muscles, a murmur of excitement rippled through the crowd, punctuated by a few cries of encouragement. Jason was seeing spots dance before his eyes as he desperately tried to break the big man's hold. A fog of black was closing in from the corners of his vision. This time, he thought hazily, he just may have bitten off more than he could chew. What had happened to the survival instinct that up until this afternoon had never failed him? Why hadn't he remembered the size of this ape before leaping so eagerly into the fray?

Finally he managed to get one arm free of the punishing circle of steel arms. In a last-ditch effort, he rammed the rock-hard palm of his hand up under the big ape's chin, snapping his head back and momentarily breaking his concentration. The arms loosened for a split second, just barely long enough for Jason to wriggle free. Without pausing for breath, he followed up with a vicious punch to the man's throat. The big man staggered and grabbed at his Adam's apple, choking and gasping for breath. One more hard-fisted blow to the chin toppled him. He crashed to the floor with the grace of a fallen elephant, sending earthquakelike tremors across the wooden plank floor. Wolf looked on and licked his chops in detached interest.

Now, finally riding free of the fort and its attendant vice

pits, Jason shook his head and wondered why he'd been so foolish as to pick a fight with such a formidable opponent. It wasn't as though the man's comments hadn't echoed those of almost every other man on post. But the rage that had exploded in his mind when he had heard Meghan's name on the lips of that low-life scum of a drunkard had known no reason. Logic and his heretofore excellent sense of self-preservation had flown out the window, and he knew he wouldn't be satisfied until Ben MacCauley was lying senseless on the floor. Never before had he acted with such dangerous foolishness.

The little Irish Indian was getting under his skin. He felt guilty for the brutal way he'd treated her after the raid on the Karr ranch. Or maybe it was something else, something he didn't much want to think about. She had a strange appeal, Irish good looks combined with the natural courage and uninhibited grace of the Cheyenne. She also combined the hot temper of an Irishwoman with the unstudied savagery of the Indian. No man in his right mind would give the girl a second thought. But however he looked at it, Meghan was a thorn in his side that he didn't need and one that he couldn't stop thinking about. He'd be glad to dump her on Pete and Carrie and ride north to vent some of his frustrations in Crook's Indian wars. That, at least, was a straightforward fight where a man could see and understand his opponent.

But of the three that rode south for Jason's ranch, Meghan was the most glum, the most confused, and the most angry. The daylight after her disastrous debut into polite society had brought not only nausea and a poundingly painful headache but acute embarrassment as well. Surely no woman had ever made such a fool of herself as she had the night before. The details were mercifully hazy, but she did remember throwing herself at the man she most despised in the entire world, and then being violently ill in a most disgraceful way. And the worst of it all, though she had brazenly offered herself with all the subtlety of a practiced whore, Jason had the effrontery to refuse her! Somehow that stung more than anything else.

Meghan had been furious when Jason told her his plans for her during the coming fall and winter. She refused point-blank, saying she wouldn't move an inch toward his goddamn ranch!

"When the hell are you going to stop cussing?" he asked her with an unaccustomed twinkle in his eye.

"I make the same use of language that you do," she sniffed. "Now that you're leaving maybe I'll try to listen to someone more refined."

He grinned amiably. "Except that you're leaving with me."

"Like hell!"

"There you go again. What would Bess think if she heard you talk this way?"

"Bess isn't here. Besides, Bess treats me like a human being. She likes me."

"I treat you like a human being. Just a damn difficult one, that's all."

She frosted him with a green glare. "Bess likes me. She'd let me stay with her."

Jason shook his head and smiled. "I wouldn't wish you on anyone as nice as Bess Carmody. You're coming with me."

"You can't make me!" she asserted confidently.

He sighed. The beginnings of impatience colored his voice. "Everyone on this post knows that your uncle put you in my charge ... for a good price of course." He grinned at her furious look. "Wouldn't want to take on such a chore without a suitable fee."

"I hate you!" she sneered, feeling the word was less than adequate for what she really felt.

"Maybe. But it doesn't matter. If I decided to hog-tie you to the back of a horse and drag you with me, I doubt anyone would have a thing to say about it. Except maybe the women might think you'd gotten what you deserved. They might be real entertained."

Meghan had pictured the smug satisfaction on the faces of the "good women" of Fort Laramie if she allowed Jason to make a spectacle of dragging her from the fort. She had no doubt he would do it, and probably enjoy every minute. The knowing smile that curved his finely molded lips made her want to scream in fury or slap him full in the face to wipe out that expression of victory. But she knew too well that either action would be useless, and the consequences might be most unpleasant. So she fumed in silence.

Now, riding with him beside her toward new people and a new place even more frightening than Fort Laramie, she despaired of ever understanding herself again. When she had been with the Cheyenne, with the people she loved and who loved her, she had been sure of her place in the world and sure of the people who occupied it with her. Now her life was confusion. New people, new places, new customs, new expectations. And new and disturbing feelings that were pushing their way past all the barriers she could erect against them.

She wanted to hate Jason Sinclair. It was only reasonable that she should hate him. But in her more honest moments she realized she didn't. At times she was furious with him and frustrated. She hated what he'd done to her—taking her from her family, forcing her to a way of life she didn't want, seducing her, then, worst of all, teaching her the passions of her body. She had every reason in the world to hate him. But she couldn't. She didn't want to think about what she felt for him, because it was something she'd never felt before, and she didn't know what it was. But she felt it take control of her soul more and more every day that she was forced to be in his company. She had lost control of her own destiny. Now she was losing control of herself as well. How would she survive a winter in his house, with his friends, knowing that sooner or later he would ride back for her? How would she survive that and still emerge as the person she could recognize as herself?

* * *

They'd been riding two days when Jason first realized that someone was following them. He hadn't expected trouble on this leg of their trip. The Indians in the territory between Denver and Cheyenne were generally friendly to whites. The Pawnee, in fact, were serving with distinction as scouts for the army. But there was always the chance of a stray band of hotheads from up north wandering down this way, or some of the local young bucks rebelling against older and wiser authority.

The followers, whoever they were, kept their distance for most of the afternoon. For the most part they were over the horizon and out of sight. Only an occasional telltale wisp of dust convinced Jason they were still there. He began to think they were simply travelers like themselves following a parallel course. Still, he kept his eye out for a likely spot to hold off an attack. Just as a precaution. Junior rode on unaware of Jason's concerns, but Meghan glanced at the eastern horizon from time to time with a little frown creasing her brow. Jason guessed she had spotted the others also. His mind went uneasily to the disastrous events resulting from the last time they were followed. They were too far south, he knew, for any of Meghan's Indian friends or family to be staging another rescue attempt. Still, an uneasiness nibbled at the edges of his mind, and he was unable to ignore it or throw it off.

The attack came as a complete surprise. The group had been paralleling their course for so long that Jason was convinced no trouble was brewing. It was unlike Indians to take the morning and half the afternoon to make up their minds to attack. So even Jason was caught off guard as five screaming warriors rode over a low ridge at full gallop, rifles spurting flame.

The Indians' aim was remarkably bad, and though bullets whizzed around the trio like angry flies, nobody was hit. In half a second Jason had his rifle to his shoulder and returned the fire. His aim was more telling, and one of the braves lurched, then fell from his horse. His scream was lost in the raucous yelling of his fellows as they turned in a flurry of dust and retreated to beyond Jason's rifle range.

"Go!" Jason wheeled the black stallion and urged his companions to a burst of speed. The whoops and yells behind them told him the Indians had worked up their courage once again. He turned and fired, but this time his shot went wild. The braves yodeled in delight and only came on faster.

Jason's stallion could easily have outdistanced the pursuing Indians, but Meghan's mare and Junior's fat little buckskin were already wheezing from the strain of the race. Jason had no desire to stand and fight with a child and an unpredictable Cheyenne war goddess at his back. But the Indians were closing the distance steadily, and the choice was soon taken from his hands. He turned and fired once again. The report of his rifle joined with the crack of a shot from the leader of the band. Meghan screamed as her horse stumbled, then somersaulted, a lead slug in its belly. She rolled as she hit the ground, as Crooked Toe had once taught her. The ground was painfully solid though, and her vision swam as she tried to regain her feet. Dark wings of unconsciousness beat at her mind as she slipped back to a half-sitting position on the ground.

The explosion of a rifle shattered the air as Jason whirled his stallion around and fired into the charging band. A warrior clutched at his throat and leaned for a moment over his pony's scraggly mane, spattering the horse's foam-streaked neck with blood. Then he fell. His comrades ignored him and came on. Jason leaned down and caught Meghan's arm as she tried once again to rise to her feet. Holding tightly to her wrist, he wheeled the stallion again, letting the horse's momentum swing her up behind him.

"Hold on!" He spurred the horse forward as Meghan's slender arms wrapped tightly around his waist. Dammit!

he thought furiously. Even in the heat of a crisis her body pressed against his back was enough to stir him. He gave the stallion an unnecessary spurring as Meghan molded herself more closely to his body, moving with him as if they were one person as the horse sprang forward.

Just as the thundering stallion caught up to Junior's laboring buckskin, Jason spotted a ravine that might prove their salvation.

"This way!" he yelled at Junior, swinging his horse toward the nearest cutbank. He plunged down it with no regard for life or limb, and Junior did the same. Pulling to a sliding halt in the deepest part of the cut, he pulled Meghan off and pushed her up against the bank.

"Stay there!" Quickly he glanced at Junior to make sure he had found himself a sheltered nook, then reloaded his rifle. "Come ahead, you bastards! Come ahead and get yourselves a gutful of lead!"

He sighted over the lip of the ravine and fired. His shot was greeted by raucous yelling as the Indians retreated out of range. Even they were not foolish enough to charge into Jason's rifle fire without being able to hit him in return. They fired some token shots in the direction of the ravine, then settled down to wait until the white fools were driven out of hiding by thirst. The afternoon sun was hot, and the water provisions the stupid whites carried couldn't last long. The leader of the band, a young brave by the name of Painted Horse, was confident the whites would make a break for it soon. In the meantime the band could enjoy the wait by finishing off the stolen bottles of whiskey they'd been sampling all day.

"They're drunk!" Jason concluded as he carefully looked over the lip of their sheltering ravine. "So that's it, the crazy fools!"

The sound of the band's wild partying carried through the hotly shimmering late-afternoon air. Meghan managed to peep over the lip herself before Jason's big hand landed on the top of her fiery head and pushed her down.

"What do you think you're doing?" he growled.

"Looking."

"I'll do the looking. You keep your head down."

One look at the marauding band was enough to convince Meghan they were not Southern Cheyenne, as she'd hoped. Cheyenne, she thought proudly, would never stoop to making fools of themselves by drinking and carrying on in such a manner. She didn't know who these braves were, but a faint hope had started to glow in her mind as the minutes and then the hours of the siege passed. If she could get to these foolish braves and let them know who she was, they might be able to get her to the Southern Cheyenne, who could in turn arrange for her to travel back to her own people. Hope that had been abandoned when she reached Fort Laramie began to bloom again. She could be rid of Jason and the disturbing feelings that roiled within her in his company. She could be rid of the awful prospect of living with white men the rest of her life. She could see Stone Eagle again, and Long Stepping Woman, and little Magpie. She could see Red Shield, and Comes in Sight, and forget that her heart had ever been disturbed by a white man, forget that her body had been possessed and branded by a white man's passion, forget that she herself, fool that she was, had in a drunken haze offered herself willingly to a man who had Cheyenne blood on his hands. What right had she to label these drunken braves fools, when she herself had been in the same state only days before?

"These are not Cheyenne," she commented to Jason.

He smiled grimly. "Were you hoping they were?"

"Maybe," she commented cheekily.

"Well, forget it. Those boys are Pawnee."

Meghan sniffed in disbelief. "They couldn't be Pawnee. The cowardly Pawnee are friends of the white man."

Jason chuckled unpleasantly. "The Pawnee aren't cowards, that's for sure. And I suspect these are wild Pawnee. Maybe some young bucks who don't much like what their elders are doing to their tribe, or maybe they're just heated up with liquor. Doesn't matter. End result is the same."

Meghan was silent, thinking her own thoughts. She didn't believe these braves were Pawnee. Jason had lived with the Pawnee for several years, she knew. He'd told her himself. She didn't believe the Pawnee would attack him. Even if these young braves didn't know him personally, they would know about him. Jason was trying to make her believe these Indians were the foes of the Cheyenne to discourage her from escaping.

Junior sidled over to them with wide eyes. "Are they still out there, Jason?"

"Yeah, they're still there, all right."

"What're we going to do?"

Jason gave the boy a reassuring smile. "Figure we'll just wait until they get impatient and come in to get us. Then we'll pick them off one by one. You got your rifle ready, boy?"

"Yessir! But why don't they come now? Why're they waitin'?"

"Figure they think we'll have to come out first. Guess they don't know that there's a few pools of water in this ravine. We can wait just as long as they can. And I'm a damn sight more patient than they are."

Jason glanced at the sun, which was now only a glowing half ball resting on the horizon. "Don't figure they'll attack tonight. They're having too much fun boozing. Come morning they'll be over here."

Come morning they'd better get this over with, Jason thought. Though there was water in the ravine now, that might dry up over the course of another hot day like today. And their food was limited. Too limited. He counted on hunting to provide himself with most of his sustenance, being a man who liked to travel light. He wasn't used to being tied down by people and horses who couldn't move as fast as he could. Alone he could have outrun these drunken, blood-happy bastards. Now, having to stay back with the slower horses, he found himself in a fine fix. He wasn't nearly so confident as he made out to Junior. He wished he were.

Meghan studied Jason and Junior as they talked in low tones. The more she thought of it, the more she knew that this was her opportunity to escape. A clearer chance could not have been handed her. Bess Carmody would have called it a gift from God. And who was Meghan O'Brian—no, Autumnfire Woman—to turn down an offering from the white people's deity.

She sat for a moment deciding whether she should simply make a run for it, trusting Jason not to pursue for fear of rifle fire from the Indians, or whether she should take one of the horses. She decided just to run. If she took a horse, the band of Indians might mistake her for a white person trying to escape. If she were on foot, it would be clear that she was running toward them, not from them. And she had to make her break before dark set in, when the band could clearly see her and not mistake her actions for flight.

Jason sat listening to Junior's chattering. The boy wasn't afraid. He had a ridiculous amount of confidence in his protector. Jason hoped that when he grew up, if he grew up, the boy would have more sense. A low growl from Wolf, lying by his side, made him turn his head. A flicker of movement caught his attention.

"Hey!" Jason couldn't believe his eyes. Meghan was on her feet and running, heading for a low part of the ravine lip. Before he understood what was happening, she had climbed out of the wash and was running full speed toward the drunken band of Indians.

"What the hell? Meghan!"

"Meghan!" Junior repeated Jason's call.

Meghan didn't turn to look back. She just kept on running. The Indians had seen her now and seemed just as shocked as Jason had been. But it didn't take long for them to react. One raised his rifle, but another knocked it away.

Jason thought fast and reached an unpleasant conclusion. Meghan was a fool, but he couldn't let her fall into the hands of those braves. He knew only too well why that rifle was knocked away. He knew only too well what those braves would do to her once she'd foolishly delivered herself into their untender care. They were standing there waiting for her, grinning, laughing, motioning her on with grotesque gestures. They might not know why the fool white woman was running to them, but they were not going to turn away such an opportunity for entertainment by gunning her down prematurely.

Jason cursed emphatically and proficiently. If he were fool enough to run after her, he would only be inviting a barrage of rifle fire that would probably kill them both. There was really only one alternative. He didn't hesitate, but his face was grim. He raised his rifle to his shoulder, sighted carefully on the running girl, and squeezed the trigger.

# Chapter Thirteen

"You shot me!" Meghan's voice was incredulous as she looked up at Jason from where he had unceremoniously dumped her on the foor of the ravine. "You filthy swine! You shot me!"

Jason knelt by her side, still panting from the race to get her back into the ravine before an Indian bullet found its mark in his body. A line of blood marked his sleeve where one bullet had passed too close. The rest of the blood on his shirt was hers, smeared onto his clothing when he'd picked her up and carried her back to safety.

"You bet I shot you, you goddamn little fool! What in hell's name do you think you were doing?" He examined her leg and confirmed that his aim had been true. She was in no danger of anything but a serious case of outrage.

"What do you think I was doing?" she sobbed. "I was going to my own people." She jerked as his fingers probed gently at her bloody calf just below the knee. "Ouch! Stop it!"

"Damn bullet's still in there," he said more to himself than to her. "Just a flesh wound though."

"You tried to kill me!"

"If I'd been trying to kill you, little idiot, you'd be dead. Just be grateful my aim was good."

"Ow! Dammit! Quit that!"

"Sorry." He leaned back on his heels. "That bullet's going to have to come out."

"You brute! You had no right. Why didn't you let me go! You've got no right—"

"Shut up! Those aren't your people out there. I told you, those are Pawnee. Do you have any idea what they would have done to you if they'd gotten hold of you?"

She was silent.

"They would've made what happened to Grace and Amy and Christine look like a picnic." He spared a glance for Junior, who crouched below the lip of the ravine out of hearing range and sporadically returned the Indians' fire. Both parties were out of range of the other, so the firing was more an empty gesture of anger than anything else, but Jason let the boy continue. They would run out of food and water long before they ran out of ammunition.

"They would have returned me to my people," Meghan insisted stubbornly.

"Stupid, muddleheaded idiot!" Jason's face was tight with anger and frustration. "You're a white woman! They would've treated you like any other white woman. Do you think you look like an Indian? And if they believed you were Cheyenne, they'd have gotten an even bigger kick out of their vicious little games. When are you going to grow some brains or some sense?"

She sniffed, suddenly hit by the foolishness of her

actions. She'd been so desperate to escape from Jason that she hadn't thought clearly. Of course that band of drunken Indians would've thought she was a white woman. And if they were truly Pawnee, as Jason said . . . A shivering nausea gripped her at the thought. The Pawnee and Cheyenne were ancient enemies. The Pawnee were great warriors and vicious antagonists. Her death at their hands would not have been easy.

"You could've killed me," she accused lamely, trying to forget her own foolishness by concentrating on Jason's wrongdoings.

"If I had," he said tiredly, "it would've been a cleaner death than what those boys would've dished out."

She sneered, marshaling every last ounce of bitterness in her to ward off the realization that she'd been a fool. Now she was in debt to Jason for risking his own life to save hers. "Better to die at the hands of the Pawnee than to live with the white man."

Jason shook his head in exasperation. "Lord save me from stubborn foolish women. If I ever manage to get you to your uncle, I feel sorry for that poor man."

The stars shone clear and sharp in the night sky, but Meghan's eyes couldn't focus on the elusive pinpoints of light as she lay looking up the the Hanging Road to Seyan. She felt almost as if she were floating, not lying on the hard sand floor of the ravine. The stars swam before her eyes, and she suspected that some of them were in her head and not in the sky.

"You think she's ready?" Junior queried, looking curiously down into Meghan's face. He didn't understand the events of this afternoon. Why would Meghan want to run off from Jason? Especially when a dirty pack of redskins was sitting right out of rifle range. He knew Meghan had lived with the Cheyenne, but surely that must make her hate the Injuns even more. Jason was in no mood to answer his questions, and Meghan was too drunk, having imbibed on Jason's insistence a healthy portion of the bottle of whiskey that Jason had had in his saddlepack. Women, Junior decided, were creatures that defied explanation.

"She's ready. Are you?"

"I guess." Junior grimaced doubtfully. "You sure you don't want me to keep a look-see on those Injuns instead?"

"I need you to hold her still. Those Indians are having too good a time to attack tonight."

"Awright. But shouldn't we maybe wait till morning? Cain't see anything now, it's so dark."

"Don't need to see much to do this." Jason poured what was left of the whiskey onto his hands. "Do it mostly by feel anyway."

Meghan giggled as Jason propped her up against the ravine embankment and Junior steadied her. The pain in her leg had faded, dulled by a pleasant alcohol-induced euphoria. Jason placed a piece of worn leather between her teeth, then brushed a loose lock of hair from her eyes in a gesture almost tender.

"This'll only take a minute, little Meghan," he said softly, then turned away to focus on her injured leg. She caught sight of the knife in his hands and closed her eyes, a rush of apprehension chasing away the warm, carefree feeling created by the whiskey. He bent over her and gently tore away the blood-caked ruffled pantaloons that Bess had given her. "Bite down on that leather when you have to," he instructed. "Hold still, and try not to scream. We don't want those Pawnee bastards to think we're having more fun than they are and come over to investigate."

"You ready?" He raised a questioning brow at Junior.

"Yeah."

He looked at Meghan, and for a moment his amber eyes caught her green ones and held them prisoner. What Meghan saw there for those few seconds turned her mind from the ordeal ahead. She saw the man beneath the tough exterior, the feelings encased in the shell. Then there was no more time to think and wonder. He knelt closer, and there was pain, white-hot pain. She gasped and bit down hard on the leather between her teeth. Concentrating her gaze on the broad shoulder that was so close above her face, she tried desperately not to move and not to scream. She felt Junior awkwardly grasp her arms in an attempt to hold her still, then she felt nothing but the unbelievable fire that ignited in her leg and flooded out from there to explode through every nerve in her body. Suddenly, the fire flashed out. All was mercifully black.

"Why'd she run away, Jason?" Junior asked, his eyes wide, inquiring, and confused. He'd put Meghan on a pedestal, and now he found he didn't understand her as well as he thought. The pedestal was crumbling.

Ruddy light from the little campfire flickered across the bronzed planes of Jason's face as he stared thoughtfully into the flames. "Guess she figured those hooligans out there could help her get home," he answered quietly.

"Home?" Junior screwed up his face in confusion. "But we're going home, aren't we?" He'd really adopted the thought of Jason's ranch as home—much more than Jason ever had.

"Home to Montana. Home to the Cheyenne, to her family." Jason raised his eyes to Junior's face. "When you lost your ma and sisters, you wanted them back, didn't you? Didn't you want everything to go back to the way it was before?"

"Yeah, I guess. But they're dead." The boy's face tightened momentarily. "Cain't go back. But I guess I got a powerful urge to see 'em again."

"Well, I figure Meghan feels the same way. Far as she's concerned, her family might as well be dead. She won't see them ever again, most likely. Only she hasn't come to see that yet. She's still trying to go back."

"But them's Injuns! Not her ma and pa!"

"She thinks of them as family. And she feels every bit

as bad about not seeing them again as you do about not
seeing your ma and sisters.''

"No kiddin'? Injuns?"

"Just people, like anybody else.'' Jason brushed back
the tawny mass that had fallen over his brow, then rubbed
his eyes wearily. "Indians fall in love and get married and
have kids and love them every bit as much as your ma and
pa loved you. And the kids love their parents as much as
you loved yours. Meghan's not only lost her family, but
her whole way of life. Sometimes it makes her a little
crazy. You have to understand and treat her like anybody
else you love who's real sad.''

Junior's eyes were wide. "Yeah," he whispered. Jason's
words put a whole new light on the situation. He figured
Meghan needed his help. That made him feel grown-up, like
a man. He liked her better as sad and lonely and needing his
help than he had as beautiful and remote and perfect.

"Do you love her?" the boy asked artlessly.

Jason's mouth tightened grimly, and he was silent for a
long moment. Finally he answered, "I don't love anybody.
Can't afford to.''

The harsh tones of Jason's voice forestalled any further
conversation. The silence stretched out.

"You feel like taking watch for a while?" Jason finally
asked.

"Sure!" the boy answered proudly.

"Okay. I'm going to get some sleep.'' He glanced at
Meghan, still lying unconscious in a sheltered nook of the
ravine bank. Jason had covered her with blankets and
placed a rolled slicker under her head for a pillow. "You
come get me if she wakes up, you understand? Or if
anything looks wrong. Got it?''

"Got it!" Junior said with a grin. He placed his rifle
across his knees, feeling very grown-up and responsible as
Jason settled himself in a dark corner of the ravine.

\* \* \*

Meghan woke to throbbing pain in her leg and a chill that permeated her whole body. Her movements to wrap the blankets more tightly around herself brought Junior to her side. He looked down curiously into her shadowed face.

"You awake?"

"Yes."

"I'll get Jason."

"You don't need to." She didn't really feel like facing Jason with the knowledge of her foolishness still fresh in her mind. And the knowledge that he'd calmly and without qualms shot her down, even if it was to save her from a worse fate, still rankled.

"Jason said to get him whenever you woke up. I'd better get him."

"You don't need to," she repeated with an irritated frown. Then, in a softer voice, she said, "Why don't you sit here with me for a while."

It was an invitation Junior couldn't resist. He plunked himself awkwardly down on the sand beside her. "Jason said you'd lost your family," the boy said with the blunt directness of youth. "Just like me. He said you were sad and lonely. And that's why you ran away."

"Did he?" Meghan was surprised that Jason bothered to think about what she was feeling.

"He said you get crazy sometimes."

Bitter laughter rose into her throat. That last sounded more like the Jason she knew.

"I'm not crazy. Just stupid."

"Yeah," Junior agreed. "Maybe that's what he meant." He paused a moment, then surreptitiously rubbed an already grimy sleeve across his nose. "I miss my ma and sisters a lot," he sighed. "I get real sad sometimes. 'Specially before Jason told me I could stay at his ranch. Seemed like there just wasn't no future no more, ya know?"

Meghan did know, because that was exactly the way she felt. There was no future, at least not one she felt she could face with any sort of happiness or even simple contentment. And unlike Junior, no one had come along to offer her an alternative to the sad state of affairs.

"Jason said you get real sad," the boy persisted. "Are you sad like me, Meghan?"

She looked at him silently. A Cheyenne didn't admit to his inner feelings to strangers. A Cheyenne always presented a brave and stoic face to the world. But she wasn't feeling brave or stoic right now. She felt like a vulnerable, helpless, idiotic fool. And she hurt. The boy was trying to be a friend even though he had plenty of difficulties to cope with for himself.

"Yes," she answered softly. "Sometimes I get sad. Sometimes I get angry. And sometimes, like Jason said, I guess I get just plain crazy."

"That's the truth if I've ever heard it," a deep voice agreed. Jason had come up so silently neither of them had been aware of his approach. "Thought I told you to wake me, Junior."

"I . . . well . . . I was about to. Really."

"I told him there was no need," Meghan said tartly. "Do you always sneak up on people while they're having private conversations?"

"Guess I'm in the habit of walking quiet," Jason conceded. He turned toward Junior. "If you want to travel with me, boy, you get used to doing what I tell you. No matter what anyone else tells you. Got it?"

"Yessir." Junior looked properly chastened.

"Go get some sleep now. I'll wake you at dawn."

The boy gave Meghan a sheepish smile and ambled off.

"You were kind of hard on him, weren't you?" Meghan commented with a tiny frown. She was inexplicably glad of his presence, in spite of her earlier reluctance to face him. She hoped her feelings were successfully hidden under her disapproving comment.

"The boy has to learn." He looked down into her face and frowned. "How do you feel?"

"Like hell."

"Well"—he noted her pale face—"you sort of look like hell, too." The shadows under her eyes were discernible even in the dim moonlight.

"Thanks."

"Don't mention it. It's not everyone I'd waste a bullet on just to save their miserable hide."

"I suppose I should be grateful."

"You might."

"I guess I'm grateful, then."

He grinned. "Spoken like a true lady."

She turned away, not in the mood for banter. "Don't make fun of me."

His grin faded. "I'm not making fun. Not much, at least."

"Why won't you leave me alone." Her voice was barely a whisper, her face still turned away.

He reached out a hand and gently ran a finger along her tense jawline, then turned her face toward him. "You don't really want me to leave you alone, do you?"

She was silent, her heart pounding. Did he know the confusing whirlpool of feelings that had grasped her? Could he look inside her eyes and see the fear, the vulnerability, the reluctant desire for his strength and his nearness? She felt her face grow hot with the awareness that somehow he could see into her soul much more deeply than she wanted him to see. She dragged her eyes from his and turned her face away once again.

"How are we going to get out of here?" She finally broke the awkward silence. The sounds of the Pawnee partying were far away, but still could be plainly heard.

He sighed, feeling somehow a spell had been broken. "They'll come at us tomorrow morning. We'll fight. We'll win."

"What if we don't? What if they stay out there and pin us down?"

The smile that touched Jason's face was wolfish, making Meghan wonder if he weren't truly blood kin to the silver-gray predator curled in the shadows on the other side of the little campfire. "If they do that, we'll have to make a break for it and fight."

"You and a green kid and crippled woman against three Pawnee warriors in the prime of their strength. We'll all die."

"Maybe," he agreed with equanimity. "But we'll take them with us, I guarantee that."

She shivered, because of his cold-blooded words or the chill in the air she didn't know. "I'm cold," she said. She was cold inside as well as outside. Death seemed very close, and she discovered she didn't want to die. So many things were left unresolved. So many things were yet to do. She was young. She'd never known love or children or the tender embrace of a man who loved her.

"You're shivering." He gazed at her for a moment with unreadable eyes, then stood and unfastened his holster and carefully placed his pistols beside the pile of blankets that was her bed. His hands then went to unfasten his belt.

"What're you doing?" she whispered, her green eyes glittering with suspicion.

"Undressing."

"Why?" she asked in a flat voice, her heart pounding.

His shirt and trousers joined his pistols by the bed. "You want to keep warm?"

"Not like that!" She managed with some difficulty to drag her eyes away from his heavily muscled form.

"Like what?" He grinned. "All I had in mind to lend you was my warmth. If you want something more . . ."

She hid her face in her hands. "Don't!"

"What?" He was taken aback by her obvious distress. From Meghan he expected scorn and harsh words, not tears, which were starting to dribble from between her fingers. He knelt and pried her hands away from her face. "What's wrong?" He wiped a trickling tear from her face with one callused finger. "Besides the obvious, that is."

She gulped, tired of fighting her need for him. "We're

going to die tomorrow. And there are so many things . . . so many things I haven't done or seen.''

He raised one brow, then gently brushed a stray lock of gold-red hair from her brow. ''We're not going to die tomorrow, little Meghan. You're just tired and cold and maybe weak from some bastard putting a slug into your leg. Things will look better in the morning.''

She gave a hiccuping sob, thoroughly ashamed of the tears coursing down her face. But what the hell? They were going to die. Nothing mattered from here on out. These were probably the last hours of her life. She stopped fighting the feelings that urged her closer to him and leaned forward, resting her cheek on his well-muscled chest. They seemed to naturally flow together as he sank to the blankets with her beside him. One arm holding her close, he pulled a blanket around them, shutting out the cold night air.

''Where's Junior?'' she whispered against his shoulder.

''Fast asleep.'' He hesitated, feeling the warmth of her flow through his body, feeling the tattoo of her heart pound in gentle rhythm against his ribs. ''So should you be,'' he told her, feeling impossibly noble.

''Hold me.'' She snuggled closer, melting his attempt at nobility in one movement. What had started as the merest ache flared to rampant desire as her uninjured leg pressed against his groin in unconscious sensuality.

''Meghan,'' he groaned, ''do you know what you're doing?''

She knew. She could feel the hard thrust of his manhood against her leg. It frightened her, and also tantalized her. In the light of having no tomorrow, some things were becoming painfully clear. Her feelings for this white man ran deep. He'd earned her hate, but had gotten . . . what had he gotten? Her love? Impossible! And yet . . . no matter. She feared him, but more than that, she wanted him. Right now she wanted him more than she had wanted anything in her life. She wanted to be his in these last hours of life. She wanted his brand of possession on her, wanted his seed within her, wanted to merge with him in a straining dance of passion that would leave her mark on his soul forever, or for as much of forever as they had left. She ignored a feeling of maidenly horror at her own boldness. There were no tomorrows. She had only tonight to know the tender embrace of a man who loved her. She would pretend Jason loved her. She would let herself love him. That would have to be good enough.

Hesitantly, somewhat abashed by her own daring, she moved her hand to the swollen proof of his desire and circled it gently with her fingers. It throbbed in her light grasp, and Jason groaned.

"Meghan." His lips were warm against her ear. "You sweet, innocent, little hussy . . ."

"Jason," she whispered against the muscular column of his neck, "I want . . . please . . ."

He chuckled. "Sweet little Meghan, it's obvious what you want."

"I—"

"Ssshhh." He nuzzled her throat, then moved his mouth in a tingling path down her neck, unbuttoning the front of her bodice as he went. "I've wanted to do this for so long," he murmured, unfastening the last button and pulling the garment down over her shoulders. "I've waited . . . so long."

He fastened his mouth on the rosy tip of one breast and gently sucked. She gasped, surprised at the delicious feel of his mouth. Curling her fingers in his thick, tawny hair, she pressed him closer and instinctively arched against him.

He raised his head and looked at her. The openness of his gaze and the warmth of tenderness in those usually cold and opaque amber eyes was a unique tribute to her, one he'd given to no other woman. "Patience, my love." He smiled, then his smile grew wry. "There is so much I'd like to teach you in so short a time."

He pressed a gentle kiss on her brow, then on her lips. Gentleness gave way to passion by degrees as his kiss grew deeper. His tongue invaded her mouth and ravaged its sweetness. She felt sucked into the maelstrom of his desire, out of control now and burning with the fire she herself had started. His hands moved down to massage her breasts. They were rough and callused but amazingly gentle as they moved over the tender skin. His thumbs paused and circled the soft, tingling nipples and teased them to rigid excitement. She moaned into his ravaging mouth, feeling her body catch fire from his, feeling an unbearable tension grow in the woman part of her and spread to flood her entire being.

"God you are beautiful!" he breathed. "So beautiful. God help me but I want you more than I've ever wanted anything."

She looked up at his shadowed face hovering so close over her. She could feel the heat of his wanting. A little smile curled the corners of her mouth as she savored, womanlike, the joy of his desire for her. Gently he eased her dress down over her hips, along with the rest of her underthings, taking great care not to bump or scrape against her tender leg. His breathing grew ragged as he admired the full complement of her femininity. "Damned if you aren't the prettiest freckled-faced, redheaded Indian I ever did see." He smiled.

He reached out a hand and touched one breast as if it were a delicate treasure that would break with anything but the gentlest of handling. Then he ran the hand slowly down over her silken skin, traversing the flat plain of her belly and gliding gently over one slender thigh. His eyes caught hers and held them prisoner as his hand worked its way up the inside of her thigh, then gently brushed the mounded curls that hid her most intimate of secrets. Meghan didn't resist when he separated her legs and twined his fingers in the soft curls, tantalizingly brushing the moist and eager flesh. His eyes still burned into hers as his fingers probed carefully into the place that was waiting for him. She moaned and arched against him, completely under the spell he was weaving.

"Jason . . . ," she almost begged. "Please!"

"Sweet little Meghan." He smiled. Pushing her thighs even farther apart, he moved over her. His lips brushed her breasts, then her neck, then fastened on her mouth. For a moment he allowed himself to pause at her warm entrance, letting the tension build between them. Then, gently, slowly, he eased into her moist recesses, letting out a deep sigh of pleasure as he felt her welcoming flesh enfold him. When his entire length was buried deep inside her, he stopped. His lips covered hers again, and his tongue thrust urgently into her mouth, seconding his rigid manhood in demanding her submission.

Meghan was lost in a world of throbbing need. As he started to move within her she curled her slender legs around his hips, urging him to plunge still deeper in his invasion. She felt herself stretching to accommodate his size, but there was no pain, only a delicious feeling of fullness. Closing her eyes, she roamed with her hands over the hard ridges of his superbly muscled body, enjoying immensely the feeling of such unleashed strength under her hands. He moved inside her in an ever-increasing rhythm of power and desire, and as she moved with him, an unbearable tension coiled within her. Finally, when it seemed she could hardly breathe and at any moment her heart must stop, his final thrusts sent her soaring through an intangible barrier. Every muscle of her body seemed to convulse in a spasm of ecstasy. His mouth captured hers and swallowed the moan that might have awakened the boy sleeping soundly on the other side of the ravine. As the sweet symphony of fulfillment built to a thundering crescendo, she felt him go rigid. Deep within her he pumped the offering of his desire.

Ever so slowly they drifted back to earth, back to reality. He shifted to relieve her of his weight, but didn't separate their bodies. Side by side, still united in a oneness of flesh that extended to the soul, they listened to the slowing beat of their hearts and the quietness of their own breathing. After a few moments he reached down and pulled the blanket up around them, pulling her closely against him as he did so. There was no need for words. Their bodies had said it all far more eloquently than any words ever could have. Wrapped in a cocoon of contentment and warmth, Meghan finally fell asleep, her face pressed against the hollow of his shoulder. Jason lay beside her unmoving, staring into the darkness of the night.

The eastern sky was just beginning to pale when Jason shook Junior from his sleep. The boy screwed up his face and squinted at the figure above him, then jerked to a sitting position.

"Huh? What?"

Jason chuckled. "Calm down. It's morning."

"The Injuns?"

"Quiet so far. Have been for a couple of hours. Get yourself some coffee."

The boy wandered sleepily over to the little cookfire where Meghan was pouring him a cup of coffee. Jason went to the lip of the ravine. By the faint light of predawn he checked the loading of both pistols and his rifle. Surreptitiously he took two shells from his belt and put them in his pocket. If defeat should overtake them, he didn't want to expend all his ammunition on the enemy and leave nothing for him to give his companions a clean and painless death.

# Chapter Fourteen

They were gone. The rising sun brought only the tranquility of the rolling grassy hills, the lilting voice of early morning birdsong, the sigh of the ever-present prairie wind. The only traces of the little band of Pawnee were the still-warm ashes of their fire and a few scattered and broken empty whiskey bottles.

"Guess when their hangovers appeared, fighting didn't look like so much fun anymore," Jason speculated, kicking at a still-smoldering pile of coals as Wolf sniffed cautiously at a broken bottle. His pistol was ready in his hand in case this was simply a ruse to get them from their place of shelter, but it appeared the Pawnee braves had really gone. "See anything from up there?"

Meghan scanned the horizon from her perch atop Jason's black stallion. "No. Nothing."

In silence the trio headed back for the ravine to pack. Meghan sat the stallion loosely, keeping her knees well away from his sides and letting him amble like a tame dog at Jason's heels. It was still early morning and she was already tired. The trauma of the day before combined with her loss of blood to make her weak, and the night's passion had left little time for sleep.

The thought of her behavior the night before brought a warm flush to her face, and she was glad Jason was walking in front of her with his back turned. She had thought death would come with the rising sun, but that was truly no excuse. A Cheyenne woman did not lie with a

man who was not her husband. From what she had learned
from Grace and at Fort Laramie, Meghan suspected white
women were ruled by similar injunctions. By either the
Cheyenne or white code she had sinned grievously. Still,
she admitted to herself with characteristic honesty, if she
had it to do over she would behave the same. And though
she felt embarrassed about the boldness of her passion, she
couldn't in her heart of hearts feel that there was anything
lewd or evil about what Jason and she had done. Somewhere in the throes of their lovemaking she had come to
feel loved and needed. Jason didn't love her, of course.
But he had handled her with such tenderness. He did feel
something for her, Meghan was sure, and last night he had
needed her just as she had needed him.

Her own feelings were harder to face. The revelations of
the night before, when she thought death was peering over
her shoulder, were just as true in the brightness of daylight. Her feelings for Jason ran deep. She had given him
more than her body. Much, much more. She had surrendered
herself, not just her physical self, but the more elusive
spiritual and emotional self as well. She had delivered
herself into his power, willingly. What else could this
foolishness be but love?

She was in love with Jason Sinclair, a cold-eyed predator known by his own people to be a man-killer, a
hard-bitten animal of a man whose rock-hard soul would
never feel warmth or tenderness for anybody, except for
maybe a brief flicker of affection in the grip of his body's
passion. May all the powers of the earth and sky help her!
For this dilemma she might even have to beg the help of
the white people's god.

They packed quickly and began once again their south-
ward journey, anxious to be as far away as possible from
the Indians, who, when their hangovers had subsided,
would likely once again be after their blood. Junior trotted
cheerfully ahead, somewhat disappointed that the great
adventure had ended so anticlimactically. He had never
doubted that Jason, his hero, could have whipped twice

as many Injuns all on his own, if he'd had to. The boy was possessed with a foolhardy urge to hunt down those Pawnee just out of anger over what they'd done, forcing Jason to hurt Meghan as he'd done. Still, Jason seemed to be able to forget and let the Injuns go their own way, so Junior figured he could be big about it too.

Jason and Meghan rode double on Jason's big black stud, Meghan perched in front of Jason and held steady by his arm wrapped around her waist. Her horse was dead, and she herself was in no shape to ride on her own. The stud was easily able to bear the weight of both of them and still strain at the bit, held back with Junior's fat little buckskin.

Jason, however, was more than a bit uncomfortable with the arrangement. Meghan's nearness disturbed him, reminding him forcefully of the night before and producing a physical reaction that was impossible to conceal with her fitted so snugly against him in the saddle. Reminders of the night before made him distinctly uneasy. Always he had admitted Meghan's physical attraction to him, a thing as inevitable as a dog wolf sniffing around a bitch in heat. Last night, though . . . last night something other than lust had entered the picture. He'd known pleasure with many women. Last night wasn't pleasure. Last night was ecstasy. Passion had never before been so fierce and at the same time so tender. He'd never felt so driven, so swollen with fire and need and power. He'd never felt so high with sweet satisfaction when the deed was done. And still there had been room for tenderness. Instead of seeking the quick slaking of his appetite, he'd longed to draw out their coupling and savor the anticipation. He'd wanted to caress every inch of that delectable body, to worship the petal-soft skin with his lips, to pay homage to the perfection of her breasts, thighs, hips, arms, lips, with his insistent kisses. But most of all, he'd wanted to drive away her fear and hurt with the comfort and strength of his own body. He wanted to make her forget all the unpleasantness of the world he'd brought her into, for he found suddenly that he couldn't bear the thought of her unhappiness. The death-knowledge in her eyes had filled him with fear for her, not for himself. He'd wanted to erase that knowledge with the power of his body. And that was what he had done.

The knowledge of what had passed between them last night, of what Meghan must have seen revealed in his for-once-unguarded eyes, scared Jason, and he was not a man easily frightened. He didn't know what it was he felt for the girl perched in front of him, but he was getting messily involved, and that knowledge sent a rush of panic coursing through his veins, something no Indian attack or gunfight had ever done. He wasn't about to lose his independence and freedom to a bad-tempered, red-headed Irishwoman who thought she was an Indian. He had to get away from her, far away from the lure of her green eyes, the pull of her smile, the enticement of that sweet-smelling gold-red hair, and the snare of her perfect woman's body. And he had to get away fast!

Three more days of hard riding brought them to Jason's ranch with its well-kept whitewashed buildings and corrals, roomy barns, and green pastures stretching away to the shining silver ribbon of the South Platte. Junior sat with mouth agape as they reined in the horses on a bluff just north of the ranch house, a sprawling, one-story building with a covered veranda running along three sides. To the west the horizon reared up to meet the towering Indian peaks, still patchily decorated with gleaming snowfields. To the east, green pastures stretched out to the winding South Platte River and beyond, rolling green hills marched to where the land faded hazily into the sky. This would be his home, this piece of paradise on earth. He could find no words to express his feelings to Jason as they sat astride their horses side by side looking down on the peaceful scene.

Meghan strained to see around Jason's broad back to see the place he'd simply referred to as "the ranch." After the first day on the trail she'd ridden behind Jason instead of in front. She was feeling much stronger and could've easily ridden on her own, but they'd passed no ranches where Jason wanted to take the time to buy another horse, so she'd continued to double on the black stallion. She couldn't help but be aware of Jason's discomfort with her pressing so closely against him on the front of the saddle. So she insisted on riding behind. He'd made no objection. In fact, he'd had very little to say to her since the night they'd spent coupled together in the heat of passion. He was polite, but distant, and the look in his eyes whenever she caught him looking at her was wary, like a wild animal eying the bait of the hunter's trap. She had enough to worry about on her own without wondering at his attitude. With her new knowledge of her own vulnerability to his masculine appeal, she was content to maintain a distance, an emotional distance at least.

Now he moved slightly to one side to give her a view of their destination. Meghan didn't know what to think. Her only experience with the dwellings of whites was Grace Karr's impoverished little ranch and dim memories of the run-down little clapboard house in St. Louis where she'd spent her early childhood. This ranch seemed an awfully grand place to belong to one man, especially a man such as Jason, a wanderer, a fighter, a restless hell-raiser living on the sharp edge of the law. Finally, Junior put her question to words.

"This is yours, Jason? Honest?"

Jason smiled with a hint of bitterness. "Yeah. It's mine."

"Golly!" Junior gaped. "You got a lot of money? You never said you was . . . I wouldn'ta thought . . ."

"You wouldn't have thought I had much more than a gun, a knife, a saddle, and a horse to go under it?"

"Well . . ."

Jason laughed as the boy's face turned red. "That's all right, Junior. I got lucky some years ago with a gold strike up on Clear Creek. I've still got a claim working a couple of miles from Central City. So now I've got a mine, a ranch, and plenty of money. Some friends of mine, a couple I met back when I was about your age, they run it for me. Do a damned good job of it too.'' He pulled his eyes away from the sprawling ranch and smiled at the shining face of the boy. "I imagine they can use another young and energetic hand around the place. So don't think you're getting a free ride, Junior. I figure you know what hard work is, and I know old Pete and Walks Alone can use the help.''

Junior seemed to swell with manly pride. "You can count on me, Jason.''

Jason's smile held only a trace of amusement. "I figured I could.''


Carrie Wellner gave the trio a quiet welcome when they rode up to the front of the sprawling ranch house. She was a woman well into middle age, but her appearance and quiet energy were more suited to a woman of thirty. Dark brown hair lightly salted with gray was pulled back from an aristocratic-looking face and fastened into a heavy pile of shining braids at the crown, similar to the style that Amy and Christine had pushed on Meghan, but producing, Meghan was sure, a much more pleasing effect on this elegant woman. Her face was somewhat angular, with high cheekbones, dark-winged brows, and a broad, high forehead. Her skin was clear and youthful. Only the faint laugh lines that radiated from her eyes hinted that she was no longer a girl. All in all, even in her plain workaday dress, Carrie Walker was surrounded by an aura of elegance that seemed to belong in a more refined and gentler place than a working ranch deep in a still mostly uncivilized frontier. Her quiet refinement made Meghan feel dirty, drab, and considerably embarrassed at the picture she must present riding behind Jason's saddle, her skirt hiked up almost to her knees and exposing dusty calves and dirty, well-worn boots. Flaming, unruly hair hanging down her back in two hastily plaited braids and a bloody bandage wrapped around her calf completed the picture of disreputability. She regretted momentarily her decision to leave off the trousers she had worn earlier under her skirt. It had been hot, and the air felt good against her bare legs, but she hadn't counted on meeting up with this coolly refined model of womanhood, either.

But the paragon's smile was warm and welcoming as she stepped off the veranda to greet them. In fact, Meghan detected a faint twinkle in her eye as her glance passed over her own unruly appearance and then came to rest on the wide-eyed boy on the fat buckskin.

"Jason," she chided lightly, seemingly not at all surprised or discomposed by his unexpected appearance with two companions he might well have pulled out of a gutter. "Whatever have you brought me?" Her smile seemed to convey that she regarded the intrusion as a pleasure rather than an imposition.

Jason smiled in return and swung off his stallion, leaving Meghan feeling somehow exposed perched alone on the horse's back. "I've brought you a gift, Carrie." He grinned. "Company for the winter."

Carrie's smile grew inquisitive as she regarded Meghan, who was trying not to squirm with embarrassment under her gentle scrutiny. But her face was still open and friendly when she turned back to the still-grinning Jason. "Well, you can tell me all about it inside. You're not going to keep these two children out in this sun any longer. Come on, now. Come inside. I've got some cool lemonade that will wash the dust out of your throats."

Meghan suffered the further embarrassment of Jason's helping her dismount, as her leg still wasn't working properly, and followed the woman into the cool of the house. Their hostess wasn't quite as tall as herself, Meghan noted, but her carriage somehow made her seem taller.

Meghan was not destined to hear how Jason explained her presence, and that of Junior, and his plans for dumping them both in Carrie Wellner's lap. As soon as Carrie was able to take a good look at Meghan's ragged dress, pale face, and the shadows that still clung under her eyes, her face puckered slightly in a little frown of distress. She summoned a short Mexican woman of ample waistline and dark flashing eyes to escort Meghan to the guest room and see that she got the comfort of a bath and clean clothes.

Almost gratefully Meghan suffered the ministrations of the plump señora, who she found out later was the cook, housekeeper, and general helper to Carrie in running a household of hungry ranch hands. The woman didn't comment as she helped Meghan strip off the dirty, sweat-pungent clothes. Without a sign of repugnance she cut off the blood-caked rags that served as a bandage for her leg and examined the still-angry wound. Then she handed Meghan a robe and sent a brown little boy scurrying to fetch heated water for the wooden tub.

Minutes later Meghan sank gratefully into the steaming depths of a bath. Without being asked the Mexican woman helped her wash the heavy length of her hair. That done, Meghan scrubbed every inch of her body until her skin was rosy and glowing. When she emerged from the bath, feeling clean and languorously relaxed, the señora wrapped her in a cool cotton robe and soothingly, rhythmically brushed her hair until it was dry. By the time she was finished, Meghan was almost asleep. The Mexican woman smiled when Meghan staggered slightly on getting up from the stool where she sat. She gestured toward the soft-looking bed.

"La señorita will sleep now," she commanded in a no-nonsense tone, the first words she'd spoken.

Meghan glanced out the window at the sun, still high and bright in the sky, and frowned. She wasn't accustomed to taking her ease in the full bloom of day, but the mattress looked so inviting. It seemed to call to her to lie down, to rest, to give herself over to the exhaustion that had been her constant companion for the past three days. She sighed and moved toward the bed.

"Jason! That poor girl! It's a wonder she doesn't look worse than she does!"

Jason chuckled at the angry glint in Carrie's brown eyes. "Don't you go underestimating that girl, now, Carrie," he warned. "She's not some delicate, demure miss who's been brought up sitting in somebody's parlor stitching samplers. She can take care of herself, and she's goddamned independent." He ignored Carrie's disapproving frown at his language. "I hesitate to dump her on you. The boy—Junior— he'll be no trouble. Likely to be some help, even. But Meghan, she's a wild one, and I wouldn't even put it past her to try to run off. But I've got to get back up to Crook in Montana, and I don't know what else to do with her."

"She must be having a terrible time of it, poor thing. Imagine being snatched away from everything she loves, and then having to travel all those miles with you, of all people." Carrie fixed him with a glare that was half accusing, half amused.

Jason just grinned. He'd explained the circumstances of Meghan's "rescue" and the treatment she'd gotten at Fort Laramie. He'd explained the whole story, in fact, leaving out only the stormy intimacy between himself and his reluctant charge.

"And you shot her, of all things." Carrie's fine-winged brows drew together in a frown. "Honestly, Jason! As long as I have known you, I don't think I'll ever understand how your mind works!"

Jason shrugged. "What was I supposed to do? Let her run into the hands of those devils? Or maybe run after her and get us both shot down?"

"Only you would think of putting a bullet through someone for her own benefit!" she replied in exasperation.

Carrie wasn't entirely displeased by Jason's account of his situation, though. She understood Jason better than her words implied. She'd known him since that harsh winter he'd spent with Pete and herself in their little mining camp in the Sierra Nevada, the winter when he was just a boy of fifteen. He'd worked hard to earn his keep, helping Pete at the mine and then coming home to labor at chores around the crude cabin where they lived. There'd been nothing of the boy in him then, even. But he was not as harsh and lonely as he was now. The mine had been a failure in the end. But Jason had learned the art of placering gold from Pete, and years later, when he himself struck a rich placer deposit in Colorado and had used the proceeds to buy a large ranch, he had remembered his friends from the little camp in the Sierra Nevada; and when he had discovered that he himself had no taste for staying in one place and managing the business, he had asked them to manage his holdings for him. Carrie had seen him only once or twice a year since then, but with a mothering instinct she'd never been able to use on children of her own, she took his problems and concerns to heart. She despaired in the more recent years, watching him become more and more of a loner. The more civilized the frontier became, the wilder he seemed to grow.

But now she saw something in his eyes when he spoke of this half-wild Irish girl, something he tried to conceal, but which her sharp eyes didn't fail to notice. Hope sparked anew in her motherly breast. Maybe in this girl, unlikely though it seemed, he could find someone who would settle him into the man she knew he could be.

When Meghan woke, the sun was a mere sliver of red about to duck below the mountains to the west. The air was noticeably cooler, and the hazy, amber light of dusk filled her room with a golden glow. She lay still for a long time, savoring the comfort of her bed, happily thinking that she could simply close her eyes and drift back into restful sleep if she chose. The muted sound of conversation from the front parlor drew her though. Jason's voice mingled in low, muffled tones with other masculine voices she didn't recognize.

Giving up the idea of returning to sleep, Meghan swung her legs over the bed and looked for her clothes. They were nowhere to be seen. The dress that Grace and her daughters had given her was so tattered, she supposed, that the Mexican woman had thrown it out. Her second dress was still packed away with the ruined Indian tunic that she'd refused to discard. The señora had laid out clothes for her though. Draped across the footrail of the bed was a green dress of some finely woven soft material Meghan had never seen before, complete with frilly undergarments, stockings, and shoes. It was somewhat short on her, reaching only to her ankles, and more than roomy in the waist and bodice; but on the whole the fit was acceptable, and the softness of the undergarments next to her clean and sweetly scented skin thrilled her with its pure luxury. She smiled as she regarded herself in the mirror, thinking that there were some advantages to being a white woman, after all. This soft material was even more comfortable than her soft buckskin tunic, and the green of the material set off the flame of her hair and the warm golden bronze of her skin. Her eyes looked larger than ever, enhanced as they were by the matching emerald of the dress.

"Ah, señorita!" A soft voice startled her out of her bemused self-scrutiny. "You are awake."

Meghan whirled around to see the plump señora standing in the doorway. She felt as if she'd been caught doing something slightly naughty, and a warm flush rose to color her cheeks.

The señora smiled. "La señora Wellner said you would look good in that dress." She chuckled warmly. "She was right, señorita. You are lovely."

Meghan felt her face grow even warmer. "I . . . thank you," she stammered.

"You feel better, after your siesta?"

Meghan nodded.

"Good. Supper will be soon. We eat early, here. There's always plenty of work left to be done after the meal." She bustled around the room, smoothing the bedcovers, straightening the ceramic pitcher and bowl on the washstand. Meghan stood awkwardly to one side, feeling very much out of place. Finally the señora smiled and gave her a knowing but friendly look.

"Would you like help with you hair, señorita? It looks very pretty hanging loose, but perhaps you would like it more confined for the evening meal?"

Meghan grimaced and grew red. She knew the señora was saying, in a most tactful manner, that she looked like a wild woman with her hair cascading down to her waist in a jumbled confusion of waves. Perceptively, the Mexican woman had guessed that Meghan had little knowledge of proper grooming for white women.

"I . . . you don't need . . . uh . . ." Meghan felt like backing into a corner under the woman's careful but friendly scrutiny.

The señora smiled warmly. "Sit." She gestured to the stool in front of the dressing table mirror. "I will show you a style that is very easy and will be most becoming, I think."

Meghan sat as she was bidden and relaxed as the señora started to brush her hair in long, smooth strokes.

"I am Señora Hernandez." She grinned at Meghan in the mirror, revealing fine white teeth with a noticeable gap between the front two. Somehow, to Meghan, it made her more human and less intimidating. "Maria Anita Christina Inez Martinez Hernandez. But you may call me Maria."

Meghan hesitantly returned the friendly smile. "I am Meghan—Meghan O'Brian."

"Sí, I know." Maria pulled her hair loosely back and was fastening it with pins at the crown of her head. "I heard la señor Jason talking to la señora Wellner." She grinned amiably. "He is much a man, that one. *Muy macho*. But wild. You are very brave, Señorita Meghan, to travel so far with him."

Meghan wondered how much Jason had told Carrie Wellner. She couldn't tell from Maria Hernandez's face how much she'd heard, or what had been said, and she certainly wasn't going to ask. At least this warm-faced, jovial woman was not primly disapproving as the ladies at Fort Laramie had been.

Maria patted the last strand of gold-red hair into place. "There," she said with obvious satisfaction. "You see?

You just take this like so . . . then fasten there and here. Pretty, no?''

"Yes," Meghan agreed, though she privately wished she could simply braid her hair as she was accustomed to doing. She supposed while she was here she would have to attempt this more sophisticated style to keep from hurting Maria's feelings.

Maria hurried off, saying that she must attend to the meal and chiding Meghan in a motherly tone not to be late to the table.

Meghan regarded herself in the mirror for a few moments longer, finally deciding she rather liked the effect of having her hair swept back from her face and fastened in a shining twisted mass at the crown. It made her look older, like a woman instead of a girl. And after all, she was a woman now. Jason had made her a woman. He'd shown her what her woman's body could do and feel. He'd initiated her into the arts of physical desire and had ended by teaching her how to love. How to love the wrong man. How to love a man whose heart and soul were as hard as his steel-thewed body.

Meghan studied herself in the mirror. Other than the changes of hairstyle and dress, she could see no telling differences between the Meghan who stared at her out of the glass and the Autumnfire who had ridden to battle with her friends that day, so long ago, in the beginning of summer. The face that she saw in the mirror showed no hint of depravity, immorality, or shameless degeneration. In spite of the attitude of the good women of Fort Laramie, in spite of her own heedless and foolish behavior since then, she still felt herself to be much the same girl who'd innocently flirted with Red Shield, and who'd puzzled over the problem of what to do about Comes in Sight. She didn't feel dirty or wicked or lewd. All she felt was confused.

Did her love for Jason excuse her body's eager response to a man not her husband? Even if it did, what could excuse her affection for an enemy, a man who'd kidnapped her, seduced her, almost killed her? How could pride allow her heart to fall into this tender and inescapable trap?

Meghan sighed and then frowned angrily at the girl in the mirror, cursing her for a fool. She had enough problems without worrying about her wayward woman's heart. Jason would soon leave. Then she wouldn't have to concern herself about him anymore. She could concentrate on pulling her life back into some semblance of order and deciding where she must go, and what she must do, from here.

The kitchen was full of delicious aromas as Meghan walked through the door. Masculine voices were still conversing in the front parlor, so she avoided going there, not wanting to see Jason in her present mood and shy of meeting any more strangers than she already had this day.

"Meghan!" Junior's smile almost split his face in two at her entrance. "Meghan! Isn't this the greatest place you've ever in your whole life seen?"

Meghan had to smile at the boy's enthusiasm. She was glad he was happy. She was glad someone was happy.

Then the other person in the kitchen turned. She froze instinctively. The band of Indians who'd attacked them—she hadn't recognized them as Pawnee. They'd been young with no war paint and for the most part far away. But this tall man who stood facing her with a solemn face—there was no mistaking his features. Pawnee. The generations-old enemy of the Cheyenne. For a moment Meghan forgot she was a white woman. Her Cheyenne heart swelled in anger at the presence of her enemy. Her eyes burned.

But the Pawnee only nodded, as if he'd seen something in her that he'd expected to find. "Meghan O'Brian," he said without a smile. He paused, as if letting the name soak through to her brain, reminding her that she was white, not Cheyenne. "I am Walks Alone. Jason has told me of you."

Meghan stared at him, torn between her inbred Cheyenne hatred and the sure knowledge that this man was not really her enemy—that as a white woman and a guest in this house, she should acknowledge his friendly greeting. He simply stood, saying nothing, looking at her as if he knew what was going through her mind.

"Meghan." Jason's voice jerked her from what was becoming a deadlocked stillness. His boots thudded heavily on the kitchen tiles. "I see you two have met."

"Yes." Walks Alone smiled. "You did not tell me, my friend, what a beautiful prize you captured."

"Rescued," Jason corrected with a grin.

Walks Alone looked at Meghan with eyes so penetrating they made her distinctly uncomfortable. "There is no need between us, my brother, for these lies that soothe the feathers of your white friends. This woman is more Cheyenne than she is white, so she could not have come with you willingly. There is rebellion in her eyes still." He grinned at his blood brother. "How is it you have been together all this time and you have not yet tamed her to your will?"

The question was half in jest, but Jason frowned just the same. "Don't think I haven't tried," he said under his breath. Then he gave the Pawnee a friendly blow on the shoulder that would have staggered a smaller man. "You just keep your thoughts to yourself, you red-devil son of a bitch."

He smiled at Meghan. "Walks Alone is my blood brother. He's also foreman here. Nobody knows horses better than he does, unless it's me." He grinned at the indignant look on the Pawnee's face.

"You are Pawnee," she said, ignoring Jason. Her voice was hot with accusation.

"Yes, he is," Jason answered quickly. "And *you* are not Cheyenne. Not anymore. So get that damned Cheyenne-uppity look off your face."

She whirled on Jason in a rage, but the look in those amber eyes made her swallow the scathing remark she was about to hurl.

"Glad to see you're learning to control your temper," he said gently, the dangerous smile she knew only too well curving his mouth. "Walks Alone is my brother, and my friend. It follows that he's your friend, too. I won't have you raising a ruckus in this house, or anywhere on this ranch, and causing Pete and Carrie concern and grief. So you just mind that hot temper of yours and remember you're a white woman. You're supposed to be meek and demure, remember?''

Neither his words nor the look in his eyes was calculated to soothe, but Meghan tried her best to keep cool, knowing that a tantrum would only get her in trouble. The battle was lost before it was fairly begun, though. Her temper won, filling her to the brim and overflowing in a rush of bitterness.

"You go to hell! Both of you!" She flounced out of the kitchen, suddenly finding the prospect of being with strangers preferable to staying near Jason and his Pawnee blood brother for one more moment.

They were the last words she said to him. The next morning she scrambled out of bed barely in time to stand at her window and watch Jason ride over the hill. He hadn't even said good-bye. She stood motionless at the window and watched him disappear over the bluff north of the house. Her heart chilled with despair as she watched him go, leaving her alone and friendless in a cold and alien world.

# Chapter Fifteen

"I can't do it!" Meghan threw the half-made skirt with its infuriating, uncooperative seams halfway across the room. It slid along the wood floor and came to rest against the rag rug at Carrie's feet.

Carrie regarded her hot-eyed charge patiently. "Of course you can do it, dear. It only takes practice. And patience."

Meghan had had very little patience for anything in the two weeks since Jason had ridden away. She rebelled at doing anything other than sitting in her room and pouting. When she was forced to leave her self-imposed isolation, she made life as miserable as possible for anyone unfortunate enough to be around her. She was by turns haughtily aloof or impatient and surly. Pete Wellner, Carrie's tall, thin, gentle-mannered husband, had taken to avoiding Meghan altogether. The ranch hands went out of their way to keep out of her path. Even Junior, happily engrossed in the joys of his newfound home, had taken to ducking out of her way whenever he saw her coming.

Carrie persisted, though. Jason had entrusted her with this strange but appealing girl, expressing the hope she could polish her manners and skills in a way that would make life easier for her when she finally reached her relatives in California. And Carrie was not one to give up. Maria Hernandez, also, ignored Meghan's surliness and treated her with a motherly concern and tenderness.

"I don't see why I have to do this," Meghan complained, glaring at Carrie.

Carrie smiled gently. "Come pick up the skirt, Meghan. Every young woman must at least learn to sew a straight seam. You've improved some, but you need more practice before we can begin on a wardrobe for you to take to California."

Meghan stuck out her chin stubbornly. "I know how to sew. I've been sewing hides and buckskins for years."

"And I'm sure you did very nice work, dear. But the skills are a bit different for cotton, linen, and silk than for hides."

Meghan got no satisfaction out of Carrie's calm, unperturbed face. She growled in irritation and huffed over to pick up the skirt. Then, after spearing Carrie with a glare she was sure the older woman saw but didn't acknowledge, she reluctantly started to ply her needle again, immediately managing to drive it into her finger instead of the rumpled material.

"Goddammit!" She was tempted to throw the work on the floor again, but knew Carrie would just calmly insist she pick it up.

Carrie refused to be nettled as she looked at the tight-lipped girl sitting across the room. "You must learn to control your tongue, Meghan. People don't expect a young woman to curse." Her mouth curved in the beginnings of a smile. "At least not in public."

"To hell with what people think!"

"Ah!" Carrie admonished. "But people can make your life miserable or very happy. It all depends on what they think of you. So you want to give the best impression possible."

"Jason says whatever he wants! And no one gives him any trouble."

Carrie's brow lifted in reproval. "Jason is a man. And obviously you've been around him far too long. He is certainly not the person a young woman should use as an example of proper behavior."

Meghan grimaced. "I just say what I think, that's all. Everything just seems to come out of my mouth without my knowing it."

"Then you must learn to control that wild temper of yours. Harness your thinking to your will. Control your heart. Your life will be much easier."

Meghan sighed. She wished she could control her feelings and her heart. Even she had not been prepared for the burden of fear, loneliness, and alienation that had lowered on her when Jason disappeared behind the bluff. She didn't like the way she was behaving. Sometimes part of her stood aside and viewed her own childish actions with disgust. When that happened, unhappiness with her own behavior only added to the distress that already weighed down her spirit. As a result, she behaved even worse. She wanted to strike out and hurt someone, or at least make someone angry. But Carrie and Maria were determined to bear her childish rebellion with irritating cheerfulness. And everyone else stayed out of her way.

She tried to curb her impatience and make her stitches small and neat and straight as Carrie showed her. She wouldn't be allowed to go, she knew, until Carrie was satisfied that she was at least making an effort. For the next fifteen minutes she labored, and managed to sew an entire seam without having to rip out any stitches. With a strange feeling of satisfaction, she held the work up to the window to examine it more carefully.

"That's quite nice," Carrie commented. "I told you it only takes a little practice."

Meghan didn't answer, not wanting to give the older woman the satisfaction of seeing the pride she took in this last seam.

"Why don't you take a break from this," Carrie offered. "See if Maria needs any help in the kitchen. And check the bread I set out to see if it's rising all right. Maria always forgets. She's too accustomed to making tortillas instead of bread."

Meghan gratefully fled the room, but she didn't go to the kitchen as instructed. She detoured down the front hall and went out the front door. The blazing sun struck her almost blind as she took the veranda steps in one leap, but she reveled in the feel of its hot glare after the cool dimness of the house. When her eyes had adjusted to the bright light, she looked around. No one was in sight except the yellow hound that belonged to one of the hands. He merely lifted his head at her passing, then sighed and rested it once more on his outstretched paws when she reached out a finger to give him a friendly scratch on his muzzle.

The main barn was cool and dim after the blaze of the early August sun. The warm smell of horses surrounded her as she ambled slowly along the central aisle between the roomy stalls, enjoying the sight of so much high-quality horseflesh. She had to admit that someone connected with this ranch knew what he was doing. The horses they ran—the studs, the mares, and the foals—and the purebred Hereford cattle, were some of the finest animals she'd ever seen. She could sense Jason's hand in some of this. From the two horses she remembered seeing him ride, the half-wild bay stud who'd scared the daylights out of everyone on the Simmons train and the magnificent black brute who now followed him around like a tame pony, she knew he had an eye for quality horseflesh. The cattle, though—they couldn't have been chosen by Jason. That would take someone with more patience. Maybe Pete Wellner, who seemed a farseeing man of many talents. Maybe Walks Alone, who seemed to have a way much like Jason's with every animal he approached.

As if her thoughts had conjured him out of the dusty air, Walks Alone rose from where he'd been squatting inside a large stall, looking after a foal that had been born only the night before. Meghan frowned, a sharp pang of disappointment pricking her at the foreman's presence. She'd hoped to spend an hour in peaceful respite wandering around the barn and enjoying the strange communion she'd always had with horses. But now she'd have to go back to the house or find another place to hide away from Carrie and Maria. She turned quickly and silently to go before he could spot her.

"Wait," he commanded softly.

Too late. Now she'd have to go back to the house, or he'd tell Carrie where she'd been. She eyed him resentfully as he came to stand beside her.

"Wait?" she asked archly. "What for?"

He was silent for a moment, looking at her. Then he spoke with an unexpected invitation. "Come. Walk with me."

She narrowed her eyes suspiciously. "Why should I?"

A hint of a smile softened his narrow, angular face. "We should talk, you and I."

She reluctantly fell into step beside him as he passed out the far door and into the sunlight, her interest piqued in spite of herself. "What is it you want to talk about?"

He stopped and leaned against the aspen logs that railed off the barn corral. Absently Meghan noted how clean the logs had been scoured by the horses, who seemed to love aspen bark. She had noted the same thing on the occasions her band of Cheyenne had journeyed into the high mountains of Montana. She had often watched the horses penned inside makeshift corrals of aspen logs strip the rails of their delicious black-and-white-mottled bark. The memory sent a sharp pang of homesickness to twist at her insides.

"Well?" she inquired sharply, noticing suddenly the intent gaze that rested on her face.

"You are unhappy," he began without preamble.

She was taken aback at the unexpected statement.

"You are very unhappy, I think. It does not please me to see you this way."

Meghan frowned mightily and lifted her chin. "It's none of your business how I feel."

"Perhaps it is."

"No. It's not." She turned to leave, but his thin hand on her arm prevented her.

"It would please me to see you happy."

She turned and regarded him with interest. "Why?"

"Because the troubles that led you here are not of your own making. You are a woman of courage. But you have let your unhappiness become a barrier to wisdom. And if you continue to be unwise, you will shrivel and die, and others may shrivel and die with you."

Meghan frowned in irritation. "You talk in riddles."

"You are blinded by your foolishness."

"I am not a fool!" she snapped. "And I am not a child as everyone here seems to think! I am a woman! You hear? A woman! I have a will of my own. You . . . they have no right to keep me prisoner here and . . . and try to make me be something I don't want to be."

"You are a woman, true." He smiled. "But a foolish one right now. How do you think you will get along in the white man's world without the things Carrie tries to teach you?''

"I don't want to get along in the white man's world!" she insisted in a frantic voice. "I am Cheyenne! I want to return to my people!"

Walks Alone looked at her solemnly. "You are not Cheyenne. You are white. And in that you are lucky."

She glared at him, but he continued. "The day of the Cheyenne, and the Cherokee and the Apache and the Sioux, and yes, the day of the Pawnee also—that day is over. You should be glad you are white, Meghan O'Brian. You should be glad of these people who are bringing you back to your own world. The world you have lived in—the world you want to return to—is dying."

"No."

"It is true. When you see clearly again, you will know it is true."

"You lie. The Pawnee has been friend to the white man for years. You are nothing more than a white man in red man's skin."

He sighed. "Perhaps we Pawnee are wiser than some. We change so we will not be destroyed."

"And yet," she accused, "your brothers attacked us three days north of her. They were drunk—a disgrace to their tribe."

He nodded sadly. "Some do not see the wisdom of our leaders. They were young, and very foolish. If they had harmed you, Jason would have killed them."

"Humph!" she snorted her disbelief, both that Jason could have overcome three warriors in their prime, drunk or not, and that he would have been inspired to revenge for any hurt inflicted upon her. Hadn't he himself put a bullet into her? "At least they know who the enemy is, which is more than I can say for you!"

He chuckled. "And who is my enemy, do you think?"

"The white man! All white men. I am your enemy if my skin is white."

"Your skin is white, Meghan O'Brian. But even if the

white man was my enemy, which he is not, I could not be enemy to the woman of my blood brother.''

She looked at him in consternation. ''I am not Jason Sinclair's woman!''

Walks Alone raised one brow in an expression distressingly like one she had often seen on Jason's face. ''Sometimes the lovers are the last to know. But I know. I see you in him. I see him in you. When he returns you will be happy again. Do not let your foolishness throw happiness away.''

Another week passed. The thunderstorms of August were turning the prairie and foothills green again. Wildflowers poked their heads through the grass. Horses and cattle grew sleek and fat. And Meghan's unhappiness did not abate.

Her sewing and spinning improved with enforced practice. Her seams were straight and neat, and the fibers on the spinning wheel no longer continually broke under hands too impatient to maintain proper tension. Maria complimented her on her growing talents in the kitchen and garden, and it no longer took her thirty minutes to put her hair into acceptable and stylish order.

Through the routine that Carrie pressed on her—learning and practicing and becoming, as Carrie put it, a proper lady—Walks Alone's warning haunted her, eating at her nerves. She'd rejected his words with an angry scowl and walked huffily away before he could say more. In the days since then she'd avoided the foreman, giving up even her cherished visits to the barns and corrals for fear of running into him. The clarity with which the Pawnee saw into her soul and sensed her hopeless love for the man he called brother frightened her. Why wasn't he equally perceptive when it came to Jason? Why couldn't he see that she was no more to Jason than a nuisance to be dealt with as quickly as possible. On a few occasions he'd desired her, it was true. But that meant nothing. Of course it meant nothing! A man of Jason's strong appetites, a young, healthy, virile male, could no doubt enjoy himself enormously with any female available, especially after a long period of abstention. His desire for her was no more than animal lust. Jason was like a randy stud horse—like the big sorrel stallion Pete had penned next to the barn. He would service any mare presented to him and do it with an enthusiasm that set the cowboys to laughing. Then he'd go his merry way without a thought for the mare he'd just covered.

Walks Alone was wrong about Jason, Meghan thought. There would be no happiness on his return, only another wrenching away from a place she'd now grown accustomed to, another journey to strange places and strange people. And then a final parting. He would leave her alone with the strangers who had paid him to bring her to them. He would desert her in an alien world and an alien way of life. She would never see him again.

*"Chica!"* Maria interrupted the dark flow of her thoughts. "Don't you think you've kneaded that dough enough? Even la señora Wellner does not beat it to a bloody pulp before putting it in the pan!"

Meghan looked down at the bread dough she'd been working with such furious energy. The longer she kneaded the more it seemed to grow under her fingers like some malignant mass. "Oh, damn! What's the use!" She pounded the floury mess down on the table and fled from the room. Maria was surprised to see tears coursing down her cheeks as she ran out the door.

*"Dios!"* she exclaimed, looking at the toughened lump of dough. "It's not that bad!"

Meghan found refuge in the main barn, huddled in the corner of Sytobian's roomy stall. Sytobian, a soft-eyed dapple-gray mare, had foaled the week before, and her little stud colt regarded Meghan's presence with curious wonder. His antics took her mind from her grief. He almost made her forget the misery that had driven her from the kitchen and from the house. First he tried to hide behind his gentle mother. Then, as he perceived that the stranger was no threat, he wobbled up to her on still-awkward legs to poke his velvety little muzzle into her face. Having satisfied his curiosity, he left her alone, called away by the rumbling of his stomach and the temptation of his mother's warm teats.

Left to her own thoughts, Meghan found her misery flooding back. Sitting in the fragrant clean hay with her back braced against a corner of the stall, she hugged her knees to her chest and let the tears flow. All the anguish of the past weeks poured out as she rocked slowly back and forth, resting her head on her knees. Her life was a disaster, her heart was a shambles, and the future looked dim indeed.

The soft scuff of a shoe brought her head up with a jerk. Carrie stood looking over the stall partition, concern clouding her face.

"Maria said you were upset," she said softly. "I see she was right."

Meghan regarded her silently as she opened the latch on the door and stepped in. She sniffed, then wiped her eyes with one corner of her skirt. She didn't want Carrie to be here. She wanted to be alone.

"Meghan"—Carrie dropped down beside her—"tell me what is wrong. Perhaps I can help."

Meghan looked away, maintaining a stubborn silence. Sytobian regarded them both with a somewhat impatient eye. Her stall was becoming a bit crowded, and the foal had broken off nursing to regard this new stranger with startled alarm.

Carrie tried again. "Meghan . . . please don't regard me as your adversary. I've become so fond of you . . . almost as if you were the daughter I never had. If something is troubling you, believe me, I would do anything I can to help. Sometimes . . . keeping things inside ourselves only makes them worse."

Meghan rested her head once again on her knees. The stud colt had overcome his fear of this second intruder and was now nuzzling at Carrie's hair, coaxing a grin and then a giggle from his victim as his soft lips tickled her ear.

"Oh, you sweet baby boy," Carrie cooed, rubbing his ears. "You're going to be a lover, aren't you?"

Meghan let some of the tension flow out of her as she watched the older woman play with the foal. She liked Carrie Wellner. The woman was elegant and proper, but underneath she was all energy and warmth and caring. Affection had warmed her eyes from the first day Meghan rode in on the back of Jason's stallion, looking like a bloody rag doll that had been dragged through several Indian wars. With all Meghan's rebelliousness, stubbornness, and surly rudeness, she had never lost patience. Her persistence had made Meghan realize that she could, if she tried, fit into the white man's world. But no skills she learned from Carrie's patient teaching could ease the pain of homesickness, the loss of loving family, and the shame and heartache that plagued her every thought of Jason Sinclair.

"Meghan?" Carrie softly resumed her plea as the foal tired of his new toy and settled down close to his mother for a nap.

The need to tell someone what she was feeling was irresistible. Meghan wanted sympathy and commiseration. She wanted someone to cry with her over her losses and mourn with her over the bleak future—and then to tell her everything was going to be all right, all her dilemmas would magically be solved. Even though Meghan knew that was impossible, that's what she wanted.

"My life is over!" Meghan burst out dramatically.

"Meghan . . . ," Carrie answered softly. "You're young and beautiful and talented. Tell me how your life is over."

Tears were flowing freely again. "My past is gone. I have no future. I don't know what to do. I miss my family so much . . . so much. And my friends . . ."

Carrie reached out and laid a warm hand on Meghan's shaking shoulder. "I know you miss your family, Meghan. No one can ever replace those dear ones in your heart. But

I hope . . . I wish . . . you could come to feel that we, Pete and I, could have a place in your heart also. We're so very fond of you, both of us. I know Pete doesn't say much, but he feels very deeply for you. And so do I. And there's your family in California—your uncle and aunt and cousins. Maybe, if you give them a chance, you could grow to love them almost as much as you loved your Cheyenne father and mother.''

"No!" Meghan denied hotly. "My uncle hired Jason to take me away from my people! I will never forgive him for that!''

"Never is a long time, dear. I suspect your uncle didn't know you were happy where you were. Sometimes we have to put ourselves in somebody else's shoes . . . try to figure out how it is that they're thinking, before we understand what their true motives are. Your uncle might have thought he was rescuing you from a life of slavery and misery.''

"I was not a slave! I was . . .''

"I know.'' Carrie smiled. "You were the honored daughter of a Cheyenne chief. And now you will be the honored niece of a California gold tycoon, from what I understand.''

"If my uncle really wanted me, he would have come for me by now,'' Meghan said with a frown.

"He trusts Jason to bring you to him. And maybe he knows you need some time to adjust to the idea before meeting your new family.''

Meghan made an impolite sound at that idea. She couldn't think of her uncle in so charitable a light. And the mention of Jason had set her heart beating. If only she didn't have to see him again. If only she didn't have to dread his return and wonder at what her reaction would be.

"Why do I have to wait for Jason?'' Meghan said resentfully. "Why can't I just go on to California and get all this over with?''

Carrie was startled by the abrupt about-face. First she didn't want to go to California. Now she couldn't wait to get there. A suspicion sparked in her mind.

"It's not safe for a woman to travel alone, Meghan, even in today's modern world. And neither Pete nor I have the time to go with you, even though I'd like to meet your family."

Meghan looked at her anxiously, hopefully sensing an ally. "Could you go with me when Jason gets back? I'd rather go with you, or with Pete, than with him."

The suspicion became almost a certainty. Carrie sighed. "Meghan, is there something about Jason . . . ?"

"I hate him!" she said flatly.

"Do you? That's not what I hear in your voice."

"I hate him."

"All right," Carrie conceded. There were tears misting the girl's eyes again, and Carrie knew from experience the tears were not from hate. When Jason had brought the girl to the ranch, she'd heard evidence in his voice that said their relationship was not quite as Jason had outlined it. She hoped at the time that Jason had finally found a girl who might civilize him, curb the violent streak in his nature and set his energies to more worthwhile pursuits than wandering and fighting. Now, as she heard the same evidence in Meghan's voice and saw the look in her eyes, she felt an odd need to protect the girl. She was so innocent, so vulnerable behind her facade of pride and anger. She was a tender morsel that Jason Sinclair could snap up in one bite and utterly destroy. And knowing Jason, he could do that without a thought to what he was doing. How wrong she'd been to hope there was something between the two of them. She'd been ready to set a wolf loose on a lamb, expecting the lamb to bring the wolf to heel.

"Meghan, you can tell me this is none of my business, but . . . well, I know Jason quite well, you see. I think quite a lot of him, but I know what sort of man he is. Did he—"

"Yes, he did," Meghan said without shame before Carrie could finish her question. If she was going to trust this woman with her feelings, she saw no reason to draw a limit at this most painful of subjects.

Carrie's softly molded lips tightened to a grim line, and for some reason Meghan felt the need to defend Jason.

"It wasn't all his fault, Carrie," she almost whispered, remembering. "He thought I'd done something horrible, and he was terribly angry. All that anger—it just exploded into something else, for both of us." She paused, remembering the terror, the humiliation, and finally, the passion. "All he had to do was touch me, Carrie, and I was begging for more. Then, when it was over, I was so ashamed. I wished he had killed me instead of . . . of . . ."

Carrie's expression only got grimmer.

"When he found out he had made a mistake about what had actually happened, he apologized. Of course," Meghan hastened to assure her listener, "I didn't forgive him, or myself either. What we'd done was awful. Worse than awful. A honorable Cheyenne woman does not lie with a man not her husband."

Carrie's eyes darkened. "Did he hurt you so badly?"

"Worse." Meghan avoided her eyes, feeling a hot rush of blood to her face. "He didn't hurt me. It wasn't that simple. He made me . . . made me want him. It was as much me as him. When he shot me . . . and the Pawnee had us pinned down . . . I thought we were going to die." She turned and looked Carrie full in the eyes. "Right then I didn't want anything as much as I wanted him. I—"

Carrie interrupted, looking embarrassed. But the condemnation Meghan had expected to see wasn't in her eyes. "Meghan, dear, are you in love with that wolf of a man?"

Meghan considered a moment, hearing the sincere concern in the other woman's voice. She'd admitted it to herself. Could she admit it to someone else as well? "Can you love someone and hate them at the same time?"

Carrie smiled sadly. "The two are very close, I think."

"Then I suppose I am in love with Jason."

Carrie sighed. "That's what I was afraid of."

\* \* \*

The conversation in the barn lifted some of the burden of despair and loneliness from Meghan's heart. Carrie understood her situation and sympathized. She knew everything and still wanted to be her friend. She'd come no closer to solving her problem, but having an understanding friend helped immeasurably.

Slowly, Meghan grew skilled at running a household. She sewed a modest wardrobe for herself, helped Maria in the kitchen, and sat with Carrie long into the night in woman-to-woman conversations. The ranch hands no longer avoided her. Junior became her friend once again. She even managed to maintain an uneasy cordiality with Walks Alone. Slowly she came to understand the white man's way of thinking. She could now carry on a suitable conversation with even the most conservative matron, she knew, without uttering a single offensive word or mentioning a single taboo topic.

Carrie was delighted with her transformation, and even Pete was charmed by her new self. But Autumnfire Woman still lurked just below the surface of what was becoming a polished Meghan O'Brian.

Carrie didn't object and seemed to understand when she asked permission to help the hands tend the horses. Occasionally she would give in to temptation and ride out onto the rolling prairie. No one had any fear that she would try to escape, now. But the freedom of the untended grasslands beyond the river, the feel of a powerful horse between her legs, the fresh smell of wind, and the exultation of galloping over the plain sparked the warmth of memory of her free and wild years with the Cheyenne and renewed the pain that those days were gone forever.

Summer faded into autumn, and the green slopes of the Indian Peaks were streaked with the vibrant gold of the aspen. The first snow flew in October, followed by an unusual cold snap that set the winter coats growing on the horses. Pete and Walks Alone conferred frequently about supplies and plans to_see the cattle through what was shaping up to be a long hard winter.

Meghan found she was content, going about her daily routine with people who had become dear to her. Only the thought of Jason's return in the spring marred her new-found happiness. She didn't want to say good-bye to these people she had come to trust and to love. And she didn't want to have him near her again to set her heart to beating and her body to yearning for his. But she had until spring, she thought, to be happy.

It was fortunate she didn't know her problems were just beginning.

# Chapter Sixteen

Meghan leaned weakly against the footrail of the bed as another spasm of nausea gripped her. With a moan of despair she bent once more over the chamber pot. Tears streamed down her face as the dry heaves subsided, leaving her aching and dizzy. Not once in her life had she ever been sick. But for the last week she'd been plagued by nausea, dizziness, and lack of appetite.

There was no doubt in her mind what was causing her discomfort. For two months in a row now her menstrual flow had not come. It was due again in another week, but she'd given up the hope of seeing evidence she had escaped unscathed from Jason's virile offerings. At first she'd attributed her lack of bleeding to the emotional upheaval in her life. She'd known a woman once who'd stopped flowing for seven months after her husband was killed in battle. But now with the sickness, the tender swelling of her breasts, and her snappish and weepy moods, she had to face the truth. She was carrying Jason's child. Only three times had he spilled his seed inside her, twice in anger, once in need and passion. Only three times, yet he'd left her with a child growing under her heart.

She sat down weakly on the bed and looked out at the bluff that Jason had disappeared behind so many weeks ago. Would he laugh when he found out? Would he care? He'd probably be proud of his goddamn masculine virility, Meghan thought bitterly, without a thought of what that virility had done to her. What would she do? What could she do? If she were still with the Cheyenne, she would be ostracized for her sin. The same thing would happen among the whites. These people she'd come to love—Pete and Carrie and Junior, and even Walks Alone—would shun her. Now as she was just gathering her life together again, as she was just learning to make her way in the white man's world, Jason had stepped in again to ruin her life. He'd taken her carelessly and thoughtlessly with no heed given to the consequences. He'd taught her passion. He'd woven such a spell of desire with his male body that in the end she'd begged him to slake the appetites he'd inspired.

In a way she had brought about her own downfall. She couldn't lay all the blame at Jason's door, she told herself bitterly. Her woman's body had responded so readily to his teachings that the only thing she'd wanted, when she was about to die, was to have him inside her once more. And her body had taken what he'd offered and nurtured it, until now a child grew in her belly. She sat on the bed and wept.

The sun was just rising when Meghan opened the door to the main barn. The warm mustiness of the interior was a welcome respite from the sharp October chill in the morning air. She recognized the broad cheerful face of Rodrigo

Chavez as he poked his head out of the tack room to see who had come in.

"Is there anyone that especially needs exercise?"

He grinned. "They all need exercise, señorita. But it's a cold morning for a ride. Maria says snow is coming, and she can always tell." He chuckled. "She says it's in her bones."

Meghan gave him a wan smile in return. "I won't be long. But I would like to ride."

"Take Satan, then. He grows fat in his stall. He won't be able to do his job, I tell him, when Ladybug comes in season. But he just ignores me and keeps eating."

Satan was not nearly as rotund as Rodrigo implied, but neither did he live up to his fearsome name. Black as night with no white on him anywhere, he had soft and gentle eyes that were unusual in a stallion. He nickered softly as Meghan approached his stall with saddle and bridle and made no objection as she pushed the steel bit into his mouth.

The wind was sharp as she led Satan out of the barn, but Meghan ignored its bite. She had to get away from the house, away from people. Only in the open air would her mind be clear enough to think. And she had to think, had to put aside the turmoil of her emotions and consider with intelligence and keenness what she should do. Now she had not only her own life to think about. She had another life as well.

She rode east to the river, then galloped south along its banks. As she urged Satan to a faster pace, an unwelcome thought pushed its way insidiously into her mind. If she rode hard enough and long enough, would she lose the babe? Wouldn't that solve her problem? No one would ever need to know. She could continue just as before. Her mind recoiled at the idea and she abruptly reined Satan in on the crest of a bluff overlooking the river.

The sun was well above the horizon now and was beginning to take the edge off the chill in the air. The frost that rimed the prairie grasses was rapidly disappearing. It promised to be a beautiful October day. The snow and cold of the week before was melting into a beautiful Indian summer.

Meghan was in no mood to appreciate the beauties of nature as she sat herself down on the edge of the bluff and looked out to the silvery ribbon of the South Platte. The brisk gallop had cleared the cobwebs from her brain, but her situation looked no better in the light of clear thinking. The deed was done, and she would have to pay for Jason's passion, and hers too. She would grow huge and awkward and everyone looking at her would know what she had done. She would give birth to Jason's child, and he would no doubt come out of her womb tawny-haired and amber-eyed and grow up to be a wanderer and a killer who could tame wolves and horses with a touch and tame women with a look. Just like his father.

Tears coursed down Meghan's wind-reddened cheeks, and she gave in to the impulse to draw up her knees and bury her face against the softness of her riding skirt. She wasn't up to this, she told herself. She wasn't up to facing the world's condemnation and Jason's indifference. She wasn't up to raising a child on her own in a world she could hardly cope with herself. If only she could wave her hand, and magically everything would be as it was before her world had shattered. She would be back with Stone Eagle, flirting with Red Shield, laughing with Buffalo Calf Road Woman. If only she could go back to that time when she'd not known the meaning of fear, and hate and passion and love. She'd been a child when she'd ridden off with Two Moon's band to confront the white men on Rosebud Creek. She'd thought of herself as a woman grown, but she'd been a child, Meghan realized. How beautiful it would be to be a child again.

She raised her head from her knees and wiped her eyes. Life seemed impossibly hard. She looked down the steep slope of the bluff. There would be one solution, she thought. A few moments of pain, then nothing. She would never have to face the accusations, the condemnation, the pity. She would never have to face Jason. It was a long fall to the bottom of the bluff. The rocks were sharp. There would be no chance of surviving. It would be a quick and sure solution.

She stood up, poised on the very edge of disaster. A sudden gust of cold wind pressed against her back, urging her out and over. She tottered, almost losing her balance. Then her eyes opened wide and she sat down abruptly.

Meghan trembled with the knowledge of what she had almost done. She, Autumnfire Woman, who'd ridden to war with Two Moon, who'd survived capture and degradation with a proud and courageous spirit, was about to throw herself off a cliff because a heedless man had gotten her with child. She, who'd always prided herself on her independence and self-reliance, was ready to kill herself because she felt deserted by the man who'd wronged her and despised by a society of prim matrons and their leering, two-faced husbands. Who were they to make her quail before their scorn? Who was Jason that she should fear his desertion, or even his indifference? She would survive, goddammit! She would not only survive, she would show them all. And most of all she would show Jason. He owed her. He'd taken her from her family and destroyed her innocence for his own pleasure. He'd dragged her into this world and then made it impossible for her to succeed. But he would make it right, Meghan vowed. She would demand that he make it right. When he returned in the spring to take her to California, she would demand that he marry her. She would have Carrie and Pete to back her demand. He must give the babe a name and give her the security of being his wife. Then he could do whatever he pleased. He could even divorce her if he insisted. And he would certainly be welcome to leave her. Meghan wanted no part of trying to tie down the wind, and that would be easier than making Jason Sinclair stay in one place and cleave to one woman. He was a throwback, a man who lived by his strength and his wits, a man who felt closed in by four walls and who preferred the open prairie or the mountain wilderness to the company of his fellow human beings.

In a way, Meghan realized, Jason was wilder than the Indians the whites labeled savages. Such a man would never tolerate a woman and a child tagging at his heels. And Meghan certainly didn't want to be a burden to a man who didn't want her. Given the respectability of marriage, she could raise the child on her own. And he wouldn't grow up to follow in his father's footsteps. He wouldn't grow into a man whose speed with a gun and accuracy with a knife were the only things that stood between him and a violent death. He wouldn't grow into a man who fought for the sheer hell of it, killed without a second thought, and preferred the company of a wild wolf over the companionship of his fellow man.

Her son, Meghan vowed, would grow into a proper white man, with a proper education. He'd be able to fit into the white man's world so well that no one would ever guess his father was a half-civilized gunman and his mother a onetime warrior woman of the Cheyenne.

"Meghan!" The sharp voice interrupted her silent planning. She turned to see Walks Alone leading his horse toward the edge of the bluff where she sat.

"Rodrigo told me you'd gone out early this morning. I've been looking all over for you!"

Meghan bristled at his tone. "Why? I'm quite all right. I can take care of myself."

"Not if you don't have sense enough to let someone know where you're going, you can't! Rodrigo told you there's snow coming in. What do you think you're doing riding out alone when there's a storm coming?"

"It's a beautiful day! There's not a hint of . . ." She broke off at the exasperated look on the Pawnee's face. Then she noticed the bite to the wind. She had been so engrossed in her own problems she hadn't noticed the change in the wind's direction. She looked to the south, whence it blew. Heavy gray clouds hung low on the horizon. Wind-torn forerunners scudded in front of the oncoming weather and showed the speed at which it was moving. "Well," she continued somewhat lamely, "it *was* a beautiful day."

"What would you have done if you'd been caught out here in an autumn blizzard? You'd never have found your way back."

Meghan wrinkled her freckle-dusted nose in disbelief as she mounted the patient Satan. "Piffle!" she said, borrowing Carrie's favorite word. "I'd have found my way back."

They rode abreast at an easy trot as the first outrunners of hard, icy snow pelted their backs. Walks Alone glanced over his shoulder at the massing of clouds moving swiftly toward them. "Experienced men have been known to lose their way in these storms, and this one looks like a good one. If any harm had come to you, Jason would've had all our hides."

Meghan laughed. Now that her vow was made, she found that the mention of Jason's name no longer sent such a stab of pain through her heart. "It would only serve to rid him of a nuisance," she declared. "He wouldn't have cared."

The Indian looked at her and shook his head, then nudged his horse into a canter. He shouted over his shoulder as she dug her heels into Satan's sides, urging him to catch up. "Meghan O'Brian! You're a bigger fool than I thought you were."

The storm was a bad one. An hour after the first icy flakes pelted down from the sky, the green pasture grass was buried under a blanket of white. Now, a full day later, the sky was still a sullen gray. The air was no longer white with swirling eddies of frozen flakes, but a light snow was still falling. Meghan's room was frigid, but she didn't dare leave its privacy until her nausea had subsided. Her morning distress had become a regular event in the last few days, and Meghan thought wearily that if the entire nine months of pregnancy was like this, she couldn't understand why any woman would want a child. She'd noticed in the mirror this morning that the shadows under her eyes were becoming more and more pronounced, and her face was beginning to take on a gaunt look.

In spite of her determined vow to brave the world's scorn, she wanted to keep her condition a secret as long as possible. No sense running to meet trouble just because you see it looming ahead, she told herself. The ground might open in a great chasm tomorrow and swallow them all, then her worries would all be irrelevant. Of course, she conceded, that wasn't likely to happen, and before long someone was going to wonder why she hadn't been coming to breakfast and had been only picking at her other meals. But until then she would be sick in the privacy of her own room and be grateful that her profile still looked slim as any maiden's.

The day of reckoning came sooner than she had bargained for. If her sickness had been confined to the morning hours, she might have avoided discovery for another month, but when the nausea began to plague her off and on throughout the entire day, she was hard-pressed to carry out her normal routine under the watchful eyes of Carrie and Maria. Even with all her precautions to hide her discomfort, Carrie had remarked to her several times that she was looking worn and hollow-eyed and should try to get more rest and eat more.

It was the last day of October and the snapping cold that had accompanied the last storm had once more given way to mild sunny days. The sunlight streaming in the large south-facing windows combined with the heat of the wood-burning cookstove to make the kitchen hot. Meghan labored over the kneading of a double batch of sourdough bread, while Maria hummed as she cut up vegetables to drop into the stew simmering on the stove.

Junior came through the door with a load of split stovewood in his arms. He dumped the wood in the box by the stove, then stood up and took a deep sniff of kitchen aroma.

"You need someone to try out that stew, Maria?" he offered with a grin.

Maria scowled with mock menace. "You stay away from this stew, boy! You'll get enough at dinner."

"Awww."

"Be off with you!" she warned, stifling a smile. "You eat more than anybody else as it is! You go back to work. Earn your dinner."

"That boy!" she said as he left. "He must have a lot of growing left to do, the way he makes food disappear."

The subject of food was not sitting well on Meghan's stomach. The heat of the kitchen, combined with the effort of kneading the heavy mass of dough, was making her woozy. The aroma of Maria's beef stew, a dish she had always loved up until today, was making her stomach cringe in rebellion. She clenched her jaw to keep the waves of nausea at bay, but as she continued doggedly at her task, minute by minute the heat seemed to grow more stifling and the aroma of the stew more sickening.

Carrie stuck her head in the door from the hallway. "Meghan, when you're through there, could you lend me your hands to help wind this skein of yarn?"

"Certainly," Meghan replied through clenched teeth, knowing there was no way she was going to make it that long. She looked up to give Carrie a compliant smile, hoping against hope that by some miracle her sickness would subside long enough for her to make an excuse to Maria and hurry to her room. As she raised her head the edges of her vision went black. Her eyes felt as if they were crossing. The kitchen suddenly seemed to tilt, throwing her to one side. Before she could regain her balance the room tilted in the opposite direction. The floor came up to meet her and everything went black.

Carrie bent over Meghan's prostrate form on the bed and gently wiped a cool wet cloth over her brow and cheeks.

"Are you awake now, dear?"

Meghan opened her eyes and sighed. For a moment the bed seemed to spin, then it settled into its proper state of stability.

"What happened?" she asked weakly.

Carrie smiled. "I was about to ask you the same question."

Meghan raised herself on one elbow and looked around her in confusion. "I fainted?"

"Yes," Carrie told her with a hint of concern in her eye. "You did."

"Oh." Meghan dropped back onto the pillows, still feeling light-headed.

"Meghan," Carrie began carefully. "Is there something you might want to tell me?"

Meghan wondered briefly if she could get away with lying, then she decided against it. Carrie was too astute a woman, and from the look in her eye she'd already guessed the truth. Trying to deny it would only make the situation worse. "I guess there is something you should know," she admitted unhappily.

Meghan was silent for a moment. She sought for words to reveal her situation in a delicate manner that wouldn't offend the sensibilities of a woman as refined as Carrie. There were none, she finally decided.

"Well?" Carrie arched a delicately winged brow in gentle query.

"I'm pregnant," Meghan blurted out.

Carrie was silent a moment. Then she sighed. "So I feared. Jason is the father, of course."

Meghan's pale face twisted in a mirthless smile. "Of course." She hesitantly met Carrie's eyes, ready to shy away if the contempt she expected was there. It wasn't. Carrie was smiling gently. Her soft brown eyes seemed to hold sorrow, regret, concern, but nothing more.

"How long have you known this, dear? How long have you been hiding your sickness and keeping this secret bottled up inside you?"

"Not long," Meghan murmured. "I've only been sure

for about two weeks . . . when I started to get sick." She was urged on by Carrie's sympathetic eyes. "In another way, I guess I've suspected for a long time. The last time we . . . we were together . . . Jason and I . . . something inside me felt his seed had taken root." She blushed lightly. "Coming here, meeting new people, new problems, the feeling sort of went into the back of my mind. I didn't think about it again until I started feeling sick. I've missed my flow three months in a row. I'd hoped maybe it was just the hurt of being taken away by Jason . . . but now . . . now I know that's not it."

"Dear Meghan," Carrie comforted. "Such a burden to bear alone. I wish you'd come to me earlier."

The door opened a crack and Maria peered in.

"Come in, Maria. She's awake."

The ample señora came to the bed and frowned down at Meghan. "*Chica!* You gave me such a scare!"

Carrie patted Meghan's hand reassuringly. "She's fine, Maria. Do you remember that herbal brew you made for yourself when you were so sick with little Anita? Do you think you could brew some up for our little Meghan here?"

Maria lifted her brows in surprise. "Sí, señora, but . . ." Her face lit with comprehension, then consternation. "Oh, my poor little *chica*. My poor little señorita. What are we . . . ?"

Carrie stopped her outpouring of sympathy. "You get your special tea, Maria. Meghan will be just fine."

The señora left the room in a dither, and Carrie turned back to Meghan. "Now, we must make you feel better, then decide what we are going to do about all this."

Meghan's face took on a stubborn set. She hoped for Carrie's support, but no matter what, she planned to stick by her own decision.

"When do you think the babe is due, Meghan?"

"Early spring," she replied in a resigned voice. "April at the latest. Jason won't be back in time for the delivery of his son."

Carrie laughed softly. "A son, is it?"

"It must be a boy." Meghan grimaced. "A girl wouldn't think of making her mother so sick."

Carrie laughed, then her face became solemn again as she picked up Meghan's hand and held it in her own. "Perhaps we'll be lucky and Jason will be back. But whether he's back or not will make no difference. Of course Jason will have to marry you."

Meghan looked at Carrie in surprise.

"Why look so startled, dear? We can't send you off to your relatives in California an unwed mother, can we?"

"It's just that," Meghan stammered, "when I was sure I was going to have a baby, I thought the same thing. I must get Jason to marry me. I just haven't figured out how to do that, yet." She was more relieved than she cared to admit that Carrie's thinking was the same as her own.

Carrie stood up and took the basin of water from the nightstand. "Don't worry about that. Jason will marry you. You just worry about keeping yourself healthy over the next few months."

Maria pushed through the door with a steaming cup of aromatic liquid. "You drink this, Señorita Meghan. You will feel better in no time. I know. I have seven children. With all of them I was very sick at first."

Meghan took the steaming cup and sipped at the contents. Even the aroma rising from the cup cleared her head and settled her stomach back into place.

"Well, Maria"—Carrie stood and smiled, her hands on her hips and looking very businesslike—"we must think of a way of bringing our yellow-haired wolf to heel."

"Sí," Maria agreed, looking at Meghan with motherly concern. She had a soft spot in her heart for Jason, but this time he'd gone too far. "We'll bait the trap, no?" She gave a gap-toothed grin. "See, we already have the bait I think."

"Yes, I think we do, Maria. I think indeed we do."

Meghan could swear that Carrie actually looked happy.

\* \* \*

Meghan's life returned to near normal as a dose of Maria's special tea every morning relieved her sickness for the most part. She worked diligently around the house and in the barn, trying as best she could to keep her mind from straying down alleyways that led only to depression and despair. Carrie and Maria, however, had never been more cheerful. They pampered her unmercifully, forbidding her to ride, scolding her for working too hard, hovering over her to make sure she ate a balanced diet. Meghan was grateful for their loving support, but sometimes she was tempted to think she'd be better off with their indifference.

Carrie and she fell into the habit of closing each day with a long, intimate chat. She felt comfortable with the older woman, more comfortable than she'd ever been with anyone, even Long Stepping Woman. She talked freely of her life with the Cheyenne without fear of her listener's contempt or hostility. She confided her fears, her hurts. She could even talk about the dilemma of her confusing love. Carrie could offer no solutions. But she listened with a sympathetic and even loving ear.

During one of these talks, Carrie warned Meghan not to say anything to anyone at the ranch about her relationship with Jason. It would be best, she told the girl, to arrange a wedding in secret and pass the story that Jason and Meghan had been married at Fort Laramie. That way there would be no unwelcome snickers. Maria and Junior and Walks Alone would know the truth, of course. But they were trusted friends. No word would ever leak from them about the wedding's taking place after the baby was born. There was a man working on a neighboring homestead who was ordained by some small sect back East. Occasionally he performed weddings, funerals, and baptisms for the local folk who were scattered in this region. He wasn't more than a couple hours' ride away. And he would be paid well to keep his silence.

Meghan wished she felt Carrie's confidence about Jason's acquiescence in the face of all these feminine plans. She couldn't imagine his being willing to give up his valued freedom, even if it was in name only. And Carrie and Maria both seemed to assume that Jason and she would live together as man and wife after a visit to her relatives in California. In fact, Maria had even voiced the hope that they would decide to stay at the ranch full-time.

Meghan knew better. Jason didn't want a wife, didn't need a wife. And she certainly didn't want to be tied to a man who didn't want her, a man whose chief thought was to be rid of her. She'd come to accept the fact that she loved him. But she would never tie him down. Let him drift here and there to satisfy the wanderlust in his soul. Let him flee to the wilderness to find the peace and isolation he desired. She would find a place for herself and their child. She could take care of herself.

Meghan nodded agreeably when Carrie or Maria expressed their hopes for her future. But privately she thought she had as much chance of making a real marriage with Jason as she did of capturing a panther tom and turning it into a tame house cat. She knew it couldn't be done.

# Chapter Seventeen

Jason lay flat on his stomach, ignoring the cold that was stiffening his limbs and making his feet and hands numb. His heavy buckskins blended in with the yellow-brown soil around him. Even his bronzed face and amber eyes were the same color as the dead pine needles carpeting the little hollow where he stretched out. Only his eyes moved, taking in the activity below his hidden perch. Crouched beside him, Wolf was just as still.

Jason had half-expected he was following another false lead, but apparently this time they had hit pay dirt. A large Cheyenne village stretched out below him in its customary pattern, with the break in the circle of lodges facing east. Women were going peacefully about their tasks, and children ran and played among the lodges and along the banks of the stream, only loosely supervised by the indulgent women. Perched as he was on the steep hillside above the camp, Jason could hear the women's chatter and the children's shrill laughter. A few old men lounged in front of their lodges, and Jason guessed that most of the young men were off hunting. A group of three aged warriors sat in front of one lodge chatting and whittling. Puffs of smoke from their pipes rose into the still winter air.

Less than a week ago Jason and a small group of his scouts had brought a captive to General Ranald MacKenzie's headquarters at Fort Reno. The young Cheyenne, a warrior by the name of Beaver Dam, had been surly and silent at first, but after seeing the overwhelming odds against him he was ready enough to talk. Among the things he said, one piece of information sent MacKenzie's troops into a flurry of activity. Crazy Horse was camped with his people on the Rosebud River. MacKenzie conferred hurriedly with his officers. Jason, being the head of the contingent of scouts, was among them.

Over the next days the whole command was moved to the Crazy Woman's fork of the Powder River, from where MacKenzie would launch an expedition against Crazy Horse. Before the general's plans could be acted upon, however, another Cheyenne rode into camp, this one of his own free will. He was from the Red Cloud Indian Agency. Beaver Dam's people, he reported, were moving to join Crazy Horse on the Rosebud. And a large Cheyenne village was camped at the head of the very stream on which the soldiers were now camped.

Jason had had his doubts about the Red Cloud Indian's veracity, but MacKenzie abruptly changed his plans. They would attack the village at the head of Crazy Woman's fork.

On November 24, General MacKenzie took his cavalry units, Jason's scouts, and the Indian scouts upstream to find the Cheyenne village. Jason and his men ranged ahead of the column to prevent a surprise attack, but all was peaceful. The first day the column covered twelve miles. The second day the country became more broken. The going was rough over steep-sided ravines cluttered with windfalls.

Jason had gotten far ahead of the troop, and now in the pale afternoon sun he lay in silent watchfulness above the village that was their quarry. The Cheyenne from Red Cloud had been telling the truth. The village was here, and it was a large one. Jason guessed from the tranquility of the scene that the Indians had no notion that soldiers were advancing on their peaceful camp. His military instincts told him if they were to surprise the village when it was least prepared, say in the first light of dawn, victory would be certain. He tried to ignore the part of him that flinched at the picture that flashed into his mind—a picture of women and children rudely awakened from their sleep to face the bullets and swords of soldiers all too anxious to slaughter anyone with copper skin, regardless of sex or age. The happy scene he was watching now would be transformed into the chaos of blood and fear and anger, flashing steel and smoking guns.

Jason mentally shook himself. He'd seen enough cruelty and killing in his lifetime to inure him to the razing of one insignificant village of Indians. Still, he wished that they hadn't found the village and that these people could be left alone to go on their peaceful way. But that wasn't the way things worked out, he told himself sternly as he silently extricated himself from his nest of leaves and pine needles. The sun was nearing the horizon. The column would be stopping soon and General MacKenzie would expect a report.

Jason's report and evaluation of the situation met with approval. The troops groaned when told they would be moving again as soon as the moon rose. But as rumors flew about the unsuspecting vulnerability of the village the groans stopped. It had been a hard and frustrating campaign this summer and fall of 1876, and the men were eager to douse their weary frustrations in the blood of their enemy. It appeared that this would be their chance.

Jason sat leaning against the rough trunk of a pine and ate a cold dinner. Cookfires were forbidden. No telltale trace of smoke must rise into the dusky evening sky to warn the village of their coming. No scent of burning wood must be carried on the breeze to alert the Indians to their danger. So Jason sat alone and ate his cold jerked beef and biscuits. The other scouts were straggling in, but only Jason had seen trace of the enemy. The village was well hidden, and he'd been lucky to spot it. Or maybe not so lucky, he mused.

Meghan probably knew some of the people in that village, he thought. Maybe even some of them were men and women she thought of as relatives. It was hard to think of the chatting women, laughing and yelling children, and old men that he'd seen today as enemies. It would be easier to face the warriors. They at least had as much blood on their hands as the white soldiers.

Jason took another bite of biscuit and chewed it unenthusiastically. It tasted as though it had been in a saddlebag for several months. Knowing the army, it might have been, but he suspected his lack of appetite had more to do with the coming skirmish than the quality of the rations. He was growing soft, Jason told himself, and since meeting Meghan he'd grown especially soft on Indians. That female was playing havoc with his thinking.

Back when he'd had Meghan constantly under his eye and hand, Jason had told himself that once he was rid of her, normality would return to his life. He'd never met a woman who could extend her influence much beyond the doorway of her bedroom. Out of sight, out of mind.

But images of Meghan continued to plague him—Meghan laughing, Meghan pouting, Meghan crying, Meghan angry. Thoughts of her warm lissome body lying next to his, under his, flashed through his mind at the most awkward times, producing a physical reaction that could make him uncomfortable for hours. His nights were harried with moment by moment recollections of the last time they'd made love—she, bloody and in pain and fully believing that death would come with the sunrise, and still unbowed. He, hot as a stallion who'd been held off a mare ripely in season and yet still eager to show tenderness and comfort. It had been that night he fully realized what danger lurked in those deep green eyes, those inviting lips, that young and eager and oh-so-female body. The girl didn't realize what power she possessed, he thought, and it was a damn good thing she didn't! He almost wished he'd left her at Fort Laramie and told the commandant to hell with what he wanted. Bess would've been glad to take her in for a few months, and the commandant would've taken responsibility for the girl if he'd simply up and deserted her. Why he hadn't was beyond him. He was asking for trouble going back and escorting Meghan to California. He had a feeling he was going to be sorry.

The dusk had thickened into night. Stars were popping out of the dark vault overhead, and a dim glow on the horizon signaled the imminent appearance of the moon. The camp stirred with the movements of men getting ready to ride and trying to be quiet about it. Only an occasional clink of a spur or creak of leather disturbed the night. Here and there the murmur of low-voiced conversation drifted by on the light breeze. By the time the magnified orange ball of the moon rested on the horizon, the column was on its quiet way. Jason hadn't seen the men so disciplined in a long time. They're anxious for blood tonight, he thought. In a way he couldn't blame them, but part of him still cried out for the innocents up ahead, going about quiet lives with no inkling of the fate riding down on them.

The night stretched out. They'd ridden for an hour when a stray breeze carried the sound of drums and singing. The camp was celebrating something—a wedding perhaps or a social get-together for the unmarried men and maidens of the tribe. It'll be your last celebration, Jason thought bitterly. So live it up while you can.

They rode for three hours. When they stopped, the revelry was still in full swing, and now the sounds of celebration were audible even when the erratic breeze blew in the wrong direction. That meant they were close enough for the noise of the advancing column to carry to the village. With all the shouting and singing and drumming they would probably never hear the evidence of their advancing enemy. But General Mackenzie was a cautious man. He told the men to get what sleep they could and warned that the first man to make an unnecessary noise would be court-martialed personally by MacKenzie himself.

They were in position before dawn, sitting cold and silent and motionless in their saddles. Finally in the dim gray light they could discern the village, upwards of fifty lodges clustered in their circle with high cliffs at their back and steep, rugged slopes on either side. The enclosing slopes were broken in only a few places by ravines and swales. It was a well-hidden campsite, and a dead-end trap for the Indians if anyone attacked them from downstream, which MacKenzie's force was about to do.

MacKenzie sat in his saddle and regarded the village with canny eyes, noting the few routes of escape, noting the size and position of the lodges in an attempt to pick out the ones belonging to the leaders. The village was quiet. Only from one lodge on the far side of the circle did smoke rise from the smokehole, indicating the women of the lodge were stirring. Even the dogs were asleep, it seemed, for no barking alerted the Cheyenne to the presence of the enemy in the valley just below their camp.

MacKenzie raised an arm, then dropped it. "Charge!"

His command echoed in the dawn's gray stillness. The morning silence was abruptly broken by the muffled thundering of hundreds of hooves and raucous voices shouting in chorus as the cavalry and scouts galloped down upon the sleeping village. The Indians woke in panic. Dogs barked at the oncoming tide of horses and soldiers. Women screamed and children cried. The first shot in defense of the village was fired as a groggy warrior emerged from one of the lodges closest to the charge, stark naked, cartridge belt in one hand, rifle in the other. That brave and the others who joined him seconds later were plowed down by bullets and trampled by steel-shod hooves. In less than a minute the wave of soldiers was halfway through the encampment, shooting anything and anyone who moved without regard to age or sex, pulling lodges down around their startled and half-asleep occupants.

Some warriors stood their ground, firing steadily at the soldiers, horses, or anything else they could get in their rifle sights that looked as if it belonged to a white man. Others herded the women and children up the steep slopes and ravines away from the fighting. Within minutes of the attack the Indians had an organized defense mounted. But even they realized it was hopeless. The bluecoats had the advantage of both numbers and position. The only good escape route was blocked. The Indians could escape up the slopes only as a band of separated stragglers, not an organized force. And first they must get their women and children to safety. Already several pathetic bodies of little ones littered the ground, one covered by the dead body of a young woman, as if even in death she was trying to protect him. Seeing these testimonies to the ruthlessness of the bluecoat attackers, the braves fought even more fiercely, even though the more battle-wise among them knew they were doomed to lose.

Jason was in the rear of the attack. He had no stomach for shooting sitting ducks or sleeping Indians, so gun still holstered, he broke off from the line and headed for the horse corral, intending to set the herd to flight. His stallion swerved abruptly as a brown-skinned form darted in front of him. His hand automatically flew to his pistol. In a swift blur of motion the gun was in his hand and his finger was tightening on the trigger.

"Goddammit to hell!" He fired into the air instead of at the cowering figure so nearly missed by the stallion's flying hooves. The young squaw stared at him in wild-eyed terror, her eyes big and brown as a startled doe's. She stood rooted to the spot and didn't move even at the sharp report of the gun in his hand.

"Run, woman! Get your children and run, goddammit!" He urged the black forward and nudged the terrified woman with his foot. "Git!"

It suddenly dawned on the woman that this white man with the strange eyes was not going to kill her. He was, in fact, urging her to make her escape. Her face broke into a smile, then she turned and fled into the dawn, light-footed and agile as a young deer. Jason watched her until she reached the cover of a brushy ravine and joined another woman who was fleeing the same way. He knew he would gun down any soldier who fired on them. They melted into the brush. He watched until he was certain they were safe. The distraction was nearly fatal.

The brave seemed to come from nowhere to launch himself at Jason's back. Unprepared, Jason was knocked from his stallion and landed hard on his back, driving the breath from his body. While he was still gasping for air, the Cheyenne pounced on him, knife poised to slash his throat. Jason was barely able to deflect the blow, and the brave's knee on his chest wasn't helping him get his breath back. In a desperate effort he heaved up and toppled the brave off, then rolled away as the Cheyenne knife once more descended to taste his blood.

Now Jason was on his feet. His vision cleared as his chest heaved to take in much-needed air. The formerly peaceful valley was filled with gunshots, screams, and shouts, but his world narrowed to the brave who stood poised and grinning before him. He had dropped his pistol when he'd fallen, but his fingers moved to close around the familiar hilt of the long-bladed knife whose tooled-leather scabbard always rested against his hip. It came into his hand smoothly, almost of its own will. Its contours were as familiar as the curves and hollows of his own hand. The razor-sharp steel caught the morning sun and glittered dangerously.

The Cheyenne brave's grin broadened as he noted the ease with which the long-bladed knife slipped into the white man's grip. Here was an opponent, he thought, who was worth killing. He would cherish this one's scalp and sing praises of his prowess to the gods. He would petition the spirits to help him along the road to his own after-world. But first he must kill him.

The Cheyenne made the first move, slashing in unexpectedly to open Jason's chest and spill out his heart. Jason was no longer there when the knife arrived though, and the brave couldn't dodge away fast enough to avoid the blood-hungry blade that whipped along his ribs. The Indian whirled away from the burning in his side, but recovered sufficiently to make a kick that connected with Jason's chest and sent him sprawling. The brave followed up his advantage and was on Jason in a split second, but Jason's upraised knee plowed into his groin and doubled him up in agony. He landed on his back, writhing in pain and grabbing desperately between his legs.

Jason used the time to roll to his feet. The Cheyenne staggered to his feet also, his face white with strain under its natural coppery tint. They circled each other warily, each aware that his opponent was a man of rare stamina and fighting ability. Jason feinted and got a slash to his upper arm for his efforts. He backed away and told himself to use more caution with this man, or he'd end up spilling his life's blood onto the ground. He watched his opponent's eyes with a concentration that refused to be distracted by the hypnotic weavings of the man's knife. He saw the eyes flicker just before the Indian struck, and he was ready. Instead of trying to dodge the blow, Jason moved with lightning swiftness to grab the Indian's wrist with his left hand. He held on for dear life and twisted. The crack of bone and a scream from the brave testified to the success of his ploy. He followed it up with a knife thrust to the chest.

The brave's life would have ended right then, but Jason's knife was deflected by a rib and missed the heart. Still, the knife sunk into muscle, bone, and cartilage up to the hilt. The Cheyenne gasped and turned ashen. His right arm hung useless at his side, and blood poured from a knife slit in the side of his chest. His enemy could finish him off with no effort now, and the Indian could make hardly a move to defend himself. He expected to see death in the strange amber eyes of the white man, but only weariness was there. He'd seen that weariness before in the eyes of warriors who'd seen too many battles, who'd left too many men dead in their wake.

Jason kicked the Cheyenne's knife far out of the man's reach and wiped his own bloody blade on his fringed buckskin trousers. "Get out of here, you shit-assed son of a bitch!"

The brave needed no second invitation. He turned and staggered away without a single look back. Jason sheathed his knife, then picked up the brave's from where it lay in the dirt and stuck it in his belt. No telling when another knife might come in handy. He watched the Cheyenne warrior disappear into the brush at the edge of the village. He was getting goddamned soft, he told himself with disgust. He should've killed the bastard without even thinking about it. Probably end up getting killed for it, he thought with disgust.

He moved to retrieve the black stallion, who was standing deceptively placid amidst the confusion and noise. An enterprising Cheyenne brave had approached him while Jason was fighting for his life and had barely missed being pounded with steel-shod hooves for his efforts.

Before Jason reached his horse though, a shadowy figure moved out from behind a lodge. He was as tall as Jason, and though his face was lined with the seams of age, his body was still hard and muscular.

"Come kill me, white man. If you can."

"Shit!" Jason turned and drew his knife from its sheath once again, wishing he'd had time to find and retrieve his pistol. One well-aimed bullet would put an end to this challenger, and he was tired beyond measure. He was tired of killing, tired of fighting, tired of spilling his own blood onto the dust and watching other men pour out theirs as well. "Why don't you go into the hills, old man? There's no victory for you here today."

"A warrior does not run into the hills with the women," the older man replied calmly. "If you think it is a good day to die, come fight me."

Jason sighed, then with grim face he advanced with knife in hand.

The fight was impossibly long. They were well-matched, Jason and this warrior challenger. They were both veterans of many kills. They both knew all the tricks a man can play to place his opponent at a disadvantage. They each played them all. And none of them worked. After twenty minutes they were both panting, dirt-smeared, and bloody from numerous scratches that had not been deep enough to serve their purpose. The chaos around them had lessened. There were no more screams of women and children, for all that lived had fled up the steep brushy slopes and into the ravines. The soldiers and Indians had both dug into their respective positions, and rifle and pistol fire was regular and orderly. Only a few clots of men still struggled together in hand-to-hand fighting. But Jason and the warrior didn't have the spare time or energy to notice the progress of the battle. They were both fighting for their lives against an enemy whose strength seemed to surmount impossible fatigue, and whose mind seemed to anticipate every move before it was made.

They both stood panting, regarding each other cautiously from a distance of about ten feet. The eyes of the Indian flickered briefly, but didn't signal another attack. Instead, the grim lines of his face relaxed very slightly. The light in his eyes faded from anger to resignation. Slowly he straightened from his crouch, his black eyes gazing at Jason with unwavering intensity.

"I know you, Panther Who Walks on Two Legs," the

Cheyenne said in a gravelly voice. "I wanted to kill you. But now I see the gods have reserved you for a longer life. So be it."

Jason didn't relax his vigilance. A chill shivered down his spine. He'd never seen this middle-aged, good-looking brave before. He had the look of a chief, with a carriage and dignity that would make him hard to forget. There were many ways the Indian could have known the name the Pawnee had given him when he'd lived with them years before, but why would this man in particular want him dead? He could think of no reason, other than one.

"Who calls me by my Pawnee name?"

The Cheyenne slipped his knife back in its sheath, seeming confident that Jason would not use his advantage to attack. "I am Stone Eagle," he replied, "war chief of the Cheyenne, father of Autumnfire Woman, who you took from us at the battle on Rosebud Creek."

Jason schooled his face to impassivity. Of all the people to run into! Meghan's Cheyenne father! His grip tightened on his knife.

"Is my daughter well?" Stone Eagle asked.

"She is well." Jason didn't bother to deny it had been he who had stolen her.

"And happy?"

Jason was silent. Stone Eagle acknowledged with a nod of his head the answer that was conveyed by Jason's silence. A ghost of a smile played about his lips.

"Autumnfire is stubborn. She is slow to realize what is in her heart. It has always been so."

Jason relaxed his stance and deftly resheathed his blade. It was obvious now that Stone Eagle had given up the idea of trying to kill him. Their fight had taken them to an edge of the village circle where it was almost quiet. They stood in a shadow of one of the lodges, hidden from the view of both the soldiers and the Cheyenne.

The Indian was regarding him with intently assessing eyes. Finally he spoke again. "I think perhaps I see the will of the gods in allowing you to live, Panther Who Walks.''

Jason raised a tawny brow inquiringly.

"When I saw you and realized you were he who took my daughter, fury swelled inside me and blinded my thought. Now I see that you are a strong warrior and an honorable man. It is good you took Autumnfire.''

Good for who? Jason was tempted to ask. He figured the chief would have a good laugh if he knew how thoughts of the girl plagued his every waking moment, making his life miserable.

"The sun of the Cheyenne is setting," Stone Eagle glanced around him at the torn and toppled lodges and the bodies, both white and red, littering the ground. "It is good Autumnfire woman is with her people, where she will be safe. If she were here, she would know only grief. She will make you a good wife.''

"What?"

Stone Eagle all but smiled at his incredulous tone. His face softened as he recalled his daughter, and for the first time Jason could picture this fierce warrior as the father Meghan loved so dearly.

"You both have fire in your eyes," Stone Eagle told him solemnly. "Your fire will merge and make strong warriors of your children, sons who will be worthy of their father's strength, daughters who will reflect their mother's beauty.''

The two men looked at each other for a long moment. Jason had never seen an Indian wear his heart in his eyes, but that was what Stone Eagle was doing. He wondered if his feelings were as equally revealed. He wondered what his feelings were.

"Tell Autumnfire her mother and sister are safe. Tell her we love her.''

With that the Indian faded into the brush behind the lodge. One moment he was standing before Jason bold as life itself. The next moment he was gone. Jason wondered briefly if he were dreaming.

By early afternoon, after hours of fighting in which Indians and whites alike were slaughtered, the surviving Cheyenne retreated for the most part to the mountainsides above the village. General MacKenzie, seeing that victory was at hand, ordered the village destroyed. Jason worked with the others to pull down the lodges. They piled the lodgepoles and skins in the center of the circle, along with everything they could find of clothing, weapons, dried meat, and other foodstuffs. At the same time the wounded were tended and the dead were buried in a grassy flat area slightly downstream of the campsite. The Indian corpses were left where they lay to be victims of the scavengers that would come when the soldiers had left.

Jason flung one more lodgeskin onto the rapidly growing pile. He was sick to the soul and vowed this would be the last village he helped to destroy. Fighting mounted warriors on the field of battle or fighting for your life against an opponent as skilled and strong as yourself was one thing, but this harassing of women and children, this destruction of a very way of life, this was something else.

Something fell with a thump into the dirt by his boots as he ripped the next thick hide from the lodge. He bent down to pick it up. It was a wooden doll barely bigger than his hand. Her body was wrapped in a crudely cut and fringed piece of skin such as a very young child might fashion. His face twisted in disgust and he threw the doll on the ground. With a curse he turned and headed for where MacKenzie stood with a group of his officers.

"Are you really going to do this?" he demanded of MacKenzie in a voice sick with disgust. "It's almost December. You're signing a death warrant for those people out there!"

MacKenzie looked at him through narrowed eyes. "That's what I intend to do, Sinclair. Those are the enemy out there, in case you've forgotten."

"Those are women and children out there, in case *you've* forgotten!"

"Seems to me," MacKenzie said coldly, "that you've

had some experience with what the Indians have done to white women and children.''

Jason's mouth drew into a tight line. Indeed he had. But somehow that didn't justify in his mind what was happening here.

"You're a civilian, Sinclair. If you don't like the way I do things, you can ride on out. No one here is holding you.''

Jason didn't ride out though. He stayed to see the deed done. Pictures of the village as he'd seen it the day before, with the women going peacefully about their tasks and the children running wild and free and happy along the banks of the stream, kept flashing through his mind the rest of the afternoon. And the old men sitting in front of their families' lodges smoking their pipes and whittling the afternoon away—was one of those old grandfathers the one who had carved the doll he'd found? And the little girl who'd played with the doll, was she one of the bloody corpses they were leaving to the mercies of vultures and wolves? Or was she even now shivering on the mountainside, watching the soldiers prepare to burn her home to the ground?

The sun went behind the mountains early, throwing the valley into shadow. Darkness followed swiftly, and an advancing bank of heavy clouds veiled the stars. By the time MacKenzie ordered the fires lit, snow was shifting from the heavily laden sky, mixed with hard crystals of ice. A cold wind fanned the flames rapidly to life.

Jason sat on the black stallion and watched with a sick heart. Every item of clothing, every weapon, every bit of stored food had been piled into the center of the village circle along with the hides and lodgepoles. The entire livelihood of the village was being consumed in flames. He wondered what the Indians were feeling and what they were thinking as they crouched up on the mountainside watching the total destruction of their home, as he knew they were. How did they feel, chased out of their lodges by gunfire in the cold of winter, robbed of everything they'd accumulated to keep them alive through the coming months? How did the women feel, clutching shivering babies and frightened children to their breasts and watching the huge bonfire in the valley below?

An image of Meghan's face formed in his mind. Every detail of her was there—the flame-colored hair, the green eyes, the pert, freckle-dusted nose. She was watching the fire, and watching the Indians concealed on the mountainside. And she was crying.

# Chapter Eighteen

In the pastures stretching out from the big white house, tender shoots of spring grass poked their blades through the patchy snow, and here and there an early wildflower decorated the new green with a spot of bright color. Crocuses had sprung up in the flower bed next to the veranda. In the pastures closest to the barns new foals cavorted on spindly legs, and on the range tiny brown and white calves trailed close behind their placid mothers. New life abounded everywhere. Nowhere more so than in the big house itself.

Meghan sat alone on the veranda sewing a frilly mattress coverlet for the cradle Pete had made for her soon-to-be-born child. Her bulging stomach made a convenient perch for her sewing, and Meghan had jokingly mentioned to Carrie that she didn't know how she had learned to sew without her built-in table.

She was glad to see the coming of spring. It had been a long winter, and for her, a hard one. Her swelling abdomen was a constant reminder of her precarious future. Though she had tried to keep a brave face to the world, the uncertainty of her circumstances had weighed on her mind. Many a night she had lain awake, staring into the dark and wondering what would become of her, and her baby, if Jason out-and-out refused to give her the respectability of his name. The ranch hands all thought she was already Jason's wife, a deception insisted upon by Pete and Carrie, although Meghan had objected strenuously to living a lie. If Jason refused to make the fiction a reality, her humiliation would be all the more complete.

She sighed and put her sewing in the box beside her chair. She was in the process of heaving herself out of her seat when the front door banged shut behind Carrie.

"Oh, don't get up," Carrie pleaded. "I was just about to come out and sit with you for a while."

Meghan sighed and sank back down. "Your timing is bad," she complained. "You should've come out before I made the effort to get out of my chair."

Carrie laughed. "You are getting a bit big to be moving around much. But soon you'll have your old figure back. It can't be too long now."

"I hope!" Meghan answered with a wry smile.

The two women sat in companionable silence while Meghan took up her sewing again and Carrie pulled out some knitting. It was a shame, Meghan thought, that the peace and quiet and friendship she'd found at this place couldn't go on forever. But the end was near. Spring had come, and Jason would be hard on its heels, eager, no doubt, to see the end of his obligation—and the last of her. Was he ever going to get a surprise!

The thought of Jason's coming increased the tempo of her heartbeat in spite of her efforts to remain objective. All winter long she had tried hard to discipline her unruly heart, the heart that continued to swell with love whenever thoughts of that tawny-haired renegade came into her mind. And her body was even worse, going weak with longing at her memories of his hard, bronzed body covering hers. Well, she thought with a touch of wry humor, there certainly wouldn't be a problem with that when he returned. The sight of her as she was now, bloated and awkward, would dash cold water on his rampant desire. And after the baby came—her certainly wouldn't want to invite even more complications.

It would be just as well, Meghan told herself sternly, if he would fulfill his obligations, marry her, see her safely to her relatives, then ride out of her life. In the world of the Cheyenne Jason would have made an ideal husband—a deadly warrior, a great hunter. But in the white man's world, where a married man was expected to settle down and look after his wife and children, Jason wasn't husband material at all. Expecting him to play the proper husband would be like putting a panther in a cage and expecting the big cat not to chafe at its captivity. And to expect her to play the role of the white man's properly docile wife, she who had ridden to war with the great Cheyenne, who had run free and unfettered for the last ten years—that was impossible also. Marry her he must to erase her shame and to give their child a name. Then she must set him free. And somehow she must also set herself free of this unwelcome love that ruled her heart. She would start a new life with her relatives in California, or perhaps she could convince Jason to let her return to her people in Montana. It wouldn't be the same life she had known before, because she was no longer the same person. Nevertheless, they were her family. They were the people she loved. They were the ones who could heal the hurts she'd been dealt and had dealt herself over the past year.

Jason reined in the black stallion on top of the grassy bluff that rose just north of the ranch house. Tongue lolling, Wolf plopped down beside him. The scene stretched out before him was the same as it had always been— white-painted house, barns, and corrals. Green pastures stretching to the river, wild prairie range stretching beyond.

He wondered how well Meghan had survived the winter. With a half-smile he wondered also how Pete and Carrie had survived Meghan. When he'd left last fall he hadn't said good-bye. Now he realized he'd been afraid. Confronted with those flashing green eyes and appealing face, he might not have left at all. Now he was equally afraid to say hello, he, who had faced all the dangers of the wilderness, was afraid of a slip of a redhead who, without having half his strength or bulk, could usually manage to stun him with a single look or a single word.

The sight of the ranch had an appeal for Jason that it had never had before. The snug house, big barns, neat fences, and greening pastures seemed to be calling him. He felt almost as though he wanted to stay this time, a feeling he'd certainly never had before. The winter campaign against the Indians must have worn him down, he figured. He'd seen enough killing, enough senseless suffering. It seemed pointless after a while. The Indians were fighting a losing battle, and by now they knew it. The waste of life on both sides filled him with disgust. He was getting weak, he told himself, and soft. Time to stop scouting for the army. He'd get Meghan to California and then—who knew? Maybe he'd come back to Colorado and help out at his mine for a while or even settle down for a few months on the ranch. Or maybe he'd just head up into the mountains and hole up in a little cabin he knew about. In a place where no one except the deer and the bear and the wolverines came, he could wipe his mind free of the stench of blood and death. And he could wipe his heart free of its obsession with a green-eyed, redheaded, freckle-faced Irish Indian.

He touched the stallion with his heels and urged him down the steep incline toward the house. They slid a good part of the way down, since the sun had melted all the snow on the south-facing slope and turned it into a sea of mud. As the stallion trotted around the corner of the house, a lone figure at work in one of the corrals turned to watch.

"Ho, there! Walks Alone!" Jason called out in Pawnee.

Walks Alone shielded his eyes from the sun. "Jason!" His brown face split in a grin. "Welcome home, my brother."

Jason swung off the stallion and looped a rein over a fence post. The two men gripped each other in a bear hug then stood back.

"How is it with you?" Walks Alone's eyes were alight with a twinkle that Jason couldn't quite decipher. "We weren't expecting you for another month or so."

"Got tired of fighting," Jason commented casually. "How are things here?" There was an undertone of meaning to the question that Walks Alone understood perfectly. He understood his blood brother better than Jason understood himself.

"Things are... interesting," Walks Alone answered enigmatically. His lips twitched in amusement.

Jason raised a brow. "That's what I was afraid of. Maybe I'd better leave and come back in a couple of months."

"I wouldn't do that if I were you."

"That bad, huh?"

Walks Alone grinned an entirely un-Indian grin. "You'll see."

Carrie had witnessed Jason's arrival out the kitchen window as she stood peeling potatoes for the evening meal. "Oh, dear!" she sighed.

Meghan, sitting at the kitchen table cutting up vegetables for a stew, turned her head at her friend's exclamation. "What is it? Did that sorrel stud break out again?"

"Not exactly, dear." Carrie frowned and wiped her hands on her apron. She hadn't really expected Jason to return until after the baby had been born. She'd been hoping to break the news to him gradually and obtain his cooperation without the confusion of having him presented with a pregnant Meghan about to deliver.

"So what is it then?" Meghan asked, curious as to what had caused Carrie's agitation.

"Jason's here."

Meghan's knife clattered onto the table, barely missing a finger. She felt the blood drain from her face.

"Jason's here?" Surely not. Not now. She wasn't prepared, hadn't rehearsed what she would say to him, wasn't prepared mentally to withstand his onslaught on her senses.

"I'm afraid so. He just rode in. He's out there talking to Walks Alone."

Meghan pushed herself to a standing position. Every day it was getting more difficult to move around. And today especially she felt as if she were carrying a lump of iron low in her belly. But the trembling in her knees wasn't only from the weight in her stomach, she knew. Trying to ignore her trepidation, she waddled over to the window.

"Oh, no," she sighed. It was unmistakably Jason. She'd recognize that tawny head of hair and that broad-shouldered figure anywhere.

"You just go sit down again, Meghan. And don't be getting yourself upset. I'll take care of this."

"No, Carrie." Meghan straightened with difficulty and stuck out her chin in what she hoped was a determined manner. "This is my problem. This thing is between Jason and me. It's I who should confront him."

Carrie chuckled. "Well, it certainly was once between you and him." She was rewarded by a faint blush from Meghan. "But not anymore, dear. I really think it would be best if you stayed in here awhile or maybe lay down in your room. Give me some time to talk to him."

Meghan sat down again and Carrie took her silence for assent. She took off her apron and straightened her hair in the mirror in the front hall. Then, feeling almost as if it were her own future at stake instead of Meghan's, she stiffened her spine and walked through the door prepared to beard the fearsome lion.

Jason was leading his horse into the barn as Carrie stepped off the veranda.

"Jason!" she called, hurrying to catch up with him.

"What a pleasant surprise. We didn't expect you for at least a month yet."

Jason turned and waited for her with a smile. "So I hear. You're all making me feel as if I should've stayed and fought the Indians a little longer."

"Oh, no! I didn't mean that!" She was breathless when she reached him, as much from nervousness as from running across the yard. "I'm glad you're here early."

"Yeah, I figured you would be. I figured you'd be glad to get her off your hands. She's a handful, I know."

"Who?"

Jason tied the stallion to a ring in the barn wall and pulled the saddle from his back.

"Meghan. Who else?"

Carrie put her hands on her hips and regarded him sourly. "Why, you unfeeling lout!"

"Huh?" Jason turned in surprise and brushed against the stallion, who shied away in surprise, jerking the halter rope out of its tether. "Get over here, you damned piece of black horsemeat!" He turned to Carrie. "What do you mean, lout?"

"Imagine saying such a thing about a sweet girl like Meghan!"

Jason laughed. "Meghan? Sweet?"

"Yes, she's sweet! She's been a pleasure to have around. If it weren't that she ought to go meet her relatives, I'd beg you to leave her here. She's a wonderful help around the house and in the barns too. All the hands adore her."

Jason smiled as he led the black into a stall. Then he whistled Wolf to his side from where he was sniffing around a pile of dung one of the hands had carelessly piled outside a stall. "Are we talking about the same girl. Redheaded? Freckled? Mean-tempered?"

"She is not mean-tempered! You're more thickheaded than I thought. Why, it would take a heart of stone not to love that girl! She's a treasure! She's . . ."

"Wait a minute! What's going on here?" He took off his hat and ran his fingers through his thick tawny hair.

Then he fixed her with a jaundiced glare. "Here I ride in fresh from freezing my rear off in the Montana mountains and getting shot at all winter, and what kind of welcome do I get? Not so much as a 'howdy-do' or 'how was your winter' or 'glad to see you're safe and sound.' For some reason all you can talk about is what a paragon Meghan is. Now what's up?"

"Guess what's up!" The soft voice came from the barn door.

"Oh, no!" Carrie breathed.

Meghan moved from the doorway into the barn. Wolf whined a greeting and she absently stroked her fingers along his head when he ran up to sniff her. Silhouetted against the outside glare, her shape couldn't be mistaken.

"Holy hell!"

Meghan regarded him unwaveringly. Her face was pale, but her head was high. A defiant posture was difficult to maintain with her stomach preceding her by so many inches, but she did her best. He would not see her beg, she vowed. She would keep her dignity at all costs.

The first wave of incredulous amazement faded from his face. He smiled. Then he laughed, a deep, melodious sound that seemed to bounce off the walls of the barn.

Meghan and Carrie both regarded him angrily. It was hard for Meghan to hold on to her much-prized dignity in the face of his disrespectful hilarity. She had expected indifference or scorn or maybe even chagrin or embarrassment, but she hadn't expected laughter.

"What's so funny?" Meghan demanded in a dangerous voice.

Jason's laughter faded into chuckles. "Looks like I got here just in time!"

"Time enough to be present at the birth of your child!" Meghan shot.

Jason just laughed again. The secretive twinkle in Walks Alone's eyes was explained.

"Jason!" Carrie broke in. She looked mad as a vixen

whose cubs were threatened. "You're not going to deny the baby is yours! Why, I . . . !"

"Of course not!" Jason chuckled. "My lord! I barely looked at the girl! And look what happens!"

"I suspect you did a bit more than look at her, Jason," Carrie said acidly.

He smiled unashamedly. "Maybe just a bit more." He swept Meghan with a gaze that made her remember distinctly just how she'd come by her present condition.

Meghan's face colored to match her hair. She didn't know what to think. The most she'd expected was a reluctant acknowledgment of his responsibility. Jason almost looked as if he was enjoying himself!

"Come on, ladies." Jason took each of them by the arm and headed toward the doorway. "From the looks of this little girl, I suspect she should be in the house close to a stove where water can be boiled. And I guess you and I have some things to talk over, Carrie."

Meghan allowed herself to be escorted toward the house. The touch of his hand on her arm brought fresh heat to her face. She'd almost forgotten, during the long winter of his absence, just how strongly his nearness affected her. She'd forgotten how his broad shoulders stretched the buckskin of his shirt, how his tawny, sun-streaked locks fell in attractive disarray over his wide brow, and how his compelling, pantherlike eyes could make her giddy with a glance. His chiseled, bronze features seemed more beautiful to her than before he'd left. Instead of dulling her feelings for him, his absence had made him all the more dear to her. She mentally kicked herself for being the worst kind of fool. If this big man were to turn right now and take her into his arms, if he ever again so much as kissed her, she would be thoroughly lost. She would never be able to leave him with grace and dignity. She would never be able to let him leave. She vowed that would not happen.

Somewhere between the barn and the house they collected both Junior and Walks Alone, who were standing in conversation near the corral.

"Jason!" Junior greeted his hero enthusiastically. "Did you see . . .?" Then he noticed Meghan waddling by Jason's side, pulled along faster than she was wont to move by his hand on her arm. "Oh," he finished lamely. "I guess you did. Hi, Meghan."

"Hi, Junior." Meghan, still pale under her tan, smiled at the boy and breathed a sigh of relief as Jason stopped his long-legged advance toward the house. "Slow down, Jason," she puffed. "I can't move as fast as I used to."

He raised a tawny brow and regarded her with amusement. "So I see." He slapped Junior on the shoulder, a man-to-man gesture that made the boy throw out his skinny chest with pride. "Have you been taking care of things here while I was gone, boy?"

"Yessir! Except . . ." Junior looked at Meghan doubtfully. He certainly didn't want to be blamed for that!

Jason chuckled at the expression on his face. "I'm glad something's the same as when I left it."

Walks Alone strolled over to join the group with a knowing grin splitting his brown face. "My brother, I see you have found your homecoming present."

Jason grinned affably. "Quite a surprise."

"You deserved it," Walks Alone returned, his black eyes twinkling.

Meghan pulled her arm from Jason's grasp. She was tired of being the butt of something these men obviously thought was a huge joke. It was no joke to her. She was miserable and depressed, and her back ached horribly. She wasn't going to stand out in the cold April wind any longer listening to these overgrown boys laugh at her condition.

"Men!" she spat scathingly. "You're all a bunch of pea-brained animals! Come on, Carrie!" She took the older woman by the arm and pulled her toward the house. "I've got no mind to stand out here and listen to these grinning jackasses. Let's go in the house." She heaved herself up the veranda steps, then with a sidelong glance at Jason, she whistled Wolf to her side.

"Come on, Wolf," she called, ignoring Carrie's horrified expression at the prospect of having the beast in the house. "You've got too much class to hang around with those clowns."

The silver-gray beast gave his master a wolfishly apologetic grin and then trotted placidly to Meghan's side, looking at her with adoring eyes. Without hesitation he followed her into the house while Meghan shot Jason a smile of triumph.

"Well, if that doesn't beat all!" Jason growled, but his eyes were lacking their usual cold opaqueness. "First she wooes my own blood brother to her side, and now it's Wolf."

Walks Alone smiled knowingly. "I may be mistaken, my brother, but I think she has charmed the big bad Jason Sinclair also."

Jason frowned ominously. "Mind your own business, Brother."

Walks Alone ignored the warning. "Why else would she be carrying your child? I have never before known you to be so careless with one who is innocent."

"That girl's about as innocent as a rattlesnake," he murmured with a faint smile as he stepped onto the porch. "And I have a feeling I've just been snakebit but good."

The parlor was warm and cosy compared to the still-chilly April air outside. A fire was stoked up in the potbellied stove that stood in one corner. Close by the stove Meghan sat in an overstuffed chair, sewing spread out on her lap. She glanced up only briefly as Jason, Walks Alone, and Junior came through the door. Wolf lay at her feet, looking distinctly uneasy surrounded by four walls. His yellow eyes sent Jason an appeal for help. With a glance at Meghan he got up and trotted over to where Jason had paused by the door.

"Turncoat wolf!" Jason said gently, his tone belying his

words. "You deserve to stay in here and be a miserable layabout house dog."

Wolf whined and managed to look ashamed.

Jason motionned to the front door. "Well, go on, if you know what's good for you. Go redeem yourself by bringing home something for dinner."

Like an overanxious kid released from the schoolroom, Wolf pushed open the door and was out like a shot.

"You're turning him soft," Jason told Meghan, walking over to the cupboard that held the liquor. Too bad he couldn't escape as easily as Wolf had, he thought. He was caught but good this time, he figured. No way to get out and still call himself a man. Still, when he'd seen Meghan's bloated shape for some reason a burden had fallen off his shoulders. Why should he feel so lighthearted? He had avoided entanglements like a plague all his life. And here he was tangled up but good, and with a little spitfire who probably would maek his life miserable. So why wasn't he cursing the day he'd snatched her out of the valley of Rosebud Creek? He poured himself a whiskey, downed it, then poured another.

Pete clumped into the parlor, dusting the grime from his trousers with his hat. He looked at Jason, and at the whiskey in his hand.

"Kind of early in the day for that, isn't it?" Pete asked in a surprised voice. Then he looked at Carrie, and at Meghan, sitting tight-lipped over her sewing. He turned back and saw the tinge of ashen color under Jason's natural bronze. "Well, maybe not," he conceded.

Carrie sighed. Things were not going as she'd planned. She'd had a nice little speech rehearsed to say to Jason when he came back this spring, a speech that would be gentle and nonaccusing, but would leave Jason no doubt about his responsibilities toward Meghan and the child. Then she'd gotten nervous and started mouthing inanities that had gotten him in a suspicious dither. And Meghan had ignored her instructions and walked out to the barn bold as brass, challenging him with her swollen body.

He'd taken it rather coolly, she admitted. In fact, he'd even had the nerve to stand outside joking with Walks Alone about the circumstances of his return. She had at least expected him to be shocked. With a mental sigh she admitted she would never understand this enigmatic man for as long as she lived. She hoped Meghan had more luck than she did.

"Why don't you menfolk sit down," Carrie said. "Seems we have a lot to talk about."

Jason sat as instructed, but his first comment was a surprise. "I don't see much to talk about." His eyes locked with Meghan's, and for a moment it seemed that no one else was in the room. "Looks as if we better get a preacher out here right away. Wouldn't do to have my kid popping out without an official daddy."

Stunned silence followed his suggestion. Both Meghan and Carrie were prepared for an argument.

"But . . . !" Meghan was left with her mouth half open. She wanted to have to persuade him. That way she could set the terms of their marriage. She could tell him he would be free to go after she safely had his name.

"But what?" He raised a tawny brow at her and she felt her heart sink. She felt out of control, felt herself slipping into his power without being able to do a thing about it.

"But nothing!" Carrie interrupted hastily. She saw the growing rebellion on Meghan's face. What could be bothering the girl? She'd been afraid all along of Jason's refusing to give her child a name, and here the man was volunteering with no trouble at all. But from the look on Meghan's face Carrie suspected the girl was about to do something foolish. "Of course you two must be married immediately. In fact, Jason, I took the liberty of spreading the story that you and Meghan were already married . . . at Fort Laramie . . . so she wouldn't be subjected to any unpleasantness before you returned. So I think it's best we keep this ceremony strictly to ourselves."

"Good idea," Jason agreed readily. "And if any of the

hands get the idea they don't believe the story, they'll have me to deal with.''

"None of them are going to say a thing against Meghan," Walks Alone assured them. "They all like her. In fact," he chortled, "I'm sure if you hadn't returned to do the right thing by her, we would've had plenty of volunteers."

"Well, you just be sure they know she's been claimed," Jason growled in an unexpected display of possessiveness.

Walks Alone smiled, and Carrie's face grew thoughtful. This situation might work out better than she'd anticipated. Jason was showing all the signs of being a man smitten, albeit reluctantly.

"Is old Preacher Bailey still working over at the Harcourt place?" Jason asked.

"Yeah," Pete answered. "In fact, they lent him to us for a couple of weeks to help with the calving. He's out on the northeast range today, looking at some new calves."

"I guess he'd be as legal as anyone else," Jason said. "I don't much see Meghan's going into Denver in her condition. Junior, you go saddle yourself a fast horse and ride out to the northeast range and tell old Bailey he's got some preacher's work waiting for him at the house. Tell him to get a move on. I want to get this over with."

"Wait a minute!" Meghan objected.

Junior hesitated at the door.

"Go on," Jason ordered. "Do as I tell you."

Junior left without another word. Meghan glared at Jason. "Don't I get any say about this?" Things were moving much too fast for her. She wanted Jason's protection, but she also wanted to get some things understood before she was irrevocably bound to this man.

Jason shot her an impudent grin. "Not really."

Meghan's eyes flashed a warning of green fire. Jason's unperturbed smile didn't fade.

Carrie cleared her throat uneasily. "Why don't we leave these two alone for a while," she suggested to the others. "I'm sure they have plenty to discuss."

When Jason and Meghan were finally alone, his smile faded and he sat looking at her with intent amber eyes.

"Don't look at me like that!" she demanded testily.

"Like what?" He raised one eyebrow in query.

Meghan threw down her sewing in helpless agitation. "Like . . . like you think I'm trying to set some sort of a trap for you."

"I didn't say that," he said gently. "In fact, I didn't even think that." He could understand her agitation. She must have gone through hell knowing she was going to have his baby and not knowing when he was going to return, or what he would do when he did. She was strong, though. She'd survived with her feisty spirit intact.

He'd almost forgotten how beautiful she was. Even bloated in the last stages of pregnancy she was beautiful, with her gold-red hair glistening in the shaft of sunlight that poured through the window. Her skin had taken on an almost translucent quality, and even now, pale with worry, it glowed with life and health. Her pert nose was still sprinkled with a light dusting of tan freckles. He knew Carrie would've urged her to stay out of the sun like a proper lady, and he knew Meghan would've ignored her. He couldn't get too upset at the prospect of tying himself down to this woman. She was a fit mate for any man. Thoughts of the passion they'd shared made him smile. He was bound to get caught someday, and he could've done a lot worse. A lot worse indeed!

Meghan found the courage to meet his eyes with hers. "I want you to know that all I want from you is the protection of your name," she said in a flat voice.

Something in Jason became poised and still, as if afraid for her to continue. Meghan steeled her determination and went on. She would not be a burden to any man, no matter how much her heart wanted him.

"After we're married, if you still insist on taking me to California, that's fine. But what you do from there on out is your business. I won't tie you down, Jason. You can leave if you want. I'm fully prepared to make a life for myself . . . and for my child.''

"My child, too."

"One you certainly never intended to create."

Jason smiled sourely. "And did you?"

Meghan flushed and pulled her eyes away from his. "Just the same, I suppose I should be grateful you're so ready to lend me the safety of your name, but I wanted you to know that I'll make no claim on you for more. I'll be no man's burden.''

"Most men don't regard a wife as a burden," he countered with a wry smile.

Meghan met his eye levelly, hoping the battle in her soul didn't show on her face. "You're not like most men. I don't want a noble sacrifice from you, Jason. Your name is enough."

He looked at her intently, as though trying to read her heart. "We'll see what happens," he finally said with a frown.

She fought back tears. She would never want another man after Jason. He was the only one her heart would cleave to. But it wouldn't do to let him know. She didn't want him staying with her out of some sense of obligation, then end up hating her for caging him away from the free and adventurous life he loved.

Jason stood up and walked to the window, looking out at the barn and corrals. He'd certainly left her bitter, he thought with regret. But then what had he expected? For some reason her rejection hurt. But, he supposed, her way might be better. Even though for a moment he'd almost convinced himself this was the woman he wanted to stay with for the rest of his life. She might be better off without him.

He turned back to Meghan, who was studying the floor in fierce concentration. "This is no time to make a decision about the future." He sighed. "You just get through having our baby, then when you're feeling good again we'll head out to your uncle's place in California. Once you meet your relatives and settle your affairs there, then maybe we'll both know better what would be best.''

Meghan stared at him silently, her eyes a deep green jumble of unreadable emotions.

The front door banged shut. A commotion in the front hall followed. Junior burst into the room, all grins. He was followed by Pete, Carrie, and Walks Alone. The preacher had arrived.

# Chapter Nineteen

Old Joshua Bailey didn't look much like a preacher. He was a big, rawboned man with a bulbous nose and crooked, rotting teeth. His clothes were grimed with the dust and sweat of the morning's work on the range. Sparse locks of graying and greasy hair stuck out at all angles from beneath his battered hat, which he swept off in a grandiose bow to the ladies that was definitely not in keeping with his less-than-impressive appearance.

"Afternoon ladies, gents. It's a rare fine pleasure to be here, to be able to help you in your needs in the Lord. I always—''

"Good afternoon, Mr. . . . uh . . . Reverend Bailey.'' Carrie sensed the danger of an impromptu sermon and interrupted as graciously as she could. "We're sorry to have interrupted your work, but—''

"Dear lady!'' Bailey said with a magnanimous wave of his arm that served to waft his less than pleasant body odor toward her face. "No trouble at all. That's my purpose in being in this land of the godforsaken and heathen, after all.'' He preened himself as Carrie tried not to wrinkle her nose.

Joshua Bailey was ordained by a little-known offshoot church whose main following was on the Eastern seaboard. Early in his undistinguished career, he moved west. There was more need for a God-fearing man out west, he insisted, than in the relatively civilized East. What better way to bring the Lord to the uncivilized and heathen than to live among those poor souls? How better to understand the temptations that lured the weak than to place himself in the path of the same danger? What he failed to mention was how much healthier it was for himself far away from the irate father of an unhappily pregnant daughter, a new convert to Bailey's church to whom he'd given very personal attention.

From Bailey's ample waistline and florid complexion it was obvious he was diligently partaking of the temptations that plagued the poor souls he'd vowed to help, the better to understand those temptations, of course. And since the uncivilized and godless inhabitants of the West had so far failed to provide him with enough converts to open a church, he labored for his bread like any ordinary man. For fifteen years he'd been working for Jess Harcourt on his small homestead in the middle of what Bailey considered nowhere. When the scattered white population north of Denver heard that he was an ordained preacher, they started taking advantage of his status for weddings and funerals. Having Bailey perform the ceremonies saved the long trip to Denver for the services of someone more qualified, for the itinerant preachers through this area were few and far between.

"Hello, Bailey." Jason saved Carrie from further conversation with the preacher by taking the man by the arm and politely guiding him toward the door into the office where all the accounts of the ranch were kept.

"Ah, Mr. Sinclair. I see you're home again." Bailey had always despised Jason Sinclair as a man who represented all that was sinful in this lawless West. But it wasn't wise to provoke a man as deadly and unpredictable as Jason was known to be, so he'd always been exceedingly careful in what he said to the man. "What can I do for you? Not a funeral, I hope." He wondered if Sinclair had brought home the body of some unfortunate who'd crossed him and paid the ultimate price.

"Not a funeral," Jason told him. "A wedding."

"Oh, good! I love weddings. The more weddings in a place, the more civilized the place is, I always say. Always more than happy to do a wedding. Who's the lucky couple?"

Bailey looked around the room, but Jason pushed him through the door of the office before he could decide who it was he was supposed to be marrying. The only people he saw in the parlor were Mr. and Mrs. Wellner, who of course were already hitched, a boy too young to be making the plunge, that damned Pawnee Sinclair kept on as foreman of his place, and a young woman who obviously already had a husband, because she looked ready to pop out a baby any minute. Maybe the lucky bride was in one of the bedrooms changing into her wedding finery.

Jason pushed Bailey down into a chair and then sat himself on the corner of the desk, his arms folded across his chest and his chiseled mouth set in a tight line. "You and I need to talk before we get on with this wedding," he said ominously.

"By all means, my boy," Bailey said in a condescending tone. "Are you the lucky groom?"

"Yeah," Jason said with a twisted smile. "I'm the lucky groom."

"And when will we see the lovely bride?"

"You've already seen her. She's the young lady out in the parlor. The pretty one with red hair and green eyes."

The door opened and Carrie slipped in, but Bailey ignored her. He fixed Jason with a formidable look of indignation, his black eyes snapping in righteous disapproval.

"Mr. Bailey . . . oh . . . Reverend Bailey . . . excuse me." Carrie walked over to stand by Jason and managed to look uneasy and determined at the same time. "Everybody thinks Jason and Meghan were married at Fort Laramie before she came to the ranch. It was the only way I could think of to protect the poor girl's reputation. You know how thoughtless and cruel people can be.'' She gave the frowning man a significant look.

"Yes," Jason continued in a dangerous voice. "You know how nasty some people can be." He paused to let his full meaning sink in. "And since we know how Christian and bighearted you are, we know you won't object to postdating the legal papers and putting the place of the wedding as Fort Laramie."

Bailey sputtered indignantly. "I'll do no such thing! In fact, in view of the little hussy's condition, I'm not even sure I want to perform the ceremony at all. It would be a travesty of—"

"Hold it right there," Jason said in a deceptively quiet voice. "You'll perform the ceremony, you old crow, because you know what an ungentlemanly sort I am when I'm crossed."

Bailey's mouth opened and closed several times in rapid succession without a sound's coming out.

"And you'll postdate the papers just the way I tell you, or you'll have reason to regret not having more of that Christian charity you preachers are always talking about." He paused to let his words register, all the while casually fingering the hilt of his long-bladed knife. "Do you understand what I'm saying?"

Bailey's mouth flapped in several spasms of agitation before he finally gave up and just nodded his head.

"Jason"—Carrie gave him a gentle frown—"I'm sure it's not necessary to use threats. Reverend Bailey must surely see the need for discretion."

Jason shot Bailey a wicked grin. "I'm sure he does . . . now."

"Well, I'm sure the quicker we get the wedding over with, the happier we all will be," Carrie sighed, still half afraid that Jason might back out.

"Just one more thing. Reverend"—Jason spoke the title

with a cynical smile—"I don't want to hear one word or see one gesture from you to upset that girl out there. She's as innocent as a lamb in all this. If you're itching to give a sermon about morality and sex, you give it to me. You understand?"

Bailey swallowed the lump in his throat, thinking that he certainly didn't want to stick around to give a sermon to anyone, much less this wild man. He'd get Sinclair hitched up to his redheaded whore and then light out. If he never saw Sinclair or his uppity Pawnee foreman again it would be too soon.

"Understand?" Jason insisted on an answer.

"You won't get no trouble from me, Mr. Sinclair. Respect for all womanhood is part of my creed, even those that have fallen from the pure and sacred pedestal of chastity."

"One slip from you and you might find yourself hitting the dirt. So watch it."

The wedding was not the one that Meghan had fantasized about for much of her life. It wasn't the colorful and joyous Cheyenne ceremony that she'd seen her friends go through, nor was it the solemn and dignified ritual she'd heard white women talk about. In fact, it was a rather drab and ordinary event. Carrie had urged her to change into the "Sunday dress" she'd made the month before, but Meghan had declined, wanting to get the ordeal over with as soon as possible.

She didn't feel well at all, and only with great effort did she heave herself to her feet to stand beside Jason in front of the repellent man they called the Reverend Mr. Bailey. He didn't look like any kind of a holy man to Meghan. The odor emanating from his body made her sensitive stomach turn, and suddenly she wished desperately for some of Maria's special tea. But she supposed it was appropriate for them to be married by such a man. Certainly this wasn't a marriage rejoiced in by the gods, or by the God of the white man either. It was fitting that they be

officially joined by this man who was the antithesis of all
things holy.

The Reverend Mr. Bailey opened a Bible and with great
solemnity started to read a few of his favorite passages
concerning women and their duty of submission to their
husbands. He was cut short, however, by Jason's impatient
frown.

"Let's get on with it, Reverend." He put a strange
emphasis on the man's title, and Meghan looked at him
questioningly. She sensed he didn't like this man any more
than she did. Was it because he was the one who was
officially tying him to her, supposedly for the rest of his
life?

Jason looked down into Meghan's pale face and smiled
reassuringly. His big callused hand folded around her small
one and held it in a gentle grip. She blinked and for a
moment seemed to sway, then steadied herself with an
effort when Bailey cleared his throat and hastily started the
marriage ceremony itself.

The whole day was beginning to seem like a nightmare
to Meghan, culminating with the ceremony that was now
taking place. She felt trapped, with her hand so firmly and
possessively held by the big man beside her. Every time
the man in front of them opened his mouth to read another
phrase of the ceremony that would bind her to Jason as his
wife, his breath came close to gagging her. The stench of
his ill-cared-for body already had nauseated her, and her
back ached so abominably that she wasn't sure she could
remain on her feet until the awful preacher was through.
She swayed against Jason and felt the corded muscles of
his arm tense as he steadied her.

Suddenly, when Meghan was sure she could endure no
more of this, the ache in her back grew to a sharp
throbbing pain. The pain spread to her abdomen like a
knife twisting in her belly. She felt something wet and
warm trickle down the inside of her thighs. She gasped in
surprise and placed a hand on her protruding stomach,
where the pain finally came to rest. Her face lost what

little color it had and faded to an ashen hue that made her nose and cheeks swarm with formerly invisible freckles.

"Oh, my God!" Carrie stepped forward, but a tight-faced Jason waved her away.

Preacher Bailey's eyes grew wide in his florid face. His cheeks grew redder.

"I would suggest you speed it up, Bailey," Jason urged in a taut voice. "Speed it up a lot." One of his strong arms circled Meghan's swollen waist to support her. The other hand gripped her arm in a firm but gentle grip.

The rest of the preacher's words came out of his mouth so fast they were barely recognizable. "Do you take this woman?" he finally spat at Jason. On the firm affirmative reply he turned in haste to the wide-eyed and swaying Meghan. "Do you?"

"What?" she asked in a quavering voice. Then her face twisted in agony as another pain seared through her belly.

"She does!" cried Carrie, stepping up in haste to support Meghan on her other side.

"Yes," Meghan whispered tiredly as the spasm subsided. "I do."

"Then you're hitched," Bailey said with relief. He slammed his book closed with a loud whump and thrust the marriage document out to Jason. "Here's your paper, all signed and legal. Those two"—he waved in the direction of Pete and Carrie—"can sign as witnesses. Now, Mr. Sinclair, if you don't mind, I'm getting the hell out of here."

Meghan, who'd been lowered by Carrie into a nearby chair, gave another cry of distress. Pete and Junior were both turning pale, Carrie was wringing her hands, and Walks Alone was looking thoughtful. Jason reached Meghan's side in two long strides.

"Hang on, little Meghan," he urged her, gently slipping his arms under her body and lifting her from the chair. "Which room?" he asked Carrie.

"On the right. The last one."

Carrie followed close behind him, hands fluttering in

nervous agitation as Jason set his wife gently down on the lacy blue-and-white counterpane of the bed. "Oh, dear!" she breathed as Meghan opened her eyes in wide-eyed panic.

"What do you mean, 'oh, dear'?" Jason demanded in an irritated voice. "You're just scaring her, Carrie. Let's get down to business here."

"Oh, Jason!" Carrie cried, trying hard to keep calm. "I don't know anything about birthing a baby!"

"Well, what about Maria? Damn! She's had seven kids, or is it eight? She ought to know what needs to be done."

"She went to care for a sick sister in Longmont."

Jason groaned. "A fine time for her to be gone!"

"She felt the baby before she left yesterday. She said it wouldn't come for another week. Maybe two."

"Well," Jason commented acidly, "she was wrong! Dammit!"

"What are we going to do?"

Jason took a deep breath and regarded her with eyes grown calm. "We're going to deliver a baby. That's what we're going to do. Walks Alone!" he called out the door. "Get in here! You!" he turned to Carrie. "Go boil some water or whatever it is people do to stay out of the way. You're white as a fresh layer of snow already!"

Carrie exited with a worried look on her face and passed a stoic and solemn-looking Walks Alone coming through the door.

"It looks like you and I are the ones around here who know the most about birthing, Walks Alone," Jason told him with a smile.

"So I suspected," his blood brother returned calmly.

Meghan's face contorted in another spasm of pain. Jason sat down next to her on the bed. "Take it easy, honey." He ran his fingers over her brow in a gentle gesture of comfort.

"Where's Carrie?" she gritted out from between clenched teeth.

"Carrie's not going to be any help. She's a wonderful lady, but this sort of thing is out of her league."

"Oh, no," Meghan breathed as the pain left her once more.

"Don't you worry." Jason smiled down into her face. "Walks Alone there has four younger sisters, and he helped deliver every one of them. And him and me both have delivered more foals than you can count and never lost a mother yet. You aren't that much different than a mare, honey. You're going to be just fine." He hoped his own worry wasn't reflected on his face.

The afternoon wore on. Jason stripped the counterpane off the bed and replaced it with a clean white sheet. Walks Alone kept a basin of cool water and a cloth ready to sponge the sweat from Meghan's face and neck. The pains came regularly and the intervals between them grew shorter. Meghan alternately screamed and cursed, not caring at all that she wasn't living up to the Cheyenne ideal of stoic endurance.

As another of the pains subsided from its crescendo, she looked up at Jason, who was holding both her hands tightly. Beads of sweat were on his brow, and the strands of tawny gold that hung down were damp with it. His face was growing pale under his dark bronze tan, and the miserable look in his eyes told her that he was enjoying this almost as little as she was. Perversely she wished every pain could strike him as hard as it was striking her.

"You did this to me, you son of a bitch." Her voice quavered with exhaustion.

He smiled weakly. "You got me there."

"No," she groaned. "You got me. But never again. No man will ever touch me again. I'm not going through this a second time!"

"You'll feel different later on," he assured her, repeating the maxim he'd heard somewhere, he wasn't sure where.

"Like hell! Touch me again, you bastard, and I'll cut off

that bold weapon between your legs. You use it better than your knife, and you're prouder of it too!''

Jason chuckled, unperturbed. "And I thought Carrie taught you to be a lady!"

"This is no time to be acting like a lady." She gasped as another wave of agony began to build.

As the sun began to drop behind the mountains to the west, Jason convinced Meghan to let Walks Alone examine the position of the baby.

"He's my blood brother, after all. And you're my wife. That sort of makes you his sister, doesn't it?"

"You shouldn't worry," Walks Alone added. "I don't find white women attractive." He smiled teasingly. "Especially freckle-faced redheads. And I could only look upon the woman of my brother like I would look upon my little sister."

"Oh, go ahead," Meghan conceded in a resigned tone. She was too tired and too miserable to care about modesty anyway.

The babe was in a good position, Walks Alone assured Jason a few minutes later, and would come when it was good and ready. Meghan was a strong woman and he shouldn't worry. She was doing fine. Before morning he should be a proud father.

Afternoon stretched into night. Carrie came in several times to check on Meghan's progress and to sit by her bedside, giving Jason and Walks Alone a short respite and saying soothing things to the miserable girl in the bed. Meghan could never remember being in such pain. She never suspected such pain existed in the world. With each contraction she felt as though her body would split apart. Carrie's soothing words fell unheard on her ears, and when Jason returned she would vent her misery on him. He absorbed her insults stoically and returned good-natured encouragements and reassurances. Around midnight the two men looked at each other wearily.

"At least mares don't scream at you when you're helping them deliver a foal,'' Walks Alone commented with a wry smile.

Jason sighed. ''They might if you'd been the one to get them pregnant.'' He looked worriedly at Meghan's pale face. Her fiery hair was dark and damp with sweat, and her mouth stretched across her face in a tight line of pain. The image of another pain-racked face rose unbidden into his mind. Meadow Flower—sweet, innocent daughter of the Pawnee who'd been so proud when she learned she carried his child. She'd wanted to give him a son, and after twenty long hours of agonized trying, she'd died with the child still trapped inside her.

As if seeing into Jason's mind, Walks Alone told him softly, ''Meghan is a strong woman, Jason. She will give you many children and be the stronger for it. She is not Meadow Flower.''

It seemed the Pawnee was right. Shortly after two A.M., Meghan was delivered of a healthy baby boy. Walks Alone pulled him from his mother's body and rubbed him briskly with a soft piece of toweling until his little lungs expanded and he let loose with a squall that set both men to smiling.

''He's yours all right.'' Walks Alone grinned. ''Already mad at the world.'' He ran his hand carefully over the soft tawny-colored fuzz that covered the babe's head, then smiled as he looked into tiny, squinting, baby blue eyes. He guessed the eyes would turn to amber as the babe grew. The shape of his face held a hint of his mother, but the rest of him was definitely Jason Sinclair. ''I guess you can tell who his daddy is, all right,'' the Pawnee said. ''Guess there's no doubt about it at all.''

But Jason's attention would not be diverted from Meghan, who after the effort and pain of pushing her son into the world lay still and pale on the bed, her hand still convulsively gripping Jason's.

''Walks Alone!'' Jason called in a strained voice as Meghan's eyes closed in exhaustion. ''There's too much blood here!''

The initial rush of blood that had accompanied the new

baby into the world had not stopped, merely subsided to a slow but steady stream. Meghan was hemorrhaging.

Walks Alone handed the baby to Carrie and came to Meghan's side, frowning when he saw how pale Meghan's face was on the pillow, matching the sheets in lack of color. Her eyes were half closed, and her face was expressionless, as if she'd closed out the world around her and was already journeying to someplace far away. An ugly scarlet stain soaked the sheets on which she lay.

"Walks Alone!" There was a rising tide of panic in Jason's voice. The Pawnee's face tightened into a grim mask. He muttered an oath in Pawnee, then went quickly and efficiently to work.

"Tear up that clean sheet over there into little strips," he ordered the frantic Jason. "Soak the strips in whiskey. Hurry!"

Walks Alone worked calmly as Jason handed him the strips, packing them firmly into her as far up as he could get them without doing further injury. Meghan was unconscious now, her breathing shallow. If possible, her face was paler than it was when Jason first became aware of the crisis. Walks Alone remembered all too well that his mother had bled the same way after delivering her last child, his little sister White Feather. She had bled her life out, with Walks Alone and his father Lame Buffalo standing helplessly by while the women and the medicine man performed useless rituals designed to invoke the spirits to her aid. One old woman had urged the procedure Walks Alone was using now, but the other women had refused, saying that if their time-honored remedies did no good, and the medicine man's chants and drums did not turn her from the path she was following, then it must be that she was meant to join her ancestors. Walks Alone did not intend for Meghan to follow the same path if he could help it. He had seen too well how his blood brother looked at this woman. Meghan was his brother's hope for happiness, and Walks Alone would have moved heaven and earth had he thought it necessary to save her.

Finally he straightened from his task and sighed wearily. "The bleeding is stopped."

Jason stood by the bed with Meghan's delicate, cool hand enfolded in his own. His features were set and grim as he raised his face and looked into his blood brother's eyes.

"She's lost a lot of blood, Jason," Walks Alone said sadly. "We'll just have to wait and see. I don't know if she has the strength left to recover."

"She'll recover," Jason whispered, his voice cracked with anxiety. "She damn well better recover."

Walks Alone put a comforting hand on his blood brother's shoulder. "There's nothing more we can do right now. I'll go help Carrie clean up the baby." He paused awkwardly. "Do you know what you're going to name him?"

"No," Jason answered quietly. "We'll wait for Meghan to name him."

"As you wish," Walks Alone granted doubtfully.

Jason sat still and quiet for several minutes after Walks Alone left the room. His eyes were fixed on Meghan's face, white and almost deathlike against the pillow. He reached out a hand and tenderly fingered a strand of the gold-red hair that fanned out in a splash of riotous color against the white bed linen. Then his finger moved to trace the delicate curve of her lips. Her mouth twitched slightly at his touch.

"You better fight, little Meghan," he finally whispered in an emotion-hoarse voice. "You better fight to live, because if you die, I'll follow you to heaven or hell or wherever and bring you back. I swear I will."

He smiled slightly at the ridiculousness of his claim, but another glance at the pale face on the pillow wiped the smile from his face. She couldn't die, not when he was just discovering how much she meant to him, not when he was just on the threshold of finding out what happiness really was.

He buried his face in his hands. He felt like crying, but he couldn't. There had been too many years of holding back his tears. The well was dry. Now he knew why he'd felt so lighthearted when he had realized she was pregnant. He hadn't really wanted to give her up. And why it had hurt so when she'd defiantly told him all she wanted of him was his name. She wanted his name. He wanted her. Not until now, faced with her death, did he realize what had been working in him all the time since he'd first seen her, standing so proud and defiant on the slopes of the Rosebud's valley.

He took her limp hand into his again, willing the abundant life and strength in his body to flow to hers. "Don't die, Meghan." This time it sounded more like a plea than a demand. "The baby needs you. Dammit! I need you!" He gazed intently at her face, as if willing his resolve into her spirit. He hoped it was not his imagination that painted a little more color into her skin, a little stronger rhythm to her breathing. "Live, Meghan, and I'll find a way to make you happy. I'll find a way, no matter what it takes."

Three days later Meghan sat propped up in her bed, her baby son rooting hungrily at her breast. She leaned weakly back on the pile of pillows, letting the sweet strange fulfillment of the infant's greedy sucking permeate her body.

Carrie, sitting by the bedside, laughed in delight. "My goodness he's hungry! How does he hold so much? Seems I never see him but what he isn't either eating or yelling that he wants to eat."

Meghan smiled as she looked down at the little tawny head nestled against her swollen breast. "Well, you know, quite a bit comes out the other end too." She gently detached the baby from her nipple and sat him bent forward on her lap, patting his back gently. When he'd given a man-sized belch she set him at her other breast.

Two days before, Meghan had awakened to find a

haggard and unshaven Jason sitting by her bedside looking every bit as if he was attending a deathwatch, which, she learned later, he was. No one had thought she would live after losing so much blood. She was surprised Jason looked so concerned. Maybe he did care for her in his own way. Or maybe he'd been scared to death of being stuck with a newborn baby. She hadn't had enough energy to do anything more than open her eyes and look at him. When she woke again he was no longer there.

Carrie told her he'd slept the clock around after it was clear that Meghan would recover. He'd been in several times to see the babe, and Meghan had to admit surprise in how much tender affection he showed the tawny-haired infant, and the almost affectionate consideration he displayed around her. He visited once while the babe was nursing and had watched in fascination at the sight of the hungry little mouth pulling at her nipple. From the look on his face, Meghan would've sworn that if she'd pulled the babe away, Jason would have jumped to take his place.

Carrie plumped the fat pillows behind Meghan's back, then gently brushed a finger over the busily nursing infant's fuzzy head. "What a fine little boy," Carrie sighed. "Have you decided on a name yet?"

"No," Meghan admitted. "Neither Jason nor I have any male relatives we're proud of, so I guess a family name isn't going to work."

"From what you've said, I guess you don't have many good memories of your father. But what about your uncle— John O'Brian. He might feel very honored to have the boy named after him."

Meghan's face clouded for an instant. She certainly wasn't going to name her son after the man who'd instigated so much unhappiness in her life. "No," she sighed, "I don't think so."

Carrie smiled, picking up a tiny hand and letting it curl around her finger. The baby hiccuped and blew a bubble, then rested quietly on his mother's lap, his tummy full of his mother's milk. "I'm sure you'll think of something appropriate. He is so adorable."

Carrie kissed Meghan on the forehead and lovingly chucked the infant under his double chins. "Rest well, dear. I'll be right in the next room if you need me." With a smile she quietly closed the door behind her.

Meghan gazed with helpless motherly love at the infant drifting to sleep on her lap. She hadn't guessed she would feel this way about the child, this protective, all-consuming love that was so different from any feeling she'd ever known. She ran her hand over the tawny fuzz on his head, the exact color of Jason's thatch of thick yellow waves. Even now she imagined she could see a resemblance to his father's strong, chiseled features.

Hard to believe this innocent babe was the sprout of Jason's seed, she thought. Would he grow up to be a panther-eyed savage who was faster with a knife than most men were with a gun, and faster with a gun than any man had a right to be? Would he grow to be a man who could capture a woman's heart with one look and make her forget all she ever knew of pride and decency for want of him? Would he grow to be like his father, even without his father around to teach him to follow in his footprints?

Meghan lay back on the pillows, the hollow look in her eyes not entirely due to the strain of childbirth and her near brush with death immediately following. She cradled the baby closer to her breast and closed her eyes.

"Damn you, Jason Sinclair!" she whispered harshly. "Damn you for making me love you!"

# Chapter Twenty

"What the hell do you mean you won't go by train?"

Jason angrily paced the length of the front parlor, his long-legged strides making the room seem much smaller than it really was.

"Just what I said," Meghan answered calmly, hugging little Andrew closer to her breast and covering his head to shield him from his father's temper. "I will not go near that iron monster."

Jason loosed his breath in a great sigh of exasperation. In the month since his son's birth Meghan had seemed to go out of her way to put a distance between them. This was simply one more ploy in a long line of petty rebellions.

"Would you care to tell me why?" he asked with tight-lipped sarcasm.

Meghan viewed him haughtily down the length of her pert nose, an affectation rendered less effective by her seated position, placing her far below his towering height. "The iron horse has disrupted the buffalo and helped to end the way of life valued by my people. I will not ride on the beast."

Jason snorted. "Don't give me that 'iron horse' crap! You've been here almost a year, and you speak English as well as I do."

"Which isn't saying much."

"So now you're a grammar critic?"

"If you can object to my speech, I can do the same."

Jason felt like pulling out his hair in frustration, or better still, pulling out some of the thick red mane of the sweet-faced termagant sitting so primly on the settee.

"You're changing the subject," he growled. "You don't have a single good reason for not wanting to go to California by train. I'm sure as hell not going to take you over South Pass by wagon. You're in no shape for that kind of trip, and I don't have the time."

Meghan's eyes flashed green fire and her face froze into an expressionless mask of Indian stubbornness, a move that never failed to make Jason furious.

"I will not go to California by train," she repeated with finality, as if that statement were the close of the subject.

Jason leaned over until his face was only inches from hers. She could see the twitch of a muscle in his jaw. She could see the angry amber sparks swarming in his eyes. "You will go to California," he insisted. "By train."

Meghan felt her ever-ready temper flare to life. "And you can go to hell, Jason Sinclair, by whatever means you wish!" Her green eyes narrowed slightly as they locked on his. She didn't want to go to California. If she had to leave the ranch, she wanted to return to her people. Jason had told her she probably had a sizable inheritance awaiting her in Placerville, but she didn't care. The more she thought about facing her unknown family, the more frightened she became.

For a moment he looked as if he wanted to hit her, and she instinctively braced herself, though she knew he wouldn't raise his hand against her, particularly with Andrew held fast in her arms. But Meghan flinched from his irate gaze. Her eyes lowered as she leaned back on the settee, carefully shifting little Andrew so as not to wake him.

"You can't make me go," she finally said in a low voice.

"Don't bet on it."

"If you don't want to take me across the Pass by horse and wagon, then let me go back to my people."

"Your people, you stubborn little idiot, are in California!"

"My people are in Montana!"

"I have never met a female as bullheaded and just plain pig-brained as you are!"

"Then get rid of me!"

"Don't tempt me!" Their voices were climbing into the shouting range now. "You are going to California!"

"Not on the iron horse!"

Jason turned around and passed a hand over his face, trying to wipe the frustration from his mind. When he turned back around his face was calmer, but his voice was still tinged with anger. "You will either go with me peacefully on the train, or I will carry you over my shoulder like a sack of grain. And I don't give a damn how much of your dignity is left when I get through with you. If you want everyone on the train to see you being manhandled like a misbehaving child, then so be it. You brought it on yourself."

"You wouldn't dare!" she challenged.

He smiled, a dangerous smile that inspired her heart to a thump of apprehension. "Who's going to stop me?"

She opened her mouth, but could think of no reply.

"Three days. Three days and you be ready to board that train."

Before she could think of an answer, he turned on his heel and strode out of the room.

Jason saddled the black stallion without a word to Walks Alone, whom he passed in the barn, and set spurs to the horse in a manner that sent the stud flying toward the foothills at a furious pace, Wolf loping happily at his heels. The headlong gallop fit Jason's mood, but after a few minutes he reined the black back to a more sedate lope. The stallion's neck was already streaked with lather, and Jason could feel the ribs under the stirrup leathers heave for breath.

"You're out of shape, big boy." Jason pulled the horse down to a walk. "Guess you've been lounging around here too long. I certainly have."

He sighed as he headed the stallion into a narrow canyon that he knew wound through the orange and yellow sandstones of the foothills and ended up at a lake surrounded by a thick stand of pine. The place had always held an attraction for him, and now he needed a measure of peace that perhaps the quiet little lake could give him.

He'd never met a woman who could get him as riled as Meghan, and since their child was born, her temper seemed more explosive than ever. But damn her stubborn hide! Why couldn't she see that she owed it to herself to find out what was waiting for her in California? Then she could make the big decisions about her future.

Meghan had made it plain, once she'd recovered from the birth, that her decision to make no further claims on him still stood. He wasn't sure if he was grateful or sorry. Until he'd come face to face with losing her he hadn't realized how thoroughly she was enmeshed in his life.

The first time he saw her after the long ordeal of birth and near death, the sight of her propped up in bed with their son nestled warmly in her arms had played sweet havoc with his heart. Her face seemed white and almost translucent against the fire of her hair, and the green eyes looked dark and shadowed when she turned to look at him.

"You're all right?" Half question, half statement, it had been the first thing to come to his mind. Of course she was all right. He had sat at her bedside day and night until she was well on the way to recovery and Carrie had dragged him off, forced a hot meal down him, and sternly ordered him to bed.

"Yes," she had answered simply. "It looks like you're stuck with me after all." Her voice held a bitterness he hadn't quite understood.

Guessing that her unhappiness came from the babe she held in her arms, he knew a sharp disappointment. In spite of the circumstances, he'd never imagined a girl as essentially warmhearted as Meghan would reject her own child simply because it was his. So he'd made the logical suggestion—leave the baby with Carrie, who would be glad to raise it in her stead. Meghan had flown into a fury and almost climbed out of bed to get at him. Only the fragile burden in her arms had held her back.

Jason stopped and dismounted when he reached the trickling stream that led down the canyon from the lake above. He let the black drink sparingly, then stretched out on the bank of the stream to take a drink himself. The water felt cool against his dusty face and soothed the parched dryness of his throat. He swung himself into the saddle again and urged the stallion up the trail.

"Might as well see what the lake looks like this year," he told the horse. "Might even bait a line and try to bring home some fish for Maria to fry for dinner."

Jason figured he'd never understand women, much less Meghan. Now that they were married, she seemed more wary of him than ever before, as if she had a new vulnerability she was striving to protect. But she doted on that baby, not letting Maria or Carrie help with even the dirtiest of chores concerning the little guy. She clung to the babe almost as though he were her only anchor in the world. She was so proud of little Andrew that she even softened toward Jason when he let curiosity and fatherly interest prod him into picking up the little bundle of warm flesh and holding him carefully against his broad, hard chest. Jason had noted the shine of tears in Meghan's eyes when the babe had grasped his big callused finger in a tiny fist. He wondered at the emotion that swam in her clear green eyes as she watched him play gently with his son. What prompted her to tears? What prompted her to anger? In so many ways this woman who was now his wife was as much a mystery as she had been when he had first seen her standing in the valley of the Rosebud.

Another hour of riding and Jason saw the glimmer of the lake through the trees. Then the trees thinned out and the vista into the valley below was unimpeded. The little lake nestled in the bottom of an oval rocky bowl rimmed on the east by a sharp tree-studded ridge and on the west by low hills that swept up to join the lower slopes of Indian Peaks. Jason reined in on the top of the ridge and just sat for a few minutes, drinking in the silence. A fresh breeze riffled the blue of the water and sent sparks of sunlight dancing across the surface. The same breeze combed through his tawny locks when he took off his hat and mounted it on the saddle horn in front of him. The fresh, pine-scented air seemed to clear the frustration choking his mind and leave his brain functioning again. He nudged the stallion with his knees and allowed the horse to ease down the trail toward the lake at his own pace. The water looked inviting. Maybe he would even indulge himself and take a swim.

June was just around the corner, but the water was icy. The hills that rimmed the valley to the west rose until they joined the towering heights of Indian Peaks, and those heights were still covered with snow, snow that was melting in the springtime sun, sending cascades of ice water down the slopes into the stream that fed the little foothills lake.

The shock of the cold as Jason dove naked into the sun-dappled water was enough to drive the breath from his body, and after a few minutes of energetic swimming he gave up the effort and pulled himself onto a warm rocky shelf that bordered the lake. The day was warm, but not that warm! Wolf looked at him as if to say he was crazy.

"You're right," Jason told the wolf as he stretched his hard-muscled bronze body out to dry. "I'm crazy. Why didn't you remind me it was only May?"

Wolf pricked his ears obligingly at the words, then turned several circles and settled down by Jason's side. Jason absently buried his fingers into the warmth of the wolf's ruff and was rewarded by the brief flick of a tongue against his arm.

"Don't ever take a mate, my friend."

Wolf laid his sharp-nosed head on his paws and looked at the man as though he understood every word.

"Were the bitches in your pack as bitchy as the female who's plaguing me?" Jason asked with a smile. "Maybe that's why you decided you preferred my company after I pulled you out of that trap, huh? But then, you weren't really old enough to appreciate the temptations of the female way back then, were you?"

Wolf whined in seeming agreement.

"Well, now, my man. You take my advice. Don't ever let a female get the upper hand. You do, you're dead meat."

Wolf raised his head and gave Jason a wolfish grin.

"You don't fool me." Jason smiled. "I know what

you've been doing—going out into the hills for days at a time, coming back with that big grin on your face. You just don't forget the trouble you can get yourself into." He sighed. "Take me as an example. Here I am, minding my own business, raising a little hell now and then, trying to keep my skin in one piece, but basically not bothering much of anyone. And what happens? I try to do the honorable thing, do someone a good turn. Old John O'Brian says, it's your fault the girl got kidnapped and raised by the dirty savages. So I go charging in and get her out. And what does it get me. A pain in the neck, that's what."

The look in Wolf's eyes seemed all sympathy.

"Who could've known that sweet-faced little girl would turn out to be such a piece of trouble? Hell! I had less trouble getting out of that scrape with that grizzly bear three years ago. Don't ever let anyone tell you that females are soft, silly, little creatures who can't do any real harm because they don't have a brain in their heads. Hell, no! They get mean when they're riled. And I mean to tell you mean! And the trouble is, they'll never tell you exactly why they've got their backs up."

Wolf was still all ears.

"Not that I haven't brought part of it on myself. Guess I'm not exactly a prize catch as a husband. But goddamn! What's a man supposed to do? Every time I see that woman I want to shake her till she rattles, then kiss her till she melts. There's just something about her. Even when she was pregnant. That first time I saw her when I came back, with her backlit by the sun, just a shadow in the barn doorway, I knew right then I couldn't let her go. And when she came on in with her stomach sticking out as if she'd swallowed a pillow, looking like a defiant mouse giving what for to a hungry eagle, I figured the jig was up. Right then I figured we had to get hitched, and it wasn't only because she was going to have a baby. Guess I knew then I was addicted."

Wolf got up, stretched, then sniffed the wind. His

nostrils flared briefly, then he sat back down and stared in the direction of the trail.

"Something coming?"

Jason sat up and fastened his eyes on the trail that descended the east ridge, the trail they'd followed into the valley. There was no movement other than the gentle breeze and the occasional flutter of a bird taking to the air. He checked for his pistol to make sure it was within easy reach. He didn't mind being surprised without his clothes on, but he sure as hell didn't want to be caught without a gun at hand. Still, nothing disturbed the quiet of the little valley other than the murmur of the pines being caressed by the breeze, and he stretched out once again on the warm rock. Wolf settled beside him, but kept a wary eye on the empty trail.

It was a hell of a thing, he thought, to lose his freedom to a snip of a girl who was as savage and uncivilized as he himself was. Who would've thought he'd end up married to a half-wild Irish hellion who'd learned the fine art of war at the knee of the Cheyenne Dog Soldiers. And the damnable thing about it was that he'd brought about his own downfall, standing quiet as a tame nag as she slipped the bit in his mouth.

Jason had to admit it to himself. He was in love with the little savage. When he left her she plagued his mind. When he was with her his eyes couldn't get enough of her, even when she was ranting at him, baiting him, provoking him to fury as she'd been doing all month. His body surged toward hers as naturally as iron toward a magnet, a bee toward honey, or more appropriately a moth toward a flame. She was poison to the thing he'd always valued the most—his freedom. And he'd drunk of her willingly, anxiously. He'd stood by and watched himself become enmeshed in her female spell. He'd watched as she, all unknowingly, had turned his lust into love. And he'd not been able to lift a finger to keep it from happening.

Somehow freedom didn't quite have the lure it once did. Four walls with Meghan inside them didn't seem quite so cramped and confining, and domesticity didn't seem like such a dirty word when it meant he would be with Meghan. No doubt about it. He was trapped but good.

Wolf was suddenly alert again. He rose to his feet, eyes riveted on the trail descending the east ridge, hackles rising along the midline of his neck and back. Jason reached for his gun and crouched beside him, straining to see what the keener wolf eyes detected. Just coming out of the trees, a horse and rider were picking their way down the rocky trail. Jason squinted for a moment, then relaxed. He set the pistol back in its holster. A sudden change of wind direction brought the scent of the newcomer to Wolf's twitching nose, and he too relaxed.

"Yo! Walks Alone!" Jason stood up and waved his arms above his head. The horse and rider changed direction toward the spot where Jason stood. Jason pulled on his clothes, then whistled the black stallion over to him from where he had been peacefully cropping grass a hundred yards away.

"Fine herd stallion you'd be!" Jason chided him as he threw the saddle on and tugged the cinch tight. "They'd have ridden right up to us before you'd have given a whinny. I'm going to have to trade you in on a meaner stud. That I am."

The stallion swung his big beautifully molded head around as Jason swung into the saddle, eying his rider in a manner that seemed to suggest that he'd known all along the intruder was friend and not foe.

"My brother," Walks Alone greeted him as they met on the trail. He didn't mention Jason's thunderous exodus from the ranch.

"Walks Alone." Jason was glad to see his Pawnee blood brother, for the direction of his thoughts had been such that he didn't want to be left alone to follow them through. "You followed me."

The Pawnee shrugged. "It is a good day for hunting."

Jason guided the stallion to fall in alongside Walks

Alone's bay mare. "Fishing was more what I had in mind."

"Maria would like a rabbit for the table or maybe a deer for venison steaks."

Jason snorted, glad to be thinking of something other than Meghan. "The rabbit and deer are too skinny this time of year. The trout are fat."

Walks Alone laughed. "As you wish, my brother. Maria will have to make do with fish."

They rode around the lake and dropped their lines into a shaded pool whose color spoke of depth. Jason was the first to feel a tug on his line, but before thirty minutes were up both men had pulled five fish from the pool. Then they sat another fifteen minutes without a nibble.

"They know we are here," Walks Alone concluded and pulled in his line to go to another pool.

"Seems so." Jason followed suit.

The men walked in companionable silence along the lakeshore, looking for another likely-looking fishing spot. It was Walks Alone who broke the silence.

"I heard Autumnfire Woman weeping when I passed by her window before I left."

The warmth and ease in Jason's amber eyes faded to the rigid hardness of yellow resin. "Her name is Meghan."

"Many months ago she asked me to call her by her Cheyenne name."

"She is no longer Cheyenne."

"True. But neither is she white. And if the name gives her comfort, why should I not use it?"

"I would think you would resent her Cheyenne background," Jason said coldly, irritated at having his mind pushed back to this most painful subject. "The Pawnee and the Cheyenne are enemies. "

Walks Alone snorted. "Today I think the Cheyenne are enemy only to the whites, and soon they will be defeated. The Cheyenne will be no more. One does not hate an enemy who is bravely fighting for his life."

"Meghan is not Cheyenne. You make it harder for her by calling her by a Cheyenne name."

"Perhaps, but I am not the one who makes her cry."

"If she was crying," Jason said curtly, "she made herself cry. She cries out of anger, not hurt."

"Who knows why white women cry?" Walks Alone mused. "They cry for every reason under the sun. Sometimes I think they cry just to cry, because that is what white women do. But Autumnfire . . . Meghan . . . did not cry until you returned."

Jason was silent.

Walks Alone frowned. "Is there trouble already between you?"

Jason fixed him with an amber stare that would have made any other man back down. "You're getting pretty nosy, even for a brother."

Walks Alone's gaze didn't falter. "I am troubled by what you are doing to yourself, my brother. It is only my love for you that makes me interfere."

Jason's face twisted into a wry, unpleasant grin. "And what am I doing to myself that troubles you so?"

"You are building a barricade around yourself. You are cutting out your heart and replacing it with a stone that sees no good in anyone or anything."

Jason didn't bother to deny it. He wished he could turn his heart to stone. Then he wouldn't be troubled by the effect of a fire-haired Irish witch on his life.

"Meghan loves you," Walks Alone stated simply. "You love her. Yet you run away."

Jason laughed bitterly. "You're wrong, my brother. I thought you had sharper eyes. Right now Meghan thinks I'm the slime that's left when the stock ponds dry up in August. She wants only to go back to her people. She's angry because I'm making her go to California to straighten things out with her relatives."

Walks Alone shook his head. "My eyes are sharper than yours. I see what you will not see. Meghan loves you. I do not believe she really wants to return to the Cheyenne. But she is very proud. Or perhaps she is afraid.''

''Damn well she should be afraid,'' Jason growled. ''I kidnapped her, shot her, seduced her, then deserted her among strangers with my child in her belly. Good reason for her to be afraid. She'd be better off without me, that's for sure.''

''Perhaps if you let her know your feelings.''

''I don't have feelings,'' Jason sneered, wishing the statement were true.

The men halted at a spot where a rocky lcdgc jutted out over the lake. There they baitcd their lines and dropped them into the water. Several minutes of awkward silence were finally broken once again by Walks Alone.

''My brother,'' he started, his face grim. ''I never before knew you to be a coward. But now I think you are not brave enough to face the fact that someone has once again captured your heart.''

Jason looked at him with narrowed eyes set in a face turned to stone. Even Walks Alone, the only man who'd ever been able to claim true friendship with this hard and mostly uncivilized man, hesitated when he sensed the anger building behind the opaque amber gaze.

''I saw you with my sister Meadow Flower, who was your wife. I saw the happy days you had together. I saw your grief when she died trying to give you a child. So I know you can love, my brother. And I know you have reason to run from loving again.''

''Meadow Flower has nothing to do with this,'' Jason gritted through a clenched jaw.

''No, she doesn't.'' Just then a tug on Walks Alone's line forestalled further conversation. But when the fish was safely on the shore he persisted. ''Meadow Flower has gone to join our ancestors. She can no longer walk beside you as she did the years you lived among my people. But the gods are kind to you. They have given you another fine woman to love, and a fine son as well.''

Jason sneered. ''I've never before known an Indian to

be a romantic. You see things only as you wish to see them.''

''I see them as they are. You have grown as wild as the silver wolf who follows you. You no longer see with the eyes of wisdom.''

''Bullshit!'' Jason yanked on his line. ''There're no fish here. Might as well head back to the ranch.''

Walks Alone grinned, knowing that in spite of his friend's denial, he had scored a few points. ''Tell Maria I will bring her enough trout to feed the crew tonight.''

Jason stalked off without answering, mounted the black stallion, and galloped off in a spray of dust and gravel, Wolf loping easily alongside. He'd come up to the valley for peace of mind, and thanks to that damn Indian he'd gotten only an earful of romantic gobbledygook that would make a grown man puke. Walks Alone had a hell of a nerve nosing in on his personal feelings. No matter that he had admitted to himself that he loved his wife. Admitting something to yourself and having someone else put the thing into words were two different things entirely. Imagine Walks Alone's saying he was too cowardly to face up to his feelings! Blood brother or not, Jason thought, the damn Indian was lucky he was in a forgiving mood. Walks Alone probably thought he was saying all that garbage for Jason's own good, so about the only thing he could do was ride away before his temper got the best of him.

Jason topped the eastern ridge and started down into the canyon. He didn't feel like going back to the ranch just yet. Meghan had probably thought up some new devilry to irritate him with. Why on earth would Walks Alone, usually an astute judge of character, think Meghan loved him when she'd done nothing but try to drive him away ever since he'd come back to the ranch? Was it possible that the Pawnee saw something Jason himself hadn't? Was there a reason for all those tears besides anger and hurt pride? What if Meghan did love him after all? That night in the ravine with the Pawnees breathing down their necks and a hole in her leg from Jason's bullet—she'd actually seduced him that night, not the other way around. She'd given herself to him with a passion that surpassed anything Jason had ever experienced. It had stirred him to aching need and then left him with a satiated contentment that was as unfamiliar as it was wonderful. There was much more than simple lust in their lovemaking that night. Could there have been love?

And what if Meghan did love him? Did that really change anything? Could he ever make a suitable husband for any white woman? Meghan, with a fiery temper to match that flaming hair, would be more than a handful for any man to handle. Would he be doing her a favor by staying by her side? Or would he always be discontented in his lot, longing to see what was on the other side of the mountain or the far side of the river? He loved her. That was a fact. But no matter how much passion and tenderness he felt for that little redheaded, green-eyed piece of temptation, it might be better all around if he got her settled with her relatives then left her to live her own life. God knows he'd brought trouble enough to her as it was.

Jason reined in at one of the last little pools in the canyon. The stallion and wolf both drank thirstily, and Jason dismounted and did the same. Then he sat himself on a rock and tried to think of a legitimate reason to keep him out until evening. He could think of nothing. Especially since he'd promised Pete he'd help him mend a couple of the corrals that afternoon. The day before, a stud had gotten overanxious for his lady love and had knocked down the poles dividing two of the pens.

"Well, my friend"—Jason reached out and scratched one of Wolf's pointed ears—"it's time to go back and face the music."

Wolf lolled his tongue and grinned in answer.

Jason looked up in the sky where a hawk circled lazily in an updraft. That was the life, he thought somewhat cynically, trying hard to convince himself. Free as that hawk up above.

When they got to California, Meghan could make a

rational decision about her future. Then if things weren't working out between them, he could go back to his old life and try to forget that he'd ever fallen in love with her. She would be safe and secure with her family, and her uncle would help her put her inheritance in order.

Jason frowned as he remembered Jonathan O'Brian sitting in that room at Fort Laramie, a big slippery-eyed Irishman trying to persuade Jason he had an obligation to rescue his niece. For all his fancy clothes and polished manners, the man wasn't that different from his blowhard brother, and what Jason had managed to learn here and there about Jonathan O'Brian and the way he did business didn't make him seem any more likable. He couldn't for the life of him imagine why a man like that had gone to such trouble to find a long-lost niece, especially when finding her was going to mean giving up some of his hard-earned money. It might be wise, Jason thought, to stick around California for a while even if Meghan was anxious to push him out the door—just to make sure Meghan and the baby were doing okay. It wouldn't hurt to make sure she was treated well. And after all . . . he was legally, morally, and every other way Meghan's husband. There was really no need to rush off.

Feeling more at ease with himself than he had all month, Jason swung into the saddle and urged the stallion down the canyon.

# Chapter Twenty-one

The train trip to Sacramento was a hard one and full of surprises. Meghan was truly determined not to set foot on the train, but in the end Jason's determination was greater than hers. She really believed he would have carried out his threat to drag her onto the train thrown over his shoulder like a misbehaving child had she not relented. She'd learned that Jason wasn't a man to make threats he wouldn't carry out.

Meghan was prepared to hate the iron monster that in so many ways represented the ascendancy of the white man and the decline of the Indian. But she hadn't counted on the thrill of speed and power as the great lumbering engine pulled them along the tracks. Fuzzy childhood memories of the seemingly endless trek across the inhospitable prairie contrasted sharply with her brief glimpse of the palace cars, where the well-heeled could now ride across the continent in the luxury they were accustomed to at home and travel from coast to coast in only a week.

Andrew cried at the noise and the smell and the frightful vibration as they sped along on their way, but Jason comforted him, holding him secure in his strong arms until his fear was gone and then bouncing him on his knee until a smile and a chortle bubbled forth from his pudgy baby face.

Jason was unexpectedly considerate during the trip from Colorado, almost affectionate. Meghan was a bit frightened by this new gentleness she sensed in him. She'd been trying diligently to drive him away, knowing that if he showed the least kindness toward her, the least affection, she wouldn't have the strength to send him on his way once this journey was done. One touch of passion from him, one kiss from that mobile mouth was all it would take. She would be lost. She would beg him to stay by her side, which was something she couldn't lower herself to do. He'd given their baby an honorable name. Her pride wouldn't allow her to ask for more.

Her uncle's confidential secretary, a nervous little man by the name of William Sykes, met them in Sacramento with a well-sprung, plushly upholstered coach pulled by a beautifully matched team of bay geldings. The meeting was awkward. The man had been instructed to expect Meghan and the hired man who'd escorted her from Montana. Instead he'd been confronted with a cold-eyed gunman (Mr. Sykes considered himself an expert on character judgments, especially of the rougher types who inhabited the country west of the Mississippi) who claimed to be the husband of his employer's niece. And there was a baby to prove it.

Meghan halfway expected Jason to leave after delivering her to her uncle's secretary in Sacramento. He'd fulfilled his obligation, and there wasn't much chance she would attempt to run away again, not in a strange land and burdened by an infant. But Jason stayed, smiling at the secretary's discomfiture and treating her as any happily married man might treat his beloved wife. Meghan didn't understand at first, until she remembered that her uncle had offered Jason payment for escorting her from Colorado to California. He probably just wanted to be sure he'd be paid the promised amount.

It took a day and a half in the coach over dusty and rutted roads before she got her first glimpse of Placerville, where her father had hoped to make his fortune in a gold mine won at the gambling table. Her father's death had been his brother's good fortune, for he had come to California to claim the mine his dead brother had won, believing himself to be the only remaining member of his brother's family.

The original mine was a placer operation on Hangtown Creek, a mere trickle of water that ran almost directly through the center of town. Under Jonathan O'Brian's management the mine had prospered, but like all placer operations had run its course in a very few years. Jonathan had taken the money earned from the original mine and developed the other claims that had been in his brother's winnings, this time using hydraulic mining to wash out the banks of a steep ravine on the South Fork of the American River, just upstream from where John Marshall had first discovered gold at Sutter's Mill in 1848. That mine had also prospered, and now there was another as well, an underground operation cutting the gold directly from bedrock only a mile from the hydraulic mine on South Fork. Now Jonathan O'Brian was a rich man. He had one of the biggest houses in El Dorado County. His wife was a leading lady of society, and his two daughters, Clara and Samantha, had every advantage that money could buy.

When the coach drove up the long tree-lined driveway to O'Brian House, Meghan thought she'd never seen anything so grand in her entire life. The mansion made Jason's unpretentious ranch house, which she thought so impressive, look like a mere hovel in comparison. Three stories high and constructed of brick, the white-painted house was fronted by two-story Grecian columns. The ornate columns supported a roof that sheltered a porch and balustraded balcony. These stretched the full front of the house. Old oaks spread their branches out over the green-tiled roof and shaded the entire house with their foliage. A carefully trimmed lawn stretched from the house down to a low stone wall two hundred feet down the hill.

Jason remarked that the house looked as though it had been built for some English lord rather than for a California gold prospector. The tone of contempt in his voice drew a frown from Mr. Sykes, who'd spoken very little during their trip from Sacramento. Meghan wondered at the tone herself. It sounded as though Jason didn't think much of her uncle, even though they'd met only once. It made Meghan more apprehensive than ever at the prospect of meeting this man who was her father's brother and who'd seen fit to hire a notoriously dangerous gunman to escort his niece on the long journey from the Indian territories of Montana.

Her apprehensions were well-founded. The man who greeted them in the parlor of the impressive brick house was as imposing as the house itself. Tall and big-boned, with a ruddy face and coal-dark eyes, he sparked a memory in Meghan's dimly recalled past, a memory of her father, big and dark and brutal. But her uncle Jonathan wasn't a poor, hard-drinking, hard-gambling Irish ne'er-do-well. He was immaculately groomed, wearing an expensively tailored suit consisting of summerweight light brown trousers, matching waistcoat, and a fashionably cut frock coat in a hue of darker brown. What was left of his hair was carefully combed and worn long enough to drape over his collar. Fuzzy long sideburns framed the ruddy face that grew thunderously dark as Mr. Sykes hesitantly explained that he had escorted from Sacramento not only Meghan, but her husband and child as well.

Meghan watched the scene from the velveteen settee on which she had been seated by her uncle's butler. Her lips tightened into a determined line as she saw the trepidation in the little secretary's face on being confronted by her uncle. Apparently her uncle Jonathan was a man somewhat feared by the people around him. She was determined that she would not be cowed. In her concentration on appearing unafraid and in perfect possession of herself, she failed to notice the glares Jason and Jonathan exchanged across the room, hostility sparking from them as it would from two dog wolves sparring for territory.

Jonathan O'Brian had composed his face into a semblance of friendliness by the time he turned to greet his long-sought niece. He welcomed her in a friendly fashion, but the friendly facade didn't soften those hard black eyes, and Meghan's heart sank. This man and his family were her only living relatives. She was expected to love them, become part of their family, and regard this intimidating uncle as her rescuer. Where was the warmth and affection Carrie Wellner had led her to hope for? Why had this steely-eyed old man been so determined to retrieve her from the Indians? She could see no affection in his gaze, or even any fondness for the sake of her dead father's memory.

The meeting and greeting of Jonathan's wife, Erin, and their two daughters, Clara and Samantha, was a bit easier. Her aunt and cousins were cordial, if somewhat reserved, and the younger daughter, Samantha, was utterly and immediately in awe of Jason, stumbling over herself with adolescent embarrassment whenever he so much as glanced her way.

But Meghan was allowed no time for idle chitchat with the family. Her uncle came straight to the point, not even giving her a moment to catch her breath after all the introductions before plunging into the business at hand, so eager was he to get it over with.

"When I learned you were alive"—his eyes bored into hers, making her extremely uncomfortable—"I spared no effort to bring you home. It was my moral duty, after all," he explained piously.

"I don't understand," Meghan said in a low voice. She was not liking this man at all. She didn't like the tone of his voice. She didn't like the way he looked at her as if she were a piece of gold he'd found in the river.

"How could I leave you to rot away with the Cheyenne when all this was awaiting you?" He gestured expansively to the tastefully furnished parlor and the well-manicured grounds that could be seen through the windows.

"I wasn't exactly rotting," Meghan replied acidly.

"Jonathan," his wife Erin interjected timidly from where she sat on a plushly upholstered love seat. "I'm sure Meghan is tired from her journey. Perhaps if we went into this later—"

"Nonsense!" Jonathan boomed. "It's best to get this out in the open right now, so there's no confusion."

Erin sighed. On one side of her Samantha looked bored. On the other side Clara looked slightly hostile.

"Confusion about what, Uncle Jonathan?"

"The mines, my dear. I want nobody to say that Jonathan O'Brian cheated his own niece out of what belonged to her. The mines are all yours, Meghan, down to the last little flake of gold."

Meghan thought her uncle looked a bit strained at this last statement, but she could understand why.

"The claims that are being worked in this business I have here belonged to your father. Of course, we all thought you were dead, killed by the Indians. But when I learned you were alive . . . well, you know what I did. You are a very wealthy young woman, Meghan."

Jason's eyes narrowed suspiciously. He'd suspected that Meghan was due at least some part of her uncle's business, but all the mines? No one was that honest! "You mean that all the mines in the O'Brian Mining Company belong to my wife?"

Jonathan turned a cold stare on his niece's presumptuous husband, but Jason's gaze didn't lower.

"There are only two operating right now, but morally speaking, they're both hers."

Jason arched a wary brow. "Morally?"

"Well, yes." Jonathan hesitated. "Legally, it gets a bit messy. You see, after seven years, Meghan was declared dead in the eyes of the law."

"Oh?" Jason asked. "And who started that legal procedure?"

"I did, of course," Jonathan answered coldly.

"Of course." Jason smiled.

"And now we must have her legally reinstated before the property can actually pass to her."

"And I suppose you'll see to that?" Jason ventured.

"Certainly I will." Jonathan frowned.

Jason pictured the legal delays that could ensue, buying more time for Jonathan. Every instinct told him not to trust this man, and his instincts had never steered him wrong before.

"Maybe that's a chore I can take off your hands," he offered blandly.

"Thank you, Mr. Sinclair." Jonathan smiled politely. "But that's not necessary. I know my way around Sacramento. I have connections there. It will be easier for me."

Jason smiled with equal politeness. "I insist."

The two men's eyes met and clashed. Jason figured they understood each other and also figured he'd better watch his back from here on out.

\* \* \*

The June air seemed to vibrate with the heat, but it was cool on the covered porch of O'Brian House. Meghan sat in a hand-carved rocker imported from Ireland, trying to concentrate on her stitchery, but more often than not her eyes were drawn to the vista in front of her. Her uncle's house was set on a hillside well above the crowded bustle of Placerville, and, from where she sat, Meghan could look out over the quiet hills. The gently rounded knolls were gold in color, as if reflecting the frenzy that had brought so many tens of thousands into these hills in search of the elusive metal. Here and there the gold of the wild grasses was overpainted by the lush green of clumps of pine, oak, manzanita, red madrona, and wild olive trees. All in all, Meghan thought, the landscape was almost too parklike to be natural, as if some ambitious gardner had plied his art on a gigantic scale.

She leaned back in the rocker and gave up her attempt at concentration on the fancy stitches that her aunt Erin had taught her. After four days at O'Brian House she still felt like a fish cast up on a riverbank, gasping for air in an alien and hostile environment. She dropped the sampler in her lap and stared into the distance, not really seeing the golden hills and blue, shimmering sky. There were too many jumbled thoughts running around her mind for her to concentrate on such a monotonous task. Too much had happened in the last year. And now Jason was gone, leaving her bereft of the one common thread that tied her new world to the old.

They'd been allowed only a few short moments alone before he rode off. Erin had thoughtfully shooed everyone about their business, leaving the two of them together in the dim coolness of the parlor. Jason's attention immediately riveted onto her, where before he'd seemed not even aware of her presence in the room. He leaned casually on the fireplace mantel, regarding her with eyes suddenly gone hot. His size and the restless energy that emanated from him made the spacious room seem small and confining. Relaxed as he seemed, the taut lines of his body had signaled his tension. Then suddenly he had moved to stand in front of her, close enough for her to feel the heat flowing from his body. He reached out, took Andrew from her arms, and laid him carefully on the seat beside her. Then he pulled her to her feet.

Nothing was said between them, only he looked at her with such intensity that for a moment she grew frightened. She started to back away, but his hands tightened on her shoulders, drawing her closer. Then his mouth descended to claim hers. Without thought of resistance she opened her lips to receive him, allowing his tongue to plunder the softness within. Of its own will her body crowded closer to his, molding her slender frame to his larger one. He dropped one hand to her buttocks and pressed her hard against him. As she felt the bold thrust of his desire, her loins seemed to turn to hot liquid and her blood beat through her veins in a demand for what only he could give.

They were both breathing in short, painful gasps when he finally released her and set her back from him. His eyes raked her face and form as though memorizing every feature, every curve, every line. She swayed dizzily and his hand tightened on her arm.

"Something to keep you until I come back, little Meghan." He didn't say how long he would be in Sacramento, or if he would be staying when he came back. And she didn't ask.

A gurgle from Andrew drew both their eyes to the infant wriggling on the settee. Jason picked up the baby and brushed his lips against the downy fuzz on his head. "You take care of your mother, boy," he whispered with a smile.

Meghan could do nothing but look at him dumbly. She said nothing when he turned and walked out the double doors leading into the hall and then into the foyer. She sat and automatically picked up her son, holding him tightly to her breast as she listened to the hoofbeats of the horse

Jason had borrowed from her uncle. As the tattoo of hooves faded into the distance, she buried her face in the warm little body she held against her, and her tears wet the infant's soft skin.

"Oh! There you are!" Meghan's cousin Samantha exclaimed as she stepped out the front door and onto the porch. "My mother's been looking for you."

The spell of Meghan's reminiscing was broken by the girl's merry voice. "I was just practicing the fancy embroidery stitches your mother taught me yesterday."

Samantha peered at Meghan's crumpled sampler with amusement. "Looks . . . well . . . what've you been doing? Using it as a handkerchief?" Then she smiled brightly. "You'll get better. Mother'll be glad you were practicing." She wrinkled her turned-up nose in a little moue of disgust. "She'll probably lecture me to be following your example."

Samantha flopped down in the chair beside Meghan, her full skirt with its many petticoats billowing up around her in the seat. "Mother told me you made all your dresses. They're very fine work."

Meghan smiled, remembering the labor that had gone into learning to sew well enough to outfit herself. "I had help with them . . . a very fine lady on Jason's ranch in Colorado. She taught me how to do practical needlework. We didn't try anything fancy like this, though." She held up the sampler and looked at it critically. "I can't really see much use in stuff like this. All this labor on something you'll only hang on a wall to look at."

Samantha smiled with a pixieish gleam in her blue eyes. "You should tell that to Mother. She won't have us doing anything practical. We have all our clothes made by Mrs. Standish in town. But Mother insists we all do this. . . ." She waved a hand at the sampler. "Says it's ladylike work for our idle hands."

Meghan couldn't help but smile, thinking of the difference in life-style at her uncle's mansion and the ranch where she'd spent the winter. There, everyone had worked at tasks that were suitable for his or her age and strength, even the children, and there had been no trouble finding work for idle hands. Here it was considered improper for the ladies of the house to do any useful work. As far as she could discern, her aunt and cousins spent all their time paying social calls and performing light tasks that were purely decorative in nature.

Seeing the wistful smile curving her cousin's lips, Samantha was instantly all sympathy. "Do you miss Jason's ranch, Meghan?"

Meghan shrugged and smiled. "There are many things I miss. I suppose that's one of them." She reached out and gave the younger girl's hand a gentle squeeze. "Don't look so concerned. I'll survive."

Samantha's blue eyes sparkled at Meghan's gesture of friendship. She was the younger of Jonathan O'Brian's two daughters, and fortunately, Meghan decided, she didn't at all take after her father. Blond ringlets framed a delicately boned, finely feminine face made bright by naturally rosy cheeks and sparkling blue eyes. At fifteen, she was still chubby and rather a tomboy, but she already showed promise of great beauty and sensitivity.

"I just think it's so exciting . . . and sad too, of course . . . the life you've led!" Her eyes sparkled with excitement. "Living with the Indians and being rescued during a great battle, and"—and here a sigh escaped Samantha's lips—"and now you're married to Jason Sinclair, of all people!"

Jason's reputation in California wasn't as widespread as it was farther east in the Rockies, but it was sufficient to make the imagination of a young girl such as Samantha run wild. Her brief encounter with Jason was enough to convince her that Meghan was the luckiest woman in the world.

"It must have been so exciting traveling wih him!" Samantha imagined out loud. "Did you see any gunfights? Is he really as terribly dangerous as everyone says?"

Meghan sighed. Her cousin's misplaced hero worship

was getting tiring after four days of the same sort of drivel.
Not only that, but enthusiasm over Jason's attractiveness
struck a bitter and painful note in Meghan's breast. She
knew how handsome, how virile, how charming, and how
very dangerous Jason was. And she didn't want to talk
about it.

"It was all very tame," Meghan lied patiently. She'd
seen violence enough and blood enough on the journey
from Montana to Colorado to be well-acquainted with the
dangerous nature of the man who was her husband. But
how to explain to this innocent girl that Jason had almost
killed her after killing four Cheyenne in bloody hand-to-
hand fighting? How to explain to the girl that Meghan
herself had been on the receiving end of Jason's fabled
marksmanship and had herself wished him dead more than
once? How could Samantha understand that after so much
violence and hate Meghan had grown to love the man
she'd so fiercely despised?

"Was it really so tame?" Samantha queried suspiciously,
seeing the sad shadows of memories in Meghan's eyes.

Meghan schooled her face to pleasantness and smiled.
"Yes. Nothing much exciting."

Samantha huffed out a sigh. "Nobody ever tells me
anything. They all say I'm too young."

"And so they should!" Erin O'Brian's voice brought
them both up with a start. She stood holding the front door
open, looking at them both with a touch of impatience.
"Samantha, how often have I told you not to pry into other
people's business? Just because Meghan is your cousin
doesn't mean you don't have to show her respect. You
must learn to leave people some privacy, my dear."

"It's all right, Aunt Erin." Meghan promptly leapt to
Samantha's defense. "She wasn't bothering me. I enjoy
her company."

Samantha preened herself under this compliment, but a
look from her mother cut her enjoyment short. "Yes,
ma'am," she answered hastily. "I'm sorry, Meghan. I

really am a pest at times." But her eyes continued to sparkle in a most unrepentant manner.

"That's better," Erin told her daughter, not noticing that the look in her eyes did not match the apologetic words. Erin strolled over to where Meghan sat and looked down at the wrinkled half-finished sampler covering her lap. She sighed daintily as she observed that while the stitches were carefully done, the material looked as though it had been wadded up and used as a washcloth. She managed to muster an encouraging smile for her husband's niece. "Those stitches are done very nicely, Meghan. You have a real talent for such fine work. You'll find yourself liking it before long and not wanting to crumple it like a dustrag."

"Oh—" Meghan started to apologize.

"Think nothing of it, dear," Erin interrupted with a smile. "I didn't come out here to inspect your stitchery, though I'm pleased you've been practicing. I came to tell you that we've been invited to a dinner party at the home of Eustace Bailey and his wife. Friday night. I'm sorry I didn't tell you earlier, but it quite slipped my mind."

"Oh!" Samantha jumped up and clapped her hands in glee. "A dinner party at the Baileys'. Oh, Meghan! They give such lovely parties! And their house is beautiful, though not quite so grand as ours of course! You'll love it!"

Meghan didn't bother to hide her distress. Her one experience with a formal dinner party had been at Fort Laramie, Wyoming, and that affair had turned out to be a disaster. "Aunt Erin, I would really rather not. I certainly don't wish to offend anyone, but I just don't feel . . . ready to be social yet."

"Nonsense!" Erin said firmly. "There's no reason in the world for you to be shy. You're a charming girl. And everyone wants to meet you. I won't hear of your staying home."

"I don't have anything suitable to wear," Meghan objected, thinking that this problem at least would dis-

suade her uncle's wife, who apparently never went anywhere unless attired in the very latest fashion from Europe.

"Yes, well . . ." Erin looked thoughtful for a moment.
"Perhaps something of Samantha's could be altered to fit.
Clara's gowns would be much too large. Later you can go
upstairs with Samantha and see if something of hers might
do. Right now, dear, you'd better go see to Andrew. Li
Ching told me right before I found you that he's getting
fussy. Perhaps he needs to be fed."

"Oh, dear." Meghan frowned. "I'm afraid I let time
run away from me. He should have been fed almost an
hour ago."

Erin followed Meghan into the house but didn't follow
her up the stairs. Instead, she opened the door to her
husband's study and, seeing he was alone, stepped in.
Jonathan looked up from his account book and scowled at
the interruption. His expression softened only a little when
he saw the intruder was his wife.

"Yes, dear?"

"Jonathan," Erin sighed and sat herself down in the
chair opposite the polished oak desk. "I do wish you
might have a chat with your niece."

"What about? She seems to be settling in quite well."

"I suppose it must look that way. She's quiet and
unobtrusive. And she seems to get along with Clara
and Samantha. But she's so . . . so inward looking, Jonathan.
She needs to be encouraged to get out more."

"Good heavens, Erin! The girl's only been here four
days, and you're expecting her to go gallivanting with you
and the girls in your social whirl? Keep in mind Meghan's
been living with civilized white people for only a year, and
then on some rustic ranch in Colorado. She's not a
well-bred young lady who enjoys the same sort of things
as you and the girls. Besides, she's a married woman with
a child."

Erin sighed heavily. "Poor girl. She's such a lovely
young thing, though for my taste her coloring is a bit
flamboyant to be truly ladylike. But she is charming and

quite attractive in an earthy sort of way. Such a shame she has so many disadvantages. Being raised by the savages was bad enough. But now, being married to a man with such a . . . a dangerous reputation. I truly don't know what will become of her, Jonathan.''

Jonathan laughed indulgently. "Don't you worry about Meghan, my dear. She's a rich woman, and she still has her looks." He sighed. "I suppose we are going to have to do something about Sinclair, though. A man like that . . . It's obvious he married her to get his hands on my . . . on her money." He smiled at his wife's look of alarm. "But I'm sure a girl as smart as Meghan will eventually see his true colors and make arrangements to free herself." He rose, patted his wife's soft white hand, and escorted her to the door. Then he sat down once again at his desk and rested his chin thoughtfully on the steeple of his hands.

Sinclair was a problem. One that must be dealt with before he made too much trouble. Jonathan had gone to a lot of trouble to bring his niece to California, and he wasn't about to let some gun-hardened, fortune-hunting bastard lay waste to his careful plans. Yes, indeed, Jonathan thought to himself. Sinclair must be dealt with one way or another before the law declared Meghan eligible to receive her inheritance.

Meghan drew her legs up under her Indian fashion as she sat on Samantha's bed, watching her young cousin pull one dress after another out of her closet. The room was all done in frilly white—white lace curtains, white flounced counterpane, white canopy over the bed. Even the two expensive Oriental rugs on the oak floor displayed only a hint of color on a white and cream background.

Samantha pulled another gown out and added it to the pile on the bed. She scowled as she examined them one by one.

"This isn't right for your coloring," she sighed, holding

a lavender gown up beside Meghan's face. "And this one . . . no, this one looks as if it should be on a ten-year-old. Fiddlesticks! Clara should be doing this. She knows more about fashion than I do."

The third dress she picked up was a yellow taffeta with a moderately low-cut bodice and full sleeves designed to end right below the elbow. The bodice was cut wide in the shoulder and tapered to a tight-fitting, V-shaped waist.

Samantha giggled. "Mother said this was too old for me, but I persuaded her to buy it anyway. It might be perfect. Try it on."

The gown had looked so pretty lying on the bed, but it was a total loss once Meghan slipped it on. It was too tight through the chest and much too loose in the waist, even though Meghan was not wearing a corset.

"Well!" Samantha gave the gown and Meghan a jaundiced look. "Guess that shows what kind of figure I have. I'm going to start fasting tomorrow."

Meghan had simply shrugged and taken the gown off.

"We'll just have to tell Daddy you need a complete new wardrobe, that's what! Maybe he'll let you and me and Mother and Clara go into Sacramento, even. They have the best shops there!"

Meghan grimaced. "I think it best that I just don't go to these parties you're invited to."

"Oh, no!" Samantha denied hotly. "Mother would never allow that! We can go down to town tomorrow and get something from Mrs. Standish. I'm sure she'll have something she can alter by Friday night. You'll like her shop. Really. She has the finest things, though Clara claims it's not nearly as nice as the shops in Sacramento." Samantha sighed wistfully. "Mother and Daddy gave a ball just for Clara last spring. And Mother took Clara for a whole week to Sacramento to pick out all her new clothes. I didn't get to go, but next summer will be my ball, and I'm going to shop in every store in that city. I swear I am!"

Meghan sighed and pulled on her own plain day dress.

She was not at all convinced she could adjust to this strange way of life. She had begun to love her life at Jason's ranch, but life in her uncle's house was different altogether. She once again longed for the simplicity of a Cheyenne village and the buckskin tunic and leggings she had worn there.

But now she knew that longing was simply a wishful dream. In the year since she had left the Cheyenne, she had witnessed the awesome numbers and power of the white man. She was convinced that Walks Alone had been right. The sun was setting on the day of the Indians. Her son must have a place among the victors, which meant that she must learn to survive here.

She listened with only a tiny part of her mind to Samantha's endless chatter while she looked out the bedroom window to the golden hills beyond the lawn. For her son's sake, she vowed, she would learn to do more than survive here. She would be more than one of these silly, useless white women thinking of nothing but parties and clothes. She would do more than survive; for her son's sake, for Jason's son's sake, she would conquer.

# Chapter Twenty-two

The heyday of the gold rush was over for Placerville, California, the bustling little town nestled in the golden foothills of the rugged Sierra Nevada, but the town still hummed with activity. There was still gold in the rivers and creeks, and gold in the surrounding hills. And there were still swarms of miners trying to get it out of the earth and into their pockets.

Erin, Samantha, and Meghan strolled along the plank walks that bordered Main Street. The day was pleasant, with a cool breeze that swept up from the distant sea and relieved the heat. The day was so pleasant, in fact, that they left their carriage on the edge of town, deciding to avoid the midday traffic. From there they proceeded on a pleasant walk down Main Street, Erin and Samantha pointing out the local sights to Meghan and filling her in on the history of the little town that for the past ten years had been the O'Brian family's home.

Meghan had to admit that Placerville was a pleasant place. Erin told her that people first settled the valley in 1849, shortly after John Marshall discovered gold on the South Fork of the American River, eight miles north of town. A frenzy of haphazard growth had followed, with building and mining both proceeding at a furious pace. Then in 1856 the town had burned to ashes. Only three buildings had remained. Now, though, traces of the fire were all but obliterated, and fine brick buildings stood in place of the wooden ones that had been destroyed. Placerville had come a long way since those riotous days of the 1850's when it was called Hangtown because of the numerous vigilant executions at the Hangman's Tree that stood in Elstner's Hay Yard.

Meghan found herself liking the town as she strolled along with her aunt and cousin. She peered into Leatherby's Ice Cream Parlor and into the old hardware store, one of the few buildings that had escaped the ravages of the fire of '56. The office of the *Mountain Democrat* also drew her notice. A young man from that enterprising newspaper had called at O'Brian House only two days before to ask if she would grant an interview on the thrilling story of her rescue from the Indians. She had been about to refuse curtly when a warning glance from Erin made her hesitate. Her uncle's wife had deftly stepped into the gap left by her hesitation and told the reporter that of course her niece would be happy to tell her story, but they must give her a bit more time to settle in. When confronted by Meghan's angry glare after the man had left, Erin had explained that it was never wise to insult the press, and there was no rule saying she had to tell the whole truth if it made her uncomfortable. This was a chance, Erin said, to vindicate herself in the eyes of polite society, even to make herself the darling of the stodgy old matrons of Placerville if she was smart about what she said. Meghan looked through the window into the printing office of the newspaper, watching as one woman and two men labored diligently at their desks. She wondered how long she would be given to "settle in" before the young reporter would call again.

The sightseeing ended abruptly when they came to Mrs. Irma Standish's dress shop. In the window hung several full-skirted dresses, one of silk and two of taffeta, which a sign proclaimed to be the very latest fashion from Europe. Meghan could see nothing very special about the gowns. In fact, they looked grossly uncomfortable, with tiny waists and daringly low-cut bodices.

Erin had left them a block before they reached Mrs. Standish's shop, having met a lady friend on the street and agreeing to take tea with her while the girls shopped. So Samantha and Meghan were now on their own. Without the self-assured presence of her uncle's wife, Meghan felt a bit unsettled in the crowded and noisy bustle surrounding them.

"I wish Clara were here," Samantha commented as they looked at the dresses displayed in the window. "She knows so much more about clothes than I do."

Clara, a large-boned, dark-haired girl who took after her father, had elected to stay home and work on her pencil sketches, which seemed to be the very root of her life. Samantha claimed that her sister had an uncanny eye for color and style, but had been unable to persuade the girl to accompany them on their shopping trip. Clara had been somewhat standoffish with Meghan since her arrival. She was polite enough, but the courtesy was forced, unlike Samantha's genuine warmth.

"I suppose we don't really need Clara, though," Samantha

continued in a happier tone. "Mrs. Standish knows absolutely everything about clothes. Just as Mother said, you can just tell Mrs. Standish what you need and rely on her advice."

"Yes," Meghan agreed halfheartedly, "I suppose."

Mrs. Standish was all that Samantha had claimed her to be. An owllike little lady who looked as if she'd lived the better part of a hundred years, she had blue eyes that were still sharp and clear behind the thick glasses, and as she surveyed Meghan she missed no detail of her figure, face, or coloring.

"I think I may have several gowns that might be suitable and would need only a little alteration," she told them in a flutelike voice. "Wait here, girls, and I'll go to the back room and get them."

Meghan glanced around the little shop with interest. White women, she thought, paid so much attention to clothes. Cheyenne women, also, liked to be attractively adorned. But the art of self-decoration didn't occupy the whole of their minds as it seemed to do with many white women she'd met, especially her uncle's wife and his youngest daughter. If there were many ladies in Placerville like her aunt and cousin, Meghan thought, Mrs. Standish must be a busy woman.

As she walked around the tiny front room of the shop, she fingered some of the fine fabrics that were on display— silk, taffeta, satin, and for simpler clothing, plain cotton, gingham, calico, muslin, and wool. All types of caps and bonnets were hung where they could be readily seen through the window and by customers walking through the door. In a discreet little corner in the back were ladies' fine underthings—stockings, crinolines, shifts, and corsets. The number and variety of items were confusing to one who for most of her life had been satisfied with a quill-decorated buckskin tunic and leggings.

"I have just the thing!" Mrs. Standish declared, appearing suddenly from the back room. She held up a blue silk dress with half sleeves and a modest neckline. "Ezra Baker's wife ordered this two weeks ago, then didn't take it because she found out she's pregnant again, poor woman. She knows the way she gains weight she'll be two sizes larger by the time the baby's delivered. With a nip here and a tuck there, it should do very nicely for you, Meghan.''

Meghan looked at the dress doubtfully. The silk was finer than anything she'd ever worn, and the stunning blue color, in combination with her flamboyant hair, was sure to draw every eye. She wasn't sure she wanted to be the center of attention, though she had to admit the gown was indeed beautiful.

"Would you like to come into the back and try it on?"

"Oh, do, Meghan!" Samantha urged. "It's truly beautiful!"

The dress was beautiful. Meghan couldn't deny it. It was even more beautiful once she had it on. The color might have been made for her alone, and the alteration required to make it fit—several tucks in the waist and a lengthening of the hem—could easily be accomplished in time for a final fitting late that afternoon so that she could wear it to the Baileys' dinner party the following night.

Meghan decided to take the dress. Then she chose several items of fine underwear, a pair of shoes, and two hats. If her aunt Erin was going to push her out into society, she decided, she might as well be dressed for it. The packages were piling up, so Samantha suggested they take their purchases back to the carriage before venturing on to see the rest of the town.

Erin was not waiting for them at the carriage, much to Meghan's disappointment. So once they were relieved of their packages, Samantha suggested they walk to the other end of town to a hotel dining room that served what she swore was the best lemonade in the county. Meghan was full of restless energy, so she agreed readily to the excursion. Erin might be with her lady friend for the entire afternoon, and Meghan had no desire to wait idly by the carriage for several hours.

The lemonade was as delicious as Samantha had promised, and they welcomed the cool drink after walking the entire dusty length of Main Street. When they had almost finished their first glass and were thinking of ordering a second, Erin walked in.

"I thought I might find you here," she said with a smile. "Did you find a suitable dress for tomorrow night, Meghan dear?"

Meghan said she had, and when Erin learned the dress should be ready for the final fitting in just over an hour, they all agreed to spend the time sitting in the pleasantly cool hotel dining room sipping another lemonade. Once again Meghan wondered at the leisure of the lives of her aunt and cousins. It was the life that her father had fancifully promised to her mother, Meghan remembered, as they were leaving on the wagon train for California. She wondered what would have happened had her father lived: If the attack on the wagon train had never taken place, would her father have been as successful as Jonathan in creating an empire out of a small placer mine and two undeveloped claims? From all that she remembered of her father, she doubted it.

The sun was far down toward the western horizon when they left the hotel. The buildings along Main Street cast long-reaching shadows across the street, and the daytime bustle was beginning to give over to the activities of the evening. Miners still grimy from the day's toil ambled down the street in twos and threes, wandering toward the lower part of town that sported saloons and houses where ladies of easy virtue could be persuaded to grant their favors to a hard-working man with gold in his pocket.

The three women proceeded down the street at a lively pace, for, as Erin confided to Meghan, it wasn't seemly for a lady to be walking the streets after sundown without a gentleman on her arm. Of course it was still a long time until sunset, but, Erin commented, the town did seem a bit rowdy this afternoon.

Mrs. Standish's shop was on the corner of Main and Benham streets, with the entrance around the corner instead of opening directly on the main avenue. Benham Street was in shadow when they went into the shop, and when they came out thirty minutes later, the shadows were even deeper. Erin lingered in the shop doorway to chat with Mrs. Standish about a new walking dress she had just ordered. Samantha and Meghan looked up Benham Street curiously while they waited for the conversation to end.

Benham Street was one of the more notorious avenues in Placerville. It was here that most of the Chinese lived and kept their shops, and at all times of the day men with long black queues hanging down their backs could be seen going about their business, oftentimes carrying on their shoulders long poles with loaded baskets balanced on both ends. It was also on Benham Street that the miners came to seek their pleasure, for the lower end of the avenue was lined with saloons, whorehouses, and hotels of doubtful reputation.

With the late afternoon shadows stretching toward night, Benham Street was coming alive. The tinny tinkling of a piano, accompanied occasionally by drunken singing and shouted comments, drifted on the breeze to the curious, listening girls. Samantha giggled and, casting a cautious glance at her mother, urged Meghan farther down the street where they could better hear the celebrating.

"I've never been here so late before," she tittered. "Can you imagine what sorts of wicked things are going on down there?"

Meghan sighed impatiently. She had no desire to think about the vices of the white man's society. For all she knew, Jason could be in a similar place in Sacramento. He probably was, she thought unhappily. He was probably drinking his fool head off and fondling the lush and somewhat soiled curves of some female who pretended to serve up drinks but really served up sex. The thought cast a pall on what had been a lovely afternoon.

Meghan's morose thoughts were interrupted by a loud laugh, followed by the off-key rendering of a bawdy song that related the adventures of a female gold digger. The voices were alarmingly close. As Meghan took hold of Samantha's arm to urge her back toward Mrs. Standish's shop, three burly men appeared from the mouth of a dark alleyway between two of the Chinese shops. They held on to each other as if for balance, and the unsteadiness of their steps testified to the fact that they'd just come from one of the saloons farther down the street.

"Look, George." One of the men punched a comrade for attention. "What have we here?" He pointed a grimy finger at the two girls. Meghan was distressed to see how far down the street they'd wandered. They couldn't reach the safety of Main Street before the men could intercept them, not even if they ran, and she knew that fleeing would only set the men after them in earnest. So she ignored their taunts and kept walking in a steady, unhurried manner.

Samantha tugged uneasily at her sleeve. "Come on, Meghan. Let's get out of here!"

"Stay calm," Meghan said in a low voice, giving Samantha's hand a reassuring squeeze. "Don't let them know you're frightened."

"Well, if it isn't big ole Jonathan O'Brian's little girl," George slurred. "And look, Harry! I bet that redhead with the uppity look on her face is that white squaw the boys been talkin' about."

"Samantha! Meghan! Where are you?" Erin chose this moment to walk out of the deepening shadows. She stopped when she saw the two girls. "Oh. There you are. How many times have I told you, Samantha—" Her impromptu scolding halted in mid-speech as she noticed the three toughs who were sauntering closer with unpleasant grins on their faces.

"Whoooeee!" Harry slapped his palm on his thigh, sending up a cloud of dust. "And here's the missus. Would you believe. Bet ole O'Brian wouldn't cotton to us being this close to his womenfolk."

Erin sniffed distastefully. "Come, girls. Let's go."

"Not so fast!" George was apparently not as drunk as

he appeared, for before the women could go any farther he slid around to place himself between them and the distant safety of Main Street. "I think you ladies owe us. What do you think, boys?"

"I don't understand." Erin frowned. "I don't even know you . . . uh . . . gentlemen."

"Woooo!" the third of the trio finally added his comment. "Gentlemen, she calls us. Didya hear that?"

George swaggered closer, close enough for Erin to smell his fetid breath. "Yer ole man fired us today, missus. Just cuz we was bitchin' about that foreman Drury who don't know the business end of a shovel from a hole in the ground. Fired us without pay, too. We figures maybe we got sumpthin' comin' from the O'Brian family. Looks like yer here just in time to pay us off."

The circle of the three men closed in on them. Erin looked as if she was about to faint. "I . . . I don't have any money with me, but . . ."

Harry laughed, a guttural sound that carried no humor in it. "Well, maybe we'll jest take sumpthin' in trade. Yer a fine-lookin' piece o' women, even if'n yer a little past yer prime. And these two fillies . . ." He licked his lips and devoured Samantha and Meghan with his eyes. "I'll bet that redhead what lived with the Injuns knows tricks that even ole Mary the Whore don't know. What say you show us how those big bucks like it, honey?"

Meghan felt no fear, only raging-hot fury. Her voice quivered with scorn as she sneered contemptuously at the big man called Harry. "Touch any one of us, you filthy piece of slime, and you'll wish you'd tried to mate with a rattlesnake!"

"Whooo-whoo! George! Silas! Listen to the redhead! She's a little savage all right. What say we take her and these other goddamn O'Brians into that alleyway over there and teach 'em what a real man feels like. We're owed, by God!"

"What you gents are owed is a lesson in how to act around ladies."

Meghan's head snapped around and her eyes grew wide with surprise as a quiet voice came out of the shadows, followed by the tall form of a tawny-haired, amber-eyed Jason Sinclair. He lounged indolently up against the corner of the closest building, looking for all the world as though he were simply passing the time of day instead of interrupting potential violence by three men who all appeared to have the brute strength and tenacity of scrub bulls. "And it seems like I'm the one elected to do the lessoning."

George spat onto the dirt. "And who might you be, mister?"

"I might be Jason Sinclair," he replied with a tigerish smile. "And I don't take kindly to my wife or her friends being mauled about by the likes of you. So I guess I'm just going to have to send you gents on your way."

Harry snorted derisively and self-consciously flexed the bulky muscles of his shoulders. "You and whose army?" The man's name had rung a bell in the back of his mind, but he couldn't quite think of where he'd heard it before. It didn't matter anyway. It was their three to his one. Those were the kind of odds Harry liked.

"Yeah!" George voiced his agreement. "Come ahead, blondie. After we've taken you out we'll show your little wife what she's been missin' bein' hitched to a guy like you."

Jason grinned and unfastened the gunbelt that circled his hips. The miners were spoiling for a fight, and he didn't object to giving them what they wanted. He'd been in a surly, frustrated mood since he had left Meghan at O'Brian House five days ago, and to tell the truth he was just itching to get somebody's blood on his hands. He handed the gunbelt to Meghan as he went forward to meet the advance of what seemed like a solid wall of beefy miners.

Meghan took the gunbelt and met Jason's feral grin with a gaze of steady impassivity. The lethal savagery she saw in his eyes didn't fill her with feminine horror. Nor did it surprise her. She was still too much of a Cheyenne to be revolted at the prospect of a bloody fight, and she knew what Jason could do. Unlike the mother and daughter cowering beside her, she's seen him in action. She'd seen him fight odds as great as these against much more dangerous opponents. She herself had been the loser in one such battle.

The fight was short and brutal. The miners had sobered up considerably since they lurched out of the alleyway toward Samantha and Meghan, but even in full possession of their wits they wouldn't have been a match for Jason. They were strong, but slow. Jason was equally strong, and very fast. The three beefy brutes simply got in each other's way as Jason dispatched them one by one. He made it look easy, and by the time all three miners were laid out on the dirt, Jason's only injuries were a split knuckle and a rapidly coloring bruise alongside his jaw. And most of the blood on his hands was not his own.

Erin clutched Samantha, who hung on to Meghan in what seemed to be a death grip. Meghan stood impassively and watched as Jason checked to make sure all three opponents were out of commission then walked toward the women. She handed him his gunbelt and knife.

Erin shook herself back to awareness in time to offer effusive thanks. Jason nodded to her gravely.

"Glad to be of help, ma'am," he addressed Erin politely. It was Meghan he was looking at, though, with one brow raised as if to ask—have you learned a lesson?

Meghan knew that if she hadn't been foolish enough to allow her young cousin down this forbidden street the whole unpleasant incident wouldn't have happened. But all feelings of chagrin were crowded out of her mind by a rising tide of hurt and indignation at finding Jason here in Placerville, when he was supposed to be in Sacramento arranging her legal reinstatement. Her jade eyes darkened to almost black as she returned his mocking gaze with an angry glare.

Ignoring the angry sparks flying from Meghan's eyes, Jason turned his attention to Samantha. "It's all right,

Miss O'Brian. These men aren't going to bother you again.''

Meghan turned to her cousin and was surprised to see tears cascading down the younger girl's face. Her whole body shook with inarticulate sobs.

"Oh, Sam! Don't cry!'' Meghan murmured, temporarily putting her own feelings on hold. Meghan was used to the sight of men spilling each other's blood, but the sight of male brutaity was a shock to Samantha's sensibilities. Meghan pulled out her handkerchief and dabbed at her cousin's face. "Everything's all right.'' She took the younger girl by the arm. "Let's get you out of here. Aunt Erin? Are you all right?''

"Oh, yes, yes, of course. Poor Samantha. My poor baby.'' Erin was pale as ash but still composed. "I don't know how to thank you enough, Mr. Sinclair. Why, if you hadn't come, I can't think . . . I don't . . . well . . .''

"Aunt Erin,'' Meghan suggested, "why don't you take Sam back to the carriage. I need to have a few words with my husband.'' She slanted Jason an ominous look.

Erin gave Jason one final expression of thanks and turned to shepherd her niece toward the safety of Main Street.

"What the hell are you doing here?'' Meghan turned on Jason with indignation painting her cheeks with an angry flush.

"Beats me!'' The devil's light was in his amber eyes as he answered her anger with an innocent smile. "I was just walking along the street, minding my own business, when—''

"Not that! What are you still doing here in town? You said you were off in Sacramento!'' The picture of his being in Placerville, probably hanging around the saloons and diddling the whores while she was sitting in O'Brian House missing him, was too much to be borne. "Why did you lie to me?'' she demanded. "If you wanted to take off on your own you didn't have to make up some story about going to Sacramento to see to my legal affairs!'' She was close to tears and furious at herself for letting his duplicity disappoint her so.

"Well, I didn't lie, exactly." Jason picked up his hat from where it had fallen in the street, dusted it on his trousers, and put it on his head. "I just sort of changed my plans. Temporarily."

Meghan's eyes narrowed suspiciously. "What do you mean?" She tried to pull away as Jason casually took her arm and guided her toward Main Street, but his grasp, for all its gentleness, was unbreakable. "What do you think you're doing?"

"What any gentleman would do. Escorting you to a place more fitting for a lady."

"Since when have you been a gentleman?" she scoffed.

"Since about the same time you've been a lady," he replied softly. A mischievous smile played around his mouth.

Her eyes narrowed and shot sparks of green fire. "You're avoiding my question. What do you mean, you changed your plans?"

"I was all set to go to Sacramento like I said. Then I stopped and figured maybe I'd better stick around out of sight for a few days."

"Why?" Meghan demanded with a frown.

"To make sure Jonathan is treating you right."

She snorted impolitely. "That's the lamest excuse I've ever heard. Why shouldn't my uncle treat me right?"

"I don't trust him much. No man gives up that much money without a fight."

Meghan stopped and forcibly pulled her arm from his grasp, swinging around to glare at him. "Well, I don't trust him either, but I thought very naively that I could trust you. Now it seems there's no one I can rely on but myself."

"Meghan—"

"Just go ahead and do what you're doing, Jason!" Meghan interrupted in a voice that was close to breaking. She gave free rein to her jealous imaginings. "Go ahead and hang around your saloons and get drunk and spend time with the whores! I'll have Jonathan send Sykes up to Sacramento to take care of my affairs. And if he takes too long about it I'll damn well go myself!'' If she couldn't have a husband, she thought furiously, then at least she would have her inheritance to make a life for herself and her son—Jason's son.

''Meghan, dammit! Would you listen . . . !''

She whirled around and ran the short remaining distance to Main Street. Before he could catch her she had disappeared among the evening strollers.

''I do hope this won't ruin the dinner party for you tomorrow night, dear,'' Erin said worriedly to Meghan.

''Yes,'' Jonathan said, idly twirling a snifter of brandy. ''The Baileys always put on a good feed. It would be a shame if you couldn't go and enjoy yourself.''

''Don't worry about me, Aunt Erin. I'm fine. Really.''

Jonathan frowned thoughtfully. ''It was fortunate that Sinclair came along when he did. A remarkable coincidence.''

Meghan frowned at the mention of Jason. She was still suffering from his betrayal.

Jonathan continued in a thoughtful tone of voice. ''I'm surprised to learn that he's still in town. I thought he'd be in Sacramento by now.'' He looked at Meghan to see if she had any light to shed on the subject.

She returned his inquiring gaze with a noncommittal shrug. She didn't trust Jonathan not to do something slippery about the inheritance. But she didn't think for one minute that her own father's brother would do anything to really harm her. And she didn't believe Jason thought that either. He had just excused his actions with the first lie that had come to mind.

''I think maybe it would be best if Sykes went down to Sacramento to take care of my reinstatement,'' she said in a flat voice. ''Jason's too busy having a good time.''

Jonathan gave her a pitying glance. "Cutting a swath through Benham Street, is he?"

Meghan looked disgusted. "He was there, wasn't he?"

"Hmm, yes, well, with all the hard cases hanging around the mines, ours included," he said thoughtfully, "Jason would be wise to take his pleasures a little more discreetly. He's not without a certain notorious reputation, and if he makes himself too visible, many of these fellows would like to make a name for themselves by gunning him down. I know he's supposed to be a tough customer, but one of these days his luck's going to run out."

Meghan studied her hands in morose silence.

"You're right, I suppose," Jonathan continued. "I'll send Sykes tomorrow. I'm rather surprised Jason didn't go, though. You'd think he'd be eager for you to receive your inheritance."

"What do you mean?" Meghan asked suspiciously.

"A man like Jason, my dear, is always primarily interested in money. That's why I wasn't all that surprised when you two turned up married, once I'd thought about it. He obviously made inquiries about me and deduced that you would be due quite a tidy portion of my holdings."

Meghan stiffened. "I told you before why we got married," she said frankly. "He married me because of Andrew." And because he cares at least a little, she added silently. He had to care. All the passion they had shared surely couldn't just have been an animal need for physical release and satiation.

Jonathan sighed tolerantly. "Of course Andrew was a convenient excuse. I'm sure Jason leaped on it with enthusiasm."

Meghan lowered her eyes from her uncle's sympathetic gaze. Was that why Jason had been so surprisingly willing to make her his wife? She didn't want to believe it. She wouldn't believe it. Still . . .

"I blame myself," Jonathan continued. "I should have known better than to send such a man after you. But at the time it seemed he was the only one who had a chance to succeed. I put you in a very awkward position, and I should have guessed that Sinclair would take advantage of it. I'm sorry, Meghan. I can see that Jason has made you very unhappy.''

"Jason hasn't made me unhappy, Uncle Jonathan. You shouldn't worry about it."

Jonathan smiled. "You're a brave girl, Meghan. But we're your family here. No one has to put on a brave face for family. And it's not hopeless, you know. I'm not without influence with the legal powers in this area. I'm sure that I could arrange for a divorce without much trouble."

The look Meghan gave him made Jonathan fear he'd pushed too hard and too fast. He'd been casually hinting at such a thing ever since Jason had left O'Brian House, and Meghan had always listened politely without comment. That damned Indian poker face of hers usually didn't give a clue to what she was thinking, but now her hostility was obvious.

"If you decide that's what you want, of course," he continued in a conciliatory voice.

Meghan was tempted to shout out her refusal, but caution made her hesitate. Jason belonged to the wild freedom of the prairies and to the cool, clean isolation of the mountain wilderness. Was he hanging around the dives on Benham Street trying to drink away the legal chains she'd wrapped around him? She had his name, and she'd promised both herself and Jason that his name was all she required. Would she be doing him a favor to let her uncle obtain a divorce for them?

"I'll think about it, Uncle Jonathan," she promised in a tense, quiet voice.

"Well!" He leaned back in his chair and visibly cast the problem from his mind, at least temporarily. "Enough of this unpleasantness! Tomorrow, Meghan, we will introduce you to Placerville society, such as it is. Maybe you will meet some decent young men there, civilized men—

someone who will prove to you that not all men are savages at heart. Eh?''

Meghan smiled politely, but couldn't care less about meeting any of her uncle's "civilized" young men. The savage man who had fought for her on a dark street in Placerville still had her heart.

# Chapter Twenty-three

In the polite society of Placerville, Eustace and Elizabeth Bailey's dinner parties were considered the very height of fashion, besides being a rousing good time. Their house was situated in a fashionable part of town, in the hills just north of Main Street. Like O'Brian House, the Bailey home was a three-story brick mansion with a carriage house jutting off one end. Sharp-peaked gables gave it an old-world charm.

At the appointed hour of the party, a parade of carriages crowded the tree-lined circular drive that led to the house. Everyone who was anyone in Placerville, Coloma, Diamond Springs, and El Dorado had been invited, and everyone who was invited had been eager to come. Word had been quickly circulated that Jonathan O'Brian's niece would be in attendance, and everyone in the area was curious to see the unfortunate young woman who had so lately been rescued from the clutches of the savage red man.

For Meghan the dinner was an ordeal. It brought to mind the disastrous dinner at Fort Laramie, where she had gotten quite thoroughly drunk under the disapproving glare of Mrs. General Hutchison, as she in her mind had named that formidable lady, when Meghan had in liquor-induced giddiness thrown herself into the arms of Jason Sinclair and disgraced herself by being violently ill. Not again, she vowed. The wine that sat beside her plate went untouched, and she only picked at the rich food that was set before her, eating just enough to be polite. She was taking no risks on getting sick tonight and disgracing her uncle and his family.

Meghan picked at her food not only out of caution. She found that she had very little appetite. She was surrounded by strangers, for it was unfashionable to go into dinner with one's family at this sort of gathering. She was the uncomfortable center of attention in the group immediately around her and received numerous stares, some covert and subtle, others open and frankly curious, even from far down the table. The young man who'd been assigned as her dinner partner, a young nobleman from Austria, was the only bright spot of the seemingly endless meal. Of all the people in the room, he alone seemed not to regard her as some sort of oddity to be stared at and snickered over.

When the dancing commenced, Meghan found that she was never without a partner, and when she did manage to sit out a dance, she was crowded around by people eager to talk to her. Everyone appeared to want a close-up view of the evening's main attraction. If the dinner had been uncomfortable, the after-dinner socializing and dancing was enough to make her wish for the healthy draft of the wine she'd refused during the meal. She wished desperately she were back at Jason's ranch, surrounded by comfortable people she loved and who loved her, or back safe and secure in Stone Eagle's lodge on the rolling plains of Montana.

The matrons of polite society, decked out in their silks and satins, beruffled and bejeweled, were either icily polite or gushingly friendly. The matrons of the frozen stares and lifted noses gazed at her with contemptuous curiosity and exchanged whispers with their friends when they thought her back was turned. The matrons who gushed with friendship and sympathy were hoping to hear the titillating details of her supposedly degrading treatment at the hands of the Indians. The matrons' daughters, the young society flowers of California's gold country, were less subtle in their contempt. Their comments were less veiled and their stares more open. Meghan wondered perversely if these various ladies would have been less hostile had the gentlemen of the party not been dancing such close attendance on her.

Meghan didn't know how to dance, but her natural grace and sense of rhythm allowed her to follow her dance partners around the floor with some success. The young men who flocked around her were for the most part clean-cut and debonair, sons of the comtemptuous matrons and brothers and suitors of the hostile daughters. They were lavish in their compliments on her dress, her looks, her grace, her courage. But behind the polite compliments and discreet conversation, there were also unguarded glances, subtle touches, playful pats, and knowing smiles that were generally reserved for ladies of soiled reputation.

Meghan had willingly informed the matrons that she was married, had an infant son, and that her son's father was Jason Sinclair. The looks of shock and outrage on their faces had given her a feeling of wry satisfaction. But the men who paraded around the dance floor with her were not so easily put off. Knowledge of her circumstances only heightened their interest, it seemed. Before long she began to feel like a cornered hare surrounded by a pack of hungry dogs. She wished she had a knife to skewer the next hand that slid down on her buttocks for a subtle pinch or that brushed lingeringly against her breast while escorting her onto the dance floor. But she couldn't make a scene without embarrassing her aunt and upsetting her uncle, so she smiled politely at her hot-eyed escorts, laughed at their jokes, blushed at their compliments, and avoided their caresses. Most of all she prayed for the evening to draw to a rapid conclusion.

The evening was half over when she was rescued from the further unwelcome attentions of the local swains. She had managed to beg off the next dance to rest her feet when the young man who'd partnered her at dinner pushed through the crowd and ended up at her side. He smiled at her with none of the innuendos and knowing smirks of the other young men. His eyes were lit with genuine friendliness as he sat down by her side.

"I saw you sitting over here, looking in great need of something cool." He handed her a crystal glass filled with iced punch.

She took it gratefully, then hesitated. "Does this have alcohol in it?"

"Not a drop."

"Well," she sighed, "in that case . . ." She eagerly downed the glass.

He smiled, and the smile seemed to wipe out much of the evening's discomfort. "Would you like more?"

"Oh, yes. Please."

He returned, this time with a bigger glass. "You are certainly the belle of the ball tonight," he commented with a grin.

She grimaced. "I feel more like a prize goose about to be devoured." His manner somehow invited honesty. "I'm sorry. I've forgotten your name."

"Josef. Josef von Forstner. From Austria."

"That's right. Aren't you a . . . a . . . count or something?"

"Viscount."

"I'm sorry," she apologized with a smile. She felt more comfortable with this foreigner than with anyone else in the room. "I have no manners or social graces. But I'm sure you've noticed."

"Practiced social graces are not necessary in one with so much natural charm."

She frowned doubtfully, but his smile was sincere.

"Would you honor me with the next dance?"

She sighed. "I don't dance very well, either."

"From what I've seen, you appear to dance quite well. But perhaps you would rather take a short stroll on the patio. The air is much cooler out there."

The air was cooler on the patio, and Meghan lifted her face gratefully to the gentle breeze. Several other couples were also taking a stroll, but no one seemed to pay heed to anyone else. They were all engrossed in their private worlds.

"You shouldn't frown so, Miss O'Brian," Josef said gently. "A face as lovely as yours should always be smiling."

"Not Miss O'Brian. Mrs. Sinclair."

His brows rose in surprise. "Pardon my error. I didn't know you were married."

Meghan glanced away, unaccountably embarrassed. "I'm married, yes. Right now I'm not sure how long that will be the case."

There was silence for a moment. When Josef spoke his voice held none of the contempt she expected. "I'm so sorry. Your husband must be an absolute fool."

"What?" Her green eyes widened in surprise.

"I said, your husband is a fool."

"No. He's not. He's—"

"Dear Mrs. Sinclair. You have no reason, and no need, to explain anything to me."

She looked at him curiously. "You're not shocked by me?"

He stopped and turned her toward him. "Shocked? Certainly not."

Her eyes flashed with a hint of defiance. "Everyone else here certainly is."

Josef chuckled, a low, pleasant sound. "Everyone else here is a provincial busybody. They can't recognize a genuine jewel in their very midst. Forgive me if I am forward, but you are the loveliest, most charming lady I have met since coming into this wilderness."

Meghan turned away and resumed their stroll, not looking at him directly. "You don't know about me," she finally stated in a flat voice. She couldn't believe this foreign nobleman would be so entranced by her supposed charm if he knew her history.

"What should I know about you that brings such a shadow to your lovely face?"

She tilted her head proudly. "I'm not ashamed of my past, but everyone here seems to think I'm some sort of freak. You see, I was captured from a wagon train when I was nine, and up until a year ago I was living with the Cheyenne. They're a tribe of—"

"Oh, yes. I know who the Cheyenne are. And I've heard the story of your rescue."

"Then why are you acting so . . . Why are you being so nice?"

Josef touched her arm and stopped her in the shadow of the high stone wall that shut the patio off from the hills beyond. "My dear lady. From what I've heard, it seems to me you are the bravest, cleverest, and possibly the most interesting woman I've ever met. And now that I have met you in person, I know that is so. If you feel slighted by the locals, it is only because they haven't the discernment necessary to recognize true worth when they see it. And that is their very great loss."

Meghan regarded him dumbly, at a loss for something to say. This man was different from anyone else she'd ever met, and she didn't know how to judge his words. For the first time since she'd left Jason's ranch, she felt completely comfortable. He was so pleasant, so easy to be with, and she had to admit she found him attractive. He was several inches taller than she was, and though slender, had a wiry build that spoke of latent strength. Longish, thick brown hair was combed neatly back from his face, which was pleasantly refined without being in any way effeminate. He was very masculine in an unthreatening sort of way. And his presence didn't inspire the urgent tension that seemed to attend her every time Jason was within sight.

"Please don't call me Mrs. Sinclair. Call me Meghan."

"I would be honored, Meghan."

They walked back toward the ballroom door in silent companionship. Meghan wondered if she could manage to keep this attractive young nobleman with her for the rest of the evening. It certainly wouldn't be proper to spend so much time with one man; it was contrary to her aunt's coaching, but then there was nothing about Meghan that was quite proper, and all of El Dorado County seemed to know it.

"I hope," Josef asked just before he opened the door into the Baileys' ballroom, "that you will allow me to call on you sometime in the near future."

Meghan smiled brilliantly, feeling somehow that something very good had just come into her life. "I hope you will, Josef." She ignored the unbidden thought that she shouldn't be encouraging this man. In spite of her uncle's offer, she was still a married woman. "I'll be looking forward to it," she said almost defiantly.

She figured if Jason could play with fire, then so could she.

The small, crowded ballroom seemed all the stuffier after her respite in the fresh air, and Meghan gratefully accepted Josef's suggestion that she sit while he fetched them something cool to drink. He escorted her to one of the brocade love seats that lined the ballroom walls, smiled warmly, then departed on his errand.

Three men stood in conversation not far from where Meghan sat fanning herself. They had evidently partaken heavily of the champagne provided to cool the throats of those guests who desired a drink with more kick than the fruit punch. Their voices were raised above the general buzz of conversation and music, and Meghan couldn't help but overhear some of what they were saying. After she grasped the subject of their conversation she no longer made a pretense of not listening.

"God!" one of them exclaimed loudly. "I've never seen anything like it! Not in this town at least. It was like the stories you hear out of Dodge City or one of those other wild cow towns!"

A thin man with a long chin and narrow, ascetic-looking mouth grimaced in distaste. "That's what you get for letting that sort of man into town. We're forced to put up with the rougher elements who work at the mines, but to let a man like Jason Sinclair hang around town . . . ! The man's a known gunfighter, after all—and notorious for having trouble like this follow him around. We should have run him out of town long before this!''

"Now don't get up on your high horse, Josiah," a ruddy-faced, heavyset man urged. "After all, no harm was done. Leastwise to nobody but them what was asking for it. Myself, I saw the whole thing. I couldn't believe how fast that Sinclair was. He took two of them boys down before they got their guns halfway out of their holsters. If that third one hadn't backshot him, he'd have gotten away without a scratch. Couldn't believe it. Never seen the like!''

An ashen-faced Meghan pushed the thin-faced man aside and confronted the man who'd been speaking. "What are you talking about? What's happened?''

The heavyset man, a hardware merchant who'd made a fortune extracting gold from the flood tide of prospectors that had flowed into Placerville in the 1850's, was unused to being so abruptly confronted by agitated young women. He stared at her owlishly for a short moment, then attempted to break the tension with a wry chuckle. "Miss O'Brian, isn't it? Nothing to bother your little head about. Just some unpleasantness in town this afternoon.''

"The name is Mrs. Sinclair," she said in a dangerous tone of voice. "I believe you were talking about my husband, and I want to know what you were talking about.''

All three gentlemen were visibly taken aback. They'd heard some talk about this niece of Jonathan O'Brian's, the young woman who'd been rescued from the Cheyenne up in Montana. Something about her showing up married and with a son, and some scandal about her husband. But that was all women's gossip, and who in his right mind listened to the empty-headed chatter of women?

"I . . . well . . .'' The hardware merchant was the first to recover. He supposed if the man was really this girl's husband, she had a right to know the details. "It was this way. Three young toughs from your uncle's mine—the Alhambra I think it is—they figured to make themselves a reputation and jumped Jason Sinclair out on Benham Street today. Guess they figured if there was three of them to one of him, one of them was bound to get in a lucky shot. They just walked out into the street, plain as day, and drew on him."

Meghan's face was a tightly controlled mask. "And . . ."

"And, well, he whips around and draws like he's not even thinking about it, like some sort of an automatic reflex it was. Anyway, the two toughs who drew on him went down. Drilled neat, they were." The merchant was warming to his story now. "Hole right through the head. Never seen such shooting. But the third guy, he's behind Sinclair, and seeing his buddies go down, he ducks into an alley and opens up on him from behind. Must of put about three slugs into him before Sinclair managed to spy out where he was hiding and bring him down, too."

Meghan stopped breathing without even being aware of it. Something squeezed at her heart until she thought her chest would burst with the pain. "Is he dead?"

"Oh, they're all three dead as doornails."

The thin-faced man shot the merchant a look of contempt. "She means Sinclair, Bill."

The merchant looked shamefaced. "Oh, of course. Sinclair. He was alive last I heard. Might be dead now, though. He was drilled pretty good."

Meghan closed her eyes. The room swam around her. Then, by sheer effort of will, she pulled herself together. "Where is he?"

"Some gents carried him off toward the Old Rose Saloon. I guess someone went to fetch the doc to him. I don't know. I left soon as the show was over."

She turned and left without a word. Josef was forgotten. Everything was forgotten except one thing. Jason was sorely hurt. Maybe even dead. If he was alive she had to get to him.

"Aunt Erin! I'm taking the carriage."

Her uncle's wife peered at her in surprise. "What? Whatever for?"

"Jason's been hurt. I have to go to him."

"Mr. Sinclair's been hurt? Why that's awful, dear! But there's no need . . . it would be terribly improper . . . oh, my!"

Meghan hadn't stayed to listen to her aunt's objections. Ignoring everything but the purpose that drove her, she flew out the front door of the Bailey mansion and ran to where they had left their carriage parked to one side of the circular drive. She untethered the horse, climbed in, and slapped the reins smartly.

The Old Rose Saloon on Benham Street wasn't hard to find. It was one of the better establishments on that street of doubtful reputation, having a thriving and noisy bar and card room on the first floor and hotel rooms on the two stories above. About half of the hotel rooms were occupied by employees of the saloon, girls who danced, served drinks, and often entertained the customers in their beds. No gently bred young lady would venture into such a place if her very life depended on it. But Meghan was not a gently bred young lady. And it was not her life that depended on it. It was Jason's.

"Here now! What do you think you're doing?" The saloon hostess was a formidable woman dressed in scarlet and black. Regarding Meghan with a combination of surprise and hostility, she blocked the stairs that led to the rooms above.

"You have my husband up there."

The woman laughed, and Meghan couldn't help but be fascinated by the way her heavy and mostly exposed bosom jiggled in rhythm with her laughter. "So what's new, honey? We've got a lot of ladies' husbands up there, off and on. And I can tell you if I let their wives barge in on their fun, my business would be gone inside a week. Not that most wives give a damn."

"Jason Sinclair," Meghan explained simply.

The woman's painted mouth fell open. "You're kiddin'."

"No," Meghan denied impatiently. "I'm not." Her heart twisted. She was afraid to ask the question. "Is he alive?"

The hostess's face softened slightly at what she saw in Meghan's eyes. "Far as I know, honey. But I don't know for how long."

"What room?" Meghan demanded.

"Four. When you get to the top of the stairs, turn right, then follow the hall to your left. It's the third door."

"Thank you," Meghan whispered in a cracked voice.

A girl with frizzy yellow hair sat by Jason's bedside. Her eyes, hard, glittering gems set in the face of a painted angel, darkened dangerously when Meghan stepped in. Meghan ignored her, going straight to the bed, where Jason lay unconscious. Dirty rags were wrapped around his chest as bandages, colored by the dark crust of old blood and the bright scarlet stain of new. Meghan exclaimed in disgust.

"Who're you?" the girl demanded in a petulant voice. "Mary told me to—"

"Who put these bandages on?" Meghan interrupted in a terse voice.

"I did. Me and Mary, that is. What of it?"

"Has the doctor been there?"

"What for?" The girl shrugged. "Look at 'im. He hasn't got a chance. Too bad too. He's a man, is that one!"

Meghan felt like breaking the little hussy's porcelain face, but for once she managed to control her temper.

"Get me some hot water. And some clean bandages." With a grimace of disgust Meghan started to remove the soiled, crusted bandages from around Jason's broad chest.

"See here! You can't just—"

"Do as she says, Sabrina." The black-and-scarlet-clad saloon hostess had come into the room.

"Mary—"

"Just do it!"

The girl left in a huff.

The woman named Mary came over to the bedside and wrinkled her nose at the smell of the rags that Meghan was trying to gently remove from the bloody wounds. "It's not much use, dearie. There hasn't been a peep from him since they brought him up here. They plugged him good."

"You could've at least got a doctor to him."

"Yeah? And who's going to pay?"

"He's got money."

"Doc's out of town anyway. Won't be back till next week."

Jason made no sound or protest as Meghan pulled on the bandages that had stuck to the raw holes in his chest. His breathing was shallow, his skin clammy. Meghan's heart sank when the bandages were finally off and she surveyed the extent of the damage. The old medicine woman in Two Moon's band had been her close friend and mentor. She'd taught Meghan much about the tending of the sick and the healing of injuries, but she had none of the herbs she needed to treat such wounds, and in this strange country who knew if she could find any. She would just have to clean the wounds as best she could and hope that Jason's strength would win through to recovery.

The frizzy-haired blonde returned with a basin of steaming water and an armful of clean sheets that could be ripped into bandages. She set them down and without a word turned and flounced out of the room. Mary started ripping the sheets while Meghan soaked a clean washcloth in the hot water and started to clean the dried blood and dirt away from the oozing wounds. Carefully she examined each hole, making sure that each bullet entrance also had an exit.

"At least there doesn't seem to be any lead left in him," she finally concluded.

Mary leaned over Meghan's shoulder to peer at the damage. "God almighty! I'm surprised he even made it here alive. Honey, you might as well give up."

It took the better part of an hour to clean and rebandage

Jason's chest. When the grisly task was finally done, Meghan straightened up and stretched the cramps out of her aching back and arms.

"I'll need a room here for a few days," she told Mary.

"We don't got no rooms to spare, dearie. Besides, this ain't no place for a decent woman to be."

Meghan sighed wearily. "I don't think most of Placerville considers me a decent woman, so you don't need to be concerned for my reputation."

Mary smiled wryly. "It's not your reputation I'm concerned about, honey. You'll ruin my business being here. Men don't like to carouse when they think some prissy-minded lady's around."

"I'm not leaving him," Meghan said with quiet determination. "And if I were you, I wouldn't try to throw me out."

The light of challenge in the girl's eyes made Mary hesitate. There was something about this young woman that was different from other ladies—an air of independence, a confidence in being able to take care of herself. She wouldn't put it past the little twit to give her a very bad time if she tried to have her put out.

"Well, I suppose I can bring an old mattress up here to put on the floor. And Horace can bring up your meals. Just keep out of sight of my customers, you hear?"

"That will be fine," Meghan sighed. "I'll just go home for a few minutes and pick up some things. I'll be back within an hour."

When Meghan pulled the carriage to a halt in front of O'Brian House, a lamp was still burning in Jonathan's study and in Erin's bedroom. When she walked through the front door she was met by both her uncle and aunt. Her uncle was first to speak.

"Just what in hell is going on, young lady? Where in damnation have you been?"

"Jonathan, please—"

"Shut up, Erin! I want to know what my niece thinks she's doing running off from the party in the middle of the night, taking the carriage, and not getting back until . . . until . . . What time is it?''

"Two o'clock, dear.''

"Until two o'clock in the morning.''

"Jason's been hurt,'' Meghan explained in a tired voice. "I went to look after him. I've just come for some clothes. I've got to go back.''

Erin's voice was strained. "Back where, dear?''

"He's at the Old Rose Saloon, in a room above the bar.''

Erin's face lost all color. For a moment Meghan thought she was actually going to faint.

"The Old Rose Saloon?'' Jonathan roared. "No niece of mine is going to be seen in a place like that! You've got no business concerning yourself with—''

"With my husband. Uncle Jonathan, he's likely to die if I don't see to him. The doctor's out of town, and none of those girls in that place knows the first thing about treating wounds.''

"If that gunman went and got himself shot up it's none of your concern,'' he insisted in a steely voice. "I won't have you—''

"I don't care what you will or won't have! I didn't ask your permission!''

She turned to her aunt and her voice grew gentler. "Aunt Erin, this is something I have to do. It will only be for a few days . . . a week at the most. Will you see to Andrew for me? He'll take a bottle now, and he shouldn't be much trouble.''

"Of course,'' Erin consented in a shaking voice. "Dear, are you quite sure you want—''

"I'm quite sure. Don't worry about me.'' Without another look at her uncle she turned and fled up the stairs. She was weary beyond all telling and more worried than she cared to admit. Jason had looked so pale, so still, when she had left the room at the saloon. Would he still be alive when she returned? Would he still be alive tomorrow or in two days' time? He was young and strong, but the barrage of bullets that had torn through his body was more than most men could survive.

What would she do, Meghan thought, if he died? What if she had no Jason Sinclair to rant at, to bait, to infuriate, to hate, and most of all to love? What would she do without him? How could she live with the knowledge that nowhere in this land was there a tall, broad-shouldered, tawny-haired, amber-eyed animal of a man whose smile could rival the morning sun for brightness, whose frown could send timid men running for cover, and whose kiss could take Meghan O'Brian Sinclair into a magic world that held only the two of them?

# Chapter Twenty-four

Jason hadn't expected to wake to the sight of Meghan's pale face hovering above him, with its halo of gold-red hair catching the late-afternoon sunlight. In fact, in the last seconds of consciousness left to him when the bullets started ripping through his chest, he hadn't expected to wake at all this side of hell. But here he was, and there she was. There were shadows under her eyes that hadn't been there before, he noticed. And pronounced hollows under the fine high cheekbones gave her face an ascetic look. The pallor of her skin made the freckles seem to swarm across her nose and cheeks.

"You look like hell," he croaked.

Meghan smiled. "Still your charming self, I see. I guess you'll live all right."

Jason tried to raise his head to look around, but quickly

gave up the effort and, with a grimace of pain twisting his face, surrendered his head once more to the pillow.

"I wouldn't try to move around if I were you. Not for a while at least."

Jason grunted, then shot her a jaundiced look. "Where are we?"

"We're in your hotel room, if hotel is what you call it."

A faint smile flickered across his pale face. "What are you doing here?"

"Someone had to take care of you. No one else seemed to care for the chore."

She dipped a cloth into a basin of cool water and sponged his brow, which was beading with sweat just with the effort of staying awake. He tried to brush off her ministrations with an impatient hand, but found it too much of an effort to lift his arm from the bed.

"Son of a bitch!" he growled, impatient with the weakness that kept him pinned to the bed. "I don't need a nurse!"

"You think not?" She raised a skeptical brow.

"You shouldn't be in a place like this. What the hell is your uncle thinking—letting you come down here? Goddammit! Will you stop that?"

She removed the rag and dropped it in the basin. "Stop acting like a temperamental child. You had a fever. You still have one. This will help." She wrung out the cloth and put it on his brow once again. "My uncle didn't exactly approve of my coming here, but I came anyway. After all, he doesn't own me. No one owns me," she asserted with a saucy twinkle in her eye. "And no one tells me what to do."

"Guess I should've learned that by now," Jason grunted and dropped his eyes. "You ought to go. I can take care of myself now."

"The hell you can. Besides, I figure I owe you, in a way. I'll stay until you're back on your feet."

"Yeah?" Jason eyed her doubtfully. "You may figure

you owe me, all right. What I'm afraid of is just how you plan to get even.''

A slow smile spread across her face. "I wasn't exactly thinking in terms of vengeance. But now that you mention it . . . I think I might enjoy having you weak and at my mercy. It's been the other way around so many times."

Jason groaned. "I knew it."

Meghan just grinned.

He didn't wake again until a knock on the door heralded the arrival of the sheriff. The local representative of the law was a corpulent, ruddy-faced man whose eyes widened in momentary surprise when Meghan opened the door to Jason's room. He touched his hat politely and stepped into the room, giving Jason an assessing look as he moved over to the bed.

"Well, Jason, boy. Rumor has it that you might live."

Jason gave him a sour look. "I might. Have any objections?"

The sheriff chuckled. "To tell the truth, I thought maybe I had you off my hands. Can't say I was surprised to hear you were shot down by those bully boys from the Alhambra Mine. Man like you in a town like this, why all you have to do to ask for trouble is breathe."

"I wasn't asking for any trouble, Sheriff. What's your business here, anyway? You didn't come just to tell me how glad you are I'm alive."

"No, well . . . I figured as long as you were still on this side of eternity, I'd just drop by to tell you there won't be no charges brought for the killings."

Jason's face turned to stone. Only his eyes showed a flicker of emotion that might have been regret. "Got all of them, did I?"

"Yeah, you got all of them. Much as I'd like to throw you in the slammer, there was too many witnessess saying those boys jumped you. So I guess you're in the clear, for now."

"For now?"

"Yeah. For now. It's bound to happen again, sooner or

later. Like I said, a man like you . . . Next time maybe you won't be so lucky.''

A cynical smile pulled at Jason's mouth. ''If I were you, Sheriff, I'd try to control the more lawless elements in my town.''

The sheriff gave him an affable grin. ''That's what I'm trying to do. I wish the hell you'd get out of town, Sinclair. You're the most lawless fellow I know.''

Jason looked innocent. ''I've been a model of good behavior ever since I hit this town. Don't know what you're complaining about.''

''You know what I mean. The mines around this town have their share of fools working for them, and a fellow with your reputation just pushes 'em into being bigger jackasses than they already are. And they don't always play fair.'' He looked significantly at the pink-tinged bandages wrapping Jason's chest. ''Don't be a bigger fool than I think you are. Take my advice and move on. Or you may end up with another bullet in your gut.''

''Sorry, Sheriff.'' Jason tried to shrug, then grimaced in pain. ''It's not in my mind to move on just yet.''

The sheriff sighed and stuck his hat back on his head with an air of finality. ''It's your funeral.''

After he had gone, Meghan emerged from the corner where she'd been standing and sat on the edge of the bed. She looked at Jason with a worried frown creasing her brow. ''You know,'' she said thoughtfully, ''my uncle said the same thing. Maybe you ought to listen to the sheriff, Jason. You might be better off getting away from here. I promised you I wouldn't tie you down.''

''Is that what you promised me?'' he returned with a faintly mocking smile. ''I thought it was to love, honor, and obey.''

She scowled. ''Be serious. If you're sticking around because of me, you don't have to. And now that Sykes has gone to Sacramento . . .''

Jason waved away the rest of her words and sighed.

Now was apparently not the time to pursue the subject of their shaky marriage. "What did your uncle say?"

"What?"

"You said your uncle said the same thing as the sheriff. What exactly did he say?"

"He said . . . well, I don't recall the exact words . . . but he said if you wanted to stay in one piece you shouldn't be so visible around town, or at least not this part of town."

"You don't say. Don't you own the Alhambra Mine?"

"I will once this legal business gets taken care of."

"Those men who jumped me were workers from the Alhambra."

Meghan looked at him blankly for a moment, then her face darkened with anger. "You couldn't think that my uncle had anything to do with . . . or that I . . . ! Why you—"

Jason grabbed her hand as she started to vault up from her seat on the bed. "Settle down. I'm not saying I think anything. Just a coincidence, that's all."

He didn't release her hand even when she relented and sat back down. Absently he caressed her palm with his thumb, sending shivers of sensation through her entire body. Her face grew red and she pulled her hand impatiently away.

"Your bandages need changing," she said abruptly.

A week's time saw Jason healing rapidly and looking stronger by the hour. Meghan almost hated to see him heal, because soon he wouldn't need her anymore. Every day he did more and more things for himself, and two days ago he had, with her help, taken his first shaky walk around the room. Another couple of days and there would be no more excuse for her to stay with him.

She had been strangely happy cooped up in this little hotel room with the man she used to fear and hate and had grown to love. In the vulnerability of his weakness he had somehow become even more dear to her. Their forced closeness, together with the intimacy of her nursing and his need for her care, had given birth to a new relationship in which they declared a tentative truce. A kind of friendship began to develop. For the first time since she'd known him, Meghan felt comfortable with Jason's nearness. Pinned to his bed by weakness, he was no longer a threat to her. She had no need to fear the violence with which he had torn her life asunder once before or the growing passion that had done more damage to her heart than his anger. For once she was the strong one, she was the one with the upper hand. She took joy in tending him, talking to him, joking with him, savoring the situation to the utmost, knowing it would end too soon and that she would go back to her uncle's house and he would go back to being fiercely independent and untamable.

Jason was angrily impatient at first, frustrated by his weakness and embarrassed at not being able to perform for himself the intimate tasks that Meghan was forced to do for him. Then he discovered how enjoyable was Meghan's touch, even over the pain of having his bandages changed and his wounds cleaned. He found himself comforted by her smiles, soothed by the musical quality of her voice, and even enjoying the conversations that filled the long idle hours. Jason had never really enjoyed talking to a woman before. His time with women was generally taken up with more urgent activities, and the women in his life had never been long on conversation. Even his passion for Meadow Flower had mostly been a physical one, and though genuine affection had been part of his feelings for his Pawnee wife, he'd never wondered about her thoughts or the workings of her mind. But lying in this dingy room with physical passion out of the question, his feelings for Meghan seemed to take on a different hue. There was much more to his relationship with this girl, he realized, than admiration for a pair of flashing green eyes and fiery gold-red hair. There was more in her magnetism for him than the natural affinity of a virile male body to a healthy, attractive female. He'd never dreamed that love could be so much more than an extension of lust. He no longer felt trapped by Meghan's allure. He was satisfied to lie there and enjoy her nearness. Her presence gave him a feeling of warmth that overcame the pain of his wounds and the frustration of his weakness.

Pain and weakness subsided as the days passed. In time Meghan's touch became more than a comfort. In time it became a sweet torture. Jason's body was healing, remembering its own strength and physical needs. His nights began to be full of vivid dreams of them together, causing him to wake with no doubt of his recovered capacities. In a way he was sorry to see this peaceful interlude come to an end, but he had learned that his relationship with Meghan would never be as uncomplicated as straightforward friendship or as simple as animal passion. Somehow he had to find a way to deal with the web of emotions that bound him more tightly with every passing day.

Meghan, too, was sorry to see their days of easy companionship draw to an end. She noted the growing hunger in Jason's eyes when he looked at her and knew she could no longer count on the safety of his weakness. He was becoming a whole man again, with all of a man's attendant desires and needs. It was time for her to go, to say good-bye and call an end to this short, sweet episode in her life. But she couldn't bring herself to leave. Not quite yet. As it was, she waited too long.

It started out innocently enough. Jason was up and pacing the room, frowning at the realization that even this small amount of exercise left him breathless. Enough of his energy had returned to make him restless, but not enough to make him strong. Meghan sat in a chair in a corner of the room, sewing lying ignored in her lap, watching Jason's fretful movements. Now was the time, she thought, to tell him she was leaving. He didn't need her attention any longer. He was able to take care of himself. But why were the words so difficult to say?

"You're going to wear a path in the floor, Jason. Why don't you get some rest?"

"I've been getting nothing but rest for a week . . . over a week."

"You're getting better fast, but you still need to take it easy. Push yourself too soon and you're going to break those wounds open again."

Jason uttered a soft oath but obediently sat down on the bed. Meghan smiled at him and came over to check his bandages. As she leaned over to check his back for bleeding, he fastened his eyes on the soft upper curves of the breasts that almost touched his cheek. He groaned as the familiar tightening in his loins sharpened to a hungry ache.

"Did I hurt you?" she asked in a surprised voice. "I'm sorry."

"You didn't hurt me," he said sharply.

"Well, then why . . . ?" She drew back and looked at him, recognizing the predatory glitter in his eyes. She jumped off the bed as though it had caught fire.

"Don't go." He grasped her arm, and his voice was a command, not a plea.

"Jason . . ."

He pulled her gently back onto the bed. "Come here, little Meghan." He'd reached the end of his endurance. She was his wife, he told himself. He had every right to take her.

"Jason don't." She tried to free herself from his grip. "You're going to hurt yourself."

He smiled. A smile of anticipation, of savoring joys to come. "I'm not going to hurt myself or you either. So quit squirming and come here to me."

She knew that smile, that heat glowing in his eyes. Her mind clamored in panic while her body yearned toward him. "Nooo!" The word was a drawn-out plea to both herself and him.

His free hand came up and began to undo the tiny buttons that fastened the front of her bodice. The brush of his callused fingers on her soft, warm flesh sent shivers of desire straight to the center of her womanhood. "No . . ."

"Yes," he murmured, his voice grown hoarse. Her dress gaped open and he slid in one hand to cup a full breast. He caught his breath sharply as the ripe orb filled his hand with softness.

She closed her eyes, willing herself to ignore the warm flood of ecstasy that centered on his gentle touch. With a great effort of will she started to draw back, but his grip still held her.

"Don't fight me, Meghan," he advised in a soft voice. "I'm your husband. Let me love you."

She tried to twist away. "This is ridiculous! You're not strong enough to . . ."

His grin mocked her as he deftly circled a nipple with his thumb, expertly bringing it erect with desire. "Shall we put it to the test—what I'm strong enough to do?" He pulled her down beside him on the bed.

"No. Don't."

His amber eyes savored the sight of her with her hair spreading out like flame on the pillow. "Stop saying no." He smiled. "We both know it's not no you mean."

His hands held her head still while his mouth descended to claim hers. She tried to lie passively as his mouth moved gently over hers. She tried not to feel, not to revel in the hardness of his body next to hers. She tried to hold back the flood tide of joy that was dammed by the determination of her good sense. But she couldn't. The dam broke. Good sense never had a chance.

His kiss grew deeper as he felt her respond. Her lips opened to his urging, and his tongue delved into the honey-sweet recesses of her mouth. With all the hunger born of months of wanting her Jason ravaged her softness, stealing her breath, trying to capture her very soul.

Abruptly he released her and with a haste bordering on frenzy pushed her bodice off her shoulders and down to her waist, freeing her full breasts to his gaze and his touch. "I've wanted to do this," he breathed, "ever since Andrew looked like he was enjoying himself so much." Gently he fastened his mouth on a desire-swollen nipple and teased with his tongue.

"Oh, Jason . . . Oh, God, Jason." Meghan almost sobbed and tangled her fingers in his hair, pulling his head closer to her. Her blood pounded seemingly in rhythm with the motions of his mouth. The ache between her thighs grew to an all-consuming need. "Don't stop!" she almost begged as his mouth released her.

"Don't worry," he assured her in a hoarse whisper. "Nothing in the world could make me stop."

Impatiently he pushed her over onto her back and took the other nipple in his mouth. At the same time he worked a hand up under her skirt and stroked lightly along the outside of her thigh, then the inside, coming tantalizingly near to the warm softness that demanded his touch. She arched against him in supplication.

Jason raised his head and looked into her eyes. They glowed with a green fire that was soft and yielding in surrender and at the same time demanding of satisfaction. "Damned if you aren't the most woman I've ever laid a hand on," he commented under his breath. "Are you still sore, Meghan?"

"Sore?"

"From having my baby." He smiled gently.

"Oh, no." She laughed. Her resistance was mere ashes in the fire of her reawakened passion. The only feeling left in her was breathless need.

"Good," he breathed. His hand moved up and into the soft nest of russet curls that adorned her womanhood.

Meghan felt as breathless and excited as an untried virgin as Jason's hand gently caressed her warm, pliant flesh. It had been such a long empty time since she'd felt his hand on her. The pressure of her need built to an unbearable tension, and when his fingers gently slipped inside her she arched up to meet him. She moved in rhythm with his caress and groaned with the need for more when he withdrew.

"I want to feel every inch of you next to me," he murmured, slipping her dress down around her hips and throwing it with her underthings in a heap beside the bed. Very quickly his own trousers were added to the pile. Slowly he lowered his hard-muscled body onto hers, letting her feel his rampant desire as he settled down upon her. She eagerly opened her thighs to receive him as he slipped between them. Her breath came in short gasps of anticipation as he felt the hot, throbbing tip of his swollen shaft poise at her entrance.

Meghan frowned impatiently as he kissed the point of her chin, then the tip of her nose. The amber eyes that looked into hers were hot with hunger, but also sparkled with mischief.

"Jason, please!" She arched against him. Her body burned with the need to be filled. All thought fled before an all-consuming desire.

He smiled teasingly. "Thought you said no."

She rolled her eyes in frustration. "Gods, help me!"

He smiled at her again. The mischief in his eyes was gone now, drowned in hunger. "They won't," he said softly. "But I will."

Slowly and deliberately he slid into her, carefully watching her face for any hint of pain. What he saw on her features was only joy as he buried himself deeply within her welcoming softness. He moved slowly at first, burying his face in the warm hollow of her throat and letting the sweet, sensuous agony roll over him as he held back his urgent need for release. "My Meghan," he murmured into the silken skin of her throat, "I have wanted you so long . . . so many months I've wanted you . . . needed you."

Gradually he increased his rhythm. They seemed to meld into one creature, straining together first in perfect harmony, then in sweet counterpoint, riding a wave of passion that held them both in an unshakable grip. When the wave crested Jason could no longer hold back. With a fierce cry of primordial delight he buried himself completely in her feminine softness and pumped his offering deep into her womb. The frantic pulsing within her brought on Meghan's own release, and she gripped him tightly with arms and legs as her body shuddered with the strength of it.

For long moments they lay entwined, unmoving, drifting together in a realm that only perfectly atuned lovers ever reach. It was Jason who first moved, shifting his weight from her slender body and withdrawing the spent instrument of his desire. He reached over to the bed table and took the clean damp cloth that Meghan had readied earlier to wash his wounds. Gently he bathed the essence of their passion from the insides of her thighs. She moved sensuously under his hand, and he smiled and kissed her gently before performing the same service for himself.

She smiled lazily, like a cat sated with rich cream. Her eyes fondly toured the features of his beloved face. The words "I love you" were poised on her lips, but she couldn't say them, not to a man who loved only freedom, who respected only survival. Not to a man who would only regard her love as a burden, just as he regarded his wealth, his ranch, and everything that tried to tie him to responsibility and one place. But how she did love him! He was a man who could satisfy both the Cheyenne and the white in her heart, a man who would come only once in a lifetime. There would never, she knew, be another who could so monopolize her passion. There would never be another who could fill all her dreams of what a man should be. What she'd thought was love in the past was a mere shadow of the real thing. Every man who'd ever caught her fancy paled in the intensity of the perfection of this one man. How could she ever let him go? Yet, how could she ask him to stay?

Jason saw the flicker of sadness in her eyes and mistook the cause. Gently he fingered a fiery lock that lay on the pillow beside his head. "Seems I've overstepped the bounds once again, little Meghan." His voice held no regret for what he'd done.

"No," she denied gently. She reached out a hand and

lovingly traced the chiseled line of his lips. "Seems as if I turn into a . . . a wanton every time I get close enough to you."

He smiled and caught her hand with his own. "Not a wanton. A woman. And such a damned beautiful woman." The amber eyes that gazed into hers were warm and more open than she'd ever seen them. "Little Meghan. I don't see how any man could resist taking advantage of you. Least of all me."

An impish smile pulled at her mouth. "So far, you're the only one who's managed with any success."

A flash of possessiveness momentarily lit his eyes. He did care, Meghan thought, warming herself in that assurance. All the more reason she must give him his happiness—his freedom. But the thought of final separation fled from her mind as his eyes grew warm and tender again and his smile warmed her battered heart. Then she caught sight of the wet scarlet stain on one of his bandages. She touched it lightly with a finger and frowned.

He glanced down at where her hand rested on his chest. "Don't worry about it. It'll close again."

"Doesn't it hurt?"

His finger touched her lips, then traced a line down the slim column of her throat. "Nothing hurts as much as wanting you and not having you." Then he smiled wryly, his hand closing warmly over her breast. "We can't seem to get this right unless one of us has a hole blown through him . . . or her."

A smile shivered on her lips as waves of renewed desire pulsed out from where his hand lay upon her breast. She tried to fight down the sensations that once again threatened to engulf her, wondering at this man's power to inflame her with only a touch.

"What do you think you're doing?" She looked pointedly at the hand that massaged her soft fullness.

He cocked one brow. "It should be obvious."

"You couldn't possibly . . ." But her statement wasn't yet finished when she saw that he was indeed ready for action again. She tried to push him away, genuinely concerned for his still-fragile condition. "You've got to be tired," she admonished. "I won't let you hurt yourself by this foolishness."

With a strength that belied his recent wounds, he resisted her push and pinned her to the bed. She could feel the hard length of his resurgent desire throb against her thigh. "This is not foolishness," he denied, an almost boyish grin of delight lighting his face. "This is most serious business. And besides, this time I'm not planning on doing much work."

"What are you doing? What . . . ?"

She didn't trust the wicked grin on his face as he pinned her shoulders to the mattress, dropped a soft kiss on each erect nipple, then trailed his tongue down the plain of her abdomen. But her uncertainties were doused by the flood of liquid fire that surged through her body when his mouth reached the soft flower of her womanhood. She no longer needed to be pinned by his hands as his tongue teased and tantalized, darting here and there into secret, sensitive places she didn't even know existed, wreaking sweet havoc with her senses until she thought her body would fairly explode.

Suddenly he left the warm nest he'd invaded, rolled over on his back and carried her with him.

"I told you I wasn't going to do much work this time. You are."

He lay flat on his back and brought her astride him. Confused as to what he intended and swamped by the sensations he had visited upon her body, she readily followed the guiding pressure of his hands as he lifted her hips over his. He closed his eyes in bliss as he gently brought her hips down, impaling her gently on his swollen shaft of desire. She gasped at the new sensation. It took only the first movement of their merged bodies to bring desire to the point of uncontrol. He exploded within her, and she followed with her own personal fireworks, stretching back sensuously and letting the crescendo of fulfillment wash over her.

How long it took them to descend from the heights of their shared passion she didn't know, but when Meghan finally floated to earth she found herself nestled in the curve of her husband's long body, his arms pressing her firmly against him. His even breathing made her think he was asleep. Warmly content to remain right where she was, she closed her eyes and surrendered herself to the welcome darkness of slumber.

Jason was not asleep; he was merely comfortably relaxed, more relaxed than he'd been in a long time. He felt as if a tightly coiled spring had been released in his body. He was filled with a feeling of warm contentment that had never before been his. This woman, he acknowledged, had spun a silken web around him. What was surprising was that he didn't want to escape. It seemed he couldn't be near her and not want her. He couldn't want her and not take her. And the taking of her—that passion fulfilled was taking the edge from his steel-hard nature. Her sweet innocent wildness was taming the savage independence that allowed him to survive in a vicious world. He was becoming an addict and loving every moment of it.

He wasn't the same man who had ridden into the battle on Rosebud Creek and snatched up the daughter of Stone Eagle. He was tired of being a savage in a world of wanton violence. He couldn't leave Meghan and Andrew, and to hell with thinking they'd be better off without him. Meghan loved him. No woman could give her body as completely as she gave hers to him and not be in love. Even with all the distrust and violence there had been between them, somehow he would convince her they could make a go of it together.

Jason softly pressed his lips to the sweet-smelling tangle of fiery waves that brushed against his chin. He wanted to shake her awake and tell her that she was his wife and he was her husband, and they were going to have years to fight and love and watch their son grow. She would moan about not tying him down and he would laugh in her face, saying he'd be tied down if he damn well wanted to be. It would be a wonderful fight! He was looking forward to it, and to the making up when Meghan finally admitted she had a husband and not just a name.

But not quite yet, Jason decided. First Jonathan must be dealt with. Sure as the cows come home the man had something planned, and he was much more likely to show his true colors if he thought Jason was out of the picture. So his declaration would have to wait. Meghan would go back to O'Brian House and he would stay at the Old Rose Saloon and they would resume their separate, lonely lives. But for this brief time while he had her close in his arms . . .

He shifted one hand to cup a warm breast. His passion was spent for now, but the silken feel of that intimate flesh in his hand possessed him with a warm glow, a feeling of fierce protectiveness that transcended physical lust. Meghan sighed in her sleep and pressed more closely against him, making him wonder why it had taken so long for him to realize they were meant to be welded into one life. The thought followed him into the dark tunnels of sleep.

# Chapter Twenty-five

"My dear Meghan," the handsome Austrian viscount said with a smile, "I've told you before. You have no need to explain anything to me. No need at all."

"I know that," Meghan told him. "Still, I feel I owe you some explanation. I left you so abruptly."

Meghan had returned home two days ago to be met by

her uncle's frosty glare and her aunt's worried frown. The story her relatives had passed around the town was that she'd taken suddenly ill and left the Baileys' party in haste. For the past week she'd supposedly been confined to her bed in O'Brian House. Meghan suspected if the good people of Placerville knew whose bed she'd actually been confined to for the latter part of that week, they would have had very little charity with her—whether or not Jason was legally her husband. Still, she felt the need to be honest with Josef, who had wasted no time calling on her now that she was once more visible around town. She liked the young nobleman and wished to have no secrets fom him. She only wished she liked him enough to divert her mind from Jason.

Josef sat beside her on the parlor's velveteen love seat, far enough away to be proper but close enough to reach over and play with Andrew, who was gurgling contentedly on his mother's lap.

"I find it perfectly understandable that you should go to your husband in his hour of need," Josef assured her. "In fact, a person of your sweet and honorable nature could have done nothing else. I don't understand why your uncle thought it necessary to invent the excuse of your being sick all these days."

A wry smile played around Meghan's soft lips. She certainly had doubts about the sweet and honorable nature of her character, but if Josef insisted on maintaining illusions, she wasn't going to dissuade him.

"My husband is not exactly a man who is approved of by polite society."

Josef grinned. "Oh, I've heard all about your husband. Jason Sinclair. A most interesting man, I would think. Such a colorful character. I hope he is recovering from his wounds?"

"He's recovering," Meghan assured him with a secret smile.

Jason was recovering very nicely, Meghan thought. He'd hardly let her leave his bed the last two days she was there, and she'd willingly succumbed to his animal allure. If there were consequences of their union she could blame no one but herself, for she'd readily surrendered to his loving and even at times enticed it. She was too in love with him to resist the physical bond between them, even though she acknowledged the unlikelihood of keeping him beside her. It would be so much easier to be in love with Josef von Forstner, who was so kind and understanding. It was a cruel fate that had delivered her into the hands of Jason Sinclair that spring day so many months ago.

"I'm happy to hear he's getting well," Josef was saying. "It was a mighty unfair fight from what I hear. It's a miracle he survived. He must be quite a man."

"He's an expert at survival," Meghan commented somewhat cynically.

"Weren't those fellows who jumped him from your Alhambra Mine? Whatever possessed them to do such a thing?"

"I don't know." Meghan thought of Jason's suspicions in the matter. His insinuations about her uncle must be unfounded, she told herself. Jonathan didn't like Jason, but her uncle was a civilized man after all. And civilized men didn't condone violence and murder.

Josef watched sadly as Meghan seemed to drift away into another world. "Would you like to take a short carriage ride down to the river?" he asked, turning the subject adroitly away from Jason.

Meghan's thoughts jerked back to the present from where they'd wandered to a room above the bar at the Old Rose Saloon. "I'm sorry, Josef." Meghan truly regretted her inattention to this kind and attractive man. "It's time for Andrew's feeding. And I'm feeling a bit tired myself. Maybe some other day."

"By all means. Tomorrow perhaps?"

"Yes," Meghan said absently. "That would be nice."

Josef stood up and fetched his low-crowned beaver hat from the hall tree. "Meghan," he started somewhat hesitantly, "I hope you don't find my ... uh ... rather persistent attentions offensive. I realize you are a married woman, and your situation is somewhat . . . well . . . unstable at the moment. But I assure you my intentions are quite honorable. I wouldn't dream of pressing my suit until you are completely free to bestow your affections on another. If you are uncomfortable with my visiting you—''

"Oh, Josef!" Meghan got up and took Josef's arm in a gesture of friendship. "I could never be uncomfortable with anything about you. Visit me whenever you like. I can't promise, though, that I can ever—''

"Say no more." Josef raised a well-manicured finger and placed it gently on her lips. "The future may bring things neither one of us expects. So for now, let us be good friends."

Good friends, Meghan thought as she took Andrew into the kitchen to prepare his bottle. Josef would be a good friend. He could also probably be a good husband and a good lover, if her heart weren't already claimed by Jason. Why couldn't she accept the fact that Jason would never belong to her? He would always belong to the road not yet traveled, the far horizon not yet explored.

"I just saw Josef's carriage go down the drive." Samantha grinned, coming into the kitchen almost skipping with glee. "Was he here long?"

"Don't be so nosy, Sam," Clara admonished, following her younger sister through the door.

"It's all right, Clara. I don't mind. He was here quite a while, and he's coming back tomorrow to take me out in his carriage."

Samantha's eyes grew dreamy. "Oh, I just knew it. He's the most beautiful man—''

"You think all men are beautiful," Clara commented dryly.

Meghan couldn't help but smile at her young cousin's ready transfer of her affections from Jason to Josef. She wished she could accomplish a similar feat. "He is nice," she agreed.

"Are you going to marry him, do you think?"

"I'm already married."

"Yes," Samantha said ingenuously, "but you're going to get a . . . a . . ." She couldn't force herself to say the awful word with her older sister listening.

"A divorce," Clara supplied emotionlessly.

"Yes, a divorce." Samantha grinned at being able to say the word out loud. "Father says so."

Meghan frowned ominously. "Your father shouldn't have said that. He would like me to get a divorce. I said I'd think about it, not that I'd do it. I haven't talked to Jason about it yet."

Samantha pouted, her visions of a genuine blue blood in the family evaporating. "How come you didn't talk to him? You were with him in that room for over a week!"

"We had other things to worry about."

Clara raised a cynical brow and gave Meghan a knowing look. "You should mind your own business, Sam. Besides, a divorce isn't that easy to get. Meghan may end up married forever to that gunfighter."

Samantha stuck out her lower lip. "How would you know about divorces?"

"I know because I listen and read while you're off in your room dreaming. Would you like me to feed Andrew, Meghan?"

"No, thank you. I can do it." Meghan sat down in the kitchen chair and snuggled Andrew against her. She had missed him while she was gone, though Clara had taken very good care of him. His warm body pressed against Meghan's breast as he drank hungrily from the bottle and drove away some of her loneliness.

"I still think it's exciting that Josef is coming to call," Samantha insisted stubbornly, refusing to be discouraged by her sister. "He's handsome and rich and very sophisticated. He'd be a perfect husband for any woman, especially Meghan."

Clara's expression made it clear that in her opinion a sophisticated husband was not what Meghan needed. Meghan flinched inwardly at the hostility she saw in her cousin's eyes, but she supposed in this case Clara had a point. What would a girl who'd lived most of her life with the savage Cheyenne do with a European nobleman as a husband? The thought was ridiculous.

"Clara's right, Sam. I've no right to be thinking of men right now. And besides, a man like Josef is used to women who are a bit more refined than I am. He'd soon grow tired of a woman who knows nothing of fashion or manners." Unlike Jason, Meghan thought cynically, Josef would expect more of a woman than passion in bed. He would expect education, sophistication, and the artifices that society expected of a woman of good breeding. He might find her a novelty now, Meghan told herself, but he would soon grow tired of her.

"Manners are something you can learn," Samantha insisted optimistically.

"Of course," Clara commented with a sour expression, "it could be that he's after your money. Some of these European nobility are pretty hard up."

"I don't think Josef is lacking for money," Meghan returned in an even voice, refusing to rise to the bait.

"Just the same," Clara said with an accusing look at her cousin, "I doubt he'd bother with a girl who wasn't well fixed. You certainly haven't seen him looking at . . . at anyone else lately!" With a show of stiff dignity Clara turned her back on Meghan and left the room.

"Don't pay any mind to her!" Samantha advised sagely. "Before you came she and Josef rode out a couple of times together, that's all. She's just using Daddy's losing the mines as an excuse. Anyone could see that no man would give her a second glance with you around."

So that was why Clara disliked her, Meghan thought. The inheritance. Everything that was once Clara's was now Meghan's, including the man she apparently fancied for herself. Did Clara really think Jonathan and his family would be paupers after the mines were turned over to Meghan? How ridiculous! Meghan had no intentions of seeing her uncle stripped of his livelihood because of this legal mess.

She should have made that clear from the very first, she supposed, but the mines and her inheritance had been the furthest things from her mind the past week. She had put off thinking about what she wanted to do with her inheritance, but she certainly intended to see that her uncle was fairly treated in this mess. Time was running out though. Mr. Sykes should be back from Sacramento any day now and the matter would come to a head. She resolved to talk to her uncle as soon as an opportunity presented itself.

Her chance to talk to Jonathan came the very next day. Samantha and Clara were both in the back parlor with Mr. Simeon, the piano instructor who doubled as Meghan's tutor in reading, writing, and ciphering. Erin had retired to her room directly after lunch, complaining of a headache. Jonathan sat alone in his study going over his accounts. He looked up as Meghan tapped on the half-open door.

"Come in, Meghan. What can I do for you?"

Meghan hardly knew where to begin. She felt awkward bringing up the matter of the mines and wished her uncle had initiated this conversation himself.

"I don't want to bother you if you're busy."

"I'm not terribly busy right now. Just going over some of the monthly accounts. What's on your mind?"

Meghan came in and glanced curiously around the room. It was the first time she'd been in her uncle's study, and she was impressed by the dignity of the room. Dark oak paneling lined two walls, and floor-to-ceiling bookcases stood against the two remaining. Just off center in the room sat a huge oak desk and plush leather-upholstered chair, placed so that as her uncle sat at his work he could look through the window out to the golden hills beyond the house. It was a stately room, the office of a successful man who obviously knew his worth and his place in the world.

Suddenly Meghan felt intimidated. What right did she have to take ownership of these profitable mines simply because her drunk and irresponsible father had once, long ago, won a piece of paper in a gambling saloon?

"So, Meghan . . ." Her uncle's voice was amiable, but his fingers tapped impatiently on the desk. "What was it you wished to see me about?"

"I was thinking it was time we talked about the mines," she said hesitantly. "Have you heard anything from Mr. Sykes about how it's going in Sacramento?"

Jonathan made a good attempt at a hearty chuckle, but nevertheless his voice had a hollow ring to it. "No word from Mr. Sykes yet, so I assume everything is going well. Try not to be impatient, dear. The wheels of the law always grind more slowly than we would like."

"Yes, of course." Meghan hesitated, thinking of Jason's warning that her uncle wouldn't give up the mines without a fight. Was her uncle delaying deliberately? And if so, what could she do about it? Jason was in no shape to go to Sacramento and check up on the slippery Mr. Sykes, and she quailed at the thought of making the trip herself.

Jonathan sensed her hesitation and continued in an assuasive voice. "There's no reason to worry, Meghan. All this is simply a formality. There's no question where you stand. The mines are yours. I'm sorry you have to put up with this legal nuisance, but naturally everyone thought you were dead after the Indian raid that killed your parents. What else could we think?"

Meghan thought she detected an underlying bitterness to his voice, but it was well hidden. "I'm not questioning what you did about the mines, Uncle Jonathan. In fact, the more I think about it, the more ridiculous this situation seems. You've built a thriving business on those claims. And now the law says you have to give it all up to me?"

"I can't pretend to be happy about it," he answered with disarming frankness. "I've put my life's work into those mines. My entire fortune is founded on this business. But the law is the law. You are your father's legal heir. The claims were never mine to begin with, though of course I thought they were."

Meghan gazed out the window for a moment. She didn't understand the white man's law. The situation seemed senseless, even though it was to her advantage. "I don't want to take the mines away from you, Uncle Jonathan. There must be enough for both of us. Maybe I could tell the people who made this law that I wanted you to have half the business. Would that work?"

Jonathan smiled indulgently, magnanimously, and, Meghan suddenly suspected, quite insincerely. "That's very generous of you, Meghan, but you shouldn't make a decision like that right now. After all, you have not only yourself to consider. Think of your son. I want no one to be able to say, sometime in the future, that I've robbed you of your rightful property." He leaned back in his chair and chuckled knowingly. "And someday, probably someday soon, you will want to marry again. Your husband should have a say in what you do with your wealth, don't you think?"

She ignored his assumption she would rid herself of Jason. Now was not the time to discuss that problem. "But what about you and your family? I wouldn't rob them of—"

"Now, Meghan." He smiled. "Calm down. Nobody's going to think you're robbing me of anything. There's no reason to be bothering your head about something that should be a man's concern. I will continue to manage the properties until you have a husband capable of seeing after your affairs." He gave her a fatherly smile. "And this time we'll make sure he's not some knife-toting, gun-hung wild man, eh?"

Meghan felt a flash of irritation. Her uncle's condescending tone was beginning to grate on her nerves, and his assumption that she needed a husband to run her affairs was insulting.

"In the meantime," he continued in the same tone, rising to escort her to the door and effectively ending the interview, "don't you worry about money. You've got enough to do anything you want. Maybe you and Erin can keep busy planning yourself a complete new wardrobe.

Wouldn't you like that? You're going to need it, you know, if you're going to take your rightful place in society, and I'm sure my wife is determined that you will. And any questions you have, you feel free to bother me at any time."

He closed the door gently behind her, an affectionate smile still on his face. His expression changed radically, however, as he sat back down at his desk. He had seen Meghan's expression when he'd mentioned her marrying again. Damn that Jason Sinclair! he thought furiously. How dare that fortune-hunting son of a bitch marry his niece and spoil his plans for bringing her under suitable control. And the way Meghan had run to the man's side when he was hurt made Jonathan wonder if his hopes for a divorce were misplaced. The twit might convince herself she was really in love with the bastard, and then what the hell was he to do?

He got up and paced restlessly over to the window, but today the splendid view didn't calm his agitation. Meghan wouldn't stay married to that damned yellow-eyed gunslinger, he'd see to that. Jason Sinclair was a dangerous unknown, and Jonathan had no intentions of putting up with the man any longer than absolutely necessary.

Jonathan stopped his pacing and tried to cool his O'Brian temper. The situation with Meghan was not beyond retrieving. If she could only be brought to look with favor upon that young Austrian. The man was handsome, cultured, rich—what any woman in her right mind would want for a husband. If anyone could divert Meghan's mind from Jason, and from her inheritance, Josef could.

The longer he thought about it, the more he liked the idea. It would be the perfect solution. Josef would want to take the chit to Europe, well away from where she could get into Jonathan's hair. And the fellow was so taken with the girl he could probably be persuaded to listen to reason about the management and control of the mines that were nominally his wife's property. Or maybe he could even persuade Meghan to relinquish her entire interest and sign over legal ownership to Jonathan. Married to Josef, her future would be secure. She would have no need to pursue her interest in the mines. With a thoughtful frown on his face Jonathan pulled the bell cord that hung conveniently close to his desk. When Li Ching arrived he was told to inform Mrs. O'Brian that her husband wished to speak with her in the study.

Erin dutifully presented herself to her husband's office and took the chair that faced the desk. She noted how drawn his face was, and remembering the stormy set of Meghan's countenance when she'd passed her on the stairs a few minutes ago, she wondered if something had passed between the two of them that was going to lead to unpleasantness. For all her preoccupation with fashion and socializing, Erin O'Brian was an intelligent woman. She was aware of the awkward situation with the mines. But Meghan was a girl of such generous and loving spirit that Erin was sure that everything would work out to everybody's satisfaction. After all, the mines were incredibly rich. The O'Brians had money and investments enough right now for Jonathan to retire and enjoy the rest of his life in opulent leisure. On the other hand, she knew what a hard, stubborn, and ambitious man Jonathan was. He would never give if he could take, and he would never back down from a stand once his position was set in his mind. And Meghan, sweet girl though she was, was a high-spirited person without the benefit of a proper upbringing. In her own way, she was just as stubborn as her uncle.

"Yes, dear?" Erin broke in on her husband's musings. "Li Ching said you wanted to speak to me."

"Yes, I do." Jonathan set down the pencil he'd been tapping restlessly on the desk. "Erin, my love, I'm becoming somewhat worried about our niece."

"How is that, dear?"

"You told me earlier you thought she was having some problems with adjusting to her new life. I think perhaps you were right."

"It's only natural, Jonathan, that she should feel somewhat confused at first. I was only concerned with her happiness. She seems so intense about some things. Very unattractive in a young lady of her age and station."

"I couldn't agree more, my love. I, too, am concerned with her happiness and well-being. I'm rather distressed at her confusion and inability to put her life in some kind of order. I think she needs a firm hand to point out the way. And I think, my dear, that she would take more kindly to your guidance than to mine."

"Well, Jonathan," Erin said cautiously, "what do you think I should do?"

Jonathan managed to look thoughtful for a moment, as if he were just now pondering possible solutions to the problem. "Perhaps that nice young Austrian is the answer," he ventured. "He seems to be from a very worthy family. Lots of money there, you know. And he certainly seems smitten with Meghan. Perhaps she should be encouraged more in his direction. I'm sure he would have an excellent influence on her attitude, and if things went well, he could make her a very fine husband."

Erin looked doubtful. Josef was doubtless a very fine gentleman; but though Meghan seemed to enjoy his company she'd been consistently casual about the relationship. That wasn't a sign of a girl about to fall in love. Still the look in Jonathan's eyes told her that her husband was set on this course of action, and she knew better than to argue.

"Perhaps you could plan some social activities that would throw the two of them together. And the girls would enjoy a few parties and get-togethers themselves, I imagine."

Erin frowned doubtfully. "That would be no problem, dear. But . . . well . . ."

"Yes?"

"Meghan is still a married woman, you know. And she's a young mother with a son. I'm not sure it would be quite proper for her to be so obviously courted by the young man."

Jonathan waved off her objections with an impatient

motion of his hand. "Don't worry about that. I think she'll come to realize what an unsuitable husband Sinclair is once she becomes better acquainted with young Josef. Right now she's confused, and I don't think she wants to admit Sinclair wants her only for her money. But she'll come around. Perhaps you might assure her there's no disgrace in divorcing a husband who's patently such an unsuitable match. It's not as though we would've tossed the chit out just because she'd had the man's by-blow. Under the circumstances she could hardly be held responsible."

Erin had a very good idea why Meghan had married Jason, and why she was so reluctant to initiate a divorce. Her heart went out to the girl in her dilemma, but she knew better than to stand against her husband once his mind was made up. "I'll see what I can arrange, Jonathan," Erin said in a resigned voice.

The very next day Josef himself sat in the chair facing the big desk. He had just paid a call on Meghan and was preparing to leave when Jonathan intercepted him in the hall and invited him into his study.

"Josef, my boy." Jonathan smiled at the man across his desk. "I'm glad I caught you. I've been meaning to have a word with you."

"What can I do for you, Mr. O'Brian?" Josef was not in the best of humors. The carriage ride with Meghan the day before had been something less than he'd hoped for, and his call today had been no more successful. Meghan had been polite but distracted. Josef was beginning to wonder if his suit had the slightest chance of success. Meghan was consistently friendly, open, and at times even affectionate. But she was so damned sisterly—with him at least! But a spark certainly lit up her eye anytime that damned Jason Sinclair's name came up in the conversation. And his name always seemed to come up, despite Josef's efforts to avoid the subject. Josef wondered if he shouldn't give up his seemingly hopeless quest and go back to Europe, where several family matters needed his attention.

"I just wanted to let you know, Josef," Jonathan was saying, "that both my wife Erin and I think very highly of you. I don't know exactly how things stand between you and my niece, but I can assure you of our approval should matters take a serious turn."

Josef looked at Jonathan with infinitesimally raised brows. The man was really quite a clod, Josef decided, speaking of such a matter before he had brought it up himself. But then, he told himself, one must make allowances for these Americans. While he was charmed by the fresh, natural honesty of a person like Meghan, he couldn't help being irritated by the pompous affectations of one who pretended to gentility but in reality had the manners of a bumpkin.

"I appreciate your regard, sir," Josef assured him in a stiff tone. "But I'm not sure your niece shares it."

"Oh, come now, man!" Jonathan all but gushed. "Don't tell me you're letting the little filly bamboozle you!"

"I beg your pardon?"

"Women!" Jonathan smiled. "They're all alike, bless their hearts, showing a man a cold shoulder while all the time they're hoping he'll pop the question."

"I don't think—"

"Now, you've got to understand Meghan," Jonathan insisted. "She's a sweet girl, but she's led a rather unusual life."

"Yes, sir. I understand all that."

"Sometimes I think she doesn't know herself what she wants. She's in need of a fellow with a level head to set her on the right course."

"Perhaps, but—"

"Now, the way I see it, Josef, you just about fit the bill for that little girl."

"Yes, sir, but your niece seems very reluctant to enter into any sort of a relationship right now."

"That's only because she's confused, poor girl. She's

led a hard life, living with the savages and all. And then that hardcase Sinclair taking advantage of her ignorance and persuading her to marry him. Don't know what he thought he would gain, but I can assure you that's history now. I've been encouraging Meghan to get a divorce, and she's assured me she's giving the matter serious thought. Now, I won't deny that Meghan needs a firm hand, but I'm more than willing to prod her in the right diection, which in my book is in your direction.''

''I'm very grateful, sir, but—''

''Now, I'm not trying to push either one of you, you understand. But I worry about the girl. She's a charmer, but she hasn't had a really proper upbringing, you know. She'll get herself into trouble with those mines, that's for sure. We both know that women are not suited to the demands of the business world. She needs her interest diverted elsewhere, and I figure you're the fellow to do it. You'll get what you want—oh, yes, I've seen how smitten you are with the girl—and Meghan will be safely under control, for her own good of course. You understand?''

Josef understood all too well. Jonathan might think he was being subtle, but the art was entirely lost the way he practiced it. He was being offered a deal. No doubt about it. Jonathan would deliver Meghan if Josef agreed to play according to her uncle's rules.

At first Josef was filled with revulsion. But then a worm of temptation wriggled its way into his mind. Meghan was a prize beyond the ordinary to Josef's way of thinking. Who would be hurt if he went along? He would make Meghan happy, give her children, wealth, love. And her uncle could have the damned mines.

Josef gave Jonathan a considering look. ''There's a lot of truth in what you say. Meghan needs a firm hand to guide her and to run her affairs. The situation with her mines . . . your mines, that is . . . is lamentable.''

Jonathan smiled. He knew the young man would catch on fast.

''You can be assured that should Meghan come around

to looking upon my suit with favor, her affairs would swiftly be put in order."

Jonathan's smile grew even wider. "I knew I could depend on you, sir."

Long after Josef had left, Jonathan sat staring at the closed door with a smirk of satisfaction on his face. His problems were all but solved. Before she knew it Meghan would be wedded and bedded and that would be that. She wouldn't even know what hit her. How could the fragile will of woman stand before the charm of European nobility and his own iron determination? Meghan didn't have a chance.

# Chapter Twenty-six

Samantha untied her bonnet and sailed it into the parlor with gay abandon. "What an absolutely wonderful picnic that was!" she chortled happily to Meghan. "Even Clara had a good time. I couldn't believe it. If I didn't know stodgy old Clara better, I'd think she was trying to take Josef away from you."

Meghan smiled gently. "Since Josef isn't mine, then it stands to reason that he can't really be taken away."

Samantha stood for a moment in frowning concentration, trying to see Meghan's logic, but only for a moment. A smile bubbled to the surface again. "Well, anyway, I'm glad Clara can't have him. Maybe that'll bring her down off her high horse. She's always so superior."

Meghan picked up Samantha's carelessly discarded bonnet and handed it to her, then unfastened her own and headed for the stairs. Samantha followed her into her room and sat down on the bed while Meghan impatiently took the pins from the elaborate coiffure Erin had persuaded her to wear to the picnic. The weight of the heavy mass of hair was making her neck ache and the heat was making her scalp prickle. Gratefully she combed her fingers through the heavy gold-red mass as it fell down her back to her waist.

"I wish I had hair like that," Samantha sighed, fingering her own yellow locks.

"Your hair is beautiful. And it's certainly much more fashionable than mine."

Samantha pouted prettily. "You look good no matter how you wear your hair though, and no matter what you wear. I don't know how Clara thinks she's going to win the viscount away from you. She doesn't hold a candle to your looks."

Meghan picked up her brush and ran it through her hair in long strokes as Samantha looked on with envy. "Clara isn't trying to take Josef away from anyone, Sam. Your imagination is running away with you. And Clara has many fine qualities. She would make an excellent wife for any man."

"Yeah." Samantha giggled. "If he didn't have eyes."

Meghan sighed in exasperation. Samantha and her older sister were ever at odds it seemed. Their personalities and priorities were so different that it was inevitable that they would clash. Samantha, sensing a sister of the soul in Meghan, had latched on to her almost from the first moment she'd come to O'Brian House. Clara, quieter and somewhat withdrawn by nature, was much more reserved. But the hostility Meghan had sensed in her older cousin had passed for the most part. Now there was a tentative friendship growing between them. Their one common interest was Andrew. Clara adored the baby, and in order to spend time with the child she had to put up with the mother. And in spending time with Meghan, Clara discovered that her cousin was not quite the rude interloper she'd thought.

For her part, Meghan was coming to admire Clara's unobtrusive virtues. Meghan herself had never been a quiet or tranquil person. She had always been too full of energy and enthusiasm to be serene. Her spirit was vigorous and undisciplined, and her years with the Cheyenne had reinforced her unruly nature. She was coming to appreciate Clara's quiet sensitivity, even though it was a quality she didn't share. Her heart went out to the older girl, for she'd seen the longing looks Clara cast toward Josef when she thought no one was looking. Clara would make Josef a much better match than she ever would, Meghan admitted. With her appreciation of quiet beauty, her sensitive and artistic nature, and her domestic efficiency, she would fit in wonderfully with the refined and aristocratic people who made up Josef's circle of family and friends. And she really wasn't that plain, Meghan thought. If the girl would only show a little interest in making herself attractive! She sewed beautifully, knew fashions and styles as well as Mrs. Standish, had a lovely figure and a quite passable face. But she garbed herself in drab colors and pulled her hair back in a severe style more appropriate for a woman of fifty than a girl of twenty-one. She would never catch Josef's eye looking like a middle-aged schoolmarm.

Meghan finished brushing her hair and began to braid it. Samantha bounced up off the bed and came to her side.

"Would you let me do that?"

"If you want."

"I saw a terrific new style in a magazine in the dry goods store yesterday. Could I try to fix your hair that way?"

Meghan sighed. "I don't want a fancy hairstyle, Sam."

"It wasn't fancy. It was all braided, see, and then pulled back and tied here." She demonstrated. "It would look beautiful for the dinner tonight."

"All right." Meghan smiled at the girl's enthusiasm. "But if I don't like it I'm going to pull it out. I don't want you to get hurt feelings."

"Oh, I won't be hurt! Here, take your dress off so we won't spoil your hair when I'm done."

Meghan did as she was bidden, feeling much cooler in just her shift.

"We certainly have been seeing a lot of Josef lately," Samantha said with studied casualness.

"Yes." Meghan smiled. "We certainly have."

It was true, Meghan thought, that the last two weeks had been crowded with picnics, dinners, luncheons, and soirees, all arranged by Erin. And Josef had been present at all of them, dancing attendance on her like a stallion on a mare. He'd been charming, gentlemanly, and persistent. Once he'd even gone so far as to steal a kiss when her aunt and uncle had conveniently left them unchaperoned on the veranda after dark. Meghan had been willing enough, eager, even, to see if the kiss of another attractive, virile man would have the same effect as Jason's kisses. Josef's kiss had been pleasant, comfortable, and completely lacking in the heart-stopping, earth-moving impact of the kiss of one tawny-haired, amber-eyed, gun-hung wild man, as Jonathan had called him.

Meghan wondered if it wouldn't be better to settle for pleasant and comfortable. Josef was so kind, so understanding. Marriage to him would be serene. He would take her far away, where she would never have to see Jason again, where wild Indians were considered an exotic adventure, not a hated enemy. And she knew Josef would make a good father for her son.

She hadn't seen Jason since she'd left him well on the way to recovery in his room in the Old Rose Saloon. Eight days ago a note for Meghan had been delivered to O'Brian House by the freckle-faced gawky boy who swept the floors and cut the firewood for a number of the dubious establishments on Benham Street.

*Going to Sacramento to light a fire under Sykes's rear end,* Jason had written. *Must talk when I return. Take care.* That was all.

Samantha finished braiding one narrow lock of hair and set it aside. "Has Josef proposed to you yet?" she asked, refusing to be put off by Meghan's contemplative silence.

Meghan smiled at the younger girl's eager inquisitiveness. She reminded her of an older version of Magpie, who had always been snooping about her boyfriends, always asking awkward and embarrassing questions, and always, always, getting in the way when she craved privacy. And Meghan had loved her dearly.

"He's mentioned marriage several times. I don't think there's any doubt about his intentions."

"How exciting!" Meghan sighed. "Imagine being married to a real lord. And he's so handsome. When he looks at me with those brown eyes I could just melt."

"You're too young to be melting when men look at you," Meghan warned with a twinkle in her eye.

"I'm just practicing. There's no harm in that, is there? Are you going to marry him?"

Meghan looked thoughtful, and a bit sad, Samantha thought. She wondered why the thought of marrying a handsome nobleman would bring such a somber look into any girl's eyes.

"I don't know, Sam. Maybe I will. I suspect he'll bring up the question again tonight at the dinner. I really haven't said yes to him, but I haven't said no, either. I guess to be fair I really ought to make up my mind."

"I wouldn't have any trouble making up my mind." Samantha put another bright lock aside and started on another. "But then, I suppose you have to choose, don't you. I almost forgot about Jason. He's really handsome too. And dangerous looking." Samantha shivered in delight. "I swear, that day he rescued us in Benham Street he looked at you like he was going to devour you right there. If any man ever looked at me that way I'd faint right on the spot."

Meghan grimaced in disbelief. "How could you remember how he looked at me? You were too busy dissolving into a little puddle of tears."

"I wasn't too busy to notice how his eyes got all hot when they were on you."

Meghan laughed. "He was just mad. Shows how much

you know about men. Besides, I don't have to choose between Jason and Josef. Jason can't abide being tied down by anyone or anything. If he wants his freedom, he deserves to have it.''

Samantha sighed romantically. ''Are you awfully in love with him?''

''I suppose so,'' Meghan admitted with a tolerant smile. ''And he loves me too, I think. At least a little. But, well, maybe you're too young to understand that sometimes— ouch!''

Samantha had yanked the lock of red hair that she was holding. ''The next time somebody tells me I'm too young for something, I'm going to scream.''

Meghan remembered with sadness her own eagerness to be initiated into the estate of full womanhood when she'd been courted by Red Shield. She'd been curious and impatient, just as Samantha. She hadn't realized the wealth of trouble and hurt that comes from a man's caress.

''Value your innocence while you can, Sam. Once it's gone, you can't get it back.''

''Oh, I won't want it back.'' Samantha giggled. ''But if you say Jason doesn't want to be tied down, then why don't you marry Josef? One must be practical about these things after all.''

''Why do I have to marry at all?'' Meghan asked with one brow arched in query.

Samantha thought this one over for a moment. ''Every woman gets married,'' she finally answered with assurance, ''except plain Janes like Clara who can't find a man. Why would any woman not want to marry?''

''I don't know,'' Meghan sighed. ''Maybe you're right.''

''I heard Mother and Daddy talking about Jason yesterday. Daddy said Jason is a fortune hunter.''

''Yes, I know what your father thinks of Jason. But no matter what he thinks, Jason didn't marry me to get his hands on my money. He's got plenty of his own.''

''Daddy said if Jason stuck around much longer, he was going to tell the sheriff to run him off. He said Jason gets some of the wilder sorts in the mines riled up just by being here.''

"Yes,'' Meghan said quietly. "He's right. Jason should probably go back to his mountains and prairies. He would be happier there.''

Samantha patted the last stray hair into place. "There,'' she declared with satisfaction, "it's finished. Do you like it?''

"It's fine, Sam. Thank you.''

"Will you wear it like that to the dinner tonight?''

Meghan looked in the mirror. The hairstyle suited her face, giving her a sophisticated look that made her seem a different person somehow. She knew Josef would like it. "Yes, I'll wear it this way.'' She couldn't keep a tinge of reluctance from her voice. Somehow, she just couldn't work up any enthusiasm for sitting through a long dinner with Josef tonight, or for making the decision that she knew he would demand of her.

As were all of Erin O'Brian's social events, the dinner was faultless. All the best of El Dorado County society were in attendance, and all agreed that the food was delicious, the orchestra matchless, and the conversation delightful. If the stray curious glances that drifted toward Meghan were somewhat less than friendly, they were very subtle in their disapproval, for no one wished to offend the host and hostess. If Jonathan and Erin O'Brian wanted to share their home with a woman of her sort, a woman who'd lived with savages and participated in heaven only knew how many perverted atrocities, a woman who'd married a hardcase man-killer such as Jason Sinclair, well, that was their business, wasn't it? But that didn't keep the good citizens of El Dorado County from disapproving. They'd be polite, for the O'Brians' sake, but only marginally polite.

Meghan sat with Josef and felt the same as she had at every other society event her aunt had pushed her into. She felt like an outsider. She was an outsider, and all these people here knew it. The only truly friendly face in the room was Josef's. How she longed to escape these stuffy people with their snobbish attitudes. She had an almost irresistible impulse to dash from the house, tear off her confining gown, throw back her head, and give voice to Two Moon's haunting war cry. That would give these people something to gossip about!

"Are you enjoying yourself, Meghan?" Josef asked, pouring her a glass of punch.

"No," she replied honestly. With Josef she didn't have to pretend. "When the dancing starts, can't we go outside instead? I feel like I'm being raked by every eye in the room."

"Certainly we can, if you prefer. I'd enjoy some fresh air myself."

Meghan smiled. She knew he would understand. Josef always understood. Josef was kind and intelligent and handsome. In some ways he was as stuffy as an old lady, but he was a good deal more open-minded than anyone she'd met in California. She should marry Josef, Meghan knew. She would be foolish not to. As Samantha had said, one should be practical about these matters. Love wasn't everything.

"This dessert is delicious," Josef commented. "Do you know what it is?"

"No," Meghan answered distractedly. "Aunt Erin hardly lets me near the kitchen since I burned a batch of pudding a few weeks ago. I learned to cook on an open fire, not on that contraption she calls a stove."

Josef laughed. "Meghan, my dear, you're wonderful. Don't ever change."

She should marry Josef, Meghan thought. She would marry him, she suddenly decided. And tomorrow she would go with her uncle to the courthouse and fill out any forms they would give her and sign her name to whatever was necessary to give Jason his precious freedom. Time to start being practical. It was the right decision. It would make Jason happy. It would provide a secure future from

Andrew and herself. Then why was her mind still in such turmoil?

A conversation from across the table caught her ear. "I heard a couple of weeks ago some troublemakers at your South Fork operation went to Jason Sinclair with complaints about the mine, Jonathan," the town's leading banker said.

Jonathan snorted. "They seem to think since he still has a tenuous connection with my niece that he has some say about what goes on there. They'll find out they're mistaken soon enough."

Meghan turned her attention toward her uncle. "Is there trouble at one of the mines, Uncle Jonathan?"

Jonathan smiled blandly. "Nothing for you to worry your head about, my dear. This is no talk for the ladies to have to hear, my friends. Let's talk of something more pleasant."

Meghan frowned. She had a right to worry about her mines if she wanted and was about to call that forcefully to her uncle's attention, forgetting for the moment that they were among guests. She opened her mouth to speak, but the gentle pressure of Josef's hand on her arm held back the words.

"Not here, Meghan," he warned softly, reading the intent on her face.

"I have a right to know!" she whispered furiously.

"I'm sure he's doing the best he can, my dear," Josef said mildly. "He's made a great success of those mines over the past years. Perhaps you should trust him a little more."

She raised surprised brows at this admonition. Did Josef, also, regard a woman as someone who should sit in the background worrying only about clothes and parties? Jason, for all his faults, treated her like a human being, not like an ornament. Her heart constricted painfully. Jason . . . how she wished she were with him, lying safely in his arms, or even confronting him in one of the many fights that had punctuated their stormy relationship. She belonged with him. Could she ever belong anywhere else?

True to his promise, Josef escorted Meghan outdoors when the rest of the party adjourned to the dance floor. The sun had set, taking the day's heat with it. A cool breeze played among the leaves of the oaks and lifted straying locks of gold-red hair from Meghan's cheeks and brows. Josef thought he'd never seen a sight so lovely. He wanted her more than he'd wanted anything in his life.

"I'm sorry you're not having a good time, Meghan," he said gently.

She shook her head. "It's certainly not your fault." She didn't want him to feel bad because she was in a dreary mood.

"Meghan, dear," he continued sympathetically, "I've told you that these provincial peons don't have the good taste or the brains to fathom what a jewel you really are. Don't let their snubs upset you."

"Oh, they don't upset me so much. I'm getting used to it, in fact."

They crossed the driveway and walked slowly down the lawn toward the stone wall. The night air was soft, and the nocturnal shadows, black on black, seemed cozy, not threatening. The hoot of an owl carried softly on the breeze. A perfect night for romance, Meghan thought. A perfect night for a proposal. Why wasn't she more excited?

"It would be quite different in Europe. People there would love you." He laughed. "I won't say they're not snobs. Even I'm a snob, my dear. I was born and bred to snobbishness. I'm sure you've noticed." She could see his fond smile glowing in the darkness of the night. "But the aristocracy are secure in their snobbishness—secure enough to welcome something new and refreshing. They would welcome someone like you, with your natural beauty and charm. They would welcome you with open arms and make you feel at home as you could never feel at home here, among people who regard you as a threat."

"A threat?" She turned to him in surprise. "Who could regard me as a threat?"

"These clods here regard you as a threat. Why do you think they treat you so shabbily? You and Jason Sinclair and the miners—you're all reminders that the only thing that separates them from the people they profess to despise is money. The people in there at your aunt's party have no class or pedigreed background, my dear. They have only money. And as you are a reminder of the rough cast that they are all made from, they put you apart, trying to convince themselves that they are made of more refined clay, even though deep in their hearts they know they're not."

Meghan laughed somewhat bitterly. "I'm not sure I understand your way of thinking, Josef. But I do know that if you think those people in there are made of rough clay, then I am surely made of mud."

Josef laughed. "No, Meghan. You, my dear, are a world above those who've been snubbing you all these weeks. You have no pretensions about being anything but what you are. And I find you utterly charming." His voice turned serious. "In fact I've come to love you very much, Meghan. And given time, so would my family." He paused, and the air between them became heavy with tension and hope. "Meghan. My dearest love. You know I want to marry you. I must return to Austria very soon, too soon for you to be set free from your husband in order to go with me. But let me go with hope in my heart. Let me go knowing I can return in time and claim you for my bride. I love you so much. I would do anything in my power to make you happy."

Meghan's heart seemed to stop in her chest. She couldn't open her mouth to answer. Where was her resolve? Where was her bold, practical decision of only hours before? She looked up into the face of the man standing beside her and saw the love shining in his eyes. He was a kind man, a good man. He would make a good husband. A fine husband.

But not for her, Meghan suddenly knew. She couldn't marry Josef. Not while her heart was still elsewhere, trapped in the amber eyes and violent, restless soul of one who had haunted her days from the first moment she'd seen him. Josef deserved a wife who adored him. Someone like Clara, who would give him unquestioning devotion to the end of her days. He didn't deserve a wife who longed for another.

"I can't marry you, Josef," she said bluntly. "I'm still in love with Jason."

Silence hung between them. Stunned silence. The light in Josef's eyes faded. His mouth tightened for a moment, and a muscle in his clean, strong jaw twitched in agitation. But his words were calm and controlled. "I appreciate your honesty."

"I should have told you before. When Jason was hurt— when he almost died—I realized then there was no room in my heart for any other man. I thought my feelings might change. But they won't."

"In time you might come to love me. I can give you more than Jason ever could."

"No," she said with finality. "I was going to say yes to you, Josef. But I can't do that to you, or to me either. You deserve someone who can see only you, who will love you with all her heart. That will never be me."

The silence dragged on. The hoot of the owl now sounded empty and haunting. The sigh of the breeze was tinged with sadness. Meghan felt Josef's disappointment like a palpable wave pounding on her heart. She wondered briefly if he was disappointed solely over losing her, or was partly saddened over losing the idea of becoming a settled, married man. It had become obvious to Meghan that at this point in his life Josef was very much wanting a wife and family. She decided to take a chance.

"Josef?"

"Yes?" His voice was hollow.

"I probably shouldn't say this. I've got no right to say this, but I will, because you should know. I'm sure, just as sure as I can be, that Clara has very deep feelings for you.''

"I beg your pardon?''

Meghan sighed. "I'm being much too bold, and Clara would kill me if she heard this conversation. But no matter how improper it is for me to tell you, I think you deserve to know, and she deserves for you to know. Clara's a lovely woman under all those drab clothes and frumpy hairstyles. She's loving and sensitive and talented. And I know she cares for you very deeply. I've read it in her eyes when she looks at you. Any man should feel honored to be loved by a woman like her. You shouldn't dismiss her simply because she's plain.''

The sound that issued from Josef's throat was a combination between a laugh and a groan. "Meghan, do you believe I can think of another woman at a time such as this?''

"I just thought you should know," Meghan said firmly. "You should think about it. You may be missing a very good thing there.''

His laugh this time was genuine. "All right, you stubborn little minx. I'll think about it. For your sake. But Meghan—''

"No, Josef. My answer will not change. I'm sorry.''

She wished she could be in love with this gentle, civilized young man instead of the half-civilized ruffian her heart was tied to. Strange thought, she realized, for a woman who just over a year ago eagerly rode to war with the savage Cheyenne.

The house was finally silent. All the guests were gone. The cook and hired help still clattered in the kitchen, but the family were all preparing for bed, tired after a successful evening of dancing and dining. The dinner and dance, Meghan had overheard her aunt say, were every bit as successful as any of the Baileys'.

Meghan sat quietly on the porch, still dressed in her evening finery. She stared into the night, thinking about the decisions she'd made this day. Momentous decisions. Decisions that would determine the course of her life. Now, she reasoned, she must take charge of herself. Now there was no one left to lean on. She must see to herself and see to her son, as best she could. Starting tonight.

Meghan suspected that her uncle would be out to see her before taking to his bed. He'd been watching as Josef led her outdoors when the dancing started. There had been a curiously satisfied smile on his face, and Meghan knew that he wanted her to marry the young nobleman. She didn't blame him, really. It would have gotten her out of his hair. And Meghan suspected somehow that his noble gesture of rescuing his niece from the hands of the savages was not working out quite as Jonathan had planned. That was fine, she thought. She'd never asked to be rescued. She'd never wanted to be torn from her home and all those she loved. If she was inconveniencing her uncle, it was only part of what he deserved.

Meghan was right. Before the last lamp in the house was doused her uncle found her on the porch.

"What have we here?" he asked genially. "Can't sleep, my dear?"

Meghan made no answer, but simply smiled as he sat down beside her.

"It was quite a night, wasn't it?" he said with satisfaction. "Did you have a good time?"

"Certainly," she lied.

"I noticed Josef was looking very handsome tonight. He's a fine young man, that one."

"Yes, he is." Meghan knew her uncle was waiting for her to tell him what he wanted to hear. She didn't mind dragging out his suspense a bit.

"Your aunt thinks very highly of him also," Jonathan hinted.

And so does Clara, Meghan thought. But Jonathan

wouldn't have noticed his own daughter's pain in all of this.

"Uncle Jonathan," Meghan finally relented, "Josef proposed to me tonight."

"That's wonderful, dear. I'm sure he'll make you a fine husband. You'll be very happy." His voice swelled with gloating, and Meghan wondered again if there was more than simple convenience in his desire that she marry Josef.

"I turned him down."

Silence. Even the nocturnal sounds seemed to be suspended.

"You turned him down," he repeated slowly. "Why?"

"I don't love him."

She sensed consternation swell in the man sitting beside her, but his voice was quiet. Only an underlying quiver of tension hinted that he had anything but a casual interest in this affair.

"You should think again, Meghan. It isn't every day a girl is offered such an opportunity. Love is something that can come with time."

"Not for me," she told him with characteristic candor. "I love Jason. If he wants a divorce he can have one. But if he doesn't—well, he and I will talk about that when he gets back from Sacramento."

Jonathan gave her a chilling look. "Jason went to Sacramento after all?"

"He wanted to see if Mr. Sykes needed any help." Meghan stretched the truth for the sake of tact. "He left a little over a week ago."

"I see." His voice was dark with something Meghan couldn't define. She couldn't see his face in the muffling shadow of the porch.

"When Jason and Mr. Sykes get back and this legal mess is done with, I'll have an agreement drawn up about the mines. I want to make sure you get treated fairly."

"That's very generous of you," he said with a hint of sarcasm. "Are you sure this is what you want?"

"Yes," Meghan said with finality. "I know you have

only my welfare at heart, Uncle Jonathan, but it's my life.''

''Yes, it's your life.''

Jonathan's eyes followed Meghan thoughtfully as she rose and went into the house. She was a fool, and she wouldn't be convinced. Time to stop playing games, he decided. He regretted what he had to do, but the little twit had brought it on herself.

# Chapter Twenty-seven

The morning was bright and clear. The air had a crisp feel to it, heralding perhaps an early autumn. Meghan guided her chestnut mare down the back trail that led into town. She wanted to stay well away from the road so she could enjoy the peace of this early-morning ride.

It was good to get out of the house. In the week since the dinner party she hadn't been riding once. Erin always had some chore for her to do or begged her company on shopping trips or social calls. Meghan was beginning to feel stifled. For the most part she didn't mind her aunt's company, but since the night of the party Erin could talk of only one thing—how foolish Meghan was to throw away the attentions of a wonderful man like Josef. The subject was beginning to wear thin. Meghan didn't want to think about it, and she certainly didn't want to talk about it. But Erin wouldn't give up hope that she could make Meghan realize her error. She was sure Josef would renew his suit if Meghan would only give him some encouragement. Sometimes there was an edge of desperation in Erin's voice that made Meghan wonder just why she was so determined.

Samantha thought the whole situation was terribly romantic. Of course, Meghan thought with a smile, Samantha thought everything was terribly romantic. She was certain that Meghan had refused Josef's proposal because she was pining for Jason. The morning after the dinner party she'd heard Jonathan raving at Erin about what he termed the deplorable situation, and she'd gone immediately to Meghan to offer her sympathy and to learn the juicy details.

"Oh, Meghan!" she sighed tragically. "You poor dear. I wish there was something I could do to help."

Meghan had been caught off guard. She didn't feel at all in need of anyone's sympathy. "Help with what?" she inquired innocently.

"Oh, you're so brave," Samantha gushed. "But I just knew this was going to happen."

"Knew what was going to happen?" Meghan was getting impatient.

"When you told me you still loved Jason, I knew you wouldn't be able to marry Josef, no matter how sensible it would be. But of course I should have known! Jason is such a spectacular man. But I must admit, there were times I thought for sure you'd marry Josef. He's so handsome and worldly. But of course you can't. Not if you're still longing for Jason in your heart. Oh, it's so romantic! Turning down a titled gentleman to fly into the arms of a fierce frontiersman! I could just—"

"Stop!" Meghan commanded, fending off the verbal barrage with raised hands. "Sam, you've been reading too many romances. It's not like that at all. I'm not flying into anybody's arms! Much less Jason's!"

"Oh, Meghan! You don't have to be brave with me! You can tell me everything!" Samantha perched herself on the arm of Meghan's chair and looked hopeful.

Meghan gave the younger girl an exasperated but affectionate squeeze on the arm. "Don't be silly. I haven't talked to Jason for a long time. Just because I'm not going to marry Josef doesn't mean Jason and I are going to stay together."

That part, at least, was true, Meghan thought as she turned the mare into the main road just outside of town. She wished Jason were here so they could settle things between them. Every day for the past week she'd looked for him to ride down the drive or at least send a note from town telling her he was back. She was almost tempted to ride on down to the Old Rose Saloon when she got to town, just to see for herself if he might be back.

Of course Samantha hadn't believed a word she'd said and insisted on treating her like the lovelorn heroine of a tragic novel. Clara, on the other hand, never mentioned Meghan's "foolish mistake," as Erin called it. But she showed a good deal more warmth toward her cousin than she had before and actually sought out her compainship on a few occasions. One morning they'd taken a ride into town together. Meghan had been surprised to note that Clara rode, sidesaddle of course, with a grace and coordination that made her seem a part of the horse. Her bemusement had grown when Clara suggested they stop by Mrs. Standish's shop. There she ordered several new frocks from the dressmaker—colorful, stylish dresses that were not at all like her usual tailored and drab apparel. Meghan had dared to hope this change in attitude had something to do with Josef, but she was afraid that asking would break the spell of companionable rapport that was building between her and her older cousin.

Main Street was a busy place today. She was the object of indignant stares from several matrons she'd met at the Bailey party and again at her aunt's dinner. They no doubt disapproved of her divided skirt and manner of riding astride. Let them gawk, Meghan thought. She was rapidly learning that money was a measure of a man's status in this white man's society, just as horses and battle prowess were the measure of a man's status in a Cheyenne band. She had more money than any of the old biddies who were sneering at her and any of their self-important husbands who leered behind her back. Therefore, she figured, the white man's rules said she had the right to ignore them. And ignore them she would.

The sheriff was taking in the cool morning air in a chair outside his office. He tipped his hat as she rode by, his face expressionless. She was reminded of his visit to Jason's room and wondered if he would try to boot Jason out of town when he returned from Sacramento. That would make Jonathan happy. Her uncle was not a man who easily gave up, and Meghan suspected that behind his facade of icy civility he still nourished hopes that she would marry Josef, though just why it was so important to him she couldn't guess.

Meghan pulled the chestnut mare to a stop in front of the bank. She had told her uncle and aunt last night not to expect her for the noon meal today. She intended to be gone on a ride from early morning until the afternoon. Her uncle had asked her to stop by the bank to deliver several sheaves of papers concerning the mines. Since these were the first halfway friendly words he'd spoken to her since the night she'd turned down Josef's proposal, she'd consented readily. Maybe, she thought, things were going to be all right between her uncle and herself. She hoped so. She hoped that once Jonathan realized she was determined on her course of action, his attitude toward her would soften. Once the mines were transferred to her, she intended to draw up an agreement giving Jonathan the lion's share of profits from the mines until Andrew reached his majority. At that time all ownership reverted to her son. She had reserved for herself only enough to see her comfortable and independent and able to provide the advantages Andrew would need to give him a head start in this hard-knocks world.

Papers safely delivered, Meghan headed back down Main Street to where it intercepted a trail into the hills, giving the mare her head in a gentle canter. She didn't see the two men riding together who followed her out of town.

The air was warming now, giving testimony to the fact

that summer was still in force. Meghan let the mare canter easily along the trail, pulling her down to a slower gait only when the going was very rough. She reveled in the feel of the horse under her and knew the mare was enjoying stretching her legs after almost a week with no exercise. No fantasy Cheyenne rode with her this day as they frequently did on her solitary rides. Her mind was firmly in California. She was coming to accept that she was a world away from those carefree days in the country of the Bighorn and Powder rivers, and she would never return. More than distance separated her now from that world of wild freedom. She was no longer the same person who borrowed a war pony from Comes in Sight and ridden off with Two Moon's war band. She was a white woman, a grown woman with family and responsibilities in the white world. Her horizons had expanded, not pleasantly, perhaps, but expanded just the same. She must find her happiness, if she could, in the world of her birth.

Meghan halted the little mare in a stream bottom and dismounted while the horse drank. Looping the reins over the saddle horn so they wouldn't drag on the ground, she let the mare wander along the stream to munch on the lush late-summer grass while she took her ease in the shade of an oak. It was good to be alone, away from the family, away from Jonathan's scowls, Erin's scolding, and Samantha's mooning. Clara was taking care of Andrew, so Meghan felt comfortable with staying out as long as she wanted. She needed to be alone with her thoughts. She needed to make plans. Her life loomed up ahead of her like a featureless plain. No trail, no road led across to show her the way. She had to determine where it was she wanted to go, and what she wanted to do with herself from this point forward if Jason chose to walk out of her life.

Meghan couldn't say just what it was that brought her out of the world of her thoughts. The mare still grazed peacefully on the grassy bottom. The birds still sang and the insects still hummed. But her Cheyenne-trained instincts made her uneasy. She got up and looked down the trail, senses alert. Nothing. The puffy clouds of summer floated peacefully in the sky. The leaves danced cheerfully in the light breeze. Everything was as it should be.

Then the mare snorted and raised her graceful head, nostrils flared and delicate ears twitched forward. Meghan took the leap from being alert to being alarmed. This was a little-used trail she was on, but someone other than she was riding these hills this morning.

Assuring herself she was being silly, she mounted the mare and rode on. The morning had grown less bright in her mind, and hills were no longer so peaceful. Time and again she looked over her shoulder. No other rider appeared to her sight, but her Indian-sharp senses told her she was being followed.

Who would want to follow her? she wondered. Perhaps Jason had returned and had seen her leave town. No. He had no reason to sneak about in the bushes. And if he didn't want to be seen for some reason, she would never have suspected his presence. Someone less skilled in stealth, then. Who would have a reason for being so secretive? She told herself again that she was being silly. She didn't have exclusive right to this trail. Probably someone else was out for a mid-morning ride. Her imagination was playing games with her.

The morning's promise of coolness had not been fulfilled. As the sun approached its zenith Meghan could feel sweat starting to trickle in irritating droplets down her spine and between her breasts. She left the trail and guided the mare down into a little stream valley. Another drink would feel good, she decided. And she could wash her face and neck in the cool water. Whoever was on this same trail behind her would pass her by, she hoped. Or at least they would if they were simply other people out for a casual ride. Her hand dropped to the rifle scabbard that rode the skirts of her saddle. She was glad she'd heeded Erin's warning not to ride these hills without a weapon. She was better than most men with a rifle. If she was being followed by miscreants or outcasts looking for easy prey, someone was going to get an unpleasant surprise.

The mare drank deeply as Meghan got off and stretched her muscles. She could tell she'd been living the soft life of late. More exercise was definitely in order, she decided, if she wasn't to turn into a soft pansy of a white woman. She untied the scarf from around her neck and dipped it in the cool water of the stream. It was good to wipe the layer of dust and perspiration from her skin. Dipping the piece of cloth again, she squeezed it so the cold water ran down under her blouse to cool her breasts. She hadn't counted on the day's being so hot. She would give her unseen companions time to lose her trail, then return home, she decided.

Then the mare lifted her dripping muzzle from the stream. Ears flicked forward as she swung her head to look back down the valley in the direction of the trail. A soft whicker sounded from her throat. Meghan was instantly alert.

Two riders emerged from the trees. They came in a slow and relaxed manner, as if they had just happened to leave the trail the same place as she. Something about the two was familiar. Meghan struggled with her memory to place their faces. Then she remembered, and her heart gave a lurch of alarm. She knew these men. She knew their names. George and Harry. Two of the no-goods from the South Fork mine who had beset her and Samantha in Benham Street.

Meghan was in her saddle before the men were halfway down to the stream. She pounded the mare's sides with her heels, startling the horse into a full-out run. The mare was long-legged and strong, and she could outrun most other horses given a fair chance. And if not, there was always the rifle.

She galloped up the little valley, avoiding the trail and hoping to lose her pursuers in the thick stand of trees and undergrowth on the side of the hill. The mare balked as branches raked her sides, but her rider's heels set her to moving again. The crashing of underbrush behind her as she reached the crest of the hill told Meghan her ploy was unsuccessful. The two men were right behind her. She plunged down into the valley on the other side. Here there was no brush for cover. The golden grasses stretched to the bottom of the valley and up again on the other side. Here she must rely on speed.

Her pursuers' horses were faster than she had expected. Where did losers like George and Harry get such splendid mounts? she wondered. The mare was fast and had the endurance that came from good breeding and good care, but she was blowing hard and straining to stay ahead of those who relentlessly pursued.

Meghan rounded a bend. Temporarily she was out of sight of the men behind her. She ducked into a brush-clogged little side valley floored with scoured rock. Her tracks in here couldn't be seen by anyone less than an expert, she knew. She maneuvered the mare into a thicket of manzanita surrounded by wild olive trees. If only the two would pass her by she could head back the way she had come and disappear. Give her ten minutes in the clear and they wouldn't have a chance to find her.

Moments of silence and stillness stretched into an eternity. Then she heard the clatter of hooves as her pursuers flew by. She stayed still for moments longer, allowing herself to breathe again. Then quietly she moved her horse forward out of the thicket. George and Harry were out of sight around the curve of the valley. The drumbeat of their horses' hooves had faded. Meghan swung the mare's head in the direction from which she'd come, moving her out at a brisk trot. The little chestnut's steel-shod hooves rang momentarily on rock, then were muffled again by a cushion of dirt. Meghan cursed herself for carelessness. She wasn't used to going by stealth on a shod mount. No matter, she told herself. The two troublemakers should be much too far away to hear. They weren't though.

A wild yell echoed down the valley as George and Harry galloped around the bend.

"Damn!" Meghan muttered, digging her heels into the mare's sides. They'd seen her ruse and doubled back.

The mare leapt forward in a spurt of valiant effort. Meghan knew she didn't have enough to give, not enough to get back to town or back to O'Brian House before she collapsed. She wasn't willing to kill the mare in an effort to escape. She still had the rifle. What she needed to find now was a good spot to turn and face these ghouls.

The place she was looking for presented itself down the valley. The stream curved back on itself in a sharp bend. For a moment, when Meghan rounded that bend, she would be out of sight. There, she determined, she would turn and prepare an unpleasant surprise for those who followed.

To snatch herself time, Meghan splashed the mare across the stream and cut the distance short by cutting across a little sandbar that had grown on the inside curve of the bend. The footing was treacherous, and the mare was exhausted by the time Meghan pulled her to a halt where they were hidden by a swell of ground from the two men behind her. She swung her horse around and stood facing her pursuers. Pulling her rifle free of its scabbard, she checked the loading. Then she put it to her shoulder and trained the sights on the spot where the two men would appear from around the hill.

They came. Their horses were laboring, lathered with sweat. The men's eyes were avid, like vicious hounds hot on the trail of their prey. Sweat ran down their faces and into the open-necked vee of their shirts. Their mouths were twisted into ugly grins of the glory of the chase. All this Meghan noticed in the instant she pulled the trigger.

The thunderclap of the rifle shot echoed off the hills. The chestnut mare jumped at least two feet into the air, almost unseating her rider and pulling her aim badly off target. Meghan cursed. What a time to discover the damned horse was gun-shy! She raised the rifle again. One more chance, then they'd be on her. The mare settled before the next shot, then jolted again as the gunfire hit her ears.

Missed again. With a muttered curse that would have burned even Jason's ears, she urged the skittish mare to flight.

The little chestnut mare, valiant though she was, had nothing left to give. She broke into a slow lope, then dropped to a trot in spite of Meghan's desperate urging. The duo's equally laboring mounts trotted up behind her.

Flight was impossible, so Meghan slipped quickly to the ground, slapping the mare on the rump to get her out of the way. She raised the rifle to her shoulder, telling herself she should have done it this way to begin with. She took aim on the figure on the right. Then out of nowhere a rope dropped over her head and jerked tight around her neck. She stumbled and choked, reflexively dropping the rifle as her hands grabbed desperately at the encircling hemp.

"Ha!" George yelled. "We got 'er now!"

A hard yank on the rope pulled her off her feet. Another rope, expertly thrown, circled and tightened around a flailing ankle. She was caught and stretched between the two of them, helpless as any calf spread for branding.

Well-trained horses held the ropes taut when George and Harry dismounted to gloat over their prey.

"Har!" George bellowed in laughter. "She don't look so high and mighty now!"

Harry joined in his hilarity. "Don't see no ornery yaller-haired ass-kicker comin' to yer rescue now, honey. Whut's a matter? He get tired a humpin' yer purty little red-haired ass?"

"Hee, hee!" George chortled with glee and reached down to yank open her blouse. Impatiently he hooked a grimy finger in her shift and ripped downward, exposing her breasts to his eager view. She hit him with her hand, but he paid her no more notice than he would a fly, and at her every movement the rope closed more tightly around her neck, sending swarms of bright spots swimming before her eyes. "Heard that yaller-haired killer's a squaw man." He closed a greedy paw over her breast. "Guess that's why he took up with this here piece. Whatcha say, Harry?"

Harry eagerly crowded him out of the way. "Lemme have some of that!" His hands eagerly groped to fondle the sweet flesh that was exposed to his view. Then they dipped lower to fumble with the fastenings of her skirt. She screeched and kicked at him with her one unbound leg to no avail.

"Get your filthy hands off me, you gutter-born son of a bitch!" she rasped from her abused throat.

Harry pulled her garments down around her knees, caught her flailing leg in one hand, and buried the other hand in the soft nest of red curls that lay at the juncture of her thighs. He pulled hard and Meghan cried in pain. "I dunno," Harry leered at his companion. "If squaw meat's all this good, I'd join the army and fight the damn Injuns." He chuckled, a low and dirty sound escaping from his lips. "Mebbe I'll have a go right here. Whatcha say, George?" One hand moved to his crotch to caress the bulge that was about to burst his denims. "I'm sure ready to give this little squaw a good ridin'."

George grunted and shifted his own self in his pants. Hunger gleamed wetly in his eyes, but his caution was greater than his lust. "Nah! Later's time enough, after the old man's finished with her. We gotta get her to the cabin."

Seeing the relief in Meghan's eyes, Harry bent down close to her face and ran his hand over her breasts and down her belly. Then he fastened his fingers firmly and painfully in her soft womanhood, grinned, unbuttoned his pants with his other hand, and pulled out his turgid organ. "Don't be too disappointed, little Injun fucker. You get a taste of this before we slit you open, eh?"

Meghan's eyes grew wide and frightened for a second only. Then she schooled her face to impassivity. She wouldn't let them see her fear, she vowed. His face leered into hers as his fingers jammed into her as far as he could get them. The pain he caused didn't show on her features as she spat full into his face.

"Shit!" George laughed at his comrade as Harry delivered

a meaty fist to Meghan's head. Stars exploded before her eyes, then all went black.

When Meghan awoke all she could feel at first was the pain in her head. The throbbing ache exploded rhythmically in her brain and threatened to burst her skull with each throb. Over what seemed centuries the pain grew more bearable. She began to feel other things. Her hands were bound with coarse rope and her wrists were chafing. Her bottom rested on hard boards that made her feel the sharpness of her bones. Her back leaned against a surface equally hard and uncomfortable.

She opened her eyes, bracing herself for the renewed pain as light seemed to stab through to the back of her skull. She was in a crude cabin dimly lit by a flickering lantern. Apparently she'd been out a long time, for it was night already. She recognized the old miner's shack on Cedar Creek. She'd ridden up here several times when she'd wanted to be sure to be alone. To her knowledge no one else ever came up here. The shack had been deserted a long time, since the early days of the gold rush. On her trips up here, she'd guessed that the cabin was occasionally used by the fugitives and outlaws who sometimes roamed these hills, for she'd found remains of fresh meals scattered among the mouse droppings and accumulated dirt, and once the barely cold ashes of a fire. This was the first proof she'd had of it, though. She'd didn't want to think about what purpose she'd been brought here for, but the intent of the two kidnappers had been obvious. They'd mentioned an old man, though. She could understand the evil motives behind the two former miners' actions, for they hated the O'Brians. But who else would wish her harm?

She tested her bonds. They were tight and secure. Her movements only served to chafe her wrists into raw welts. She looked around, hoping against hope to find something within reach sharp enough to fray the ropes. The dim lanternlight concealed more than it revealed, but it was sufficient to show her a floor bare of all but dust, food scraps, and mouse droppings. No help to be had there.

Voices sounded from outside. She recognized the tones of her captors. They were arguing. She strained to listen.

"You go!" Harry whined. "I'll stay here and watch the girl."

"Like hell!" George thundered. "I know what you'll do while I'm gone. The old man don't pay us to be stickin' our peckers in the goods. After he's gone, we can do what we like. What he don't know won't get us in shit. But I know you, you damned fool. You got the balls of a bull and the brains of a flea. You'll get us both in shit if he comes up here and finds you pumping your damned ass off 'atween her legs. You go get the man, and I'll stay here!"

"And what the hell will you be doing with that swelled-up puny prick of yours while I'm gone? I seen the way you looked at her ass. By God! Yer jest lookin' for some extra time for humpin' 'er while I'm ridin' down to get 'im."

"Don't anything ever get past yer thick skull? Is humpin' the only thing you ever think about? I'm surprised yer pecker don't fall off the way you work it!"

"All right," Harry spat. "We'll make us a pact. I go fer the man and bring 'im back, like he told us. But if yer lying to me . . . if yer juice is dryin' on that squaw meat in there when I get to 'er, I'm cuttin' off yer tool. An' don't think I won't."

"Jesus Christ! You hump-brained piece of shit. I'm not goin' to fuck her till we can both have a go at it!"

"Jest remember I warned ya'!"

"Asshole!" George muttered as Meghan heard hoof-beats growing fainter in the distance.

George came into the cabin and regarded her impassively. "See yer awake, missy. Don't think of tryin' nothin'. Ya cain't get away, so's ya might as well relax fer a spell. Make it easier on the both of us."

"Why have you brought me here?" Meghan demanded. "Who hired you?"

"You'll find out soon enough, missy. Ain't nothin' you c'n do about it nohow."

"My uncle will have a search party out when I don't come back. When he gets hold of the two of you, you'll wish you were never born."

George chuckled. "Think so?"

"Yes, I think so. And he isn't the only one who'll be looking for me. If you know what's good for you, you'll turn me loose right now."

"Do tell!" George grinned, setting his bulk down on the one rickety chair that graced the room. "So ya think that yaller-haired man-killer will be comin' fer ya, huh? Ya must be a pretty good lay fer that fella to stick around so long. I know his type, an' they usually don't stick in one place for this long. Course, if I was gettin' it regular from a purty little red-assed gal like you who got broke in pleasin' those Injun studs, mebbe I'd stick around too. I hear those Injuns're hung heavy as a bull, and they mount their wimmen from behind, jest like an ole stallion fucks a mare. 'Zat true?"

She refused to be baited by his crudity, turning her head instead and trying to ignore his presence as he continued to goad her with further displays of his sick imagination. If either of those men laid hands on her again, she knew that she'd be sick. Given their tastes in entertainment, they'd probably enjoy being thrown up on. She had to find a way to escape. Even if she was killed in the attempt, it would be a kinder fate than what these two twisted animals planned for her. But how? That was the big question. Her bonds were secure, and with that big lout watching her every move she couldn't even work to get loose.

Her racing mind froze in heart-stopping dread as hooves clattered in front of the cabin. Harry was back. Her fate was at hand. Now at last one question would be answered. Who wished her ill so much as to set these dreadful hounds on her trail. The cabin door opened, admitting Harry and one other, a man she recognized, a man she knew well, a man who apparently wished her dead.

Jonathan.

# Chapter Twenty-eight

Jonathan. Of course Jonathan. How could she have been so naive? Who else would profit so much from her death? She'd believed his prattle of family loyalty and family ties. She'd believed him when he'd claimed to regard her like a daughter for the sake of his long-dead brother. She'd believed him when he'd told her he had her welfare uppermost in his mind. She'd been a fool.

"Meghan." Jonathan looked at her, bruised and dirty, bound hand and foot. "What a shame you've brought us all to this." He turned to George and Harry, who were smirking at the stunned expression on her face. "Out, you two! And don't come back in until I tell you!"

"Now," he said when the two toughs had reluctantly shuffled out the door, "we have some things to discuss, you and I. If you give me your word you won't try to escape, I'll untie you. That looks mighty uncomfortable the way they've got you trussed up."

Meghan was silent. She wouldn't give her word. Let the bastard assume she was a helpless woman and untie her. She'd rip his heart out.

Jonathan moved forward, then halted when he saw the expression in her eyes. "Perhaps not." He smiled. "I keep forgetting the wilder side of your nature. You've adjusted so well to our way of life, what with brand-new clothes and fancy manners, it's easy to forget you're just a little savage at heart. Aren't you?'

Meghan kept her silence. If she got out of this alive, Jonathan would find out just how savage she could really be, but in the white man's way, not the Cheyenne way. She'd been subjected to more savagery in the white man's world that she'd ever seen among the Indians. And now her own family was betraying her. Indian methods were too kind for Jonathan. If she got out of here, she'd use the white man's law to tear Jonathan's world apart piece by piece. She swore she would.

"No words of welcome for your dear uncle?" he mocked. "Well, perhaps you're right. Let's put the civilities aside for now. Let me get down to the purpose of this visit." He pulled up the room's single chair and sat down, looking exactly as if he were preparing to do business in his richly appointed study in O'Brian House. "Now, Meghan, I'm really very sorry that I had to have you brought here in this manner. I realize those boys outside aren't the most pleasant. In fact, I dismissed them once from the South Fork mine, but shortly afterwards I discovered that they could be very useful in other ways."

His words hit Meghan with a burst of realization. If Jonathan was in the habit of hiring unsavory misfits to do his dirty work, could he also have hired another group of no-goods to take care of Jason?

"Did you tell those thugs from the Alhambra to jump Jason?"

"Let's stick to the matter at hand, my dear."

"I want to know!" Meghan demanded. "Did you hire those three creeps to jump Jason in the street and shoot him down?"

Jonathan sighed. "Not in so many words. I did let it be known that such an action might meet with appropriate rewards. Unfortunately, the boys who took me up on the offer weren't as good as they thought they were. They didn't do the job right. Therefore they didn't stay alive to collect a reward."

"Why did you do it?"

"It should be obvious. Jason stood in the way of my plans for you. He was the one factor in your life that I couldn't control. Which brings us to the subject at hand."

"Which is?" Meghan inquired with a sneer.

"Can't you guess?"

"No. What the hell is this all about?"

Jonathan sighed. "You're not as bright as I gave you credit for. Did you think I had you brought back from Montana simply because of an overabundance of family feeling?"

Meghan's eyes narrowed. "I've wondered about that. Why did you bring me back to this mess?"

Jonathan smiled, and the smile was not pleasant. "So I could control you, my dear niece. No good businessman allows events to surprise him if it can be prevented. When I heard that surveyor's story about a red-haired white woman riding with the Cheyenne, I knew it had to be Mary Catherine O'Brian's redheaded, green-eyed daughter. I'd never seen you, but I met your mother when she married my brother back in Ireland. Never forgot her wild coloring, so I figured that girl riding with the savages had to be you all right. When I learned you were alive, I knew you were a threat to all I'd built. So I brought you back where I could watch you and where I could mold you into someone who wouldn't interfere with my life. Unfortunately, you have so far proved to be nothing but a stubborn and interfering nuisance."

Meghan eyed him with distaste. "And so . . . ?"

"And so I had you brought here, where we can work out a better arrangement, and you can be aware of the stakes in our little discussion."

"And what arrangement is that?" she asked coldly.

He smiled condescendingly. "You didn't really think I was going to give up the fortune I'd worked so hard to achieve all these years, did you? Just because my drunken, no-good, layabout brother had a daughter with the bad taste to survive that Indian raid instead of dying like everybody else.''

One corner of Meghan's mouth lifted in a twisted smile. ''So since the Indians didn't kill me you figured to have your bully boys out there take care of the job. Right?''

Jonathan looked hurt. ''You misjudge me, niece. That was never my original intention. And I hope such measures won't be necessary now—if you'll just be sensible and cooperate.''

''Cooperate with what?'' Meghan asked doubtfully.

''A very simple arrangement that is to both our benefits. You will sign the mines over to me after marrying the love of your life—Josef, of course—and losing all interest in the business.''

Meghan's face was impassive. ''What does Josef have to do with this? Why can't I just sign the mines over to you and that's that?''

''Illogical.'' Her uncle visibly preened himself. ''I've thought of everything. If you just signed over the mines, people would talk. All sorts of accusations would be flying about. But everyone would understand your giving me the mines after just having married a wealthy nobleman from Europe. This really is the best way, my dear''—he sighed solicitously—''I have no wish to see you harmed in any way. You are kin, after all.''

''I spit on your kinship,'' Meghan jeered. ''I'd rather be kin to a snake!''

''Now, Meghan,'' he said with a little smile. ''There's no need to get personal in all of this. After all, I didn't exactly ask to have you as kinfolk either. But we Irish, we value our family ties. That's why I'm going to so much trouble to give you this second chance, dear. I had those unpleasant fellows bring you here just to show you I mean business. I can get rough if necessary, Meghan, but I sincerely hope it won't be necessary.''

''Is that all you want?'' she asked cautiously.

''Essentially, my dear, that's all I want. It's very simple. You have a choice. You may marry Josef—a very nice young man if I do say so myself—go with him to Europe, and sign over ownership of the mines to me, your loving uncle, in return for all I have done for you. In addition, you will leave Andrew here with my family, as a hostage to your good behavior. We wouldn't want news of this little meeting of ours to get out, would we? Josef would be quite upset if he found out what methods I had to employ to get you to marry him.''

Meghan was tempted to spit in the man's face, but for once she managed to bridle her temper. ''What else?''

''That's all I ask. Not so much, is it? Andrew will be perfectly safe with me, as long as you keep your mouth shut about our little arrangement—and you stay in Europe. I want no one to have doubts that this deal is aboveboard and legal.''

''And if I don't?''

Jonathan sighed. ''That would be extremely foolish, Meghan.''

''Tell me just how foolish.''

''All right,'' he consented with a reluctance that was not at all convincing. ''I'm not a man of violence myself. So, much as I would hate to do it, I would be forced to leave you with the two gentlemen outside to dispose of. I will ask them to be quick and clean about it. You are kin, after all. There are plenty of old shafts in these hills where an unwanted body can be safely gotten rid of. You would never be found. And of course, your poor little son wouldn't survive you by very many days. Babies are so fragile, aren't they?''

Meghan's face was calm, but her heart was pounding. ''You'd never get away with it, Jonathan. I'd be missed. Your own family...Even Jason will come looking for me.''

''Your disappearance could be easily explained. You've such a penchant for riding out alone. Who knows what terrible things can happen in these hills? You certainly wouldn't be the first to vanish without a trace. I doubt many questions will be asked.''

420 ♦ *Emily Carmichael*

"You're mad!" Anger was possessing her so she almost trembled with it.

"No, my dear, I'm completely sane. And I'm not about to give up any part of what I've worked for all these years."

"You wouldn't even miss the part that would go to me. I've talked to the lawyer Abernathy about drawing up an agreement. You'd get almost everything until Andrew comes of age. By then you'd be an old man ready to retire."

Jonathan smiled. "It's the principle of the thing, my dear. But as you're an uneducated female who's lived most of her life with the Indians, I doubt you'd understand anything so abstract."

"Oh, I understand all right," Meghan snarled. "You're a greedy bastard who has more money than he can ever spend and still wants more. And you're willing to kill your own flesh and blood to get it."

Jonathan shook his head sadly. "You really don't understand at all."

"Go dive into an outhouse, Jonathan."

Jonathan eyed her pityingly. "I hope that's not our final answer."

She opened her mouth to deliver a stinging reply, but caution closed it again. Think! she told herself. For once in your life think! Don't just react. She needed time. Time to escape. She wasn't about to give in to Jonathan's threats. As he'd said earlier, it was the principle of the thing. She wasn't about to leave her son hostage to anyone. But if she could stall, who knew what would happen?

"I need time to think," she said with a frown.

Jonathan was getting impatient. "Your one choice should be obvious."

"Well, it's not so obvious to me!" she protested hotly. "Give me until morning."

He stood up and dusted off his expensive trousers. "As you wish, then. But don't count on anyone's coming to your aid, Meghan. Because if anyone should happen on this cabin tonight, the fellows outside have orders to finish the job. You understand?''

Meghan glared at him silently.

"I hope by morning you are thinking a bit straighter." Jonathan looked at her solicitously. "Perhaps my associates outside can help convince you to cooperate."

When Jonathan walked out the door, Meghan once again strove desperately to free her hands. But her activities came to an abrupt halt when George and Harry lumbered back into the room. Harry squatted down beside her and roughly fondled her breast through the thin fabric of her shirt. "We'uns is goin' to have us a party, missy. All night long till morning." His hand dipped to her crotch as he leered into her face. She tried to squirm away.

"My uncle will be back in the morning. He won't be happy with what you're thinking to do, you lout."

George laughed. "He don't care, little miss high and mighty. Long as there ain't no more marks on you, he says we c'n have our fun."

Curse her uncle to hell! Meghan thought. He'd set these goons on her before she'd even refused his offer. Damn him for a lying, slimy son of a bitch.

"We still gots to figger out how to do this when the time comes." George scratched his head with a grimy finger to help in the unfamiliar process of thinking. "We gots to hide the body good. Don't want no slipups. The hangin' tree's a place I don't wanta end up."

"Come on," Harry whined. "We c'n think about that later. Might not even hafta kill the little bitch. Let's get to it. Here, you untie her feet. Cain't have no fun with her legs tied together like that."

Meghan's heart turned to ice. She tried to tell herself that whatever these ghouls did to her didn't matter as long as she lived. She had to live for Andrew's sake. If she let these apes kill her, then Jonathan would surely find a way to dispose of her son as well. She closed her eyes and clenched her teeth as her legs were forced apart and rough hands pushed her divided skirt down over her hips.

"Whooeee! Wouldya look at that!" She could feel their hot eyes searing her flesh and she resisted the urge to cringe away. She wouldn't give them the satisfaction of seeing her fear and revulsion.

"I git to go first," Harry claimed. "Open yer eyes, you sweet-assed Injun fucker! See what I've got for you."

"I'd put it back in your pants, if I were you, fella. Or else it's going to get shot off."

The two apes whirled around in surprise at the unexpected voice. Meghan opened her eyes, hardly daring to believe she wasn't dreaming. Jason stood in the doorway, the dim lamplight etching his carven face with flickering shadows. The pistol in his hand was cocked, ready, and looked hungry for blood. George and Harry were caught not only with their pants down, but with their pistols out of reach.

"What the . . . !?"

"You gents ought to be more careful about leaving tracks. And about letting your victim's horse wander back into town minus a rider."

Comprehension dawned in Harry's dull eyes. "Oh . . . yeah . . ."

"As it is," Jason continued with an amiability that didn't reach his glittering eyes, "you boys are in a heap of trouble." He glanced at Meghan, noting the torn disarray of her clothing and the bruise beginning to discolor and swell on her face.

George looked at Jason and saw death written on the grim planes of his face. "We wasn't goin' to hurt the lady!" he whined.

"Is that why your pants are down around your knees?" Jason asked coldly.

"Jason!" Meghan was struggling to get to her feet, but the task was impossible with her hands tied and her skirt around her ankles.

Keeping the pistol steady on target, he moved swiftly

over to Meghan and cut her hands free. She swiftly pulled herself together as best she could, tying together her torn shirt so it at least covered her breasts and hitching her skirt into place. Then without forethought she scrambled to her feet and threw her arms around Jason, burying her face against the hard muscle of his shoulder.

"I've never been so glad to see anyone," she mumbled into his shirt.

"That's a change!" He grinned, all the while keeping his pistol unwaveringly on his two apprehensive prisoners.

"Oh, God! If you hadn't come back!" Her voice had an uncharacteristic quaver.

His arm tightened around her. "I'm back. Everything's okay."

Suddenly Meghan pulled back from him, the grim realities of the situation once more registering in her mind.

"Forget those goons! We've got to get Andrew away from Jonathan."

"What about Andrew?" Jason demanded.

"If my uncle learns that something's gone wrong here, he'll kill him, Jason. I'm sure he will! He's mad! I swear he is! He'll do anything to keep those damn mines."

"Then let's get out of here." He retrieved George and Harry's pistols, throwing the holsters over one shoulder. "Are you all right?"

His eyes softened momentarily as he surveyed the damage done, the bruises, bloody scratches, and torn clothing. Meghan thought he'd never looked so . . . so . . . husbandly. But she couldn't stop to appreciate it. Her son was in danger.

"Turn around," Jason ordered the prisoners. When they obeyed, he turned his pistol butt forward and clubbed them both smartly on the skull. "That ought to put them to sleep for a while."

Swiftly he tied them with the rope he'd cut off Meghan. Giving the knots a final yank, he felt a bitter disgust well up in his soul. These filthy rutting slobs had dared to lay hands on what was his. The thought set a demon of jealousy eating at his vitals. He itched to close his hands around their fleshy throats and slowly choke the life from their bodies, preferably when they were awake and could feel his hands squeezing until their breath was gone and their hearts had stopped. But revenge was an empty and dangerous gesture, he had learned. And hate was an emotion that could get a man killed before his time. These two would keep for a while, and there were far more important matters to take care of right now.

Meghan was watching him with a peculiar light in her eyes. Jason turned and fastened her with a questioning gaze. "Did they hurt you?"

Meghan returned his look steadily. "If you mean did they rape me, then the answer is no. They didn't get that far, thanks to you. Why?"

Jason dragged the two out of the cabin and hoisted them on their horses, belly down. " 'Cause if they did," he finally answered, "I figure I'd have to see to it they were mighty sorry. Generally I don't hold with revenge, but in this case I'd see fit to make an exception."

Meghan gave him a measuring look. "Why?"

"You're my wife." He steered Meghan to where the black stallion waited.

She put her foot in the stirrup, then hesitated while she fought herself and fought her pride. "You do care, don't you? About me and Andrew."

He grinned, a flash of white teeth against bronze skin. "You mean you didn't know?"

"I hoped. I didn't know."

"Well, you do now." He gave her a well-positioned shove on her backside as she climbed into the saddle. He swung up behind her and turned the stallion's head in the direction of O'Brian House. "I care. And as soon as we get our son out of your uncle's house, I intend to show you just how much."

\* \* \*

O'Brian House was waiting silently as they trotted up the drive, leading the two goons' horses with their unconscious burdens. Meghan hoped with all her heart, prayed with all her soul to both the Cheyenne deities and the white man's God, that Jonathan was not at home, that she could casually greet her aunt and cousins and snatch Andrew to safety, though right now she didn't pretend to know where safety was to be found. She leaned back against Jason's hard-muscled chest, seeking comfort in his strength. His arms tightened around her as he felt her need.

"I'm not going to let anything happen to our son, Meghan," he said softly.

"Oh, Jason!" she whimpered, suddenly feeling weak with her fear and tired to death of hiding it. "What if . . . what if he's already . . . ?"

"He's not." In all the trials he'd put her through, Jason had never seen Meghan so close to breaking. He himself felt icy fingers of fear claw at his heart at the thought of his innocent little son in Jonathan's hands. "Jonathan doesn't have any way of knowing you're not still in that cabin, waiting for him to come back for your answer. Andrew will be all right." The statement was meant to reassure himself as much as Meghan.

Meghan had explained the whole situation to him on the ride from the cabin. The iron muscles of his arms had tightened spasmodically around her when she'd spoken of Jonathan's plans for her and Andrew, and his alternative should she not cooperate. But that was the only outward sign of the rage that was building inside him. He held to it, keeping it tightly under control, cultivating it until the time he would need its explosive power.

The house was still lit even though the hour approached midnight. Meghan scrambled down from the saddle and ran for the front door, bursting in with a frantic haste that destroyed Jason's plans for caution. Her aunt and cousins were seated in the parlor looking as if some great tragedy had struck. At her sudden entrance they looked up in surprise. Then Erin ran to her, her face streaked with tears. She put her arms around her and hugged her to her spare bosom. Samantha followed close behind, bouncing like a coiled spring, and Clara's face bloomed with a happy smile.

"My darling girl!" Erin choked back tears that were closing off her throat. "We were so desperately worried. The sheriff rode out this evening to say your mare had wandered into town without you on her back. We were afraid something dreadful had happened! Oh, Jason!" She finally noticed the tall figure who had come to stand behind her niece. "You brought her back to us! What happened? Why . . . ?"

Meghan untangled herself from Erin's embrace. "Where's Andrew?" she asked urgently.

"He's upstairs," Clara answered. "He's sleeping like an angel. Why?"

"Where's Jonathan?" Jason asked as Meghan headed quickly for the stairs.

"He's in his study, I think," Erin replied. "What . . . ?" Erin frowned in confusion.

Jonathan's voice came from the upstairs hallway. "I'm not in my office, Meghan." He appeared at the top of the stairs, a sleeping Andrew in his arms.

Meghan stopped in her headlong dash, her face a study in despair.

"I saw you come up the drive, my dear," he explained calmly. "My office window has quite a convenient view."

"Put him down," Meghan begged. She had no pride when it came to the safety of her son.

"I intend to." With a saintly smile he glanced over the second-story balustrade to the hard wooden floor fifteen feet below. "I will put him down," he promised, "very far down, unless you do exactly as I say. Understand?"

"I understand," Meghan said softly. She was convinced her uncle was mad. No sane man could threaten such a malevolent act while looking so calm.

Erin rushed to Meghan's side, her face drawn into a

frown of confusion. "Jonathan! What on earth are you doing? Put Andrew back to bed at once and come down and talk to your niece. Here we've all been so worried!"

"Erin, my love. Tell the girls to leave the room."

"Jonathan!?"

"Do as I say!"

Erin looked at her husband as if she were seeing a stranger. She looked from Meghan to Jonathan and her eyes slowly clouded with horror as understanding of the scene flooded her mind. "Jonathan! You can't!"

"Samantha! Clara!" Jonathan's voice boomed. "Leave the room immediately!"

The two girls huddled together in confusion, frightened by the demon that seemed to possess their father. Clutching each other's arms, they backed out of the room. Samantha gave Meghan a despairing look, but Clara looked only at her father, a black mask of anger twisting her usually gentle features.

"Now, Sinclair. Drop your pistols."

Jason did as he was told.

"Very carefully, now," Jonathan cautioned as Jason's hands went slowly to his holsters. "You wouldn't want me to have to wake up your son, would you?"

Jason grasped the butts with two fingers only, slid the pistols slowly from their holsters, and holding them well away from his sides, dropped them to the floor. The crash of hard steel against polished wood sounded like a clap of thunder in the tense silence.

"Good." Jonathan's mouth twitched in a smile. "Now, Erin, pick up the guns."

"Jonathan, you can't do this!" Erin's face was haggard. She seemed to have aged ten years in five minutes.

"Do as I say, Erin. I'm doing this for our family, dear. Just trust me."

She picked up the guns gingerly, as if they might explode in her hands. "Jonathan . . ." Her voiced begged him to grasp his sanity once again.

"Go outside, Erin, and untie the two gentlemen on the horses. Give them the guns."

The life went out of Erin's eyes. She moved to the door like a woman caught in a nightmare.

"Jonathan!" Jason's voice ran in the waiting silence of the hallway. "You harm that baby and I'll see you dead. There's nowhere you can go to be safe from me. I'll make you beg for death."

Jonathan's tone was almost friendly. "What makes you think you'll be alive, Sinclair?"

"Don't you count on my being dead, O'Brian. Other men have gambled on that and lost."

The two men stared at each other for a moment, taking each other's measure. Footsteps behind them broke the silence. Erin had returned, George and Harry following groggily at her heels.

"I see I can't trust you gentlemen to see a job done right. Now, Meghan, you've had your time to make a decision. Suppose you tell me your answer."

"Uncle Jonathan," Meghan pleaded, "I'll do anything. Just don't hurt my baby. I'll sign the mines over to you. I'll never say a thing." Tears ran unchecked down her face.

"Very touching, dear. But now I'm beginning to wonder if my plan was a very good one. Little Andrew, here, might grow up questioning why his mother had signed away his inheritance, and once he was old enough to escape my clutches, so to speak, I'd have no more control over your behavior. Josef and I had a gentlemen's agreement, but I'm not sure I trust that young twit to control you. He's far too taken with you. You could probably wrap him around your little finger." He smiled slowly, and with a sinking heart Meghan realized he was actually enjoying this. "I might just have to rescind my offer."

Erin moved to the bottom of the stairs and looked up at her husband for one last try. "Jonathan, you don't need to do this. We don't need the mines anymore. We've got plenty of money. We'll never be poor, Jonathan. You don't have to do this."

She rattled on with her pleas while the dark-haired, quiet shadow moved across the upstairs hallway, positioning herself right behind Jonathan. Clara had gone up the back stairway and was determined to stage a rescue attempt for her beloved Andrew. Fortunately the angle of the hallway kept her from the sights of the still-groggy George and Harry. Meghan held her breath as her cousin slowly sidled toward the balustrade, carefully keeping out of Jonathan's line of sight as he listened to his wife's entreaties. She didn't think the girl could do anything. A noise, a quick movement from her, could startle her father and cause him to fling the baby over the rail.

"Erin, my love," Jonathan finally cut her short, ignoring her pleas. "I think it best if you leave the room now."

Erin gaped at her husband blankly, seeing Clara behind him but not registering the fact on her face. Wordlessly she turned and left the room. Her eyes were glazed. She moved past Meghan and Jason as though not seeing them.

"It was nice to hear you surrender, Meghan," Jonathan gloated. "But I think I'm going to have to change my plan." A core of ice formed in Meghan's heart as he continued. "I see now I could never really control you, and Sinclair there has already said he'll have me dead. I'm afraid I have no choice."

Meghan saw her death in his face before he gave the command, but Andrew was the only one on her mind.

"Take them away and kill them," Jonathan commanded the two thugs behind them.

Meghan launched herself forward, twisting herself away from the reaching hands of George. She took the stairs three at a time.

But Jason was faster, and deadlier. Harry couldn't grab him before he reached to his belt and in one smooth, speed-blurred motion pulled his long-bladed knife from its sheath and sent it speeding toward Jonathan's throat, where it buried itself with a meaty thunk. Clara screamed

430 ♦ Emily Carmichael

as her father slowly folded to the ground, but her hands reached out to take the baby from arms gone limp. She backed away in horror and screamed again at the sight of the bloody blade piercing Jonathan's neck. Andrew woke to terror and added his squalling to the noise. Erin and Samantha both rushed into the room.

George and Harry knew when they were beaten. They were preparing to make a hasty exit when Jason caught them, grabbing a thick neck in each hand. Raising them both above the ground in the strength of his pent-up fury, he slammed their heads into the wall, then into each other. When he released them, they slipped unresisting to the floor and lay in two untidy heaps. Satisfied, his anger somewhat appeased, Jason turned to the chaos on the stairs.

Erin and Samantha huddled over Jonathan's body, which was slumped grotesquely on the stairs. Erin wept. Samantha looked stunned. Meghan was in the second-floor hallway, cradling the screaming Andrew in one arm and comforting the distraught Clara with the other. Li Ching had appeared in a long white nightshirt and was jumping up and down in confusion and dismay. Wearily Jason plowed through the confusion and climbed the stairs. He took the baby from Meghan.

Andrew quieted in his father's arms, and Jason looked at him somberly, seeming to commit him to memory. He briefly cradled him against his chest as the baby crooned his delight, having forgotten, in the way of infants, his pique at being awakened so abruptly. He handed the babe back to its mother.

Meghan gazed at Jason with a tear-streaked face. "Thank you," she said quietly. "I'll never be able to thank you enough."

"You don't have to. He's my son too."

Meghan took the baby and placed a kiss on his brow, then on his nose. The tears started afresh when she looked at Jason. He saw the tears and the gratitude, and he saw something else as well—jagged remnants of terror and despair turning into sick unhappiness. He had brought her to this, he thought. He had torn her from a life of innocence and happiness and forced her into a world of greed and mad scheming. And still she loved him. That too was shining in those deep green eyes that he loved so well.

He turned wearily and went down the stairs. She followed him like a lost child. He stooped to pick up his gun. She stayed by him. He turned to her and drew her close, sheltering the baby between them.

"It's over, Meghan." With one callused finger he traced a tear that had run down her cheek. "No more tears. We've got our son back. You've got your mines, all nice and legal. And you've got me, Meghan, if you're so inclined."

She looked at him through the tears that were flooding her eyes. "Do you truly love me, Jason? Is that why you've stayed all these weeks?"

"I do truly love you, Meghan." He smiled.

Her eyes took in the scene around them: the two unconscious bodies piled by the door, her aunt and cousins weeping over her uncle's lifeless form. Suddenly a sickness clenched her stomach and threatened to rise into her throat. Jason was right. It was over. If she'd ever had hope of accepting the white man's world, that hope was gone.

"If you love me, Jason," she said with a level look into his amber eyes, "then take me home."

"This is your home," Jason said gently.

"No." Meghan shook her head in vigorous denial. "This was never my home. Let the white men have their gold. I want to go back to the Cheyenne."

# Chapter Twenty-nine

Autumnfire Woman sat astride her horse and looked down at the little village huddled on the banks of Lost Chokecherry Creek. It was a painfully small village, smaller than any of those she'd known in her happy childhood. Thirty lodges sat in a broken circle, thirty lodges that housed the remnants of the brave band that had defiantly set out from Oklahoma in September 1878. For over a year the Northern Cheyenne had suffered and sickened and died on the reservation of their Southern Cheyenne brethren. They had petitioned the army to allow them to return to their home, to the cool and clean hunting grounds of the northern plains. The army had been unsympathetic. The Northern Cheyenne must stay in the south. So Little Wolf, Wild Hog, Morning Star, and Old Crow had set out to march north with a band of already-weakened men, women, and children. It was better to die marching toward freedom, they said, than die like dogs in this miserable land far from their home. The brave band divided shortly after the march began. Half surrendered at the Red Cloud Indian Agency. Little Wolf's band, though, had pushed on. Now it was February. Soon the band would leave its winter camp on Lost Chokecherry Creek and continue the march to the northwest.

As always, the circle of lodges was broken in a line with the rising sun. Now, though, the sun was setting. Women were coming in from their wood gathering and root digging, chatting and laughing in small groups as they entered the village circle. Men were smoking in front of their lodges, relaxing before the evening meal. Some sat talking with their comrades, tending their weapons, discussing days long gone. None talked of the future. There was no future, and all in the village knew it.

Autumnfire felt the bite of the knife-edged Nebraska wind even through her heavy buffalo-hide cloak, and she checked to make sure that Andrew, strapped to her back in the Cheyenne fashion, was securely wrapped. Little Magpie, sitting on her spotted pony a few feet away, wrinkled her nose at the odors blowing up from the circle.

"Rabbit stew again tonight."

Autumnfire smiled. "There's nothing wrong with rabbit stew."

Magpie screwed up her chubby face. "I'm tired of it."

"Soon we'll be moving up to the Powder River country. Then we will have antelope again."

"Not soon enough for me," Magpie commented with a heavy sigh.

Long Stepping Woman came out of her lodge, saw the two girls on the bluff, and waved. Autumnfire waved back but didn't move from her spot. She wasn't ready to go in yet, even though she knew there were chores aplenty to be done. She felt a twinge of guilt for not doing her share of the women's work this day, but she had needed to get away and think. Magpie had come along as a lark but at least had managed to gather the dry wood that was tied in bundles hanging along the spotted pony's sides. Other than that, the two of them had contributed nothing to the day's effort.

Three months had passed since Autumnfire had joined her family's lodge, now a part of Little Wolf's band. Six months had gone by since she had left California. She had learned Stone Eagle's whereabouts from Two Moon, who had surrendered at Fort Keogh in April 1877. Against the old chief's advice, she had ridden to join the people she most loved. She had shed her white identity and donned the mantle of Autumnfire Woman once again. Her mind had been set, and she had known in her heart that when she was once more with the Cheyenne, or what was left of the Cheyenne, she would have peace of mind. But she'd been wrong.

As the weeks passed she became more and more certain that she'd been terribly wrong to return, wrong to run away from the loneliness and unhappiness in California, wrong to run away from Jason. She shook her head despairingly. How could she have been such a fool to throw away the love she'd yearned after for so many months?

When her uncle had met his end, Meghan had wanted to get away as far as possible from the mines and from white society in general. Jason had offered to take her anywhere she wanted to go. But he had stubbornly insisted she settle her affairs in California first. She owed it to herself, he told her, and to Erin and Clara and Samantha. She almost had to smile, remembering the fight that had ensued. Meghan had regarded his attitude as mercenary and cold and had told him so in terms borrowed from his own colorful and highly improper vocabulary. He had not one grain of understanding in his whole body, she'd yelled, and if he was so damned interested in her money and her mines he could damn well settle her affairs himself.

As usual when her temper flared to white heat, her reason evaporated. Suddenly it seemed to her that Jonathan had been right about this, at least. How had she ever thought this hardened adventurer cared for her? If he cared, wouldn't he see that she wanted nothing as much as she wanted to leave the poison of this hateful place and this corrupt society behind?

The next day reason had returned, but the hurt remained. She told Jason to leave her alone for a few days and let her think. He left without a word, with eyes hooded and expression shuttered so she had no clue to what he was feeling, and right then she hadn't cared. She hardly knew what she herself was thinking and feeling. The trauma and grief of Jonathan's evil scheming and violent death had left her numb. More than anything she wanted to be gone from this place of bitter memories.

She stayed in Placerville only long enough to see Clara

wed to Josef, which was done in haste and privacy because of recent events and Josef's need to return to his homeland. Josef had generously offered his in-laws a home in Austria, and Erin had accepted with alacrity. She wanted to escape the stares and pitying glances of her former friends and saw a chance for her and her younger daughter to start fresh in a new place.

There were no sad good-byes when Meghan left town. She feared Jason would follow if he knew of her plans, and she was still bitterly nursing the hurt of his callous attitude. So she left her aunt and cousins a loving note of apology, packed up a confused Andrew, and slipped out in the darkness of night. She also left a note for the lawyer Mr. Abernathy, instructing him to sell O'Brian House, which was the property of what was now her mining company, after Erin and Samantha departed for Austria. The money from the house was to be sent to her aunt and cousins, as was a deed for a half-interest in the mine holdings. The mines would be well managed by the mine supervisor, and she knew if Andrew ever wanted to claim it, there would be a fortune waiting for him someday in Placerville.

So Autumnfire Woman was born again. She was welcomed back by Little Wolf's band and affectionately folded into the loving embrace of her family. Stone Eagle, Long Stepping Woman, and Magpie were unchanged to her loving and anxious eyes. Elsewhere, though, things were not the same.

When she had been carried away by Jason, the Cheyenne were confident and aggressive. Now they knew the end was near. They wanted only to spend their last days in their homeland. Bitterness ate at many of them. Red Shield had taken a wife shortly after Autumnfire had been snatched away, a young woman whom she remembered as a childhood playmate. She had died on the reservation in Oklahoma. Red Shield now hated all whites with more than a warrior's passion for battle. He hated Meghan as well, it seemed, for he'd not spoken a word to her since she'd returned, and the looks he sent her way were full of resentment.

Several others in the little band felt as Red Shield did.

Though they had said nothing to the elders or to Stone Eagle, Autumnfire could feel their stares as she went about her business in the encampment. The people whom she thought of as her own now regarded her as an outsider, it seemed.

Autumnfire had ridden out today to look into her heart. She must decide her future. She must choose a path to follow that would be right for her and right for her son. She had hoped to leave the white world behind and now found that she was more Meghan than she was Autumnfire Woman. She no longer belonged with these people, as much as she loved them. Their path was separate from hers, and she could not accompany them on their journey to whatever fate awaited them. All day she had sought the answer, hoping that some message would flash at her out of the sky, or some bird would sing the right song in her ear. No message had come in the sky or in birdsong, however, and she was left with an empty, questioning heart.

She wondered if this was how Jason felt, belonging nowhere and to no one, and the thought brought more pain. She'd been a fool to leave him. He'd only wanted her to do what was right. It had been a bad time to confront her with practicalities, but then tact had never been numbered among Jason's talents. Every day she saw his image in her growing son. At night her body still ached for his touch, and his shadow still haunted her dreams. Never would she be rid of him. He had carved a space in her heart that could never be filled. He had lit a fire in her body that would never be quenched by another.

"I'm hungry." Magpie squirmed in her saddle and cast her red-haired sister a pleading look. "Even that rabbit stew is beginning to smell good."

"Let's go get some then." Autumnfire smiled.

They rode into the village, giving the ponies over to the care of a young orphan boy who lived in Stone Eagle's lodge in return for doing chores. Dinner was waiting, and Long Stepping Woman gave them both a harsh look for being so late.

They sat in silence around the fire as dinner was served, it being the Cheyenne custom to hold conversation until the meal is over. Autumnfire felt her father's eyes on her more than once, however, and wondered if he would rebuke her for dawdling the day away.

The meal was cleared away, and Long Stepping Woman gathered up Andrew and took Magpie by the arm, steering her firmly toward the lodge exit. Autumnfire started to follow, but Stone Eagle motioned her to stay.

"I would talk to you, daughter. Sit with me in the warmth of the lodge for a few minutes."

Autumnfire sank to her place beside the fire, watching as Stone Eagle lit his pipe with a glowing splinter. The lodge was homey and warm, full of the familiar odors of food, smoke, and hides. The fire crackled cheerfully. Autumnfire was content just to sit in silence as Stone Eagle regarded her from beneath his graying brows. He had aged, she thought. His hair was grayer, his face etched with deeper lines, not the lines of years but the lines of worry and despair. Her heart ached with the grief of seeing her loved ones' sorrow and not being able to help.

Stone Eagle cleared his throat and put on a solemn face. I'm in for a real lecture, Autumnfire thought with chagrin.

"Autumnfire Woman," he began formally. "When you were a child, brought to me by my brother who has now joined our ancestors, you were the sun in my day, the moon in my night."

Autumnfire was silent, knowing that many words would flow before the point of the lecture was reached.

"When you became a young woman, you were still my joy, though at times you pricked at me like a mosquito." His eyes were warm with memories, and a reluctant smile tugged at his mouth. "You were ever the mischief-maker and pest, but still you brought happiness to my life. When you were taken from us, my heart was torn in two, and your mother would not be comforted in her grieving. Suddenly our days were dark and our nights were long and lonely."

He looked at her again in silence. Autumnfire grew

438 ◆ *Emily Carmichael*

uneasy under his scrutiny. This didn't sound like a lecture on the responsibilities of doing the chores.

"When you returned to us, my daughter, my heart was restored to me. Long Stepping Woman rejoiced, saying our little girl has come back, and we will be just as before. But that is not true. Autumnfire left us as a girl, with much of the child still in her. She returns a woman."

"This is true, my father," Autumnfire agreed quietly.

A silence stretched into minutes as the old warrior regarded her searchingly.

"Your son has the eyes of his father," Stone Eagle said abruptly.

Autumnfire looked at him in surprise.

"We know of the one who carried you away from us. Panther Who Walks on Two Legs is a great warrior, with the strength of the lion who sired him and the cunning of the wolf who runs with him."

Autumnfire arched a brow in question.

"It is said," Stone Eagle told her with a half-believing grin, "that his mother was visited in the night by the great yellow panther who roams the hills. It is from their mating that Panther Who Walks was born. It is said he is a man by day and a lion by night."

Autumnfire couldn't hold back a chuckle. "My father, you have seen the lion's eyes in my son and say you know of his sire." Her eyes twinkled with mischief. "I, too, know his sire, and I can tell you he is as much a man by night as he is by day. A man like any other. No different."

Stone Eagle nodded sagely, but an irrepressible smile played around her mouth. "Time proves few legends to be true. A man, you say, like any other. But I think you are wrong. He is a man with rare strength and spirit. Like the lion. Like the wolf. May his son, my grandson, grow to be like him in manhood."

Autumnfire sighed. If Andrew grew up to follow in his father's footsteps, he would lead a hard life indeed. But Stone Eagle didn't know much of the white man's world.

He knew only his own dying world. And he admired courage and strength where he saw it.

"My daughter," Stone Eagle said finally, "I do not want to talk of your son, dear as he is to my heart. I want to talk of you."

"Yes, father." She lowered her eyes before his steady gaze.

"You are a woman now, a woman with a child. A woman belongs in her husband's lodge."

"I have no husband," Autumnfire said calmly.

"Panther Who Walks is your husband."

"He is not my husband. He was once, but no longer."

Stone Eagle looked puzzled for a moment. "Then why did he ride into our village today, saying he had come for his wife, Autumnfire Woman, the daughter of Stone Eagle?"

Meghan's heart stopped. Her mind reeled.

"He rode in alone and didn't fight when the young men took him and bound him."

"Why did they do that?" Autumnfire asked in near panic.

"He is our enemy, my daughter. All white men are our enemies now. And too, he is blood brother to the hated Pawnee, who have been our enemies for generations."

"What are you going to do to him?" Her heart pounded in her chest so loudly she thought for sure her father must hear.

"That is for you to say. If he is truly your husband he will be honored. If not . . ." He let the sentence hang and added fuel to the fire of her fear.

"I must see him! Where is he?"

"In the lodge of Two Beavers."

Without seeking her father's permission, Autumnfire fled from the lodge. She didn't see the knowing and gentle smile on the old warrior's face as his eyes followed her out the door.

*   *   *

Two Beavers' lodge was far down the circle from that of Stone Eagle. Autumnfire was breathless when she reached it, but her breathlessness was not from her running all the way. Her heart pounded in her chest like the heavy beat of the medicine drum, and her breathing raced in time. Her palms were moist and cold, and her legs seemed suddenly unable to support her. All from the idea of seeing Jason again, talking to him again. Why had he come? Why? Why? Why?

She opened the flap and ducked into the dim interior of the lodge. She straightened, face stony, composure even, and beneath the facade every nerve quivering. He stood to greet her. Her eyes ached with joy at the sight of him, broad-shouldered, hard-muscled, bronze-skinned, and tawny-haired. Her father was right. He was the lion, the sleek, the powerful, the tawny, amber-eyed hunter. Everything was as she remembered—the sweet, mobile mouth that could tighten into a hard, cruel line or curve into a gentle smile. The straight, high-bridged nose whose nostrils could flare in passion. The amber eyes, hooded and cold, but sometimes warm, open, vulnerable. Just as she remembered. Jason. Father of her son. Love of her life. Forever. Why had he come? Why?

She sat cross-legged by the fire, never leaving him with her eyes. He sat facing her. He looked calm, assured, sane. Much too sane to have ridden openly into a camp of renegade Cheyenne. She'd known Jason to be many things, but never a fool. Why had he done it? Why had he come?

"Why did you come?" The question was an extension of her thoughts. She was hardly aware of having spoken aloud.

Jason smiled. There was a gleam of devilment in his eyes. "I came for my wife."

Meghan arched an inquiring brow. "Wife?"

"Wife," he repeated firmly. Jason looked at the woman sitting across from him. The flickering of the lodge fire sent shadows racing across her face as she sat in stony silence. She wore her Indian face—calm, imperturbable, emotionless. But her eyes betrayed her. They searched his features, tense, wary, waiting for him to say the words that would hurt her again, as he had so many times in the past.

"I thought you would get a divorce after I left," she said cautiously.

"Why would I do a fool thing like that?"

She had changed, Jason thought. She'd become a woman in his absence. A woman's wisdom showed on her face and deep in her eyes. A woman indeed. Incredibly beautiful. His woman. Yet he still saw in her traces of the redheaded pixie who'd wanted to go hunting with him on that morning so many years ago. The nine-year-old imp was still there, in the way errant fiery locks escaped her braids and curled around her high-cheeked face, in the hint of mischief that now and then flashed in her emerald eyes. He loved her. God how he loved her. More than freedom, more than the far horizon, he loved her.

"Meghan." He longed to reach out and touch her, but she'd placed herself so that the fire was between them. "Will you listen to what I have to say?"

She looked at him for a long silent moment, eyes unreadable, face inscrutable. "I will listen," she finally said in a flat voice.

Jason drew a deep breath. He had his chance, he knew. Better make it good.

"I've always been a wanderer, a loner with no kin I cared about. I guess I'm a hard case, as people say." A smile twitched at his mouth. "God knows I'm ornerier than an old bear when I get my temper up. At times I'm too quick to rile and too fast with a gun. But that's what comes from living on the raw edge of despair."

She didn't comment, just looked at him with wary eyes.

Jason gritted up his courage to continue. This confession of the soul was harder than facing down a whole band of Sioux. But he'd say what he'd come to say. If she refused him . . . if she refused him . . . His thoughts refused to dwell on the possibility.

"I've had a lot of women, Meghan, and I've forgotten

most of them. But you're the one I couldn't forget." His steady gaze never left her face and held her eyes in thrall. "I knew all along you loved me." Her face tightened at this assertion, but he plunged on. "You were too innocent to know how to hide such a thing. I loved you too. I was slow to realize it. Slower still to say it. But it was always there."

He dropped his gaze and brought a hand up to massage his brow. For the first time she noticed how weary he looked.

"The night I killed Jonathan, when I looked in your eyes, you holding our son in your arms, it hit me just how empty I would be without you in my life." His mouth twisted in a wry smile. "Loving you that much scared the hell out of me, but I figured I'd get used to it. When you got all riled up and ran away, there was no doubt in my mind I had to hunt you down. Took me a while to find you, seeing as these people don't much want to be found right now. But I couldn't give up, because you were always there with me. You haunted my dreams and hounded my waking thoughts. I was free as a bird again. No obligations, no ties. But I came to hate the very idea of being free, because it was keeping me from you."

Meghan tore her eyes away from his searching, arresting gaze. She focused on the hands clenched white-knuckled in her lap.

"You're still my wife, little Meghan. I figure I'd be a fool to let you get away from me just because you're a hardheaded, hot tempered female who doesn't know how much in love with me she really is."

Meghan sat in silence, still studying her clasped hands. He loved her! He wanted her! He'd gone to all the trouble to track her down. And yet, how long would it be before the itch for independence was on him again? How long before the lobo wolf in his soul took him from her? She wanted to cry out her question, but knew it was one she must answer for herself. Did she love him enough to hance another loss?

Uneasy at her continued silence, he plunged on. "We'll go back to Colorado. Pete and Carrie are expecting us, in fact, and Junior is all excited about having Andrew there. Seems he always wanted a little brother. They've missed you. They all reamed me out good for letting you go in the first place."

Meghan was silent for a long moment. Then a smile quirked the corner of her mouth. Her decision was made. There was really no question about what she had to do. "Seems you're doing a lot of telling and not very much asking."

For once in his life Jason Sinclair was caught off balance. His amber eyes flickered with uncertainty. Then he grinned, a broad grin that softened his hard, chiseled features and gave his face an almost boyish glow. "So I'll ask. I'll beg. Come with me, Meghan. Be my wife in truth."

Meghan's look of doubt was belied by the gleam of mischief in her eye. "Why should I?"

"Because I love you more than life itself. And," he added with a wicked grin, "you can't live without me."

Meghan frowned in earnest now. "I'll be no man's burden."

He shook his head. "How could you be a burden? You're the only thing in this world that I want." He reached across the dying fire and took her hand in a firm grip, refusing to let her go. "Little Meghan. You're the first woman who's had the misfortune to love me and the wisdom to let me go. No more wandering for me. Even Wolf has left me. He knows the wildness is gone. What I want now is you and our kids and my ranch in Colorado. I promise you we'll make a world of our own, where both of us will fit in."

He rose and pulled her to her feet, no longer able to resist the urge to banish the distance between them. Gently he drew her toward him. Unresisting, she came into his strong arms, reveling in the feel and the smell of him against her, wanting him never to let her go. His lips

444 ◆ Emily Carmichael

pressed against her hair, then her brow, then descended to her lips. Her body seemed to melt as she opened her mouth to his gentle invasion. The wind quieted, the fire froze, the earth stood still. The only sound in the universe was the heavy beating of two hearts.

His face looked down at hers, seeking his answer. She smiled, her green eyes warm with content.

"Jason, my only love." Her voice was but a whisper, but it thundered in his brain. "So long I've wanted to go home. Now I know where home is. Wherever you are."